W9-CAU-060

Praise for *New York Times* bestselling author

PENNY JORDAN

"Women everywhere will find pieces
of themselves in Jordan's characters."
—*Publishers Weekly*

"*One Night with the Sheikh* is a deliciously wonderful
tale with blazing sexual chemistry, a warm and
engaging romance and two larger-than-life characters."
—*RT Book Reviews*

"Jordan's record is phenomenal."
—*The Bookseller*

"*The Christmas Bride* by Penny Jordan is a well-told
love story...The beautiful settings and sensual love
scenes add charm and zest to this holiday romance."
—*RT Book Reviews* on *The Sheikh's Blackmailed Mistress*

"[Penny Jordan's novels] touch every emotion."
—*RT Book Reviews*

Penny Jordan, one of Harlequin's most popular authors, sadly passed away on December 31st, 2011. She leaves an outstanding legacy, having sold over 100 million books around the world. Penny wrote a total of 187 novels for Harlequin, including the phenomenally successful *A Perfect Family, To Love, Honor and Betray, The Perfect Sinner* and *Power Play,* which hit the *New York Times* bestseller list. Loved for her distinctive voice, she was successful in part because she continually broke boundaries and evolved her writing to keep up with readers' changing tastes. *Publishers Weekly* said about Jordan, "Women everywhere will find pieces of themselves in Jordan's characters." It is perhaps this gift for sympathetic characterization that helps to explain her enduring appeal.

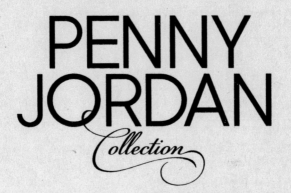

THE SHEIKH'S BABY

entertain, enrich, inspire™

If you purchased this book without a cover you should be aware that this book is stolen property. It was reported as "unsold and destroyed" to the publisher, and neither the author nor the publisher has received any payment for this "stripped book."

ISBN-13: 978-0-373-24962-6

THE SHEIKH'S BABY

Copyright © 2012 by Harlequin Books S.A.

Recycling programs for this product may not exist in your area.

The publisher acknowledges the copyright holder of the individual works as follows:

ONE NIGHT WITH THE SHEIKH
Copyright © 2003 by Penny Jordan

THE SHEIKH'S BLACKMAILED MISTRESS
Copyright © 2008 by Penny Jordan

All rights reserved. Except for use in any review, the reproduction or utilization of this work in whole or in part in any form by any electronic, mechanical or other means, now known or hereafter invented, including xerography, photocopying and recording, or in any information storage or retrieval system, is forbidden without the written permission of the publisher, Harlequin Enterprises Limited, 225 Duncan Mill Road, Don Mills, Ontario, Canada M3B 3K9.

This is a work of fiction. Names, characters, places and incidents are either the product of the author's imagination or are used fictitiously, and any resemblance to actual persons, living or dead, business establishments, events or locales is entirely coincidental.

This edition published by arrangement with Harlequin Books S.A.

For questions and comments about the quality of this book, please contact us at CustomerService@Harlequin.com.

® and TM are trademarks of Harlequin Enterprises Limited or its corporate affiliates. Trademarks indicated with ® are registered in the United States Patent and Trademark Office, the Canadian Trade Marks Office and in other countries.

www.Harlequin.com

Printed in U.S.A.

CONTENTS

ONE NIGHT WITH THE SHEIKH

PROLOGUE

'You won't forget your mummy whilst I'm away working, will you, my precious baby girl?'

Mariella watched sympathetically as her younger half-sister Tanya's eyes filled with tears as she handed her precious four-month-old daughter over to her.

'I know that Fleur couldn't have anyone better to look after her than you, Ella,' Tanya acknowledged emotionally. 'After all, you became my mother as well as my sister when Mum and Dad died. I just wish I could have got a job that didn't mean I have to be away, but this six-week contract on this cruise liner pays so well that I just can't afford to give it up! Yes, I know you would support us both,' she continued before Mariella could say anything, 'but that isn't what I want. I want to be as independent as I can be. Anyway,' she told Mariella bitterly, 'supporting Fleur financially should be her father's job and not yours! What I ever saw in that weak, lying rat of a man, I'll never know! My wonderful sexy dream fantasy of a sheikh! Some dream he turned out to be—more of a nightmare.'

Mariella let her vent her feelings, without comment, knowing just how devastated and hurt her half-sister had been when her lover had abandoned her.

'You don't have to do this, Tanya,' she told her gently

now. 'I'm earning enough to support us all, and this house is big enough for the three of us.'

'Oh, Mariella, I know that. I know you'd starve yourself to give to me and Fleur, but that isn't what I want. You've done so much for me since Mum and Dad died. You were only eighteen, after all, three years younger than I am now, when we found out that there wasn't going to be any money! I suppose Dad wanted to give us all so much that he simply didn't think about what would happen if anything happened to him, and with him remortgaging the house because of the stock market crisis.'

Silently the sisters looked at one another.

Both of them had inherited their mother's delicate bone structure and heart-shaped face, along with her strawberry-blonde hair and peach perfect complexion, but where Tanya had inherited her father's height and hazel eyes, Mariella had inherited intensely turquoise eyes from her father, the man who had decided less than a year after her birth that the responsibilities of fatherhood and marriage simply weren't for him and walked out on his wife and baby daughter.

'It's not fair,' Tanya had mock complained to her when she had announced that she was not going to go to university as Mariella had hoped she would, but wanted to pursue a career singing and dancing. 'If I had your eyes, I'd have a ready-made advantage over everyone else whenever I went for a part.'

Although she knew how headstrong and impulsive her half-sister could be, Mariella admired her for what she was doing, even whilst she worried about how she was going to cope with being away from her daughter for six long weeks.

Whatever small differences there might ever have been

between them, in their passionate and protective love for baby Fleur they were totally united.

'I'll ring every day,' Tanya promised chokily.

'And I want to know everything she does, Ella… Every tiny little thing. Oh, Ella…I feel so guilty about all of this…I know how you suffered as a little girl because your father wasn't there; because he'd abandoned you and Mum…and I know too how lucky I was to have both Mum and Dad and you there for me, and yet here is my poor little Fleur…'

Holding Fleur in one arm, Mariella hugged her sister tightly with the other.

'The taxi's here,' she warned, before releasing Tanya and tenderly brushing the tears off her face.

'ELLA! I'VE GOT the most fab commission for you.'

Recognising the voice of her agent, Mariella shifted Fleur's warm weight from one arm to the other, smiling lovingly at her as the baby guzzled happily on her bottle. 'It's racehorses, dozens of them. The client owns his own racing yard out in Zuran. He's a member of the Zuran royal family, and apparently he heard about you via that chap in Kentucky, whose Kentucky Derby winner you painted the other year. Anyway—he wants to fly you out there, all expenses paid, so that you can discuss the project with him, see the beasts *in situ* so to speak!'

Mariella laughed. Kate, with her immaculate designer clothes and equally immaculate all-white apartment, was not an animal lover. 'Ella, what is that noise?' she demanded plaintively.

Mariella laughed. 'It's Fleur. I'm just giving her her bottle. It does sound promising, but right now I'm pretty booked with commissions, and, to be honest, I don't really think that going to Zuran is on. For a start, I'm looking after Fleur for the next six weeks, and—'

'That's no problem—I am sure Prince Sayid wouldn't mind you taking her with you and February is the perfect time of year to go there; the weather will be wonderful— warm and mild. Ella, you can't turn this one down. Just what I'd earn in commission is making my mouth water,' she admitted frankly.

Ella laughed. 'Ah, I see…'

She had begun painting animal 'portraits' almost by accident. Her painting had been merely a small hobby and her 'pet portraits' done for friends, but her reputation had spread by word of mouth, and eventually she had decided to make it her full-time career.

Now she earned what to her was a very comfortable living from her work, and she knew she would normally have leapt at the chance she was being offered.

'I'd love to go, Kate,' she replied. 'But Fleur is my priority right now…'

'Well, don't turn it down out of hand,' Kate warned her. 'Like I said, there's no reason why Fleur shouldn't go with you. You won't be working on this trip, it's only a mutual look-see. You'd be gone just over a week, and forget any idiotic ideas you might have about potential health hazards to any young baby out there—Zuran is second to none when it comes to being a world-class cosmopolitan city!'

One of the reasons Mariella had originally bought her small three-storey house had been because of the excellent north-facing window on the top floor, which she had turned into her studio. With Fleur contently fed she looked out at the grey early February day. The rain that had been sheeting down all week had turned to a mere drizzle. A walk in the park and some fresh air would do them both

good, Mariella decided, putting Fleur down whilst she
went to prepare her pram.

It had been her decision to buy the baby a huge old-
fashioned 'nanny' style pram.

'You can use the running stroller if you want,' she had
informed Tanya firmly. 'But when I walk her it will be in
a traditional vehicle and at a traditional pace!'

'Ella, you talk as though you were sixty-eight, not
twenty-eight,' Tanya had protested. Perhaps she was a little bit old-fashioned, Mariella conceded as she started to
remove the blankets from the running stroller to put in
the pram. Her father's desertion and her mother's conse-
quent vulnerability and helplessness had left her with a
very strong determination to stand on her own two feet,
and an extremely strong disinclination to allow herself to
be emotionally vulnerable through loving a man too much
as her mother had done.

After all, as Tanya had proved, it was possible to in-
herit a tendency!

She frowned as her fingers brushed against a balled-up
piece of paper as she removed the bedding. It could easily
have scratched Fleur's delicate skin. She was on the point
of throwing it away, when a line of her sister's handwrit-
ing suddenly caught her eye.

The piece of paper was a letter, Mariella recognised,
and she could see the name and address on it quite plainly.

'Sheikh Xavier Al Agir, No. 24, Quaffire Beach Road,
Zuran City.'

Her heart thudded guiltily as she smoothed out the note
and read the first line.

'You have destroyed my life and Fleur's and I shall hate
you for ever for that,' she read.

The letter was obviously one Tanya had written but not
sent to Fleur's father.

Fleur had always refused to discuss her relationship with him other than to say that he was a very wealthy Middle Eastern man whom she had met whilst working in a nightclub as a singer and dancer.

Privately Mariella had always thought that he had escaped far too lightly from his responsibility to her sister and to his baby…

And now she had discovered he lived in Zuran! Frowning slightly, she carefully folded the note. She had no right to interfere, she knew that, but… Would she be interfering or merely acknowledging the validity of fate? How many, many times over the years had she longed for the opportunity to confront her own father and tell him just what she thought of him, how he had broken her mother's heart and almost destroyed her life?

Her father, like her mother, was now dead, and could never make reparation for what he had done; but Tanya's lover was very much alive, and it would give her a great deal of satisfaction to tell him just what she thought of him!

Blowing Fleur a kiss, she hurried over to the telephone and quickly dialled her agent's number.

'Kate,' she began. 'I've been thinking…about that trip to Zuran…'

'You've changed your mind! Wonderful… You won't regret it, Ella, I promise you. I mean, this guy is mega, mega rich, and what he's prepared to pay to have his four-legged friends immortalised in oils…'

Listening to her, Mariella reflected ruefully that on occasion Kate could show a depressing tendency to favour the material over the emotional, but she was an excellent agent!

CHAPTER ONE

ZURAN had to have the cleanest airport in the world, Mariella decided as she retrieved her luggage and headed for the exit area, and Kate had been right about Prince Sayid's willingness to spare no expense to get her to Zuran. In the first-class cabin of their aircraft Fleur had been treated like a little princess!

Arrangements had been made for her to be chauffeur-driven to the Beach Club Resort where she would be staying along with Fleur in their own private bungalow, and, thanks to the prince's influence with the right diplomatic departments, all the necessary arrangements to get Fleur a passport, with Tanya's permission, had also been accomplished at top speed!

Craning her neck, Mariella looked round the busy arrivals area searching for someone carrying a placard bearing her name.

Behind her she was vaguely aware of something going on, not so much because of an increase in the noise level but rather because of the way it suddenly fell away. Alerted by some sixth sense, Mariella turned round, her eyes widening as she watched the way the crowds parted to make way for the small phalanx of white-robed men. Like traditional outriders, they carved a wide path through the crowd to allow the man striding behind them to cross the marble floor unhindered. Taller than the others, he looked neither to the right nor the left so that Mariella's artist's eye was able to observe the patrician arrogance of a profile that could only belong to a man used to being in command.

Instinctively, without being able to substantiate her reaction, Mariella didn't like him. He was too arrogant, too aware of his own importance. So physically and powerfully male, perfect in a way that sent a hundred unwanted sexual messages skittering over her suddenly very sensitive nerve endings. He had drawn level with her, and, whether because she sensed her antagonism or because Mariella had gripped her just a little bit more tightly, Fleur suddenly broke the silence with a small cry.

Instantly the dark head turned in their direction whilst the equally dark eyes burned into Mariella's. Mariella registered his gaze as her body gave a small, tight shudder.

The dark eyes stripped her, not of her clothes, but of her skin, her defences, Mariella recognised shakily, leaving them shredded down to her bones; her soul! But his gaze lingered longest of all on her face. Her eyes, she realised as she returned his remote and disdainful look of contempt with one of smouldering fury.

Fleur made another small sound and immediately his gaze switched from her to the baby and stayed there for a while, before it switched back to her own as though checking something.

Whatever it had been it brought a sneering look of contempt to his mouth that curved it into an even more dangerous line, Mariella noticed as her body responded to his reaction with a slow burn of colour along her cheekbones.

How dared he look at her with such contempt? She didn't care who or what he was! Once she imagined her father must have looked so at her mother before walking out on her, before leaving her to sink into the needy despair and dependence that Mariella remembered so starkly from her childhood, until her stepfather with his love and kindness had come to lift them both out of the dark, mean place her father had left them in.

As swiftly and as silently as they had arrived the small group of men swept through the hall and left. As a production it had been ridiculously overdone and theatrical, Mariella decided as she found the chauffeur patiently waiting for her and allowed herself to be carefully driven along with Fleur in the air-conditioned luxury of the limousine.

THE BEACH CLUB Resort was everything a five-star resort should be and more, Mariella acknowledged a couple of hours later when she had finished her exploration of her new surroundings.

The bungalow she had been allocated had two large bedrooms, each with its own bathroom, a small kitchen area, a living room, a private patio complete with whirl-pool, but it was the obvious forethought that had gone into equipping the place for a very young baby that most impressed Mariella. A good-sized cot had been provided and placed next to the bed, the bathroom was equipped with what was obviously a brand-new baby bath, baby toiletries had been added to the luxurious range provided for her own use, and in the fridge was a very full selection of top-of-the-range baby foods. However, it was the letter that had been left for her stating that the Beach Club's chef would prepare fresh organic baby food for Fleur on request that really made Mariella feel she could relax.

Having settled Fleur, who fell asleep as easily and comfortably as though she was in her own home, Mariella checked her watch and then put a call through to her sister. Tanya's cruise liner was on an extended tour of the Caribbean and the Gulf of Mexico.

'Ella, how's Fleur?' Tanya demanded immediately.

'Fast asleep,' Mariella told her. 'She was fine on the flight and got thoroughly spoiled. How are you?'

'Oh…fine… Very busy…we're doing two shows each evening, with no time off, but as I said the money is excellent. Ella, I must go… Give Fleur a big kiss for me.'

A little guiltily, Mariella looked at the now-silent mobile. She hadn't said anything to Tanya about her determination to confront her sister's faithless ex-lover and tell him just what she thought about him! Tanya might have gone willingly to his bed, but Mariella knew she hadn't been lying to her when she had told her that she had believed that he loved her, and that they had a future together.

MARIELLA STRUGGLED TO wake up from a confused and disjointed dream in which she was being dragged by her guards to lie trembling at the feet of the man who was now her master. How she hated him. Hated him for the way he stood there towering over her, looking down at her, looking over her so thoroughly that she felt as though his gaze burned her flesh.

He was looking deep into her eyes. His were the colour of the storm-tossed skies and seas of her homeland, a cold, pure grey that chilled her through and through.

'You dare to challenge me?' he was demanding softly as he moved closer to her. Behind her Mariella was conscious of the threatening presence of the guards.

She hated him with every sinew of her body, every pulse of blood from her heart. He left the divan where he had been sitting and came towards her, bending down, extending his hand to her face, but as his fingers gripped her chin Mariella turned her head and bit sharply into the soft pad of flesh below his thumb.

She felt the movement of the air as the guards leapt into

action, heard them draw their swords, and her body waited for the welcome kiss of death, but instead the guards were dismissed whilst her tormentor stepped back from her. One bright spot of blood glistened on the intricately inlaid tiled floor.

'You are like a wildcat and as such need to be tamed,' she heard him telling her softly.

She could feel the cleanliness of her hair on her bare skin and froze as he slowly circled her, standing behind her and sliding his hand through her hair and then wrapping it tightly around his fingers, arching her back against his body so that her semi-naked breasts were thrown into taut profile. His free hand reached for the clasp securing her top and her whole body shook with outrage. And then abruptly he released her, turning to face her so that she could see the contempt in his eyes.

Swimming up through the layers of her dream Mariella recognised that his face was one she knew; that his cynical contempt was something she had experienced before…

In the half heartbeat of time between sleeping and waking she realised why. The man in her dream had been the arrogant, hawk-eyed man she had seen earlier at the airport!

Getting out of bed, she went into the bathroom, shaking her head to clear her thoughts, and then, when that tactic did nothing to subdue their dangerous, clinging tentacles of remembered sensuality, she turned on the shower, deliberately setting it at a punishing 'cool,' before stepping into it.

The minute the cool spray hit her overheated skin she shuddered, gritting her teeth as she washed the slick film from her body, and then stepping out of the shower, to wrap herself in a luxuriously thick, soft white towel. In the mirror in front of her she could see the pale, pearlescent gleam of her own skin, and dangerously she knew that if

she were merely to close her eyes, behind her closed eyelids she would immediately see her tormentor, tall, cynically watchful, as he mocked her before reaching out to
take the towel from her body and claim her.

Infuriated with herself, Mariella rubbed her damp skin
roughly with the towel, and then re-set the air-conditioning. In her cot Fleur slept peacefully. Going to the fridge,
Mariella removed a bottle of water and opened it. Her hand
was shaking so much some of it slopped from the bottle
onto the worktop.

MARIELLA AND FLEUR had just finished eating a leisurely
breakfast on their private patio when a message came chattering through the fax machine. Frowning, Mariella read
it. The prince had been called away on some unexpected
business and would not now be able to see her for several
days. He apologised to Mariella for having to change their
arrangements, but asked her to enjoy the facilities of the
Beach Club at his expense until his return.

Carefully smoothing sun-protection lotion onto Fleur's
happy, wriggling little body, Mariella bent her head to kiss
her tummy, acknowledging that this would be an ideal time
to seek out Fleur's father. She had his address, after all! So
all she needed to do was summon a taxi to take her there!

Kate had been quite correct when she had described
Zuran's February weather as perfect, Mariella admitted
half an hour later as she carried Fleur out into the warm
sunshine. Since she was here on business and not holiday
she had packed accordingly, and was wearing a pair of
soft white linen trousers and a protective long-sleeved top.
When she showed the taxi driver the sheikh's address he
smiled and nodded. 'It will take maybe three quarters of
an hour,' he told her. 'You have business with the sheikh?'
he asked her conversationally.

Having learned already just how friendly people were, Mariella didn't take offence, replying simply tongue in cheek, 'You could say that.'

'He is a famous man. Revered by his tribe. They admire him for the way he has supported their right to live their lives in the traditional way. Although he is an extremely successful businessman it is said that he still prefers to live simply in the desert the way his people always have. He is a very good man.'

Mariella reflected inwardly that the picture the driver had just drawn for her was considerably at odds with the one she had gained from her half-sister.

Tanya had met the man in a nightclub, after all. Mariella had never liked the fact that Tanya worked there—although she had been employed as a singer, it openly advertised the sexual charms of its dancers, and Tanya had freely admitted that the majority of the customers were male.

And, certainly, during the twelve months they had been together, Mariella had never heard Tanya mention any predilection on her sexy sheikh's part to spend quality time in the middle of the desert! In fact, if she was honest, she had gained the impression that he was something of a 'playboy,' to use a perhaps now outdated word.

It took just under forty minutes for them to reach the impressive white mansion, which the taxi driver assured her was the correct address.

A huge pair of locked wrought-iron gates prevented them from going any farther, but as if by magic an official stepped out of one of the pair of gatehouses that flanked the gates, and approached the car.

As firmly as she could Mariella explained that she wished to see the sheikh.

'I am sorry but he is not available,' the official informed

her. 'He is away at the oasis at the moment and not expected back for some time.'

This was a complication Mariella had not been expecting. Fleur had woken up and was starting to grizzle a little.

'If you would care to leave a message?' the official was offering courteously.

Ruefully Mariella acknowledged inwardly that the nature of the message she wanted to give to the sheikh was better delivered in person!

Thanking him, she asked the taxi driver to take her back to the hotel.

'If you want, I can find someone to drive you to this oasis?' he suggested.

'You know where it is?' she questioned him.

He gave a small shrug. 'Sure! But you will need a four-wheel drive vehicle, as the track can be covered with sand.'

'Could I drive there myself?' Mariella asked him.

'It is possible, yes. It would take you two, maybe three hours. You wish me to give you the directions?'

It made more sense to drive to the oasis under her own steam than to go to the expense of paying a driver for the day as well as hiring a vehicle, Mariella decided.

'Please,' she agreed.

METHODICALLY, MARIELLA CHECKED through everything she had put on one side to pack into the four-wheel drive for her trip into the desert. The Beach Club's information desk staff had assured her that it would be perfectly safe for her to drive into the desert, and had attended to all the necessary formalities for her, including ensuring that a proper baby seat was provided for Fleur.

The trip should take her around three hours—four if she stopped off at the popular oasis resort for lunch as recommended by the Beach Club. But just in case she decided not to, they had provided her with a packed lunch in the form of a picnic hamper.

If it hadn't been for the serious purpose of her trip, she could quite easily have felt she were embarking on an exciting adventure, Mariella thought. Like everything else connected with the Beach Club, the four-wheel drive was immaculately clean and was even provided with its own mobile telephone!

The road into the desert was clearly marked, and turned out to be a well-built, smooth road that was so easy to navigate that Mariella quickly felt confident.

The secluded oasis where apparently the sheikh was staying was located in the Agir mountain range.

The light breeze, which had been just stirring the air when she had left the Beach Club, had increased enough to whip a fine dust of sand over her vehicle and the road itself within an hour of her setting out on her journey. The sand particles were so fine that somehow they actually managed to find their way into the four-wheel drive, despite the fact that Mariella had the doors and windows firmly closed. She had left the main road, now branched out onto a well-marked track across the desert itself.

It was a relief when she reached the Bedouin village marked on her map. It was market day and she had to drive patiently behind a camel train through the village, but fortunately it turned off towards the oasis itself, allowing her to accelerate.

In another half an hour she would stop for some lunch— if she hadn't reached the second oasis, marked on her map, she and Fleur would have their picnic instead.

The height of the sand dunes had left her feeling surprised and awed; they were almost a mountain range in themselves. Fleur was awake and Mariella turned off the radio to play her one of her favourite nursery rhyme tapes, singing along to it.

It was taking her longer than she'd estimated to reach the tourist base at the oasis where she had planned to have lunch—it was almost two o'clock now and she had expected to be there at one. A film of sand dust had turned the sky a brassy red-gold colour, and as she crested a huge sand dune and looked down into the emptiness on the other side of it Mariella began to panic slightly. Surely she should be able to at least see the tourist base oasis from here?

Ruefully she reached for the vehicle's mobile, realising that it might be sensible to ask for help, but to her dismay when she tried to make a call to the number programmed into the phone the only response was a fierce crackling sound. Stopping the vehicle she reached for her own mobile, but it was equally ineffective.

The sky was even more obscured by sand now, the wind hitting the vehicle with such force that it was physically rocking it. As though sensing her disquiet Fleur began to cry. She was hungry and needed changing, Mariella recognised, automatically attending to the baby's needs whilst she tried to decide what she should do.

It was impossible that she could be lost, of course. The vehicle was fitted with a compass and she had been given very detailed and careful instructions, which she had followed to the letter.

So why hadn't she reached the tourist oasis?

Fleur ate her own meal eagerly, but Mariella discovered that she herself had lost her appetite!

And then just as she was beginning to feel truly afraid she saw it! A line of camels swaying out of the dust towards her led by a robed camel driver.

Relieved, Mariella drove towards the camel train. Its leader was gravely polite. She had missed the turning to the oasis, he explained, something that was easily done with such a wind blowing sand across the track. To her alarm he further explained that, because of the sudden deterioration in the weather, all tourists had been urged to return to the city instead of remaining in the desert, but since Mariella had come so far her best course of action now was to press on to her ultimate destination, which he carefully showed her how to do using the vehicle's compass.

Thanking him, she did as he had instructed her, grimly checking and re-checking the compass as she drove up and down what felt like an interminable series of the sand dunes until eventually, in the distance through the sand blowing against her windscreen, she could just about see the looming mass of the mountain range.

It was already four o'clock and the light seemed to be fading, a fact that panicked Mariella into driving a little faster. She had never dreamed that her journey would prove so hazardous and she was very much regretting having set out on it, but now at last its end was in sight.

It took her almost another hour of zigzagging across the sand dunes to reach the rocky thrust of the beginnings of the mountain range. The oasis was situated in a deep ravine, its escarpment so high that Mariella shuddered a little as she drove into its shadows. This was the last kind of place she had expected to appeal to the man who had been her sister's faithless lover.

Would his villa here be as palatial as his home in Zuran? Mariella frowned and checked as the ravine opened out and she saw the oasis ahead of her. Remote and beautiful in its own way, it was very obviously a place of deep solitude, the oasis itself enclosed with a fringing of palms illuminated by the eerie glow of the final rays of the setting sun. Shielding her eyes, Mariella stopped the vehicle to look around. Where was the villa? All she could see was one solitary pavilion tent! A good-sized pavilion, to be sure, but most definitely not a villa! Had she somehow got lost—again?

Fleur had started to cry, a cross, tired, hungry noise that alerted Mariella to the fact that for Fleur's sake if nothing else she needed to stop.

Carefully she drove the vehicle forward over the treacherously boulder-rutted track, which seemed more like a dry river bed than a roadway! Sand blowing in from the desert was covering the boulders and the thin sparse grass of the oasis.

There was a vehicle parked several yards from the pavilion and Mariella stopped next to it.

A man was emerging from the pavilion, alerted to her arrival by the sound of her vehicle.

As he strode towards her, his robe caught by the strong wind and flattened against his body revealing a torso muscle structure that caused her to suck in her own stomach in a sharply dangerous womanly response to its maleness.

And then he turned his head and looked at her, and the earth halted on its axis before swinging perilously in a sickening movement as Mariella recognised him.

It was the man from the airport. The man from her dream!

CHAPTER TWO

His hand was on the door handle of the four-wheel drive. Wrenching it open, he demanded angrily, 'Who the devil are you?'

He was looking at her eyes again, with that same look of biting contempt glittering in his own as he raked her with a gritty gaze.

'I'm looking for Sheikh Xavier Al Agir,' Mariella responded, returning his look with one of her own—plus interest!

'What? What do you want with him?'

He was curt to the point of rudeness, but then, given what she had already seen—and dreamed—of him, she wouldn't have expected anything else.

'What I want with him is no business of yours!' she told him angrily.

In her seat Fleur's cries grew louder.

Peering into the vehicle, he demanded in disbelief, 'You've brought a baby out in this?'

The disgust and anger in his voice made her face sting even more than the pieces of sand blown against it by the wind.

'What the hell possessed you? Didn't you hear the weather warning earlier? This area was reported as being strictly out of bounds to tourists because of the threat of sandstorms.'

Hot-faced, Mariella remembered how she had switched off the radio to play Fleur's tapes.

'I'm sorry if I've arrived at an inconvenient time,' she responded sarcastically to cover her own discomfort, 'but if you could just give me directions for the Oasis Istafan, then—'

'This is the Oasis Istafan,' came back the immediate and cold response.

It was? Then?

'I want to see Sheikh Xavier Al Agir,' Mariella told him again, gathering her composure together. 'I presume he is here?'

'What do you want to see him for?'

Mariella had had enough. 'That is no business of yours,' she said angrily. Inwardly she was worrying how on earth she was going to get back to the city and the comfort of her Beach Club bungalow and what on earth a man as wealthy as the sheikh was reputed to be was doing out here with this…this…this arrogant predator of a man!

'Oh, I think you'll find that anything concerning Xavier is very much my business,' came the gritted reply.

Something—Mariella wasn't sure what—must have alerted her to the truth. But she was too shocked by it to voice it, looking from his eyes to his mouth and then back again as she swallowed—hard—against the tight ball of shock tightening like ice around her heart. 'You…you… can't be the sheikh,' she told him defiantly, but her voice was trembling lightly, betraying her lack of confidence in her own denial.

Was this man her sister's lover…and Fleur's father? What was that sharp, bitter, dangerous feeling settling over her like a black cloud?

'You are the sheikh, aren't you?' she acknowledged bleakly.

A brief, sardonic inclination of his head was his only response but it was enough.

Turning away from him, she reached into the baby carrier and tenderly removed Fleur. Her whole face softened and illuminated with love as she hugged her and then kissed her before looking him straight in the eyes and saying fiercely to him, 'This is Fleur, the baby you have refused to both acknowledge and support.'

She had shocked him, Mariella realised, even though he had concealed his reaction very quickly.

As he stepped back from the vehicle for a second Mariella thought he was going to tell her to leave—and cravenly she wanted to do so! The man, the location, the situation were so not what she had been anticipating and prepared herself for. Each one of them in their different ways shattered not just her preconceptions but also her precious self-containment.

The man—try as she might she could just not envisage him in the club where Tanya had performed. The location made her ache for her painting equipment and brought her artistic senses to quick hunger. And her situation! Oh, no... Definitely no! This man had been her sister's lover, and was Fleur's father—

The shadowy fear that had stalked her adult years suddenly loomed terrifyingly sharply in front of her. She would not be like her mother; she would not ever allow herself to be vulnerable in any way to a man who could only damage her emotionally. The ability to fall in love with the wrong man might be learned, but it was not, to the best of Mariella's knowledge, inherited!

'Get out!'

Get out? With pleasure! Gripping the steering wheel,

Mariella reached for the door, slamming it closed and then switching on the ignition at the same time, then she threw the vehicle into a furious spurt of reverse speed.

The tyres spun; sand filled the air. She could hear a thunderous banging on her driver's door as the car refused to budge. Looking out of the window, she saw Xavier looking at her in icy, furious disbelief.

Realising that she was bogged down in the swirling sand, Mariella switched off the engine. If he wanted her to leave he would have to move the vehicle for her, she recognised in angry humiliation.

As the engine died he was yanking the door open, demanding, 'What the hell do you think you are trying to do?'

'You told me to get out!' Mariella reminded him, equally angry.

'I meant get out of the car, not…' As he swore beneath his breath, to her shock he suddenly reached into the vehicle and snapped off her seat belt, grasping her so tightly around her waist that it actually hurt.

As he pulled her free of her seat and swung her to the ground she had a sudden shocking image of the two of them in her dream!

'Let go of me,' she demanded chokily, pushing him away. 'Don't touch me…'

'Don't touch you?'

Now that she was on the ground she realised just how far she had to look up to see the expression in his eyes.

'From what I've heard it isn't often those words leave your lips.'

Instinctively Mariella raised her hand, taking refuge in an act of female rebuttal and retaliation as ancient as the land around her, but immediately he seized her wrist in a punishing grip, his eyes glittering savagely as he curled his fingers tighter. 'Hell cat!' he taunted her mercilessly. 'One attempt to use your claws on me and, I promise you, you will regret it.

'You can't go anywhere tonight,' he told her bluntly. 'There's a sandstorm forecast that would bury you alive before you could get even halfway back to the city. In your case it would be no loss, but for the sake of the child…'

The child…Fleur!

An agonised sound of distress choked in Mariella's throat. She could not stay here in this wilderness with this…this…savagely dangerous man, but her own common sense was telling her that she had no other option. Already the four-wheel drive was buried almost axle-deep in sand. She could taste it in her mouth, feel it on her skin. Inside the vehicle, Fleur had begun to cry again. Instinctively Mariella turned to go to her, but Xavier was there before her, lifting Fleur out.

The baby looked so tiny held in his arms. Mariella held her breath watching him… He was Fleur's father after all. Surely he must feel something? Some remorse, some guilt…something… True, he did pause to look at her, but the expression on his face was unreadable.

'She has your hair,' he told Mariella, before adding grimly, 'The wind is picking up. We need to get inside the tent. Where are you going?' he demanded as she turned back to the vehicle.

'I want to get Fleur's things,' she told him, tensing as he gave a sharp exclamation of irritation and overruled her.

'Leave them for now. I shall come back for them.'

Mariella couldn't believe how strong the wind had become! The sand felt like a million tiny particles of glass shredding her skin.

By the time they reached the safety and protection of the

pavilion, her leg muscles ached from the effort of fighting her way through the shifting sand.

Once inside the pavilion she realised that it was much larger than she had originally thought. A central area was furnished with rich carpets and low divans. Rugs were thrown over dark wood chests, and on the intricately carved tables stood oil lamps and candles. In their light Mariella could see two draped swags of cloth caught back in a dull gold rope as though they covered the entrance to two other inner rooms.

'Fleur needs something to eat, and a change of clothes,' she announced curtly, 'and I want to ring the Beach Club to tell them what has happened.'

'Use a telephone—in this intensity of sandstorm?' He laughed openly at her. 'You would be lucky to be able to use a landline, never mind a mobile. As for the child...'

'The child!' Mariella checked him bitterly. 'Even knowing the truth you still try to distance yourself from her, don't you? Well, let me tell you something—'

'No, let me tell you something... Any man could have fathered this child! I feel for her that she should have a mother of such low morals, a mother so willing to give herself to any and every man her eye alights on, but let me make it plain to you that I do not intend to be black-mailed into paying for a pleasure that was of so little value, never mind paying for a child who may or may not be the result of it!'

Mariella went white with shock and disbelief, but before she could defend her sister, Fleur started to cry in earnest.

Ignoring Xavier, Mariella soothed her, whispering tenderly. 'It's all right, sweetheart, I know you're hungry...' Automatically as she talked to her Mariella stroked her and kissed the top of her head. She was so unbearably precious to her even though she was not her child. Being there at her birth had made Mariella feel as though they shared a very special bond, and awakened a maternal urge inside her she had not previously known she had.

'I don't know what she has to eat, but there is some fruit and milk in the fridge, and a blender,' he informed her.

Fridge? Blender? Mariella's eyes widened. 'You have electricity out here?'

Immediately he gave her a very male sardonic look.

'Not as such. There's a small generator, which provides enough for my needs.' He gave a brief shrug. 'After all, I come out here to work in peace...not to wear a hair shirt! The generator can provide enough warm water for you to bathe the child, although you, I am afraid, will have to share my bathing water.'

He was waiting for her to object, Mariella could see that. He was enjoying tormenting her.

'Since I shall only be here overnight, I dare say I can manage to forgo that particular pleasure,' she told him grittily.

'I shall go to your vehicle and bring the baby's things. You will find the kitchen area through that exit and to your right.'

Mariella had brought some dried baby food with her as well as some tinned food, which she knew would probably suit Fleur's baby digestion rather better than raw fruit, no matter how well blended! Even so, it would do no harm to explore their surroundings.

As she stepped through the opening she found that she was in a narrow corridor, on the right of which was an unexpectedly well equipped although very small kitchen, and, to the left, an immaculately clean chemical lavatory, along with a small shower unit.

The other opening off the main room must lead to a sleeping area, she decided as she walked back.

'What is all this stuff?' she heard Xavier demanding as he walked in with his arms full.

In other circumstances his obvious male lack of awareness of a small baby's needs might have been endearing, but right now...

Ignoring him and still holding Fleur, she opened the cool-bag in which she had placed her foods.

'Yummy, look at this, Fleur,' she murmured to her. 'Banana pudding...our favourite... Yum-yum.'

The look of serious consideration in Fleur's hazel eyes as she looked at her made her smile, and she forgot Xavier for a second as she concentrated on the baby.

'I suppose I shouldn't be surprised that she isn't receiving the nutrition of her mother's own milk,' she heard Xavier announcing critically.

Immediately Mariella swung round, her eyes dark with anger.

'Since her mother had to go back to work that wasn't possible!'

'How virtuous you make it sound, but isn't it the truth that the nature of that work—is anything but? But of course you will deny that, just as you will claim to know who the child's father is.'

'You are totally despicable,' Mariella stopped him. 'Fleur does not deserve to be treated like this. She is an innocent baby...'

'Indeed! At last we are in agreement about something. It is a pity, though, that you did not think of that before you came out here making accusations and claims.'

How could he be so cold? So unfeeling! According to the little Tanya had said about him, she had considered him to be a very emotional and passionate man.

No doubt in bed he was, Mariella found herself acknowledging. Her face suddenly burnt hotly as she recognised the unwanted significance of her private thoughts, and even worse the images they were mentally conjuring up for her; not with her sister as Xavier's partner—but herself!

What was happening to her? She was a cool-blooded woman who analysed, rationalised and resisted any kind of damaging behaviour to herself. And yet here she was...

'Just how long is this sandstorm going to last?' she asked abruptly.

The dark eyebrows rose. 'One day...two...three...'

'Three!' Mariella was aghast. Apart from the fact that Tanya would be beside herself if she could not get in touch with her, what was the prince going to think if he returned and she wasn't there?

'I have to feed and change Fleur.'

Luckily she had brought the baby bath with her as well as the changing mat, and Fleur's pram cum carry-cot, mainly because she had not been quite sure what facilities would be available at the oasis.

'Since it is obvious that you will have to stay the night, it is probably best that you and the child sleep in my... In the sleeping quarters,' Xavier corrected himself. Mariella's mouth went dry.

'And...where will you sleep?' she asked him apprehensively.

'In here, of course. When you have fed and bathed the child I suggest that we both have something to eat. And then—'

'Thank you, but I am perfectly capable of deciding for myself when I eat,' Mariella told him sharply.

SHE WAS FAR more independent, and a good deal more fiery, than he had anticipated, Xavier acknowledged broodingly when Mariella had disappeared with Fleur. And quite definitely not his younger cousin's normal type.

Thinking of Khalid made his mouth tighten a little. He had been both furious and disbelieving when Khalid had telephoned him to announce that he had fallen in love and was thinking of marrying a girl he had met in a dubious nightclub. Khalid had been in love before, but this was the first time he had considered marriage. At twenty-four Khalid was still very immature. When he married, in Xavier's opinion it needed to be someone strong enough to keep him grounded—and wealthy enough not to be marrying him for his money.

His frown deepened. It had been his cynical French grandmother who had warned him when he was very young that the great wealth he had inherited from his father would make him a target for greedy women. When he had been in his teens his grandmother had insisted that he spent time in France meeting the chic daughters of her own distant relatives, girls who in her opinion were deserving of inheriting the 'throne' his grandmother would have had to abdicate when Xavier eventually married.

Well-born though they were, those girls had held very little appeal for him, and, practical though he knew it would be, he found himself even less enamoured of the idea of contracting an arranged marriage.

Because of this he had already decided that it would be Khalid who would ultimately provide the heir to his enormous fortune and, more importantly, take his place as leader of their historically unique tribe. But he hadn't been in any hurry to nudge Khalid in the direction of a suitable bride—until he had learned of his plans *vis-à-vis* the impossible young woman who had forced her way into his private retreat!

He didn't know which of them had angered him the

most! Khalid for his weakness in disappearing without leaving any indication of where he had gone, or the woman herself who had boldly followed up her pathetic attempt at blackmailing him via the letter she had sent Xavier, with a visit to his territory, along with the baby she was so determined to claim his cousin had fathered!

Physically he had not been able to see any hint in the child's features that she might be Khalid's; she was as prettily blonde as her mother, and as delicately feminine. The only difference was that, whilst her mother chose to affect those ridiculous, obviously false turquoise-coloured contact lenses, the baby's eyes were a warm hazel.

Like Khalid's?

There was no proof that the child was Khalid's, he reminded himself. And there was no way he was going to allow his cousin to marry her mother, without knowing for sure that Khalid was the father, especially now that he had actually met her. It was a wonder that Khalid had ever fallen so desperately in love with her in the first place!

'She has the grace of a gazelle,' he had written to him. 'The voice of an angel! She is the sweetest and most gentle of women...'

Well, Xavier begged to differ! At least on the two eulogising counts! Had he known when he had seen her at the airport just who she was he would have tried to find some way of having her deported there and then!

Remembering that occasion made him stride over to the opening to the pavilion, pulling back the cover to look outside. As had been forecast the wind was now a howling dervish of destruction, whipping up the sand so that already it was impossible to see even as far as the oasis itself. Which was a pity, because right now he could do with the refreshing swim he took each evening in the cool water of the oasis, rather than using the small shower next to the lavatory.

It both astounded and infuriated him that he could possibly want such a woman—she represented everything he most detested in the female sex: avarice, sexual laxity, selfishness—so far as he was concerned these were faults that could never be outweighed by a beautiful face or a sensual body. And he had to admit that, in that regard, his cousin had shown better taste than he had ever done previously!

Xavier allowed the flap of the tent to drop back in place and secured it. It irked him that Mariella should have the gall to approach him here of all places, where he came to retreat from the sometimes heavy burden of his responsibilities. A thin smile turned down the corners of his mouth. From what Khalid had described of the luxury-loving lifestyle they had shared, he doubted that she would enjoy being here. However little he cared about her discomfort, though there was the child to be considered.

The child! His mouth thinned a little more. Little Fleur was most definitely a complication he had not anticipated!

WITH FLEUR FED, clean and dry, Mariella suddenly discovered just how tired she felt herself.

She had not expected Xavier to be pleased to be confronted with her accusations regarding his treatment of Tanya and Fleur, but the sheer savagery and cruelty with which he had verbally savaged her sister's morals had truly shocked her. This was after all a man who had very eagerly shared Tanya's bed, and who, even worse, had sworn that he loved her and that he wanted her to share a future with him!

In her opinion Tanya and Fleur were better off without him, just as she had been better off without the father who had deserted her!

Now that she had confronted him, though—and witnessed that he was incapable of feeling even the smallest shred of remorse—she longed to be able to get away from him, instead of being forced to remain here with him in the dangerous intimacy of this desert camp where the two of them…

THOSE RIDICULOUS TURQUOISE eyes looked even more theatrical and unreal in the pale triangle of her small exhausted face, Xavier decided angrily as he watched Mariella walking patiently up and down the living area of the pavilion whilst she rocked Fleur to sleep in her arms.

No doubt Khalid must have seen her a hundred or more times with her delicate skin free of make-up and those haunting, smudged shadows beneath her eyes as he lay over her in the soft shadows of the early morning, waking her with his caresses.

The fierce burst of anger that exploded inside him infuriated him. What was the matter with him? When he broke it down what was she after all? A petite, small-boned woman with a tousled head of strawberry-blonde hair that was probably dyed, coloured contact lenses to obscure the real colour of her eyes, skin the colour of milk and a body that had no doubt known more lovers than it was sensible for any sane-thinking adult to want to own to, especially one as fastidious in such matters as he was.

It would serve her right if he proved to Khalid just exactly what she was by bedding her himself! That would certainly ensure that his feckless cousin, who had abandoned his desk in their company headquarters without telling anyone where he was going or for how long, would, when he decided to return, realise just what a fate he had protected him from!

The child, though, was a different matter. If she should

indeed prove to be his cousin's, then her place was here in Zuran where she could be brought up to respect herself as a woman should, and to despise the greedy, immoral woman who had given birth to her!

CHAPTER THREE

MARIELLA woke up before Fleur had given her first distressed, hungry cry. She wriggled out from under the cool pure linen bedding to pad barefoot and naked to where she had placed the carry-cot.

Her khaki-coloured soft shape trousers could be re-worn without laundering, but the white cotton tee shirt she had worn beneath her jacket, and her underwear—no way.

Fastidiously wrinkling her nose at the very thought, Mariella had rinsed them out, deciding that even if they had not dried by morning wearing them slightly damp was preferable to putting them back on unwashed!

Picking Fleur up, she carried her back to the bed... Xavier's bed, a huge, low-lying monster of a bed, large enough to accommodate both a man and half his harem without any problem at all!

Sliding back beneath the linen sheets, Mariella stroked Fleur's soft cheek and watched her in the glow of the single lamp she had left on. She could tell from the way the baby sucked eagerly on her finger that she was hungry!

She had seen water in the fridge, and she had Fleur's formula. All she had to do was to brave the leopard's den in order to reach the kitchen!

And in order to do that she needed to find something to wear.

Whilst she was deciding between one of the pile of soft towels Xavier had presented her with or the sheet itself, Fleur started to cry.

'Hush,' she soothed her gently. 'I know you're hungry, sweetheart…'

Xavier sighed as he heard Fleur crying. It was just gone two in the morning. The divan wasn't exactly the most comfortable thing to sleep on. Outside the wind shrieked like a hyena, testing the strength of the pavilion, but its traditional design had withstood many centuries of desert winds and Xavier had no fears of it being plucked away.

Throwing back the cover from his makeshift bed, he pulled on the soft loose robe and strode towards the kitchen, briskly removing one of the empty bottles Mariella had left in the sterilizer and mixing the formula.

His grandmother—an eccentric woman so far as many people were concerned—had sent him to work in a refugee camp for six months after his final year at school and before he went on to university.

'You know what it is to be proud,' she had told him when he had expressed his disdain for her decision. 'Now you need to learn what it is to be humble.

'Without humility it is impossible to be a great leader of men, Xavier,' she had informed him. 'You owe it to your grandfather's people to have greatness, for without it they will be swamped by this modern world and scattered like seeds in the wind.'

One of his tasks there had been to work in the crèche. For the rest of his life Xavier knew he would remember the emotions he had experienced at the sight of the children's emaciated little bodies.

Snapping the teat on the filled bottle, he headed for the bedroom.

The baby's cries were noticeably louder. Her feckless

mother was no doubt sleeping selfishly through them, Xavier decided grimly, ignoring the fact that he himself had already noticed just how devoted Fleur's mother was to her.

Fleur was crying too much and too long to be merely hungry, Mariella thought anxiously as she caught the increasing note of misery in the baby's piercing cry.

To her relief, Fleur seemed to find some comfort as Mariella sat up in the bed and cuddled her against her own body.

'What's wrong, sweetheart?' she whispered to her. 'Are you missing your...?'

She froze as the protective curtain closing off the room swung open, snatching at the sheet to cover herself, her face hot with embarrassment as she glared at Xavier.

'What do you want?' she demanded aggressively.

'So you are awake. I thought—'

Fleur's eyes widened as she saw that he was carrying Fleur's bottle.

'What have you put in there?' Mariella demanded suspiciously, holding Fleur even tighter as he held the bottle out to her.

'Formula,' he told her curtly. 'What did you think was in it...hemlock? You've been reading too many idiotic trashy books!'

As she took the bottle from him and squirted a few drops onto the back of her hand, tasting it, he watched her.

'Satisfied?'

Looking fully at him, Mariella compressed her lips.

'My word,' she heard him breathe in disbelief. 'You even go to bed in those ridiculous coloured contact lenses! Hasn't anyone ever told you that no one actually has eyes that colour? So if it's your lovers you are hoping to impress and deceive...'

As Fleur seized eagerly on her bottle Mariella froze in outraged fury.

Coloured contact lenses. How dared he?

'Oh, is that a fact?' she breathed. 'Well, for your information, whether you consider it to be ridiculous or not this just happens to be the real colour of my eyes. I am not wearing contact lenses, and as for wanting to impress or deceive a lover—'

Fleur gave a wail of protest as in her agitation Mariella unwittingly removed the teat from her mouth. Apologising to the baby, and comforting her, Mariella breathed in sharply with resentment.

Real? The only thing about her that was real was her outrageous lying! Xavier decided lowering his lashes over his eyes as he discreetly studied the smooth swell of her breasts as her agitated movements dislodged the sheet.

No wonder she had not wanted to feed her child herself. With breasts so perfectly and beautifully formed she would be reluctant to spoil their shape. He could almost see the faint pink shadowing of the areolae of her nipples.

Uncomfortably he shifted his weight from one foot to the other, all too conscious of the effect she was having on him. She was doing it deliberately, he knew that... She was that kind of woman!

When he came here it was to withdraw from the fast-paced city life and concentrate on more cerebral matters, Xavier reminded himself sharply.

The sheet slipped a little farther.

Her flesh was creamy pale, untouched by the sun. He frowned. Khalid had said specifically that he had taken her to the South of France. Surely there she must have exposed herself, as so many did, to the hot glare of its sun and the ever hotter lustful looks of the men who went there specifically to enjoy the sight of so much young, naked flesh?

Knowing his cousin as he did, he couldn't imagine that Khalid would be attracted to a woman too modest to remove her bikini top!

He, on the other hand, found something profoundly and intensely sensual about the thought of a woman only revealing her bare breasts to her lover, her only lover...

Worriedly Mariella studied Fleur's suddenly flushed face, reaching out to touch her cheek. It burned beneath the coolness of her own fingertips. Her heart jumped with anxiety.

Xavier's stomach muscles clenched as she removed her arm, revealing the full exposed curve of her breast. As he had known it would be, her nipple was rose-pink and so softly delicate that he ached to reach out and touch it, explore its soft tenderness, feel it hardening in eager demand beneath his caress.

In her anxiety for Fleur, Mariella had all but forgotten that he was there, only alerted to his sudden departure by the brief swirl of air eddying the door-hanging as he left.

The minute he had gone Fleur started to cry again and nothing Mariella could do would soothe her.

In the end, terrified that he would reappear at any minute and demand that she silence the baby or else, Mariella got out of the bed and, wrapping the sheet around herself, started to pace the floor, gently rocking Fleur as she did so.

To her relief after about ten minutes Fleur began to fall asleep. Gently carrying her back to her cot she started to lie her down, but the minute she did so the baby began to cry again.

Resolutely Mariella tried again...and again...and again...

Three hours later she finally admitted just how afraid she was. Fleur was crying pitifully now, her cheeks bright red and her whole body hot and sweaty. Mariella's own eyes ached and her arms were cramped with holding her as she walked up and down the bedroom.

Outside the wind still howled demoniacally.

'Oh, poor, poor baby,' Mariella whispered anxiously. Tanya had entrusted her precious child to her. How would she feel if she knew what Mariella had done? How she had brought her to the middle of the desert where there was no doctor and no way of getting to one? What if Fleur had something really seriously wrong with her? What if she had picked up some life-threatening infectious disease? What if…? Sick with anxiety and guilt, Mariella prayed that Fleur would be all right.

In the outer part of the pavilion Xavier could hear the fretful cry of the baby but he dared not go in to find out what was wrong. He could not trust himself to go in and find out what was wrong he admitted grimly.

AN HOUR LATER, still trying to soothe and comfort Fleur, Mariella felt desperately afraid. It was obvious that Fleur wasn't well. The fear tormenting her could not be ignored any longer. Her hands trembling, Mariella relit all the oil lamps and then carefully undressed Fleur, slowly checking her for any sign of the rash that would confirm her worst fears and indicate that the baby could somehow have contracted meningitis.

Not content with having checked her skin once without finding any sign of a rash, Mariella did so again. When once again she could not find any sign of a rash, she didn't know whether to feel relieved or simply more anxious!

Tenderly wiping the tears from Fleur's hot face, she kissed her. Fleur grabbed hold of her finger and was trying to suck on it. No, not suck, Mariella realised—she was trying to bite on it. Fleur was cutting her first tooth!

All at once relief and recognition filled her. Fleur was

teething—that was why she had been so uncomfortable.
Mariella could well remember Tanya at the same age,
her mother walking up and down with her as she tried to
soothe her, explaining to Mariella just how much those
sharp, pretty little teeth cutting through tender flesh hurt
and upset the baby.

Naturally Mariella had tucked a good supply of pae-
diatric paracetamol suspension into her baby bag before
leaving home and, still holding Fleur, she went to get it.

'This will make you feel better, sweetheart,' she
crooned, adding lovingly, 'And what a clever girl you are,
aren't you, with your lovely new tooth? A very clever girl.'

Within minutes or so of the baby having her medicine,
or so it seemed to a now totally exhausted Mariella, she
was fast asleep. Patting her flushed face, Mariella smothered a yawn. Tucking Fleur into her cot, she made for her
own bed.

XAVIER FROWNED. IT was well past daylight. He had showered and eaten his breakfast and switched on the laptop he
had brought with him to do some work, but his mind wasn't
really on it. Every time he thought about his cousin's mistress he was filled with unwanted and dangerous emotions.
There hadn't been a sound from the bedroom in hours.
No doubt working in a nightclub she was used to sleeping during the day... And very probably not on her own!

The very thought of the woman sleeping next door in
his bed drove him to such an unfamiliar and furious level
of hormone-fuelled rage that he could barely contain himself. And he was a man who was secretly proud of the fact
that he was known for his fabled self-control!

Khalid should think himself very fortunate indeed that
he had prevented him from marrying that turquoise-eyed
seductress.

But Khalid did not think himself fortunate! Khalid thought himself very far from fortunate and had, in fact, left his cousin's presence swearing that he would not give up the woman he loved, no, not even if Xavier did try to carry out his threat and disinherit him!

His cousin was quite plainly besotted with the woman, and now that Xavier had met her for himself he was beginning to understand just how dangerous she was.

But not even Khalid's love would be strong enough to withstand the knowledge that she had been his cousin's lover. That she had given herself willingly to him! That the thought of ensnaring an even richer man than Khalid, in Xavier himself, had been enough to have her crawling into his bed.

That knowledge would hurt Khalid, but better that he was hurt quickly and cleanly now than that he spent a lifetime suffering a thousand humiliations at her hands! As he undoubtedly would do!

Surely the silence from the bedroom was unnatural. The woman should be awake by now, if only for the sake of her child!

Irritably Xavier strode towards the bedroom area, and pulled back the hanging.

Mariella was lying on the bed deeply asleep, one arm flung out, her pale skin gleaming in the soft light.

The thick strawberry-blonde hair was softly tousled, a few wisps sticking to her pink-cheeked face, lashes, which surely must be dyed to achieve that density of colour, surrounding the turquoise she insisted on claiming was natural.

In her sleep she sighed and frowned and made a little moue of distress before settling back into sleep.

Unable to drag his gaze from her, Xavier continued to watch her. There was nothing about what he knew of the type of person she was that could appeal to his aesthetic and cultured taste. But physically…

Physically, hormonally, she exerted such a pull over his senses that right now…

He had taken a step towards the bed without even realising it, the ache in his groin immediately a fierce, primal surge of white-hot need. If he took her in his arms and woke her now, would it be Khalid's name he heard on her lips?

That thought alone should have been enough to freeze his arousal to nothing, but instead he was filled with a savage explosion of angry emotion at the thought of any man's name on her lips that wasn't his own!

As he battled with the realisation of just what that meant, his attention was suddenly distracted by the happy gurgling coming from the cot.

Striding over to it, he stared down at Fleur. Her child. The child another man had given her! A surge of primitive aching pain filled him.

Fleur had kicked off her blankets and was playing with her bare toes, smiling coquettishly up at him.

Xavier sucked in his breath. She was so small, so delicate…so very much like her mother.

Instinctively he bent to pick her up.

Mariella didn't know what woke her from her deep sleep, some ancient female instinct perhaps, she decided shakily as she stared across the room and saw Xavier bending over Fleur.

Gripping the bedclothes, she burst out frantically, 'Don't you dare hurt her.'

'Hurt her?' Tight-lipped, Xavier swung round. 'You dare to say that when she has already been hurt immeasurably simply by being brought into being as the child of a woman who…'

Unable to fully express his feelings, he compressed his mouth.

'I suppose she is used to being left to amuse herself whilst her mother sleeps off the effects of her night's work!'

Mariella could scarcely contain her fury.

'How dare you say such things, after the way you have behaved? You are the most loathsome, the most vile man I have ever met. You are totally lacking in any kind of compassion, or…or responsibility!'

Her eyes really were that colour, Xavier recognised in disbelief as he watched them darken from turquoise to inky blue-green.

Did they turn that colour when she was lost in passion? Was she as passionate in her sexual desire as she was in her anger? Of course she was…he knew that instinctively, just as he knew equally instinctively that if she were his…

'It is nearly eleven o'clock, the child must be hungry,' he told her tersely, infuriated by his own weakness in allowing such thoughts to creep into his head.

Eleven o'clock—how could it be? Mariella wondered guiltily, but a quick glance at her watch showed her that it was.

She couldn't wait to get back to the city and the sooner she and Fleur were on their way back there, the better, she decided as Xavier strode out of the room.

CHAPTER FOUR

MARIELLA frowned as she walked into the empty living area of the pavilion. Where was Xavier?

A laptop hummed quietly on a folding campaign table to one side of the pavilion. Xavier had obviously been working on it.

As she looked round the pavilion with its precious carpets and elegant few pieces of furniture, which she recognised as being expensively antique as well as functional, Mariella tried to imagine her dizzy half-sister in such a setting. Tanya was totally open about the fact that she was a girl who loved the bustle of cities, holidays in expensive, fashionable locations, modern apartments as opposed to traditional houses. Although she adored Fleur, self-indulgence was her byword, and Mariella was finding it increasingly hard to visualise her sister ever being compatible with a man like Xavier, who she could not imagine truly sharing Tanya's tastes. He was too austere, surely. Too...

Tanya loved him, she reminded herself stubbornly, although she was finding that equally hard to imagine! He was just so totally not Tanya's type! Tanya liked happy-go-lucky, boyish, fun-loving men!

Fleur was sound asleep, and Mariella decided she would go outside to check on what was happening. She could no longer hear the sound of the wind battering against

the walls of the pavilion, which hopefully meant that she
would be able to make her way back to the city.

As she stepped outside she saw to her relief that the
wind had indeed dropped. The air was now totally still
and the sky had a dull ochre tinge to it. She could see her
four-wheel drive, its sides covered in sand.

On the far side of the oasis, the rock face of the gorge
rose steeply, its almost vertical face scarred here and there
by the odd ledge.

There was a raw, elemental beauty about this hidden
place, Mariella acknowledged, seeing it now with an artist's eye rather than the panicky apprehension of a lost
traveller.

A scattering of palm trees fringed the water of the
oasis, and beyond them lay a rough area of sparse, spiky
grass. The rutted track she had driven down probably was
a dried-out river bed, she could see now.

The quality of the stillness and the corresponding silence were almost hypnotic.

A movement on the other side of the oasis caught her
eye, her body tensing as she recognised Xavier. He was
dressed not in traditional robes, but in jeans and a tee shirt.
He seemed to be checking the palm trees, she realised as
he paused to inspect one before walking to another. He had
obviously not seen her, but instinctively she drew farther
back into the shadow cast by the pavilion.

He had turned away from the trees now and was staring across the oasis, shading his eyes as he looked up into
the sky.

THE STORM HADN'T weakened the roots of any of the palm
trees, Xavier acknowledged. There was no reason why
he shouldn't go back to the pavilion and continue with
his work. And in fact pretty soon he would have to do so.

Right now they were in the eye of the storm, but as soon as it moved on the wind would return with even greater force.

But he couldn't go back inside. Not whilst he was still visualising *her* lying on the bed...his bed...

Angrily he stripped off his tee shirt, quickly followed by the rest of his clothes. And began to wade out into the water.

Mariella couldn't move. Like someone deeply beneath the spell of an outside force she stood, muscles clenched, hardly daring to breathe as she fought to repel the sensation coiling through her, and shivering to each and every single sensitive nerve ending as her gaze absorbed the raw male beauty of Xavier's nudity.

As an artist she was fully aware of the complexities and the beauty of the human form, she had visited Florence and wandered lost in rapt awe as she studied the work of the great masters, but now she recognised she was seeing the work of the greatest Master of all.

Xavier was wading out into the water, the dull glaring sunlight glinting on flesh so warmly and evenly hued that it was immediately obvious that such nudity was normal for him.

As he moved through the water she could see the powerful sinews in his thighs contracting against its pressure. Trying to distract herself she visualised what lay inside that heavy satin male flesh, the bones, the muscles, the tissues, but instead of calming her down, it made her awareness of him increase, her wanton thoughts fiercely pushing aside the pallid academic images she was trying to conjure, in favour of some of their own: like a close-up of that sun-warmed flesh, roped with muscle, hard, sleek, rough with the same fine dark hair she could see so clearly arrowing down the centre of his body.

Only his buttocks were a slightly paler shade than the

rest of his skin, taut and man-shaped, packed with the muscles that would drive…

Mariella shuddered violently, feeling as though she herself were sinking into a pool of sensation so deep and dangerous that she had no means of freeing herself from it.

Helplessly she watched as Xavier moved farther into the oasis until all she could see above the water were his head and shoulders. He ducked his whole body beneath the water and she held her breath, expelling it when she saw him break the surface several yards away, cleaving through it with long, powerful over-arm strokes that propelled him at a fierce and silent speed away from her.

She felt sick, shocked, furiously angry, terrifyingly vulnerable, aching from head to toe and most of all, deep down inside the most female part of her body, tormented by a need, a knowledge that ripped apart all her previous beliefs about herself.

She could not possibly want Xavier! But that…that merciless message her body had just given her could not be denied.

It sickened her to think of wanting a man who had hurt her sister so much; a man Tanya still loved so much. Such a feeling was a betrayal of everything within herself she most prided herself on. It was inconceivable that such a thing could be happening, just as it was inconceivable too that she, a woman who took such pride in her ability to mentally control the sexual and emotional side of her nature, could allow herself to feel so…so…

Dragging her gaze away from the oasis, Mariella closed her eyes.

Go on, admit it, she taunted herself mentally. You are so hungry for him that if he came to you now, you would let him do whatever he wanted with you right here and right now. Let him? You would urge him, encourage him, entice him...

Frantically Mariella shook her head, trying to shake away her own tormenting thoughts, the tormenting inner voice that was mocking her so openly.

Blindly she headed back for the pavilion, not seeing the hot breaths of wind tugging warningly at the topmost fronds of the palm trees, and not noticing, either, the bronze ring of light dulling the sun so menacingly.

Once inside the pavilion she hurried to check on Fleur who was still sleeping. She had only been outside for around half an hour, but it felt somehow as though she had passed through a whole time zone and entered another world. A world in which she no longer knew exactly who or what she was.

Quickly she started to get together their things. She didn't want to be here when Xavier came back. She couldn't bear to be here when he came back; she couldn't bear to face him, to be in the same room with him, the same space with him; in fact she wasn't sure right now if she could even bear to be in the same life with him.

She had never imagined that there could be anyone who could make her feel so threatened, so appalled by her own feelings, and so afraid of them. Flushed and sticky, she surveyed her uncharacteristically chaotic packing.

She would put their things in the four-wheel drive first, and then pop Fleur in and then she would drive back to the hotel and not stop until she got there.

Mariella took a deep breath. Once she was there she would no doubt come to her senses and think of Xavier only as the man who had betrayed her sister, the man who was Fleur's father!

The wind was beginning to bend the palms as Mariella hurried out to the vehicle with their things, but she was oblivious to it as she wrestled with the heavy door and started to load the car.

Xavier saw her as he turned to swim another length. Treading water, he watched in furious disbelief as she struggled with the vehicle's door and then started to push the bulky container she had brought with her inside it.

THERE! NOW ALL she had to do was go back for Fleur and then they could leave, hopefully whilst Xavier was too busy swimming to notice! And anyway, if he had wanted a swim that badly why couldn't he have worn…well, something? Why had he had to—to flaunt his undeniably supremely male and very, very sexy body in the way he had?

Engrossed in her thoughts, she failed to see Xavier wade out of the water and pull on his tee shirt and jeans without wasting time on anything else, before starting to run towards the pavilion into which she had already disappeared.

'Come on, my beautiful baby,' Mariella crooned lovingly to Fleur as she wrapped her up. 'You and I are going—'

'Nowhere!'

Turning round, white-faced and clutching Fleur protectively to her, Mariella glared at him. The fine cotton tee shirt was plastered to his very obviously still damp body and her skittering gaze slid helplessly downward to rest indiscreetly on the groin of his jeans at the same time as her heart came to rest against her chest wall in a massive breathtaking thud.

He was standing in the exit blocking her way, but infuriatingly, instead of registering this vitally important fact first, her senses seemed to be far too preoccupied with taking a personal inventory of the way he looked clothed and the way he had looked…before!

Reminding herself that she was an adult, mature businesswoman, well used to running her own life and making her own decisions, and not the sad female with her hormones running riot that she was currently doing a good impression of, she drew herself up to her full height and told him determinedly, 'I am taking Fleur back to the city and there is no way you are going to stop me. And anyway, I can't imagine why you would want us to stay after the way you have behaved! The things you have said!'

'Want you to stay? No, I don't!' Xavier confirmed harshly. 'But unfortunately you are going to have to, unless, of course, you want to condemn yourself and the baby to almost certain death.'

Mariella stared at him. What did he mean? Was he trying to threaten her? 'We're leaving,' she repeated, making for the exit, and trying to ignore both the furious thud of her heart and the fact that he was standing in the way.

'Are you mad? You'd be lucky to get above half a dozen miles before being buried in a sand drift. If you thought the wind coming here was bad, well, let me tell you that was nothing compared with what's blowing up out there now!'

Mariella took a deep breath.

'I've just been outside. There is no wind,' she told him patiently, slowly spacing each word with immense care. 'The storm is over.'

'And you would know, of course, being an expert on desert weather conditions, no doubt. For your information, the reason that there was no wind, as you put it, is because we are, or rather we were in the eye of the storm. And anyone who knows anything about the desert would know that. Couldn't you feel the stillness? Didn't you notice the sand haze in the sky?' The look he shot her could have lit tinder at fifty paces, Mariella recognised shakily.

'You're lying,' she told him stubbornly, determined not

to let him get the better of her. 'You just want to keep us here because—'

When she stopped he looked derisively at her.

'Yes. I want to keep you here because what?'

Because you know how dangerously much I want you, a treacherous little voice whispered insidiously inside Mariella's head, and you feel the same way.

Shuddering, she pushed her thoughts back into the realms of reality—and safety.

'You're lying,' she repeated doggedly, eyeing the exit rebelliously.

'Am I?' Moving to one side, he swept back the tent flap so that she could see outside.

The palms were bending so much beneath the strength of the wind that their fronds were brushing the sand.

As she stared in disbelief Mariella could hear the strength of the wind increasing until it whistled eerily around the oasis, physically hurting her ears.

Out of nowhere it whipped up huge spirals of sand, making them dance in front of her. She could hardly see the sun or differentiate any longer between sand and sky.

Disbelievingly she took a step outside and cried out in shock as she was almost lifted off her feet when the wind punched into her. In her arms, Fleur screamed and was immediately removed to the protection of a much stronger and safer pair as Xavier snatched Fleur from her.

The thought of what would have happened to them if they had been caught in the open desert in such conditions drove the colour from Mariella's face.

'Now do you believe me?' Xavier demanded grimly when they were both back inside and he had secured the tent flap.

Reaching out to take Fleur from him, Mariella, whose fingers had inadvertently come into contact with the damp heat of his tee-shirt-clad chest, withdrew her hand so fast she almost lost her balance.

Immediately Xavier gripped her arm to steady her, supporting whilst he did so, so that it looked almost as though he were embracing them both, holding them both safe.

Against all rationality, given what she knew about him, Mariella discovered that her eyes were burning with emotional tears. She should be crying, she acknowledged grimly, for her own stupidity in allowing her emotions to be aroused so much for so little real reason! Pulling back from him, she demanded, 'Just how long is this storm going to last?'

'At least twenty-four hours, perhaps longer. Since the storm is making it impossible to receive any kind of communication signal, it is impossible to know. Such storms are rare at this time of year, but when they do occur they are both unpredictable and fierce.'

As was Xavier himself, Mariella decided as she took Fleur from him.

CHAPTER FIVE

GETTING up from the bed where she had been lying read-ing one of the research books she had brought to Zuran with her, Mariella went to check on Fleur.

A brief glance at her watch showed her that it was nearly eight p.m. Fleur was awake but obviously quite content, and happy to oblige when Mariella checked her mouth to look at the small pearly white tooth just beginning to ap-pear. Her face was still a little bit swollen and flushed, but the paracetamol seemed to have eased the pain she had suffered the previous night.

Mariella had retreated to 'her bedroom' late in the af-ternoon, desperate to escape from the highly charged at-mosphere in the main living area.

It had become impossible for her to look at Xavier with-out imagining him as he had been earlier: naked…male.

He had retrieved the things she had carried out to the four-wheel drive and put them back in the bedroom, and when Mariella had come across a sketch-book and pencils she had forgotten she had brought, along with her book, she had fallen on the book with a surge of relief.

Apart from the fact that she genuinely found the subject interesting, it gave her a perfect excuse to distance herself from Xavier, who had been busily working on his laptop.

On the pretext of Fleur needing a nap she had come into the sleeping quarters and had remained there ever since.

A thorough understanding of anatomy was essential for any painter in her type of field, and she had quickly become totally engrossed in trying to trace the development of the modern-day racehorse from the original Arabian bloodstock.

As Kate had said, the potential commission from the prince was indeed a prestigious one.

Picking up her sketch-book, Mariella started to work. Those incredible muscles that powered every movement… Her pencil flew over the paper, her absorption in what she was doing only broken when Fleur started to demand her attention.

Smiling, she discarded the sketch-book and then frowned sharply as she looked at what she had done, her face burning mortifying and disbelieving scarlet.

How on earth had that happened? How on earth had she managed to sketch, not a horse, but a man… Xavier… Xavier, swimming, Xavier standing, Xavier: his body lean and naked, clean-muscled and powerful.

Guiltily, Mariella flipped over the page. Fleur was blowing kisses at her and becoming increasingly vociferous.

Tucking the sketch-pad safely out of sight, Mariella went to her and picked her up, fastening her into her car seat and then carrying her into the kitchen.

'Look at this yummy dinner you're going to have,' Mariella crooned to Fleur as she prepared her food.

It had been her intention to take Fleur back into the bedroom to feed her, but instead Mariella carried her into the living area.

Fleur was Xavier's daughter, after all, and perhaps they both needed reminding just what that meant, albeit for very different reasons! Perhaps too he ought to be made to see just what he was missing out on by not acknowledging her.

He was working on the laptop when Mariella walked in and put Fleur down in her seat so that she could feed her.

She was a strong, healthy baby with a good appetite, who thankfully no longer seemed to be too bothered by the tooth she had been cutting.

Absorbed in her own enjoyable task, Mariella didn't realise that Xavier had stopped work to turn and study them until some sixth sense warned her that they were being watched.

His abrupt, 'She has your nose,' made Mariella's hand tremble slightly. She and Tanya shared the same shaped nose, which they had both inherited from their mother. Fleur had their nose, but, according to Tanya, her father's deliciously long thick eyelashes.

Mariella could feel her face starting to burn. What was it about a certain type of man that enabled him to behave so uncaringly towards the child he had fathered?

The way Xavier was behaving towards Fleur was so reminiscent of the way her father had behaved towards her! She knew all too well what it was like to grow up feeling rejected and unloved by one's father and she couldn't bear to see that happen to Fleur!

Xavier ought to be made to see that she was at least in part his responsibility instead of being allowed to just walk away from her. The way she felt had nothing whatsoever to do with money, Mariella recognised, and everything to do with emotion.

Fleur had finished her meal and was beginning to drift off to sleep. Bending down to double check that she was comfortably fastened into her seat, Mariella tenderly kissed her downy cheek, then straightened up and headed for the kitchen to wash out her feeding things.

Left on his own with Fleur, Xavier studied her frown-
ingly. She was far fairer skinned than his cousin and,
whilst Xavier could see an unmistakable physical resemblance to Mariella in her, he could see none to Khalid. Fast
asleep now, Fleur gave a small quiver.

Immediately Xavier went over to her. Desert nights
could be unbelievably cold—she felt warm enough, but
perhaps she needed an extra cover?

He could hear Mariella in the kitchen and so he went
through into the bedroom area, to get an extra blanket
from the carry-cot.

Mariella had tucked her sketch-pad in between the
carry-cot and the box of baby equipment, and as Xavier
reached for a blanket he saw the sketch-pad, and its very
recognisable sketches.

Frowning, he picked it up and studied it.

Having washed Fleur's feeding cup, Mariella walked
into the bedroom intending to put it away, coming to an
abrupt halt as she saw Xavier bending towards the carry-
cot.

'Where is Fleur?' she demanded immediately.
'What—?'

'She's fast asleep where you left her,' Xavier answered
her adding, 'From looking at her, it is plain to see her resemblance to you, but as to there being a similarity to her
supposed father...'

Mariella had had enough.

'How can you deny your own flesh and blood?' she demanded bitterly. 'I can't imagine how *any* woman could
ever desire you, never mind—'

Before she could say 'Tanya' he had cut her off as he
asked with cutting brutality, 'Indeed? Then, what may I
ask, are these?'

Mariella felt the breath wheeze from her lungs like air

squeezed from a pair of bellows as he held up in front of her her own sketches.

Chagrin, embarrassment, guilt and anger fused into one burning, searing jolt of emotional intensity had her lunging frantically towards him, intent on snatching her betraying sketches from him. But Xavier was withholding them from her, holding them out of her reach with one hand whilst he fended her attempt to repossess them with the other.

Furiously Mariella redoubled her efforts, flinging herself at him, and trying to shake off his hard grip of her wrist as she did so.

'Give those back to me. They are mine,' she insisted breathlessly.

As she tried to reach up for them she overbalanced slightly, her fingers curling into his arm, her fingernails accidentally raising livid weals on his olive skin.

'Why, you little...'

Shocked as much by her own inadvertent action as his reaction to it, Mariella went stiff with disbelief as he suddenly dropped the sketches and grabbed hold of her waist with both hands.

'Other men might have been willing to let you get away with such behaviour, but I most certainly do not intend to!' She could hear Xavier grating at her as he gave her a small, angry shake.

Mariella could feel the edge of the bed behind her as she turned and twisted, frantically trying to break free, but Xavier was refusing to let her go and suddenly she was lying on the bed, with Xavier arching over her, pinning her down.

He was angry with her, Mariella recognised as she stared into the lava-grey heat of his eyes, but her senses were telling her something else as well and a savage little quiver then ran unmistakably through her own body as she realised that something else had nothing whatsoever to do with fear.

Xavier wanted her! Mariella could sense, feel it, breathe it in the sudden tension that filled the air, engulfing, locking them both in a place out of time.

This was fate, Xavier decided recklessly, a golden opportunity given to him to prove to his cousin beyond any shadow of a doubt that this woman was not worthy of his love, but, strangely, as he lowered his mouth to Mariella's it wasn't his duty towards his cousin that was filling his thoughts, driving him with an intense ferocity that a part of him recognised was more dangerous than anything he had previously experienced.

This was wrong, desperately wrong, the very worst kind of betrayal, Mariella acknowledged as her whole body was savaged by a mixture of anguish and hunger.

Xavier's mouth burned hers, its possession every bit as harsh and demanding as she had expected, barely cloaking a hunger that scorched right through her body to her fingertips.

Helplessly her mouth responded to the savage demand of his, her body quivering as his tongue probed her closed lips demanding entry. Somehow, some time she had lifted her hands to his body so that she was gripping his shoulders. To push him away, or to draw him closer?

His teeth tugged ruthlessly at her bottom lip and her resistance ebbed away, like the inner tears of shame and guilt she was silently crying inside for her inability to resist giving in to flames of her own desire as they licked and darted inside her, burning down her pathetically weak defences. Without knowing how she knew, she knew that this man, this moment was something a part of her had been waiting for, for a very long time. Even the merciless intent of his sensual need was something that a part of her was fiercely responsive to.

Her eyes, magnificent in their emotional intensity, shimmered from turquoise to dark blue-green. Xavier was mesmerised by them, caught in their brilliance. How could such cool colours glow so hotly? But not nearly so hotly as his own body.

Without knowing what she was doing, Mariella raked the taut flesh of his arm—deliberately this time—her body galvanised by deep, urgent shudders as his kiss possessed her mouth, his tongue thrusting into its warm softness.

Mariella tried to deny what she was feeling, pulling frantically away from Xavier, in a desperate attempt to escape and to save them both from the very worst kind of betrayal, but having shared her surrender Xavier refused to let her go, pinning her to the bed with the weight of his body hot and heavy on hers, making her melt, making her ache, making her writhe in helpless supplication and moan into his mouth, a tiny keening sound lost beneath the greater sounds of their bodies moving on the bed. The rustle and rasp of fabric against flesh, of two people both revealing their hunger in the accelerated sound of their breathing, and the frantic thud of their heartbeats.

Xavier's mouth grazed her skin, exploring the curve of her jaw, the soft vulnerability of her throat as she automatically arched her whole body. The hot, fevered feel of his mouth against her flesh made her arch even more, shuddering in agonised pleasure.

Just a few kisses, that was all it was… And yet she felt as possessed by him, as aching for him as though he had touched her far more intimately and for far, far longer. The desire she was feeling was so acute, so very nearly unbearable, that Mariella dared not allow herself to imagine how she was going to feel when he did touch her more intimately. And yet at the same time she knew that if he didn't—

When his hand covered her breast she cried out, unable to stop herself, and felt his responding groan shudder through his body. She could hear herself making small, whimpering sounds of distress as she tugged at his clothes, her own body consumed by a need to be completely bare to his touch, to be open to him…

And yet when he had finally removed them and she was naked, a sense of panic that was wholly primitive and instinctive ripped through her, causing her to go to cover her naked breasts protectively with her own hands. But Xavier was too quick for her, his fingers snapping round her wrists, pinioning her hands to either side of her head as he knelt over her.

Mariella felt the heavy thread of her own hungry desire. She just had time to see the molten glitter of Xavier's answering hunger before he looked down at her exposed breasts. A sinful desire slid hotly through her veins, her face burning as she watched him absorbing the taut swell of her breasts as her nipples tightened and darkened, openly inciting the need she could hear and feel in his indrawn breath, even before he lowered his head to her body.

The feeling of him slowly circling first one and then the other nipple with the moist heat of his tongue, whilst she lay powerless beneath him, should surely have inflamed her angry independence instead of sending such a sheet of white-hot sensuality pouring through her that her belly automatically concaved under its pressure whilst her sex ached and swelled.

Mariella closed her eyes. Behind her closed eyelids she could see him as she had done in the oasis, just as she wanted to see him again now, she recognised as her body began to shudder. Slow, deep, galvanic surges of desire that ripped rhythmically through her, her body moving to the suckle of his mouth against her breast.

She could feel his knee parting her thighs her body already aching for the aroused feel of him, hot, heavy, masculine as he urgently moved against her.

HE WAS LOSING himself, drowning in the way she was making him feel, his self-control in danger of being burned away to nothing. Just the sight of her swollen breasts, their nipples tight and aroused from his laving of them, made him ache to possess her, to complete and fill her, to complete himself within her.

The moment Xavier released her wrists, Mariella tugged impatiently at his clothes, answering her demanding need for him. Immediately Xavier helped her, guiding her hands over buttons and zips and then flesh itself as she moaned her pleasure against the hot skin of his throat when her fingertips finally tangled with the soft, silky hair she had ached to touch earlier.

His body, packed hard with muscle, was excitingly alien and overpoweringly male. His impatience to be a part of her made her gasp and shudder as he kissed her throat, her shoulder and then her mouth, whilst he wrapped her tightly in his arms so that they were lying intimately, naked body to naked body.

The feel of him pressing against her. Hot and hard, aroused, his movement against her urgently explicit, was more than she could withstand.

Eagerly she coiled herself around him, opening herself to him, crying out as she felt him enter her, each movement powerful and sure, strong and urgent.

Already her own body was responding to his movement, her muscles clinging to him. Sensually stroking him and savouring each thrust, she could feel him strengthening inside her, filling her to completion, picking up the rhythm of her body and carrying…driving them both with it.

'Never mind the child he has given you, has my cousin given you this? Has he made you feel like this when he holds you? When he possesses you? When he loves you? Was *this* how it was between you when you made Fleur together?'

Mariella's whole body stiffened.

'Did you give yourself to him as easily as you did to me? And how many others have there been?'

With a fierce cry, she pulled away from him, her brain barely able to take in what he was saying, her body and emotions in such deep shock that removing herself from him made her feel as though she were physically dying.

The shock of her rejection tore at Xavier's guts. He wanted to drag her back into his arms, where surely she belonged, to roll her into the bed beneath him and to fill her with himself, to make her admit that no other man had ever or could ever give her or share with her what he could. But most of all he wanted to fill her with the life force that would ultimately be his child. A part of him recognised that there was no more elemental drive than this, to fill a woman's body with one's child in order to drive out her commitment to another man and the child he had already given her. The barbaric intensity of his own emotions shocked him. He had done what he had done for Khalid's sake, to protect him, he reminded himself, and to reinforce that fact he told her, 'It's a little too late for that now! You have already proved to me just what you are, and once Khalid learns how willing you were to give yourself to me he will quickly realise how right I was to counsel him against you.'

He had taken her to bed for that? Because of that? So that he could denounce her to another man?

In the outer room Fleur suddenly started to cry. Dragging on her clothes, Mariella hurried in to her, picking her up and holding her tightly as though just holding her could somehow staunch the huge wound inside her that was haemorrhaging her life force. She was shaking from head to foot with reaction, both from what had happened and from what she had just learned.

Fleur was not Xavier's child! Xavier's cousin was Fleur's father! But Xavier believed that she was Fleur's mother. And because of that he had taken her to bed, out of a cold-hearted, despicable, damnable desire to prove to his cousin that she was a…a wanton who would give herself to any man!

Fate had been doubly kind to her, she told herself staunchly: firstly in ensuring that she had not betrayed her sister, and secondly in giving her incontrovertible proof of just what manner of man Xavier was!

CHAPTER SIX

As SHE stepped inside the welcome familiarity of her Beach Club bungalow, Mariella allowed herself to expel a shaky sigh of relief. Her first since she had left the oasis!

Now that she was safely here, perhaps she could allow herself to put the events of the last forty-eight hours firmly behind her. Lock them away in a very deep sealed drawer marked, 'Forget for ever.'

But how could she forget, how could any human being forget an act as deliberately and cold-bloodedly cruel and damaging as the one Xavier had perpetrated against her?

If she herself had been a different kind of woman she might have taken a grim sense of distorted pleasure in knowing that, for all he might try to deny it, Xavier had physically wanted her. In knowing it and in throwing that knowledge back at him! Instinctively she knew that he would be humiliated by it, and if any man deserved to be humiliated it was Xavier!

Just thinking about him was enough to have Mariella's hands curling into small, passionately angry fists. As her heart drove against her ribs in sledgehammer blows. How could he possibly not have recognised that she would never, ever, ever under any circumstances betray her love, and that if she had been another man's lover nothing he could have done would have tempted her to want him? Hadn't her body itself proclaimed to him the unlikeliness, the impossibility of her being Fleur's mother and any man's intimate lover?

But believing that he had been Tanya's lover hadn't stopped her, had it?

She would carry that shame and guilt with her to her deathbed, Mariella acknowledged.

The message light on the bungalow's communications system was flashing, indicating that she had received several telephone calls, all from the prince's personal assistant, she discovered when she went to check them. Before answering them, the first thing she intended to do now that she was safely back at the hotel was ring her sister and double check that she had not misunderstood Xavier—he was not Tanya's lover or Fleur's father!

And once she had that confirmation safely in her possession, then Xavier would be history!

It took her several attempts to get through to Tanya, who eventually answered the phone sounding breathless and flustered.

'I'm sorry, Ella,' she apologised quickly. 'But things are really hectic here and… Look, I can't really talk right now. Is Fleur okay?'

'Fleur is fine. She's cut her first tooth, but, Tanya, there's something I've got to know,' Mariella told her, firmly overriding her attempts to end the call.

'I must know Fleur's father's name, Tanya. It's desperately important!'

'Why? What's happened? Ella, I can't tell you…'

Hearing the panic in her sister's voice, Mariella took a deep breath. 'All right! But if you won't tell me who he is, Tanya, then please at least tell me that his first name isn't Xavier…'

'Who?' Tanya's outraged shriek almost hurt her eardrums. 'Xavier? You mean that horrid cousin of Khalid's? Of course he isn't Fleur's father. I hate him... He's the one responsible for parting me and Khalid! He sent Khalid away! He doesn't think that I'm good enough for him! Anyway...how do you know about Xavier, Ella? He's an arrogant, overbearing, old-fashioned, moralistic beast, who lives in the Dark Ages! Look, Ella, I've got to go... Love to Fleur and lots of kisses.'

She ended the call before Mariella could stop her, leaving her gripping the receiver tensely.

But at least she had confirmed that Xavier was not Fleur's father.

Determinedly Mariella made herself turn her attention to her messages.

The prince had now returned to Zuran and wanted her to get in touch with his personal assistant.

'DON'T WORRY,' THE prince's personal assistant reassured Mariella when she rang him a few minutes later to explain why she had not returned his calls.

'It is just that the prince is hosting a charity breakfast tomorrow morning at the stables and he wanted to invite you as his guest. His Highness is very enthusiastic about his project of having the horses painted, but of course this is something you will be having formal discussions with him about at a later date. The breakfast is a prestigious dressy event, although we do ask all our guests not to wear strong perfumes, as this can affect the horses.'

'It sounds wonderful,' Mariella responded. 'However, there is one small problem. I have brought my four-month-old niece to Zuran with me, as the prince knows. I am looking after her for my sister, and—'

'That is no problem at all,' the PA came back promptly.

'Crèche facilities are being provided with fully trained nannies in attendance. A car will be sent to collect both you and the baby, of course.'

Mariella had previously attended several glitzy society events at the invitation of her clients, including one particularly elegant trip to France for their main race of the season at Longchamps—a gift from a client, which she had repaid with a 'surprise' sketch of his four-year-old daughter on her pony, and, recalling the sophistication and glamour of the outfits worn by the Middle Eastern contingent on that occasion, she suspected that she was going to have to go shopping.

TWO HOURS LATER, sitting sipping coffee in the exclusive Zuran Designer Shopping Centre, Mariella smiled ruefully to herself as she contemplated her assorted collection of shiny shopping bags.

The largest one bore the name, not of some famous designer, but of an exclusive babywear store. Unable to choose between two equally delicious little outfits for Fleur, Mariella had ended up buying her niece both.

She had been rather less indulgent on her own account, opting only to buy a hat—an outrageously feminine and eye-catching model hat, mind you!—a pair of ridiculously spindly heeled but totally irresistible sandals, which just happened to be the exact shade of turquoise-blue of the silk dress she had decided to wear to the charity breakfast, and a handbag in the same colour, which quite incredibly had the design of a galloping horse picked out on it in sequins and beads.

And best of all she had managed not to think about Xavier at all...well, almost not at all! And when she had thought about him it had been to reiterate to herself just what a total pig he was, and how lucky she was that all she had done was give in to a now unthinkable and totally out of character, momentary madness, which would never, ever be repeated. After all, there was no danger of her ever allowing herself to become emotionally vulnerable to any man—not with her father's behaviour to remind her of the danger of falling in love—never mind a man who had condemned himself in the way that Xavier had!

Having drunk her coffee, she gathered up her bags and checked that Fleur was strapped securely in her buggy before heading for the taxi rank.

It had been a long day. She had hardly slept the night before, lying awake in Xavier's bed, her thoughts and her emotions churning. And then there had been the long drive back to Zuran this morning after her prayers had been answered and the storm had died away.

True, she had had a brief nap earlier, but now, even though it was barely eight in the evening, she was already yawning.

XAVIER PACED THE floor of the pavilion. He should, he knew, be rejoicing in his solitude and the fact that that woman had gone! And of course he would have no compunction whatsoever in telling Khalid just how easily and quickly she had betrayed the 'love' she had claimed to have for him!

That ache he could feel in his body right now meant nothing and would very quickly be banished!

But what if Khalid refused to listen to him? What if, despite everything he, Xavier, had said to him, he insisted on continuing his relationship with her?

If Fleur was Khalid's child then it was only right that he should provide for her. Xavier tried to imagine how he would feel if Khalid were to set his mistress and their child up in a home in Zuran. How he would feel know-

ing that Khalid was living with her, sharing that home…
sharing her bed?

Angrily he strode outside. Even the damned air inside
the tent was poisoned by her perfume—that and the scent
of baby powder! He would instruct his staff to dispose of
the bedding and replace it with new, just in case her scent
might somehow manage to linger and remind him of an
incident he now wanted to totally forget!

But even outside he was still haunted by his mental images of her. Her ridiculous turquoise eyes, her creamy pale
skin, her delicate bone structure, her extraordinarily passionate response to him that had driven him wild, driven
him over the edge of his control to a place he had never
been before. The sweet, hot, tight feel of her inside, as
though she had never had another lover, never mind a
child! No wonder poor, easygoing Khalid had become so
ensnared by her!

FLEUR WAS CERTAINLY attracting a lot of attention, Mariella
reflected tenderly as people turned to look at the baby
she was carrying in her arms, oblivious to the fact that it
was her own appearance that was attracting second looks
from so many members of the fashionably dressed crowd
already filling the stable yard.

Her slim silk dress had originally been bought for a
friend's wedding, its soft, swirling pattern in colours that
ranged from palest aqua right through to turquoise. Over
it, to cover her bare arms, Mariella was wearing a toning,
velvet-edged, silk-knit cardigan, several shades paler than
her hat and shoes.

A member of the prince's staff had been on hand to
greet her as she stepped out of the limousine that had
been sent to collect her, and to pass her on to a charming

young man, who was now taking her to introduce her to the prince.

The purpose-built stables were immaculate, the equine occupants of the stalls arching their long necks and doing a good deal of scene stealing, as though intent on making the point that they were the real stars of the event and not the humans who were invading their territory.

The breakfast was to be served in ornamental pavilioned areas, off which was the crèche, so Mariella had been informed.

Her stomach muscles tightened a little as she saw the group of people up ahead of her. People of consequence and standing, no matter how they were dressed, all possessed that same air of confidence, Mariella acknowledged as the crowd opened up and the man at the centre of it turned to look at her.

'Miss Sutton, this is His Royal Highness,' her young escort introduced her to the prince, her potential client.

'Miss Sutton!' His voice was warm, but Mariella was aware of the sharp, assessing look he gave her.

'Your Highness,' she responded, with a small inclination of her head.

'I have been very impressed with your work, Miss Sutton, although I have to say that, especially in the case of my friend and rival Sir John Feinnes, you have erred on the side of generosity in the stature and muscle you have given his "Oracle".'

A small smile dimpled Mariella's mouth.

'I simply reflect what I see as an artist, Highness,' she told him demurely.

'Indeed. Then wait until you have seen my animals. They are the result of a breeding programme that has taken many years' hard work, and I want them to be painted in a way that pays full tribute to their magnificence.'

And to his own, Mariella decided, but tactfully did not say so.

'My friend Sir John also tells me that you have some very innovative ideas… The finishing touches are currently being put to an exclusive enclosure at our racecourse, which will bear my family name, and it occurs to me that there could be an opportunity there for…' He paused.

Mariella suggested, tongue in cheek, 'Something innovative?'

'Indeed,' he agreed. 'But this is not a time to discuss business. I have invited you here as my guest, so that you can meet some of your subjects informally, so to speak…'

Fleur, who had been staring around in wide-eyed silence, suddenly turned her head and smiled at him.

'You have a beautiful child,' he complimented her.

'She is my niece,' Mariella informed him. 'I am looking after her for my sister. I think my agent did explain.'

'Yes. I am sure she did! I seem to remember that my personal assistant did mention the little one.'

Some new guests were waiting to be presented to him, and Mariella stepped discreetly to one side. In the distance on the racecourse she could see a string of horses being exercised, whilst here in the yard there were grooms and stable hands all wearing khaki shorts or trousers, and tee shirts in one of the prince's three racing colours denoting their status within the hierarchy of the stables.

'If you would care to take the baby to the crèche,' the prince's assistant was asking politely.

Firmly Mariella shook her head. Such was her sense of responsibility towards her niece that she preferred to keep her with her for as long as she could, and, besides, the yard was far too busy for her to be able to do even the briefest of preliminary sketches of the animals. The event was providing her with a wonderful opportunity to do some people watching, though.

SURVEYING THE CROWD filling the prince's racing yard, Xavier wondered what on earth he was doing here. This kind of social event was normally something he avoided like the plague! It was much more Khalid's style than his, and if Khalid had not taken leave of absence without warning he would have been the one to attend the event! However, since Xavier was involved in shared business interests with the prince, he had felt that perhaps he should attend the breakfast—especially as it was in aid of a charity that he fully supported.

Several people had already stopped him to talk with him, including various members of the royal family, but he now felt that he had done his duty and was on the point of leaving when he suddenly frowned as he caught sight of a silky flash of turquoise-blue as the crowd in front of him momentarily parted.

Grimly he started to stride towards it.

People were starting to move towards the pavilioned area where the breakfast was about to be served, but Mariella hesitated a little uncertainly, suspecting that it would be a diplomatic move now to take Fleur over to the crèche area rather than into the pavilions. A little uncertainly she glanced round, unsure as to what to do, and hoping that she might see the prince's helpful assistant.

Xavier saw Mariella before she saw him, his eyebrows snapping together in seething fury as he realised his suspicions had been confirmed. It was her! And he had no difficulty in guessing just what she was doing here! Some of the richest men in Zuran were here, and very few of them were unlikely to at least be tempted by the sight of her! From the top of the confection of straw and tulle she was wearing on top of her head to the tip of the dainty little pink-painted toenails revealed by shoes so fragile that he was surprised that she dared risk wearing them, especially when carrying her child, she looked a picture of innocent vulnerability. But of course she was no such thing! And dressing the baby in an outfit obviously chosen to match hers seemed to proclaim their mother and baby status to the world.

Unaware of the fact that Nemesis and all the Furies were about to bear down on her with grim zeal in the shape of a very angry and disapproving male, Mariella shifted Fleur's weight in her arm.

'Very fetching! Trust you to be here, and with the very latest European accessory—I have to tell you, though, that you've misjudged its effect in Zuran!'

'Xavier!' Mariella felt her legs wobble treacherously in her high heels as she stared at him in shock.

'I don't know how you managed to get past the security staff—although I suspect I can guess how!' he told her cynically. 'Kept women and those who sell their favours to the highest bidder are normally kept out of such events.'

Kept women! His condemnation stung not just her pride, but her sense of sisterly protection for Tanya. She knew that if this conversation were to continue, she would have to explain she was not Fleur's mother, but right now she was due in the pavilion for breakfast. She was here on business and she would not jeopardise the commission by having an argument with Xavier in front of the prince! 'I refuse to speak with you if you are going to be so rude,' she said tersely. 'Now, if you'll excuse me, I must go and join the others.' A flash of light to her left made her gasp as she realised a photographer had just caught the two of them on camera!

'Don't think I don't know what you're doing here,'

Xavier told her challengingly. 'You know that Khalid is going to come to his senses and realise just what you are, and you're looking for someone to take his place, and finance you.'

'Finance her!' The feathers nestling in the swathes of chiffon on Mariella's hat trembled as she shook with outrage.

'For your information, I do not need anyone to finance me, as you put it. I am completely financially independent.' As she saw his expression Mariella turned on her heel.

Hurrying away from him, she tensed as she suddenly felt a touch on her arm, but when she looked round it was only the prince's assistant.

'The prince would like you to join his table for breakfast, Miss Sutton,' he told her. 'If I may escort you first to the crèche,' he added tactfully.

Angrily Xavier watched as the crowd swallowed her up. How dared she lie to him and claim to be financially independent, especially when she knew he knew the truth about her?

She was the most scheming and deceitful woman he had ever met, a woman he was a total fool to spare the smallest thought for!

THE CONVERSATION AROUND the breakfast table was certainly very cosmopolitan, Mariella decided as she listened to two other women discussing the world's best spa resorts, whilst the men debated the various merits of differing bloodstock.

After the breakfast was over and people were beginning to drift away, the prince came over to Mariella.

'My assistant will telephone you to make formal arrangements for us to discuss my commission,' he told her. 'I was wondering if it would be possible for me to visit your new enclosure?' Mariella asked him. 'Or, failing that, perhaps see some plans?'

She had the beginnings of a vague idea which, if the prince approved, would be innovative, but first she needed to see the enclosure to see if it would work.

'Certainly. I shall see that it is arranged.'

As he escorted her outside Mariella saw Xavier standing several yards away, her face beginning to burn as he looked at the prince and then allowed his glance to drift with slow and deliberate insolence over her, assessing her as though…as though she were a piece of…of flesh he was contemplating buying, Mariella recognised.

'Highness!'

'Xavier.' As the two men exchanged greetings Mariella turned to leave, but somehow Xavier had moved and was blocking her way.

'I see that you do not have Fleur with you!'

'No,' Mariella agreed coldly. 'She is in the crèche. I am just on my way to collect her.'

'You know Miss Sutton, Xavier? I hadn't realised. I am about to avail myself of her exceptional services, and she has promised me something extremely innovative.'

Mariella winced as she recognised from his expression just what interpretation Xavier had put on the prince's remarks. Excusing herself, she managed to push her way past Xavier, but to her consternation he only allowed her to take a few steps into the shadows cast by one of the pavilions before catching up with her and taking hold of her arm.

'My word, but you are a witch! The prince is renowned for his devotion to his wife and yet he speaks openly of entering a relationship with you!'

Mariella did not dignify that with an answer. Instead she bared her teeth at him in a savage little smile as she told him sweetly, 'There, you see, you need not have gone to all that trouble to protect your cousin. There is no need for you to go running to him now to tell him all about your sordid and appalling behaviour towards me. After all, once he gets to hear about the fact that the prince is paying for my…expertise…'

'You dare to boast openly about it?' Xavier was gripping her with both hands now, his fingers digging into the vulnerable flesh of her upper arms.

To her own surprise Mariella discovered that winding Xavier up was great fun and she was actually enjoying herself.

'Why shouldn't I?' she taunted him. 'I am proud of the fact that my skills are so recognised and highly thought of, and that I am able to earn a very respectable living for myself by employing them!'

As his fingers bit even harder into her arms she viewed the ominous white line around his mouth with a dangerous sense of reckless euphoria.

'In fact, in some circles I have already made quite a name for myself.'

She had gone too far, Mariella realised as her euphoria was suddenly replaced with apprehension.

'You are proud of being known as a high-class whore? Personally I would have classed you merely as an expensive one!'

Mariella was just about to slap him when he said, 'If you strike me here you could well end up in prison, whereas if I do this…'

She gasped as he bent his head and subjected her to a savagely demanding kiss, arching her whole body back as she fought not to come into contact with his, and lost that fight. In the shadows of the pavilion he used his physical strength to show her what she already knew—that despite his rage and contempt he was physically aroused by her! Just as she was by him?

He released her so abruptly that she almost stumbled. As he turned away from her he reached into his robe and removed a wallet, opening it to throw down some money.

White-faced, Mariella stared at him. Deep down inside herself she knew that she had deliberately incited and goaded him, but not for this.

'Pick it up!' he told her savagely.

Mariella took a deep breath and gathered what was left of her dignity around her. 'Very well,' she agreed calmly. 'I am sure the charity will be grateful for it, Xavier. I understand it helps to support abandoned children.'

She prayed that he would think the glitter in her eyes was caused by her contempt and not by her tears.

Silently Xavier watched her go. His own behaviour had shocked him but he was too stubbornly proud to admit it—and even more stubbornly determined not to acknowledge what had actually caused it.

How could he admit to jealousy over the favours of such a woman? How could he acknowledge that his own desire to possess her went far, far beyond the physical desire for just her body? He could not and he did not intend to do so!

CHAPTER SEVEN

'A FRIEZE?'

The prince frowned as he looked at Mariella.

It was three days since the charity breakfast, and two since she had visited the new enclosure.

After what had happened with Xavier, the temptation to simply pack her bags and return home had been very strong, but stubbornly she had refused to give in to it.

It wasn't her fault that he had totally misinterpreted things. Well, at least not entirely! And besides... Besides, the commission the prince was offering her had far too much appeal for her as an artist to want to turn it down, never mind what her agent was likely to say!

So instead of worrying about Xavier she had spent the last two days working furiously on the idea she had had for the prince's new enclosure.

'The semi-circular walkway that leads to the enclosure would be perfect for such a project,' she told him. 'I could paint your horses there in a variety of different ways, either in their boxes, or in a string. I have spoken to your trainers and grooms and they have told me that they all have their individual personalities and little quirks, so if I painted them in a string I could include some of these. Solomon in particular, they tell me, does not like anyone else to lead the string, and then Saladin will not leave his box until his groom has removed the cat who is his stable companion. Shazare can't tolerate other horses with white socks, and—'

The prince laughed. 'I can see how well you have done your research, and, yes, I like what you are suggesting. It will be an extremely large project, though.'

Mariella gave a small shrug.

'It will allow me to paint the animals lifesize, certainly.'

'It will need to be done in time for the official opening of the stables.'

'And when will that be?' Mariella asked him.

'In around five months' time,' he told her.

Mariella did a quick mental calculation, and then exhaled in relief. That would give her more than enough time to get the work completed.

'It would take me about a month or two to finish. It has to be your decision, Highness,' she informed him diplomatically.

'Give me a few days to think about it. It is not that I don't like the idea. I do, but in this part of the world, we still put a great deal of store on "face", and therefore, no matter now innovative the idea, if it is not completed on time, then I shall lose face in the eyes of both my allies and my competitors. I certainly have no qualms about your work or your commitment to it, though.'

He needed time to check up on her and her past record of sticking to her contracted time schedules, Mariella knew, but that didn't worry her. She was always extremely efficient about sticking to a completion date once it was agreed.

THE NURSEMAID PROVIDED by the prince to look after Fleur whilst she had been working smiled at her as she went to collect the baby.

'She is a very good baby,' the young woman told Mariella approvingly.

Once she was back in the Beach Club bungalow, Mariella tried to ring Tanya to both update her on Fleur's progress and to tell her about her work, but she was only able to reach her sister's message service.

If the prince did give her this commission, then at least she would be earning enough to ensure that Tanya did not have to work away from home. She knew her sister wanted to be independent, but there were Fleur's needs to be considered as well, and besides…

She was going to miss Fleur dreadfully when the time came to hand her back to her mother, Mariella acknowledged. She was just beginning to realise what her determination never to become involved in a permanent relationship was going to mean to her in terms of missing out on motherhood.

A LITTLE NERVOUSLY, Mariella smoothed down the fabric of her skirt. She had arrived at the palace half an hour ago to see the prince, who was going to give her his verdict on whether or not he wanted her to go ahead with the frieze.

A shy nursemaid had already arrived to take Fleur from her, and now Mariella peeped anxiously at her watch. Fleur hadn't slept very well the previous night and Mariella suspected that she was cutting another new tooth.

'Miss Sutton, His Highness will see you now.'

'Ah, Mariella…'

'Highness,' Mariella responded as she was waved onto one of the silk-covered divans set around the walls of the huge audience room.

Almost immediately a servant appeared to offer her coffee and delicious-looking almond pastries glistening with honey and stuffed with raisins.

'I am pleased to inform you that I have decided to commission you to work on the frieze,' the prince announced. 'The sooner you can complete it, the better—we have lots of other work to do before the official opening.'

Quickly Mariella put down her coffee-cup and then covered it with her hand as she saw that the hovering servant was about to refill it.

Whilst he padded away silently the prince frowned.

'However, there is one matter that is of some concern to me.'

He was still worrying about her ability to get the work finished on time, Mariella guessed, but instead of confirming her suspicions the prince got up and picked up a newspaper from the low table in front of him.

'This is our popular local newspaper,' he told her. 'Its gossip column is a great favourite and widely read.'

As he spoke he was opening the paper.

'There is here a report of our charity breakfast, and, as you will see, a rather intimate photograph of you with Sheikh Xavier Al Agir.'

Mariella's heart bumped against the bottom of her chest, her fingers trembling slightly as she studied the photograph the prince was showing her.

It took her several seconds to recognise that it had been taken when she and Xavier had been quarrelling, because it looked for all the world as though they were indeed engaged in a very intimate conversation, their heads close together, her lips parted, Xavier's head bent towards her, his gaze fixed on her mouth, whilst Fleur, whom she was holding in her arms, beamed happily at him.

Even though she had not eaten any of the pastries, Mariella was beginning to feel sick.

The article accompanying the photograph read:

Who was the young woman who Sheikh Xavier was so intimately engaged in conversation with? The sheikh is known for his strong moral beliefs and his dedication to his role as leader of the Al Agir tribe, and yet he was seen recently at the prince's charity breakfast, engaged in what appeared to be a very private conversation with one specific female guest on two separate occasions! Could it be that the sheikh has finally chosen someone to share his life? And what of the baby the unknown young woman is holding? What is her connection with the sheikh?

'In this country, unlike your own, a young woman alone with a child does cause a certain amount of speculation and disapproval. It is plain from the tone of this article that the reporter believes you and Xavier to be Fleur's parents...' the prince told Mariella, his voice very stern.

'But that is not true, Your Highness. We are not,' Mariella protested immediately. 'Fleur is my niece.'

'Of course. I fully accept what you are saying, but I think for your own sake that some kind of formal response does need to be made to this item. Which is why I have already instructed my staff to get in touch with the paper and to give them the true facts and to explain that Fleur is in fact your niece and that you are in Zuran to work for me. Hopefully that will be an end to the matter!'

MARIELLA FROWNED AS for the third time in as many hours her sister's mobile was switched onto her message-taking service.

Why wasn't Tanya returning her calls?

Because of the length of time it was going to take her to complete the frieze, it had been decided that, instead of her returning to England as had originally been planned,

she and Fleur should remain in Zuran so that she could
commence work immediately.

The prince had announced that she would be provided
with a small apartment and the use of a car, and Mariella
was planning a shopping trip to equip both herself and
Fleur for their unexpected extended stay.

Fleur's new tooth had now come through and the baby
was back to her normal happy self.

Someone was knocking on the door of the bungalow
and Mariella went to open it, expecting to see a member
of the Beach Club's staff, but instead to her consternation
it was Xavier who was standing outside.

Without waiting for her invitation he strode into the
room, slamming the door closed behind him.

'Perhaps you can explain the meaning of *this* to me,'
he challenged her sarcastically, throwing down the copy
of the newspaper she had been reading earlier, open at the
gossip column page.

'I don't have to explain anything to you, Xavier,'
Mariella replied as calmly as she could.

'It says here that you are not Fleur's mother.'

'That's right,' she agreed. 'I'm not! I'm her aunt. My
sister Tanya is her mother…and the woman who I have had
to listen to you denouncing and abusing so slanderously
and unfairly! And, for your information, Tanya is not, as
you have tried to imply, some…some… She is a professional singer and dancer, and, whilst you may not consider
her good enough for your precious cousin, let me tell you
that in my opinion he is the one who isn't good enough for
her…not for her and certainly not for Fleur!' All the anger
and anguish Mariella had been bottling up inside her was
exploding in a surge of furious words.

'Your cousin told Tanya that he loved her and that he
was committed to her and then he left her and Fleur! Have

you any idea just what that did to Tanya? I was there when Fleur was born, I heard Tanya cry out for the man she loved. It's all so easy for a man, isn't it? If he doesn't want the responsibility of a woman's love or the child they create together, he can just walk away. You don't know what it means to be a child growing up knowing that your father didn't want or love you, and knowing too that your mother could never again be the person she was before her heart was broken. I would never, ever let any man hurt me the way Tanya has been hurt!'

'You wantonly and deliberately let me think that you and Khalid were lovers,' Xavier interrupted her savagely, ignoring her emotional outburst.

'Well, at first I thought you were Fleur's father, so I assumed you knew I wasn't Fleur's mother. But, face it, you wanted to think the worst you could about me, Xavier. You enjoyed thinking it! Revelled in it. I tried to warn you that you were getting it wrong, when you totally misinterpreted those comments by the prince! Remember?'

'Have you any idea just what problems this is causing?' he demanded harshly.

'What I have done?' Mariella gave him a disbelieving look. 'My sister is a modern young woman who lives a modern young woman's life. Her biggest mistake, in my opinion, was to fall in love with your wretched cousin, and yet you have talked about her as though—!' Mariella compressed her lips as she saw the flash of temper darkening his eyes.

'Are you trying to say to me that you too are a modern young woman who lives a modern young woman's life, because if you are I have to tell you—!'

Xavier broke off abruptly, remembering the character references the prince had insisted on him reading when he had stormed into the palace earlier in the afternoon, demanding an immediate audience with him.

Mariella was not only a very highly acclaimed artist, she was also, it seemed, a young woman of the highest moral integrity—in every facet of her life!

'That is none of your business,' Mariella told him angrily.

'To the contrary. It is very much my business!'

Mariella stared at him, her heart thumping.

'Fleur is my cousin's child, which makes her a member of my family. Since you are also of her blood, that also makes you a member of my family. As the head of that family I am, therefore, responsible for both of you. There is no way I can allow you to live here in Zuran alone, or work unchaperoned for the prince. Our family pride and honour would be at risk! It is my responsibility!'

'What?' Mariella looked at him in open angry contempt. 'How can you possibly lay claim to any right to pride or honour? You, a man who was quite prepared to take the mother of his cousin's child to bed, just so that you could enforce your wish to keep them apart? This has got to be some kind of joke! I mean, you...you abuse me verbally, and physically. You insult and denigrate me and...and now you have the gall to turn round and start preaching to me about pride or honour! And as for your so-called sense of responsibility! You don't even begin to understand the meaning of the word, as decent people understand it!'

Mariella could see the tension in his jaw, but she suspected that it was caused by anger rather than any sense of shame.

'The situation has now changed!'

'Changed? Because you have discovered that instead of being, and I quote, your cousin's "whore" paid to have sex with men, I am a career woman.'

'I have received a…a communication from Khalid confirming that he is Fleur's father, and because of that—' his mouth tightened '—I have to consider Fleur's position, her future…her reputation!'

'Her reputation!' Mariella gave him a scathing look. 'Fleur is four months old! And anyway, His Highness has already done everything that is necessary to stem any potential gossip.'

'I have been to see His Highness myself to inform him that, whilst you are here in Zuran, you will be living beneath the protection of my roof! Naturally he is in total agreement!'

Mariella couldn't believe her ears.

'Oh, no,' she denied, shaking her head vigorously from side to side. 'No, no, no. No way!'

'Mariella. Please see it as a way for me to make amends by offering you my hospitality. Besides, you have no choice—the prince expects it.'

He meant it, Mariella recognised as she searched his implacable features.

'I shall wait here until you have packed and then we will return to my home. I have arranged for my widowed great-aunt to act as your chaperone for the duration of your stay in Zuran.'

Her chaperone!

'I am twenty-eight years old,' she told him through gritted teeth. 'I do not need a chaperone.'

'You are a single woman living beneath the roof of a single man. There will already be those who will look askance at you having read that article.'

'At me, but not, of course, at you!'

'I am a man, so it is different,' he told her with a dismissively arrogant shrug that made her grind her teeth in female outrage.

Mariella couldn't wait to speak to her sister to tell her what had happened!

Right now, though, Mariella dared not take the risk of defying him! He could, after all, if he so wished, not merely put his threats into action, but also take Fleur from her here and now if he chose to do so!

IT TOOK HER less than half an hour to pack their things, a task she performed in seething silence whilst Xavier stood in front of the door, his arms folded across his chest, watching her with smoulderingly dangerous eyes.

When she had finished she went to pick Fleur up, but Xavier got there first.

Over Fleur's downy head their gazes clashed and locked, Xavier's a seething molten grey, Mariella's a brilliantly glittering jade.

THE LIMOUSINE WAITING for them was every bit as opulent looking as the one the prince had sent for her, although Mariella was surprised to discover that Xavier was driving it himself.

Somehow she had not associated him with a liking for such a luxurious showy vehicle. She had got the impression that his tastes were far, far more austere.

But, as she had discovered, beneath his outwardly cold self-control a molten, hot passion burned, which was all the more devastating for being so tightly chained.

It didn't take them long to reach the villa, but this time the gates were opened as they approached them and they swept in, crunching over a gravel drive flanked by double rows of palm trees.

The villa itself was elegantly proportioned, its design restrained, and Moorish in inspiration, Mariella noticed

with unwilling approval as she studied its simple lines
with an artist's eye.

A pair of wrought-iron gates gave way to a gravelled
walled courtyard, ornamented with a large central stone
fountain.

Stopping the car, Xavier got out and came to open her
own door. A manservant appeared to deal with her luggage, and a shy young girl whom Xavier introduced to
her as Hera, and who, he told her, would be Fleur's nanny.
Smiling reassuringly at the nanny he handed Fleur to her
before Mariella could stop him.

She certainly held Fleur as though she knew what she
was doing, Mariella recognised, but even so! A pang of
loss tightened her body as she looked at Fleur being held
in another woman's arms.

'Fleur doesn't need a nanny,' she told Xavier quickly. 'I
am perfectly capable of looking after her myself.'

'Maybe so, but it is customary here for those who can
afford to do so to provide the less well off amongst our
people with work. Hera is the eldest child in her family,
and her mother has recently been widowed. Are you really willing to deprive her of the opportunity to help to
support her siblings, simply because you are afraid of allowing anyone else to become emotionally close to Fleur?'

As he spoke he was ushering her into the semi-darkness
of the interior of the villa. Mariella was so shocked and
unprepared for his unexpectedly astute comment that she
stumbled slightly as her eyes adjusted to the abrupt change
from brilliant sunlight to shadowy darkness.

Instantly Xavier reached for her, his hand gripping her
waist as he steadied her. Her dizziness must be something to do with that abrupt switch from lightness to dark,
Mariella told herself, and so too must her accompanying
weakness, turning her into a quivering mass of over-sen-

sitive nerve endings, each one of them reacting to the fact that Xavier was touching her. Confused blurred images filled her head: Xavier, naked as he swam, Xavier leaning over her as he held her down on the bed, Xavier kissing her until she ached for him so badly her need was a physical pain.

Her need? She did not need Xavier. She would never, never need him. Never… She managed to pull herself free of him, her eyes adjusting to the light enough for her to see the cold disapproval with which he was regarding her.

'You must take more care. You are not used to our climate. By the end of this month the temperature will be reaching forty degrees Celsius, and you are very fair-skinned. You must be sure always to drink plenty of water, and that applies to Fleur as well.'

'Thank you. I do know not to allow myself to get dehydrated,' Mariella told him through gritted teeth. 'I am a woman, not a child, and as such I am perfectly capable of looking after myself. After all, I've been doing it for long enough.'

The look he gave her made her feel as though someone had taken hold of her heart and flipped it over inside her chest.

'Yes. It must have been hard for you to lose your mother and your stepfather having already lost your father at such a young age…'

'Lost my father?' Mariella gave him a bitter look. 'I didn't "lose" him. He abandoned my mother because he didn't want the responsibilities of fatherhood. He was never any true father to me, but he broke my mother's heart—'

'My own parents died when I was in my early teens—a tragic accident—but I was lucky enough to have my grandmother to help me through it. However, as we both know, the realisation that one is without parents does tend to breed a certain…independence of spirit, a certain protective defensiveness.' He was frowning, Mariella recognised, picking his words with care as though there was something he was trying to tell her. He broke off as Hera came into the reception hall carrying Fleur.

'If you will go with Hera, she will show you to your quarters. My aunt should arrive shortly.'

He had turned on his heel and was striding away from her, his back ramrod straight in the cool whiteness of his robe, leaving her no alternative other than to follow the timidly smiling young maid.

The villa obviously stretched back from its frontage to a depth she had not suspected, Mariella acknowledged ten minutes later, when she had followed the maid through several enormous reception rooms and up a flight of stairs, and then along a cloistered walkway through which a deliciously cool breeze had flowed and from which she had been able to look down into a totally enclosed private courtyard, complete with a swimming pool.

'This is the courtyard of Sheikh Xavier,' Hera had whispered to her, shyly averting her gaze from it and looking nervous when Mariella had paused to study it.

'Normally it is forbidden for us to be here, as the women of the household have their own private entrance to their quarters…'

'Let me take Fleur,' Mariella told her, firmly taking her niece back into her own arms and relishing the deliciously warm weight of her.

A door at the end of the corridor led to another cloistered walkway, this time with views over an immaculate rose garden.

'This was the special garden of the sheikh's grandparents. His grandmother was French and the roses were from France. She supervised their planting herself.'

For Mariella the rigid beds and the formality of the garden immediately summoned up a vivid impression of a woman who was very proud and correct, a true martinet. Her grandson obviously took after her!

The women's quarters, when they finally got to them, proved to be far more appealing than Mariella had expected. Here again a cloistered walkway opened onto a private garden, but here the garden was softer, filled with sweet-smelling flowers and decorated with a pretty turreted summer house as well as the customary water features.

They comprised several lavishly furnished bedrooms, each with its own equally luxurious bathroom and dressing room, a dining room, and a salon— Mariella could think of no other word to describe the delicate and ornate antique French furniture and decor of the two rooms, which she suspected must have been designed and equipped for Xavier's French grandmother.

On the bookshelves flanking the fireplace she could see leather-bound books bearing the names of some of France's most famous writers.

'The sheikh has said that you will wish to have the little one in a room next to your own,' Hera was telling her softly. 'He has made arrangements for everything that she will need to be delivered. I am not sure which room you will wish to use...'

Ignoring the temptation to tell her that she wished to use none of them, and that in fact what she wished to do was to leave the villa with Fleur right now—after all, none of this was Hera's fault and it would be unfair of her to take out her own resentment on the maid—Mariella gave in to her gentle hint and quickly inspected each of the four bedrooms.

One of them, furnished in the same Louis Fifteenth

antiques as the salon, had quite obviously been Xavier's grandmother's and she rejected it immediately. Of the three others, she automatically picked the plainest with its cool-toned walls and simple furniture. It had its own private access to the gardens with a small clear pool only a few feet away and a seat next to it from which to watch the soothing movement of the water.

'This room?'

When Mariella nodded, Hera smiled.

'The sheikh will be pleased. This was his mother's room.'

Xavier's mother's room! It was too late for her to change her mind, Mariella recognised.

'What…what nationality was she?' she asked Hera, immediately wishing she had not done so.

'She was a member of the tribe… The sheikh's father met her when he was travelling with them and fell in love with her…'

Fleur was beginning to make hungry noises, reminding Mariella that it was her niece she should be thinking about and not Xavier's family background.

CHAPTER EIGHT

MARIELLA stared worriedly at her mobile phone. She had just tried for the fourth time since her arrival at the villa to make contact with Tanya, but her sister's mobile was still switched onto messaging mode. She had left a message saying that she was staying at Xavier's villa, and had asked Tanya to contact her at the villa or call her cell phone. Mariella realised to her consternation that it was days since she had actually spoken to Tanya. A little tingle of alarm began to feather down her spine. What if something had happened to her sister? What if she wasn't well or had hurt herself. Or...

Quickly Mariella made up her mind. It took her quite some time to get the telephone number for the entertainments director of her sister's cruise liner, but eventually she managed to get through.

'I'm sorry, who is this speaking, please?' The firm male voice on the other end of the line checked her when Mariella had asked for Tanya, explaining that she had been unable to make contact with her via her mobile.

'I am Tanya's sister,' Mariella explained.

'I see... Well, I have to inform you that Tanya has actually left the ship.'

'Left the ship!' Mariella repeated in disbelief. 'But... where? Why...?'

'I'm sorry. I can't give you any more details. All I can say is that Tanya left of her own accord and without giving us any prior warning.'

From the tone of his voice Mariella could tell that he wasn't very pleased with her sister!

Thanking him for his help, she ended the call, turning to look at Fleur, who was fast asleep in her brand-new bed.

As Hera had already warned her, Xavier had instructed a local baby equipment store to provide a full nursery's worth of brand new things, all of which Mariella had immediately realised were far, far more expensive and exclusive than anything she or Tanya could have afforded.

Tanya! Where was her sister? Why had she left the ship? And why, oh, why wasn't she returning her calls?

It was imperative that she knew what was happening, and, for all her faults, her impulsiveness and hedonism, Tanya genuinely loved Fleur. It was unthinkable to Mariella that she should not make contact with her to check up on her baby.

In Tanya's shoes there was no way she would not have been on the phone every hour of every day... No way she could ever have brought herself to be parted from her baby in the first place, Mariella recognised, but then poor Tanya had had no alternative! Tanya had been determined to pay her own way.

Emotionally, she stood over Fleur looking down at her whilst she slept. Increasingly she ached inside to have a child of her own. When she had made her original vow never to put herself in a position where she could be emotionally hurt by a man, she had not foreseen this kind of complication!

XAVIER FROWNED AS he paced the floor of his study. A flood of faxes cluttered his desk, all of them giving him the same information—namely that his cousin had not been seen in any of his usual favourite haunts! Where on earth was Khalid?

Xavier was becoming increasingly suspicious that his cousin had been deliberately vague about Fleur's true paternity. Out of a desire to protect Fleur and her mother, or out of a desire to escape his responsibilities?

Surely Khalid knew him well enough to know that, even if he couldn't approve of or accept Fleur's mother, he would certainly have insisted that proper financial arrangements were made for her and Fleur, and if necessary by Xavier himself? Of course he did, which was no doubt why he had now written to Xavier informing him that he was Fleur's father.

It irked him that he had been so dramatically wrong-footed in assuming that Mariella was Fleur's mother. The security information the prince had revealed to him had made it brutally clear just how wrong he had been about her.

Here was a young woman who had shouldered the responsibility, not just of supporting herself, but of supporting her younger half-sister as well. Not a single shred of information to indicate that Mariella had led anything other than the most morally laudable life could be found! There were no unsavoury corpses mouldering away in the dusty corners of Mariella's life; in fact, the truth was that there were not even any dusty corners! Everyone who had had dealings with her spoke of her in the most glowing and complimentary terms.

And yet somehow he, a man who prided himself on his astuteness and his ability to read a person's true personality, had not been able to see any of this! True, she had deliberately deceived him, but...

But he had behaved towards her in a way that, had he

heard about it coming from another man, he would have had no hesitation in immediately denouncing and condemning him!

There were no excuses he could accept from himself! Not even the increasingly insubstantial one of wanting to protect Khalid.

Wasn't it after all true that the last thing, the last person who had been in his thoughts when he had taken Mariella to bed had been his cousin? Wasn't it also true that he had been driven, possessed...consumed by his own personal physical desire?

He could find no logical excuse or explanation for what he had done. Other than to tell himself that he had been driven by desert madness, and he felt riddled with guilt, especially for the way he had coerced her into staying with him at his villa. He would of course have to apologise formally to Mariella!

A woman who already had proved how strong her sense of duty and responsibility was. A woman with whom a man could know that the children he gave her would be loved and treasured...

He had sworn not to marry, rather than risk the hazards of a marriage that might go wrong, he reminded himself austerely.

Surely, though, it was better to offer Mariella the protection of his name in marriage rather than risk any potential damage to her reputation through gossip?

He had already provided her with sufficient protection in the form of his great-aunt as a chaperone, he reminded himself grimly. If he continued to think as he was doing right now, he might begin to suspect that he actually wanted to marry her! That he actually wanted to take her back into his bed and complete what they had already begun.

Angrily he swung round as the sudden chatter of the fax machine broke into his far too sensually charged thoughts.

'So, HERE WE are, then. Xavier has summoned me to be your chaperone, and I am to accompany you to the palace whilst you paint pictures for His Highness, *non?*'

'Well, not exactly,' Mariella responded wryly. It was impossible for her not to like the vivacious elderly Frenchwoman who was Xavier's great-aunt and who had arrived half an hour earlier, complete with an enormous pile of luggage and her own formidable looking maid.

'I am not actually working at the palace, but at the new enclosure at the racecourse, and, to be honest, I don't agree with Xavier—'

'Agree? But I am afraid that here in Zuran we have to comply with the laws of the land, *chérie,* both actual and moral.' Rolling her eyes dramatically, she continued, 'I know how difficult I found it when I first came to live here. My sister was already married to Xavier's grandfather for several years by then. She was older than me by well over a decade. Since the death of my husband, I live both in Paris and here in Zuran. The child I understand is Khalid's?' she commented, with a disconcerting change of subject. 'He is a charming young man, but unfortunately very weak! He is fortunate that Xavier is so indulgent towards him, but you probably know Xavier does not intend to marry and he intended for Khalid's son to ultimately take over his responsibilities! It is such foolishness...'

'Xavier does not intend to marry?' Mariella questioned her.

'So he claims. The death of his own parents affected him very seriously. He was at a most impressionable age when they perished and of course my sister, his grandmother, was very much a matriarch of the old school. She was determined that he would be brought up to know his responsibilities towards his people and to fulfil them. Now Xavier believes that their needs are more important than his own and that he cannot therefore risk marrying a woman who would not understand and accept his duty and the importance of his role. Such nonsense, but then that is men for you! They like to believe that we are the weaker sex, but we of course know that it is we who are the strong ones!

'You have great strength, I can see that! You will miss the child when you eventually have to hand her back to her mother,' she added shrewdly.

The speed of her conversation, along with the speed of her perceptiveness, was leaving Mariella feeling slightly dizzy.

'I see that you have chosen not to occupy my late sister's room. Extremely wise of you if I may say so…I could never understand why she insisted on attempting to recreate our parents' Avenue Foche apartment here! But then that was Sophia for you! As an eldest child she was extremely strong-willed, whilst I…' she paused to dimple a rueful smile at Mariella '…am the youngest, and, according to her at least, was extremely spoiled!

'You would not have liked her,' she pronounced, shocking Mariella a little with her outspokenness. 'She would have taken one look at you and immediately started to make plans to make you Xavier's wife. You do not believe me? I assure you that it is true. She would have seen immediately how perfect you would be for him!'

Her, perfect for Xavier? Fiercely squashing the treacherous little sensation tingling through her, Mariella told her quickly, 'I have no intention of ever getting married.'

'You see? Already it is clear just how much you and Xavier have in common! However, I am not my sister. I do not interfere in other people's lives or try to arrange them for them! *Non!* But tell me why is it that you have made up your mind not to marry? In Xavier's case it is plain that it is because of the fear instilled in him by my sister that he will not find a woman to love who will share his dedication to his commitment to preserve the traditional way of life of the tribe. Such nonsense! But Sophia herself is very much to blame. When he was a young and impressionable young man she sent Xavier to France in the hope that he would find a bride amongst the daughters of our own circle. But these girls cannot breathe any air other than that of Paris. The very thought of them doing as Xavier has done every year of his life and travelling through the desert with those members of the tribe who had chosen to adhere to the old way of life would be intolerable to them!

'Xavier needs a wife who will embrace and love the ways of his people with the same passion with which he does himself. A woman who will embrace and love him with even more passion, for, as I am sure you will already know, Xavier is an extremely passionate man.'

Mariella gave her a wary look. What was his great-aunt trying to imply? However, when she looked at her face her expression was rosily innocent and open.

Madame Flavel's comments were, though, arousing both her interest and her curiosity.

Hesitantly she told her, 'You have mentioned the tribe and Xavier's commitment to it, but I do not really know just what…'

'*Non?* It is quite simple really. The tribe into which Xavier's ancestor originally married is unique in its way of life, and it was the life's work of Xavier's grandfather, and would have been of his father had he not died, to preserve the tribe's traditional nomadic existence, but at the same time encourage those members of it who wished to

do so to integrate into modern society. To that end, every
child born into the tribe has the right to receive a proper
education and to follow the career path of their choice, but
at the same time each and every member of the tribe must
spend some small part of every year travelling the traditional nomadic routes in the traditional way. Some members of the tribe elect to live permanently in such a fashion,
and they are highly revered by every other member of the
tribe, even those who, as many have, have reached the
very peak of their chosen career elsewhere in the world.
Within the tribe recognition and admiration are won, not
through material or professional attainment, but through
preservation of the old ways and traditions.

'Xavier's role as head of the tribe means, though, that
he has a dual role to fulfil. He must ensure that he has the
business expertise to see that the money left by his grandfather generates sufficient future income to provide financially for the tribe, and yet at the same time he must be
able to hold the respect of the tribe by leading it in its ancient traditional ways. Xavier has known all his life that
he must fulfil both those roles and he does so willingly, I
know, but nevertheless it will be a very lonely path he has
chosen to follow unless he does find a woman who can
understand and share his life with him.'

Mariella had fallen silent as she listened. There was a
poignancy about what she was hearing that was touching
very deep emotional chords within. The Xavier his great-
aunt was describing to her was a man of deep and profound
feelings and beliefs, a man who, in other circumstances,
she herself could respect and admire.

'MADAME, I ASSURE you there is really no need for you to
remain here with me,' Mariella told her chaperone firmly
as she studied the long corridor that was to be her canvas.

Fleur was lying in her pram playing with her toes and Mariella had pinned up in front of her, on the easel she had brought with her, the photographs she had taken of the prince's horses.

'It is for this purpose that Xavier has summoned me to his home,' Madame Flavel reminded her.

'You will be bored sitting here watching me work,' Mariella protested.

'I am never bored. I have my tapestry and my newspaper, and in due course Ali will return to drive us back to the villa for a small repast and an afternoon nap.'

There was no way she intended to indulge in afternoon naps, Mariella decided silently as she picked up her charcoals and started to work.

In her mind she already had a picture of how she wanted the frieze to look, and within minutes she was totally engrossed in what she was doing.

The background for the horses, she had now decided, would not be the racecourse itself, but something that she hoped would prove far more compelling to those who viewed it. The background of a rolling ocean of waves from which the horses were emerging would surely prove irresistible to a people to whom water was so very, very important. Mariella hoped so. His Highness had certainly liked the idea.

It wasn't until her fingers began to ache a little with cramp that she realised how long she had been working. Madame Flavel had fallen asleep in the comfortable chair with its special footstool that Ali had brought for her, her gentle snores keeping Fleur entranced.

Smiling at her niece, Mariella opened the bottle of water she had brought with her and took a drink. Where was Tanya? Why hadn't she got in touch with her?

The door to the corridor opened to admit Hera and Ali.

'Goodness, is it lunchtime already?' Madame Flavel demanded, immediately waking up.

Reluctantly Mariella started to pack up her things. She would much rather have continued with her work than return to the villa, but she was very conscious of Madame Flavel's age and the unfairness of expecting her to remain with her for hours on end.

CHAPTER NINE

By the end of the week Mariella was beginning to find her enforced breaks from her work increasingly frustrating.

'It disturbs me that you are so determined not to marry, *chérie*,' Madame Flavel was saying to her as she worked. 'It is perhaps because of an unhappy love affair?'

'You could say that,' Mariella agreed wryly.

'He broke your heart, but you are young, and broken hearts mend...'

'It wasn't my heart he broke, but my mother's,' Mariella corrected her, 'and it never really mended, not even when she met and married my stepfather. You see, she thought when my father told her that he loved her he meant it, but he didn't! She trusted him, depended on him, but he repaid that trust by abandoning us both.'

'Ah, I see. And because of the great hurt your father caused you, you are determined never to trust any man yourself?' Madame Flavel commented shrewdly. 'Not all men are like your father, *chérie*.'

'Maybe not, but it is not a risk I am prepared to take! I never want to be as...as vulnerable as my mother was... never.'

'You say that, but I think you fear that you already are.'

Mariella was glad of Ali's arrival to put an end to what was becoming a very uncomfortable conversation.

IT WAS TWO o'clock in the afternoon and Madame Flavel was taking her afternoon nap.

Mariella walked restlessly round the garden. She was itching to get on with the frieze. She paused, frowning slightly. And then, making up her mind, hurried back inside, pausing only to pick up Fleur.

Ali made no comment when she summoned him to tell him that she intended to go back to the enclosure, politely opening the door of the car for her. Stepping outside was like standing in the blast of a hot hair-dryer at full heat.

The car was coolly air-conditioned, but outside the heat shimmered in the air, the light bouncing glaringly off the buildings that lined the road.

Like the car, the enclosure was air-conditioned, and as soon as Ali had escorted her inside and gone Mariella began to work.

A moveable scaffolding had been erected to allow her to work on the upper part of the wall, and she paused every now and again to look down from it to check on Fleur, who was fast asleep. Her throat felt dry and her hand ached, but she refused to allow herself to stop. In her mind's eye she could see the finished animal, nostrils flaring, his mane ruffled by the wind, the sea foaming behind him as he emerged from the curling breakers.

Somewhere on the edge of her awareness she was vaguely conscious of a door opening, and quiet but ominously determined footsteps. Fleur made a small sound, a gurgle of pleasure rather than complaint, which she also registered, her hand moving quickly as she fought to capture the image inside her head. This horse, the proudest and fiercest of them all, would not tolerate any competition from the sea. He would challenge its power, rearing up so that the powerful muscles of his quarters and belly were visible... Fleur was chattering happily to herself in baby talk, and Mariella was beginning to feel almost light-headed with concentration. And then just as she was finishing something a movement, an instinct made her turn her head.

To her shock she saw that Xavier was standing beside Fleur watching her.

'Xavier...'

She took a step forward and then stopped, suddenly realising that she was still on the scaffolding.

'What...what are you doing here?' she demanded belligerently to cover her own intimate and unwanted reaction to him.

'Have you any idea just how much you distressed Cecille by ignoring my instructions?' he demanded tersely.

Mariella looked away from him. She genuinely liked his great-aunt, and hated the thought that she might have upset her.

'I'm sorry if she was upset,' she told him woodenly, her own feelings breaking through her tight control as she gave a small despairing shake of her head.

'I promised His Highness that the frieze would be completed as soon as possible; your aunt is elderly. She likes to spend the afternoon resting, when I need to be here working! Whether you believe this or not, Xavier, I too have a...a reputation to protect.'

'In that case why didn't you simply come to me and explain all of this to me instead of behaving like a child and waiting until my aunt's back was turned?'

Mariella frowned. What he was saying sounded so... so reasonable and sensible she imagined that anyone listening to him would have asked her the same question!

'Your behaviour towards me has hardly encouraged me to...to anticipate your help or co-operation,' she reminded

him as she went to climb down from the scaffolding, sur-
reptitiously trying to stretch her aching muscles.

'Although she herself refuses to acknowledge it, my
aunt is an elderly lady,' Xavier was continuing, breaking
off suddenly to mutter something beneath his breath she
couldn't quite catch as he strode forward.

'Be careful,' he warned her sharply. 'You might...'

To her own chagrin, as though his warning had provoked it, the scaffolding suddenly wobbled and she began
to slip.

As she gave a small instinctive gasp of shock Xavier
grabbed hold of her, supporting her so that she could slide
safely to the floor.

Mariella knew that the small near-accident was her own
fault and that she had worked for too long in one position,
without stopping to exercise her cramped muscles, and
her face began to burn as she anticipated Xavier's triumphant justification of his insistence that she was chaper-
oned, but instead of saying anything he simply continued
to hold her, one hand grasping her waist, the other supporting the small of her back, where his fingers spread a
dangerously intoxicating heat right through her clothes
and into her skin.

Dizzily Mariella closed her eyes, trying to blot out the
effect the proximity of him was having on her, but, to her
consternation, instead of protecting her all it did was increase her vulnerability as sharply focused mental images
of him taunted and tormented her, their effect on her so
intense that she started to shake in reaction to them.

'Mariella? What is it? What's wrong?' she heard Xavier
demanding urgently. 'If you feel unwell...'

Immediately Mariella opened her eyes.

'No. I'm fine,' she began and then stopped, unable to

drag her gaze away from his mouth, where it had focused itself with hungry, yearning intensity.

She knew from his sudden fixed silence that Xavier was aware of what she was doing, but the shrill alarm bells within her own defences, which should have shaken her into action, were silenced into the merest whisper by the inner roar of her own aching longing. No power on earth, let alone that of her own will, could stem what was happening to her and what she was feeling, Mariella recognised distantly, as her senses registered the way Xavier's grip on her body subtly altered from one of non-sexually protective to one of powerfully sensual. She could feel the hot burn of his gaze as it dropped to her own mouth, and a sharp series of little shivers broke through her. Without even thinking about it she was touching her lips with the tip of her tongue, as though driven by some deep pre-programmed instinct to moisten them. She was trembling, her whole body galvanised by tiny sensual ripples of reaction and awareness that made her sway slightly towards him.

She saw a muscle twitch in his jaw and raised her hand to touch it with her fingertips, her eyes wide and helplessly enslaved.

'Mariella!'

She felt him shudder as he drew breath into his lungs, her body instinctively leaning into his as weakness washed over her.

His mouth touched hers, but not in the way she had remembered it doing before.

She had never known there could be so much sweet tenderness in a kiss, so much slow, explorative warmth, so much carefully suppressed passion just waiting to burn away all her resistance. She wanted to lose herself completely in it…in him.

She gave a small cry of protest as Xavier's ears, keener

than hers, picked up the sound of someone entering the gallery, and he pushed her away.

Caught up in the shock of what she had experienced, Mariella watched motionless as Xavier went over to where Ali, his chauffeur, was hovering.

Lifting her hand, she touched her own lips, as though unable to believe what had happened...what she had wanted to happen. She had wanted Xavier to kiss her, still wanted him to kiss her, her body aching for him in a hundred intimate ways that held her in silent shock. She and Xavier were enemies, weren't they?

He was walking back to her and somehow she had to compose herself, to conceal from him what was happening to her.

She felt as though she were drowning in her own panic.

'We must get back to the villa, immediately,' he told her curtly.

Instantly her panic was replaced by anxiety.

'What is it?' she demanded. 'Has something happened to your aunt?'

She started to gather up her things, but he stopped her, instructing her tersely, 'Leave all that.'

He was already picking up Fleur, his body language so evident of a crisis that Mariella forbore to argue. Her stomach was churning sickly. What if something had happened to his great-aunt, perhaps brought on by her own stubborn determination to ignore his dictates? She would never forgive herself!

Falling into step beside him, Mariella almost had to run to keep up with him.

They drove back to the villa in silence, Mariella's anxiety increasing to such a pitch that by the time they finally turned into the courtyard of the villa she felt physically sick.

Giving some sharp order to Ali, in Arabic, Xavier got

out of the car, turning to her and telling her equally shortly, 'Come with me.'

Even Fleur seemed to have picked up on his seriousness, and fell silent in his arms, her eyes huge and dark.

Please let Cecille be all right, Mariella prayed silently as the huge double doors to the villa were thrown open with unfamiliar formality and she followed Xavier into its sandalwood-scented coolness.

Without pausing to see if she was following him, Xavier headed for the anteroom that opened out into what Mariella now knew was the formal salon in which he conducted his business meetings.

Unusually two liveried servants were standing to either side of the entrance, their expressionless faces adding both to Mariella's anxiety and the look of stern formality she could see on Xavier's face, giving it and him an air of autocratic arrogance so reminiscent of the first time she had seen him that she automatically shivered a little.

Expecting him to stride into the room ahead of her, Mariella almost bumped into him when he suddenly turned towards her. A little uncertainly she looked at him, unable to conceal her confusion when he reached out his hand to her and beckoned her to his side.

Holding Fleur tightly, she hesitated for a second before going to join him. Wide as the entrance to the salon was, it still apparently necessitated Xavier standing so close to her that she could feel the heat of his body against her own as he gave the servants an abrupt nod.

The doors swung open, the magnificence of the room that lay beyond them dazzling Mariella for a moment, even though she had already peeped into it at Madame Flavel's insistence.

It was everything she had ever imagined such a room should be, its walls hung with richly woven silks, the cool marble floor ornamented with priceless antique rugs. The light from the huge chandeliers, which Madame Flavel had told Mariella had been made to Xavier's grandmother's personal design, dazzled the eyes as it reflected on the room's rich jewel colours and ornate gilding. Luxurious and rich, the decor of the salon had about it an unmistakable air of French elegance.

It was a room designed to awe and impress all those who entered it and to make them aware of the power of the man who owned it.

As her eyes adjusted to the brilliance Mariella realised that two people were standing in front of the room's huge marble fireplace, watching Xavier with obvious apprehension as they clung together.

Disbelievingly Mariella stared at them.

'Tanya,' she whispered, her voice raw with shock as she recognised her sister.

Her sister looked tanned and expensive, Mariella noticed, the skirt and top she was wearing showing off her body. She was wearing her hair in a new, fashionably tousled style, and it glinted with a mix of toning blonde highlights.

She was immaculately made up, her fingernails and toenails shining with polish, but it was the man standing at Tanya's side on whom Mariella focused most of her attention. He was shorter than Xavier and more heavily built, she guessed immediately that he must be Khalid, Xavier's cousin and Fleur's father.

'Khalid,' Xavier acknowledged curtly, with a brief nod in the other man's direction, confirming Mariella's guesswork. 'And this, I assume, must be…'

'My wife,' Khalid interrupted him, holding tightly to Tanya's hand as he continued, 'Tanya and I were married three days ago.'

'HONESTLY, MARIELLA, I just couldn't believe it when we docked at Kingston and Khalid came on board. At first I totally refused to have anything to do with him, but he kept on persisting and eventually…'

It was less than twenty-four hours since Mariella had learned that her sister and Khalid were now married, and Tanya was updating her on what had happened as they sat together in the garden of the villa's women's quarters, whilst Fleur gurgled happily in her carrier.

'Why didn't you tell me what was going on when I telephoned you?' Mariella asked her.

Tanya looked self-conscious.

'Well, at first I wasn't sure just what was going to happen—I mean…Khalid was there and he was being very sweet, admitting that he loved me and that he regretted what he had done, but…

'And then you left that message on my cell phone saying you were here with Xavier, and I was worried that you might say something to him and that he would find a way of parting me and Khalid again…'

'Have you any idea how worried about you I've been?' Mariella asked her.

Tanya flushed uncomfortably.

'Well, I had hoped that you'd just think I wasn't returning your calls because I was so busy… It didn't occur to me that you'd ring the entertainments director…'

'Tanya, you didn't ring me to check on Fleur for days. Of course I was worried…'

'Oh, well, I knew she'd be fine with you, and I did listen to your messages. But Khalid… Well, we needed some time to ourselves, and Khalid insisted… Please don't be cross with me, Ella. You've never been in love so you can't understand. When Khalid left me I thought my life was over. I'm not like you. I need to love and be loved. I don't think I'll ever forgive Xavier for what he did.'

'Xavier didn't physically compel Khalid to abandon you and Fleur, Tanya,' Mariella heard herself pointing out to her sister almost sharply.

The look Tanya gave her confirmed her own realisation of what she had done.

'How can you support him, Ella?' Tanya demanded. 'He threatened to stop Khalid's allowance; he would have left me and Fleur to starve,' she added dramatically.

'That's not true, Tanya, and not fair either,' Mariella felt bound to correct her, but she couldn't quite bring herself to tell her sister that it was her own opinion that Khalid was both weak and self-indulgent and that he had selfishly put his own needs before those of his lover and their child. She could see already the beginnings of a sulky pout turning down the corners of Tanya's mouth and her heart sank. She had no wish to quarrel with her sister, but at the same time she couldn't help feeling that Tanya wasn't treating her own behaviour with regard to her maternal responsibilities towards Fleur anywhere near as seriously as she should have been doing.

'Well, we're married now and there's nothing that Xavier can do about it! And he knows it!'

Mariella knew that this was not true and that Xavier could have carried out his threat to stop paying Khalid his allowance, and also remove him from his sinecure of a job. However, she also knew from what Madame Flavel had innocently told her that Xavier had not done so because of Fleur.

'Oh, and you'll never guess what,' Tanya told her excitedly. 'I haven't had the opportunity to tell you yet, but Khalid is insisting on taking me for an extended honeymoon trip. We're going to take Fleur with us, of course, and then once we get back I suppose we will have to make our home here in Zuran, but Khalid has promised me that we'll get away as often as we can. He says that we can have our own villa and that I can choose everything myself! Oh, and look at my engagement ring. Isn't it beautiful?'

'Very,' Mariella agreed cordially as she studied the huge solitaire flashing on her sister's hand.

'I can't tell you how happy I am, Ella,' Tanya breathed ecstatically. 'And you have looked after my darling baby so well for me. I have missed you so much, my sweet,' Tanya cooed, blowing kisses to her daughter. 'Your daddy and I can't wait to have you all to ourselves.'

As she listened to her sister a small shadow crossed Mariella's face, but she was determined not to spoil Tanya's happiness by letting her see how much she was dreading losing Fleur.

'It all sounds very exciting,' she responded, forcing a smile as she looked up and saw the expectant look on her sister's face.

'When will you be leaving?'

'Tomorrow! Everything's already arranged. Khalid just wanted to come to Zuran to tell Xavier about our marriage, and to collect Fleur, of course…'

'Of course,' Mariella agreed hollowly.

'ELLA, I CAN'T thank you enough for looking after Fleur for me. We're both really grateful to you, aren't we, Khalid?'

'Yes, we are,' her new brother-in-law agreed.

Mariella was still holding Fleur, not wanting to physically part with her until she absolutely had to, whilst Tanya said her goodbyes to Madame Flavel and Xavier.

Tanya was still behaving very coolly towards Xavier, only speaking to him when she had to do so.

'Darling, can you take Fleur out to the car?' she instructed Khalid.

Mariella could feel herself stiffening as Khalid went to take the baby from her, and, whether because of that or because as yet Fleur was not used to her father, as he reached for her the little baby suddenly screwed up her face and started to cry.

Immediately Khalid pulled back from her looking flustered and irritable.

'Here, let me take her!'

Xavier quietly removed Fleur from Mariella's arms, before she could object. He smiled down at Fleur and soothed her, whilst she gazed back at him wide-eyed, her tears immediately ceasing.

Out of the corner of her eye Mariella saw that Tanya had started to glower at Xavier, obviously resenting the fact that Fleur was more comfortable with him than with her father, but before she could say anything Khalid was urging her to hurry.

They went out to the car together, Xavier still holding Fleur, Mariella wincing in the blast of hot air.

As soon as she got into the car, Tanya held out her arms to him for Fleur, but to Mariella's surprise, instead of handing Fleur to Tanya, Xavier gave her to Mariella.

Mariella could feel her eyes burning with emotional tears, her throat closing up as her feelings threatened to overwhelm her. It was almost as though Xavier could sense how she felt and wanted to give her one last precious chance to hold Fleur before she had to part with her.

Bending her head, she kissed her niece and then quickly handed her over to her sister.

When the car taking them to the airport finally pulled away, Mariella could only see it through a blur.

'Let's get out of this wind,' she heard Xavier telling her
when the car had finally disappeared from sight.

If he was aware of her tears he was discreet enough not
to show it, simply ushering her back to the villa without
making any other comment.

However, once they were inside, Mariella took a deep
breath and made her voice sound as businesslike as she
could as she told him, 'I'll make arrangements to leave just
as soon as I can arrange somewhere else to stay.'

'What on earth are you talking about?' Xavier demanded sharply. 'Nothing has changed. You are still a
single young woman who is a member of my family, and
as such your place is still here beneath my roof and my protection! This should be your home whilst you're in Zuran,'
Xavier told her.

Mariella opened her mouth to argue with him and then
closed it again. It was just because she was feeling so upset
about losing Fleur that his statement was giving her this
odd sense of heady relief, she told herself defensively. It
had nothing to do with…any other reason. Nothing at all!

MARIELLA WAS DREAMING. She was dreaming that she was
all alone in an unfamiliar room, lying on a large bed and
crying for Fleur, and then suddenly the door opened and
Xavier came in. Walking over to the bed, he sat down beside her and reached out for her hand.

'You are crying for the child,' he told her softly. 'But
you must not. I shall give you a child of your own to love.
Our child!' As she looked at him he started to touch her,
smoothing the covers from her naked body with hands
that seemed to know just how to please her. Bending his
head, he started to kiss her, a slow, magically tender kiss,
which quickly began to burn with the heat of a fierce passion. She could feel her whole body trembling with need

and longing! And not just for the child he had promised her, but for Xavier himself!

His hands cupped her breasts, his grey eyes liquid with arousal as he gazed at them, shockingly sensual words of praise falling from his lips as he whispered to her how much he wanted her. He kissed each rosy crest, savouring their shape and sensitivity with his lips and tongue until she was clinging to him, digging her nails into his back as she submitted to her own desire.

Possessively she measured the strong length of his arms with her fingertips, expelling her breath on a shuddering sigh as his tongue rimmed her belly and his hand covered her sex, waiting, aching, wanting. Beneath her hand she could feel him harden as she touched him, torn between wanting to explore him and wanting to feel him deep inside her as he ignited the spark of life that would be their child. But as she reached for him, suddenly he pulled away, abandoning her. Desperately she cried out to him not to leave her, her body chilled and shaking, tears clogging her throat and spilling from her eyes. Abruptly Mariella woke up.

Somehow in her sleep she had pushed away the bedclothes, which was why she was now shivering in the coolness of the air-conditioning. The tears drying stickily on her face and tightening her skin were surely caused by the fact that she was missing Fleur and not because she had been dreaming about Xavier...about loving him and losing him! She would never allow herself to be that much of a fool! But physically she was affected by him, she could not deny that! Fiercely she tried to tense her body against its own betraying ache of longing. Xavier was a man who, even she had to acknowledge, took his responsibilities and his commitments very seriously. A man whose passions...

Stop it, she warned herself frantically. What was she doing thinking like this? Feeling like this?

Wide awake now, she got out of bed, and was halfway toward Fleur's now empty cot before she realised what she was doing. It was only right that Fleur should be with her parents, but she ached so to be holding her small body. She ached so for a child of her own, she admitted.

TIREDLY MARIELLA FLEXED the tense, aching muscles in her neck and shoulders as she sat beside the small pool in the women's courtyard. She had worked relentlessly on the frieze over the last two weeks, driven by a compulsion she hadn't been able to ignore, and now knew that she would be able to finish the project well ahead of time.

The prince had arrived to inspect her progress just before she had left and she had seen immediately from his expression just how impressed he was by what she was doing.

'It is magnificent…awe-inspiring,' he had told her enthusiastically. 'A truly heart-gripping vision.'

'I'm glad you like it,' Mariella had responded prosaically, but inwardly she had been elated.

Elated and too exhausted to eat her dinner, she reminded herself ruefully as she reached up to try and massage some relief into her aching neck, tensing as she saw Xavier walking towards her.

'I have just come from seeing His Highness,' he told her. 'He wanted to show me your work. He is most impressed, and rightly so. It is magnificent!'

His uncharacteristic praise stunned Mariella, who stared at him, her turquoise eyes shadowed and wary.

'Has your sister been in touch with you yet to reassure you that Fleur is well?' Xavier continued.

Not trusting herself to speak, Mariella shook her head and then winced as her tense, locked muscles resisted the movement.

Quick to notice her small betraying wince, Xavier demanded immediately, 'You're in pain. What is it? What's wrong?'

'My muscles are stiff, that's all,' Mariella replied.

'Stiff. Where? Let me see?'

Before she could object he was sitting down next to her, his fingers moving searchingly over her shoulders, expertly finding her locked muscles.

'Keep still,' he said when she instinctively tried to pull away. 'I am not surprised you are in so much pain. You work too hard! Drive yourself too hard. Worry too much about others and allow them to abuse your sense of responsibility towards them!'

Swiftly Mariella turned her head to look at him.

'You are a fine one to accuse me of that!' she couldn't help pointing out.

For a moment they looked at one another in mutual silence. She was learning so much about this man, discovering so many things about him that changed her whole perception of what and who he was.

HE COULDN'T HAVE been more wrong about Mariella, or misjudged her more unfairly, Xavier acknowledged as he looked down into her eyes. Her sister, in contrast, was exactly what he had expected her to be, and typical of his cousin's taste in women. The more cynical side of his nature felt that, not only were they suited to one another, but that they also deserved one another in their mutual selfishness and lack of any true emotional depth.

Mariella, on the other hand... He had never met a woman who took her responsibilities more seriously, or who was more fiercely protective of those she loved. When she committed herself to a man she would commit herself to him heart and soul. When she loved a man, she would love him with depth and passion and her love would be for ever…

'Your sister should have been in touch with you. She must know how much you are missing Fleur,' he told Mariella abruptly.

Mariella tensed, immediately flying to Tanya's defence as she told him fiercely, 'She is Fleur's mother. She doesn't have to consult me about…anything. This holiday will give the three of them an opportunity to bond together as a family. Tanya and Khalid are Fleur's parents and…'

'I miss Fleur too,' Xavier stopped her gruffly, his admission astonishing her. 'And in my opinion she would be much better off here in a secure environment with those who know her best, rather than being dragged to some fashionable resort where she will probably be left in the care of hotel staff whilst her parents spend their time enjoying themselves!'

'You are being unfair,' Mariella protested, and then winced as Xavier started to knead the knots out of her muscles, making it impossible for her to move.

'No. I am being honest,' he corrected her. 'And when Khalid returns you may be sure that I shall be making it very plain to him that Fleur needs a secure family environment!'

Xavier would make a wonderful father, Mariella conceded, and then stiffened as she tried to reject the messages that knowledge was giving her! After all, like her, Xavier had no intentions of ever getting married!

'Your muscles are very badly knotted,' she heard him telling her brusquely as his thumbs started to probe their way over the tight lumps of pain.

It was heaven having the tension massaged from her body, Mariella acknowledged, and no doubt what he was doing would be even more effective if she wasn't trying to tense herself against those dangerous sensations that had nothing whatsoever to do with any kind of work-induced muscle ache, and everything to do with Xavier himself.

The longer he touched her, the harder she was finding it to control her sexual reaction to him.

His thumbs stroked along her spine, causing her to shudder openly in response. Immediately his hands stilled.

'Mariella.'

His voice sounded rough and raw, the sensation of his breath against her skin bringing her out in a rash of sensual goose-bumps. Was she only imagining that she could hear a note of hungry male desire in his voice?

She couldn't trust herself to speak to him, just as she didn't dare to turn round, but suddenly he was turning her, holding her, finding her mouth with his own and kissing her with a silent ferocity that made her tremble from head to toe as her body dissolved in a wash of liquid pleasure that ran through her veins, melting any resistance.

The hands that had so clinically massaged her shoulders were now caressing her flesh beneath her loose top in a way that was anything but clinical! A savage, relentless ache began to torment her body. The warm, perfumed night air of the garden was suddenly replaced by the aroused male scent of Xavier's body and Mariella reacted to it blindly, wrenching her mouth from beneath his and burying her face in the open throat of his robe so that she could breathe it—him—in more deeply, her lips questing for the satin warmth of his skin, her moan of pleasure locked in her throat as she gave her senses their head.

Beneath her lips his flesh felt firm and hot, the muscles of his throat taut, the curve where it met his shoulder tempting her to bite delicately into it. She heard him groan as his hand covered her breast, her nipple swelling eagerly against his palm. She felt the warmth of the night air against her skin as he pushed her simple cotton robe out of the way, her whole body shuddering in agonised pleasure as he cupped her breast and lowered his mouth to her waiting nipple.

The pleasure that surged through her tightened her body into a helpless yearning arc of longing, exposing her slender feminine flesh to his gaze and touch, offering her up to them, Mariella recognised distantly as she shook with hunger for him. Wanting him like this seemed so natural, and right, so inevitable, as though it were something that had been destined to happen.

Lifting her hand, she touched his face, their gazes meeting and locking, silently absorbing one another's need. The look in his eyes made her body leap in eager heat, the sensation of the slightly rough rasp of his jaw against her palm as he turned his face to kiss it filling her with a thousand erotic images of how it was going to feel, to have him caressing even more sensitive and intimate parts of her body. She was, she realised, trembling violently, as Xavier stroked his hands down her back and lifted her against his body so that she could feel its hard arousal. She ached so badly for the feel of him inside her, for the fulfilment of his possession of her, the completion. His mouth was on her breast, her nipple, caressing it in a way that made her cry out for the hot, deep suckle of a more savage pleasure.

In the moonlight Xavier could see the swollen softness of her mouth and her breast, his breath catching in his lungs as his gaze travelled lower, to where the delicate mound of her sex seemed to push temptingly against the fine cotton of her briefs.

The thought of sliding his hand beneath them and holding her, parting the delicately shaped lips and opening up her moist inner self to his touch, his kiss, sent a shudder of hot need clawing through him. In the privacy of this garden he could show her, share with her, give her the pleasure he could see and feel her body was aching for. But here in his garden, in his villa, where she was under his protection, a member of his family…a woman as off limits as any of the carefully guarded daughters of his friends.

His hand was already splaying across her sex, his thumb probing tantalizingly.

Hot shafts of molten quivers darted from the point where Xavier's hand rested so intimately on her to every sensitive nerve ending in her body. Within herself Mariella could feel her own femaleness expanding rhythmically in longing. More than anything else she wanted him there inside her. More than anything else she wanted him…

Her raw sound of shocked protest broke the silence as Xavier suddenly released her.

'I already owe you one apology for my…my inappropriate behaviour towards you,' she heard him telling her curtly. 'Now it seems that I am guilty of repeating that behaviour. It will not…must not happen again!'

As he stood up and turned away from her, Mariella wondered if he was trying to reassure her—or warn her! Her face and then her whole body burned hot with mortified misery.

Her throat was too choked with emotion for her to be able to say anything, but in any case Xavier was already leaving, walking across the garden to the small, almost hidden doorway that led through into his own quarters, and to which only he had the key.

Was she too destined to be a secret garden to which only he held the key?

Fiercely she resisted the dangerous and unwanted thought. It was simply sex that had driven her…a physical need…a perfectly normal response to her own sexuality. There was nothing emotional about what she had felt. Nothing.

PACING THE FLOOR of his own room, Xavier came to an abrupt decision. Since he couldn't trust himself to be in the same place as Mariella and not want her, then he needed to put a safe distance between them, and the best way for him to do that would be for him to return to his desert oasis.

CHAPTER TEN

'It is almost a week since he left and still Xavier remains at the oasis.'

Mariella forced herself to concentrate on her work instead of reacting to Madame Flavel's comments.

The prince had come to see how she was progressing earlier in the week and he had brought his wife and their young family with him. The sight of the four dark-haired and dark-eyed children clustering round their parents had filled her with such a physical ache of longing that she had felt as though her womb had actually physically contracted.

She was desperate to have her own child, Mariella recognised. And not just because she was missing Fleur. Fleur's birth might have detonated her biological clock, setting it ticking away with such frantic urgency, but the longing she felt now was beginning to consume her, eating into her dreams and her emotions.

Now she felt she understood why she had wanted Xavier so much. Her body had recognised him as a perfect potential baby provider! Knowing that had in a way eased a lot of the anxiety she had been feeling; the fear she couldn't bear to admit that she might actually have fallen in love with him. Now, though, she felt secure that her emotional defences had not been breached. Now it was easy for her to admit to herself just how much she had wanted him and how much she still wanted him. She wanted him because she wanted him to give her a child!

It made so much sense! Didn't she remember reading somewhere that a woman naturally and instinctively responded to the ancient way in which nature had programmed her and that was to seek the best genes she could for her child? Quite obviously her body had recognised that Xavier's genes were superlative and her brain fully endorsed her body's recognition.

And this of course was why she was being bombarded by her body and her brain with messages, longings, desires, images that all pointed in the same direction. Xavier's direction! Her maternal urges were quite definitely on red alert!

'XAVIER HAS TELEPHONED to say that he will be remaining at the oasis for another week,' Xavier's great-aunt informed Mariella with a small sigh as they sat down for dinner. 'It must be dull here for you, *chérie,* with only your work to occupy you and me for company.'

'Not at all,' Mariella denied.

'*Non?* But you do miss *la petite bébé?*'

Now it was Mariella's turn to sigh.

'Yes, I do,' she admitted.

'Then perhaps you should consider having *enfants* of your own,' Madame Flavel told her. 'I certainly regret the fact that I was not blessed with children. I envied my sister very much in that respect. I have to confess I cannot understand why two people like Xavier and yourself, who anyone can see are born to be parents, should decide so determinedly against marriage.

'You are working very hard on your frieze. It would do you good to have a few days off.'

She *had* been working very hard—but if truth were told,

the frieze was practically finished. But Mariella had been painstakingly refining it to make sure it was absolutely perfect. Could she take a few days off? To do what? Have even more time to miss Fleur and to ache for a child of her own? Even more time to wish passionately that Xavier had not brought an end to their intimacy before they had... If only she had pressed him a little harder, persuaded...seduced him to the point where he had not been able to stop, she considered daringly, then right now she could already be carrying within her the beginnings of her own child!

Restlessly her thoughts started to circle inside her head. Once they had finished eating Madame Flavel retired to her own room, leaving Mariella to walk through their private garden on her own. If only Xavier were here in the villa now, she could go to him. And what? Demand that he take her to bed and impregnate her?

Oh, yes, she could just see him agreeing to that!

Why would she have to demand? She was a woman, wasn't she? And Xavier was a man... He had already shown her that he could be aroused to desire for her...

But he wasn't here, was he? He was at the oasis.

The oasis... Closing her eyes, Mariella allowed herself to picture him there. That night when he had thought that she was Tanya, he had come so close to possessing her. Her whole body was aching for him now, aching with all the ferocity of a child-hungry woman whose womb was empty!

IRRITABLY, MARIELLA THREW down her sketch-pad, chewing on her bottom lip as she glowered at the images she had drawn: babies...all of them possessing Xavier's unmistakable features. She had hardly slept all night, and when she had it had merely been to be tormented by such sensually erotic dreams of Xavier that they had made her cry out in longing for him. It was as though even her dreams, her own subconscious, were reinforcing her desire for Xavier's child.

In fact the only thing about her that was still trying to fight against that wanting was...was what? Fear... Timidity... Did she really want to look back in years to come and face the fact that she had simply not had the courage to reach out for what she wanted?

After all, it wasn't as though she would be doing anything illegal! She had no intention of ever making any kind of claim on Xavier—far from it! She actively wanted to be left to bring up her child completely on her own. All she wanted from him was a simple physical act. All she had to do...

All she had to do was to make it impossible for him to resist her! And whilst he was at the oasis he would be completely at her sensual mercy! It was even the right time of the month—she was fertile.

A wildly bold plan was beginning to take shape inside her head, and the first step towards it meant an immediate shopping trip, for certain...necessities! There was a specific shop she remembered from a previous trip to the busy souk in the centre of the city, which specialised in what she wanted!

SLIGHTLY PINK-CHEEKED, Mariella studied the fine silk kaftan she was being shown by the salesgirl, so fine that it was completely sheer. Surely the only thing that stopped it from floating away was the weight of the intricate and delicate silver beading and embroidery around the neck and hem and decorating the edges of the long sleeves.

It was a soft shade of turquoise, and designed to be worn—the salesgirl had helpfully explained without so much as batting an elegantly kohled eyelid—over a matching pair of harem trousers. Their cuffs and waistband had been embroidered to match the kaftan itself. It was quite plainly an outfit designed only to be worn in private and for the delectation of one man. The sheerness of the fabric would leave one's breasts totally revealed—and Mariella had not missed the strategically embroidered rosettes, which she doubted would do anything more than merely make a teasing pretence of covering the wearer's nipples—and as for the fact that the harem pants incorporated an embroidered and beaded v-shaped section at the front, which she had an unnerving suspicion would draw attention to rather than protect, any wearer's sex...

'And then, of course, there is this,' the salesgirl told her, showing Mariella a jewelled piece of fabric, which she helpfully explained was self-adhesive so that the wearer could easily fix it to her navel.

Mariella gulped. Her normal sleeping attire when she wore any tended to be sturdily sensible cotton pyjamas.

'Er... No...I don't think...it's quite me,' she heard herself croaking, her courage deserting her. Seducing Xavier was going to be hard enough without giving herself the kind of self-conscious hang-up wearing that kind of outfit would undoubtedly give her!

'I...I was thinking of something more...more European,' she explained ruefully to the salesgirl.

'Ah, yes, of course. There is a shop in the shopping centre run by my cousin, which specialises in French underwear. I shall tell you how to find it.'

Mariella sensed that the girl was amused by her self-consciousness, but there was no way she intended to pay a sheikh's ransom for an outfit that would take more courage to wear than going completely naked!

The souk was busy, and she paused on her way back through it to admire the wares on some of the other stalls, especially the rugs.

There was far more to seduction than merely wearing

a harem outfit, she tried to comfort herself as she headed for the modern shopping centre. Far, far more. Sight was just one of man's senses, after all.

BY THE TIME she finally returned to the villa Mariella felt totally exhausted. She was now the proud owner of a perfume blended especially for her, and a body lotion guaranteed to turn her skin into the softest silk; she had also given in to the temptation to buy herself some new underwear, from the harem outfit seller's cousin, in the shopping mall. French and delicately feminine without making her feel in any way uncomfortable. Low-cut French knickers might not be as openly provocative as beaded harem trousers but they did have the advantage of being perfect to wear underneath her jeans!

It didn't take her very long to pack. All she said to Hera when she summoned her was that she wanted her to hand the note she was giving her to Madame Flavel when she woke up from her afternoon nap.

By that time she should have safely reached the oasis, and her note was simply to calm the older lady's fears and told her only that Mariella had driven out to the oasis because there was something she wanted to discuss with Xavier.

She took a taxi to the four-wheel drive rental office, where the car she had organised earlier by telephone was waiting for her.

This time she made sure she had the radio tuned in to the local weather station, but thankfully no sandstorms were forecast.

Taking a deep breath, she started the car's engine.

WITH A SMALL oath, Xavier pushed the laptop away and stood up. He had come to the oasis to put a safe distance between himself and Mariella but all his absence from her was doing was making him think about her all the more.

Think about her! He wasn't just thinking about her, was he?

The tribe were currently camped less than thirty miles away and on a sudden impulse he decided to drive over and see them. The solitude of his own company was not proving to be its usual solace. Everywhere he looked around the oasis he could see Mariella. There might be a cultural gap between them, but, like him, she had a very strong sense of responsibility, and like him she would not give either her heart or herself easily. Like him, too, once she was committed, that commitment would be for ever. And did she also ache for what they had so nearly had and lie awake at night wanting…needing, afraid to admit that those feelings went way, way beyond the merely physical? And if she did, then… Could she love him enough to accept his duty to the tribe, and with it his commitment to his role in life…to accept it and to share it? Dared he lay before her the intensity of his feelings for her? His love? Could he live with himself if his secret fears proved to be correct and his love for her overwhelmed his sense of duty?

Switching off the laptop, he reached for his Jeep keys.

SHE COULDN'T EVER remember a time when she had felt more nervous, Mariella acknowledged as she urged the four-wheel drive along the familiar boulder-strewn track. Up ahead of her she could see the pavilion and her heart lurched, slamming into her ribs. What if Xavier simply refused to be seduced and rejected her? What if…?

For a moment she was tempted to turn the four-wheel drive round and scuttle back to the city. Quickly she reminded herself of the sexual tension stretching between them in the garden of the villa. He had wanted her then, and had admitted as much to her!

She had half expected to see him emerging from the pavilion as he heard her drive up, but there was no sign of him.

Well, at least he wouldn't be able to demand that she turn round and drive straight back, she comforted herself as she parked her vehicle and climbed out, going to the back to remove her things, and then standing nervously staring at the pavilion.

Perhaps if she had timed things so that she had arrived in the dark… Some seductress she was turning out to be, she derided herself as she took a deep breath and walked determinedly towards the chosen fate.

Five minutes later she was standing facing the oasis, unwilling to accept what was patently obvious. Xavier was not here! No Xavier, no four-wheel drive, no seduction, no baby!

A crushing sense of disappointment engulfed her. Where was he? Could he have changed his mind and returned to the city despite informing his great-aunt that he intended to stay on at the oasis? How ironic it would be if by rushing out here so impulsively she had actually denied herself the opportunity of achieving what she wanted!

But then she remembered that his laptop was still inside the pavilion, and surely he would not have left that behind if he had been returning home? So where was he?

The sun was already a dying red ball lying on the horizon. Soon it would be dark. There was no way she was going to risk driving all the way back without the benefit of daylight!

So what exactly was she going to do? Spend yet another evening enduring her rebellious body's clamouring urgency for the fulfilment of its driving need? It had simply never occurred to her that he wouldn't be here!

The pavilion was so intimately a part of him. Dreamily, she trailed her fingertips along the chair he used when working at the laptop. The air actually seemed to hold an echo of his scent, a haunting resonance of his voice, and she felt that, if she closed her eyes and concentrated hard enough, she could almost imagine that he was there... She could certainly picture him behind her tightly closed eyelids. But it wasn't his mental image she wanted so desperately, was it?

She knew she ought to eat, but she simply wasn't hungry. She was thirsty, though.

She went into the kitchen and opened a bottle of water. Fine grains of sand clung to her skin, making it feel gritty. Hardly appropriate for a would-be siren! The long drive in the brilliant glare of the desert sun had left her eyes feeling tired and heavy. Like her body, which felt tired and heavy and empty. A sense of dejection and failure percolated through her.

Slowly, she walked out of the kitchen intending to return to the living area, but instead found herself being drawn to the 'bedroom.' Standing in the entrance, she looked achingly around it.

A fierce shudder that became an even fiercer primal ache gripped her as she looked at the bed and remembered what had happened there. It was just her biology that was making her feel like this, her fiercely strong maternal desire. That was all, and of course it was only natural that that urge should manifest itself in this hungry desire for the man whose genes it had decided it wanted, she reassured herself as she was confronted with the intensity of her longing for Xavier.

Just thinking about him made her go weak, made her

want him there so that she could bury her lips in the warm
male flesh of his throat and slide her hands over the hard,
strong muscles of his arms and his back, and then down
through the soft dark hair that covered his chest and ar-
rowed over his belly to where…

She needed a shower, Mariella decided shakily. A very
cool shower!

'SAFE TRAVELLING, ASHAR.' Xavier smiled ruefully as he embraced the senior tribesman whilst the others went about
the business of breaking camp ready to begin the long slow
journey across the desert.

'You could always come with us,' Ashar responded.

'Not this time.' Xavier shook his head.

All around him he could hear the familiar sounds of
the camp, the faint music of the camel bells, the orderly
preparations for departure. The tribe would travel through
the night hours whilst it was cool, resting the herd during
the heat of the day.

Ashar's shrewd brown eyes surveyed him.

Ashar remembered Xavier's grandfather as well as his
father. Alongside his respect for Xavier as his leader ran
a very deep vein of paternal affection for him.

'Something troubles you—a woman, perhaps? The tribe
would rejoice to see you take a wife to give you sons to
follow in your footsteps as you have followed in those of
your grandfather and your father.'

'If only matters were that simple, Ashar.' Xavier grimaced.

'Why should they not be? This woman, you are afraid
perhaps that she will not respect our traditions, that she
will seek to divide your loyalties? If that is so then she is
not the one for you. But knowing you as I do, Xavier, I
cannot believe that there could be a place in your heart for

a woman such as that. You must learn to trust what is in here,' he told him, touching his own heart with his hand. 'Instead of believing only what is in here.' As he touched his hand to his head Xavier hid a wry smile. Ashar had no idea just how dangerously out of control his emotions were becoming!

He waited to see the tribe safely on their way before climbing in his vehicle to drive back to the oasis.

A sharply crescented sickle moon shared the night sky with the brilliance of the stars. Diamonds studded onto indigo velvet. For Xavier it was during the night hours that the desert was at its most awesome, and mystical, a time when he always felt most in touch with his heritage. His ancestors had travelled these sands for many, many generations before him, and it was his duty, his responsibility to ensure that they did so for many, many generations to come. And that was not something he could achieve from behind the walls of a high-rise air-conditioned office, and certainly not from the fleshpots of the world as Khalid would no doubt choose to do. No, he could only maintain and honour the tribe's traditional way of life by being a part of it, by sharing in it, and that was something he was totally committed to doing. He must not deviate from that purpose. But his feelings, his love for Mariella could not be denied, or ignored. The strength of them had initially shocked him, but he had now gone from shock to the grim recognition that it was beyond his power to change or control the way he felt.

HE SAW MARIELLA'S vehicle as he drove up to the oasis. Parking next to it, he got out and studied it warily. He did not encourage anyone to visit him when he was at the oasis and he was certainly not in the mood for uninvited guests, right now! Where and who was its driver?

Frowning, he headed for the pavilion, not needing to waste any time lighting the lamps to illuminate the darkness, his familiarity with it enough to take him from the entrance to the opening to the bedroom without breaking his stride.

Mariella was lying fast asleep in the middle of the bed, where she had curled up in exhaustion like a small child. The white robe she was wearing was Xavier's and it drowned her slender body. She had lit one of the lamps, which illuminated her face, showing her bone structure and the thick darkness of her silky eyelashes. In the enclosed heat, Xavier could smell the scent of her, and of his own instant reciprocal desire for her.

Xavier's hand tightened convulsively on the cord that fastened the curtain to the bedroom's entrance, whilst his heart tolled in slow, heavy beats. If he had any sense he would pick her up and carry her straight out to the Jeep and then drive back to the city with her without stopping!

He let the heavy curtain drop behind him, enclosing them both in the sensual semi-darkness.

Standing next to the bed, he looked down at Mariella.

SOMETHING, SOME INSTINCT and awareness, disturbed Mariella's sleep, making her frown and stir, her eyes opening.

'Xavier!'

Relief…and longing flooded through her. Automatically she struggled to sit up, her arms and legs becoming tangled in the thick folds of Xavier's robe as she did so.

'What are you doing here?' Xavier demanded harshly.

'Waiting for you,' Mariella told him. 'Waiting to tell you how much I want you, and how much I hope you want me.'

She watched as his eyes turned from steel to mercury and recognised that she had caught him off guard.

'You drove all the way out here to tell me that!'

His voice might be curt and unresponsive, but Mariella could see the way his jaw tightened as he turned his head away from her, as well as feel his betraying tension. Tiny body-language signs, that was all she knew, but instinctively she knew she had an advantage to pursue!

'Not to tell you, Xavier,' she corrected him boldly. 'To show you…like this…'

Standing up, she went to him, letting the robe slide from her body as she did so. She had never envisaged that she would ever feel such a pride in her nakedness, her femaleness, such a sense of power and certainty, an awareness of how much a man's still silence could betray how very, very tightly leashed he was keeping his desire.

She was standing in front of him and he hadn't moved. For a moment she almost lost her courage but then she saw it, the way he clenched his hand and tried to conceal his involuntary reaction.

Quickly she raised herself up on her tiptoes and cupped his face with her hands. Never in a thousand lifetimes could she have behaved like this simply for her own gratification, for the indulgence of her own sexual or emotional feelings, but she was not doing it for them, for herself, she was doing it for the child she so desperately wanted to give life! Silently she looked up into his eyes, her own openly reflecting her desire. Very deliberately she let her gaze drop to his mouth. There was no need for her to manufacture the sharp little quiver of physical reaction that pierced her, tightening her belly.

She brushed her lips against his—slowly, savouring the delicate sensual contact between them, refusing to be put off by his lack of response, drawing from her inner self to focus totally on the pleasure it was giving her to explore the shape and texture of his mouth. Very quickly her senses took over, so that it was desire that led her to stroking his bottom lip with her tongue tip rather than calculation, the same desire that drove her to trace tiny kisses along the shape of his mouth and then draw her tongue lightly along that shape.

Xavier couldn't endure what she was doing to him! Mentally he willed her to stop, but instead she opened her mouth over his and started to kiss him properly! Lost in what she was doing, what she was enjoying, Mariella took her time, putting her whole self into showing him just how hungry for him she was.

And then sickeningly, she could feel the rejecting hostility of his body, and for a heart-rocking second when he raised his hands she thought he was going to push her away. She suspected that he had thought so too, because suddenly in his eyes she saw both his shock and his raw, burning hunger.

He could never be a man who would be a passive lover, Mariella recognised on a deep shudder of pleasure as his hands imprisoned her and his mouth fought hers for control.

How little he realised that her surrender was really her victory, she rejoiced as his tongue thrust urgently between the lips she had parted for him.

'I can't believe that you've done this,' she heard him saying thickly.

'I had to,' Mariella whispered back. After all, it was the truth. 'I had to be with you, Xavier…like this…as a woman.'

He had released her to look at her, and now he lifted his hand to her face. Instantly Mariella caught hold of his wrist and turned her head to run her tongue tip over his fingertips.

She saw the way his skin stretched over his cheekbones,

running hot with colour, his chest lifting and falling as savagely as though he had been deprived of oxygen. His forefinger rubbed over her bottom lip, and when she sucked on it his whole body jerked fiercely.

'I want to see you, Xavier,' she told him softly. 'I want to touch you…taste you…I want. I want you to take me to bed and pleasure me, fill me.'

Taking his hand, she placed it against her naked breast.

'Please,' she whispered. 'Please now, Xavier. Please…'

'This is crazy. You know that, don't you?' she heard him mutter. 'You are not your sister, you do not… I have not… I am not prepared…' His voice had become thick and raw as he bent his head to kiss the exposed curve of her shoulder, her throat, his hands sliding down her back to pull her urgently against him.

'There is nothing for you to worry about,' she told him.

She felt light-headed with the intensity of her own longing—but she only felt like that because she wanted his child, she was quick to reassure herself. That, after all, was what was driving her, motivating her, even if that motivation was manifesting itself in an increasingly urgent need to touch him and be touched by him, to allow herself to luxuriate in the slow and delicious exploration of every bit of his skin, absorbing its heat, its feel, the essence of him through the sensitivity of her own pores. So that her child, their child could be impregnated through her with those memories of his father he would never otherwise be able to have?

Ruthlessly she stifled that thought. Her child would not need a father to be there. He or she only needed a father to provide that life.

What he was doing was reckless to the point of insanity, Xavier knew that, but he also knew that he couldn't resist her, that he had ached for her, yearned for her too

long to deny himself the soft, sweet, wanton feel of her in
his arms…his bed…

But once he had held her, loved her, he also knew that
he would never be able to let her go. Could she accept his
way of life…adapt to it? Would she?

She was kissing him with increasing passion, stringing
tiny, delicately tormenting little kisses around his throat,
her tongue tip carefully exploring the shape of his Adam's
apple, her fingers kneading the flesh of his upper arm with
unconscious sensuality. Xavier recognised his senses on
overload from her deliberately erotic seduction.

Mariella gave a small startled gasp as Xavier suddenly
lifted her bodily in his arms, so that her mouth was on a
level with his own as he took it in a hotly demanding and
intimate kiss.

Helplessly she succumbed to it, feeling the desire he
was arousing inside her run through her veins as sweetly
as melting honey. He lifted her higher, kissing her throat,
his lips moving lower to the valley between her breasts, before trailing with heart-hammering slowness and delicacy
to first one eagerly waiting, quivering crest and then the
other, and then back again, this time to lap tormentingly
at her nipple with his damp tongue tip; the leisurely lan-
guorous journey repeated again and again until her whole
body was crying out in agonised frustration.

Unable to stand the sensual torment any more, when his
lips teased delicately at her nipple she buried her hands in
the thick darkness of his hair and held his mouth against
her body.

Surely he must feel the fierce rhythms pulsing through
her flesh; surely he must know how much she wanted him?

Her hands tugged at his clothes, her voice whispering
a soft torrent of aroused female longing that swamped
Xavier's defences.

His hands helped hers to quickly remove the layers of clothing that separated them.

When she finally saw the naked gleam of his flesh in the lamp-lit room, Mariella sucked in her breath on a small sob of shocked pleasure.

In wonder she studied him as tiny but openly visible quivers betrayed her body's excited reaction to him. So compulsively absorbed in gazing at him, she was oblivious to the effect her sensual concentration was having on Xavier himself.

'If you are deliberately trying to torment me and test my self-control by looking at me like that, then I warn you that both it and I have just about reached my limit,' he told her thickly.

'Now! Are you going to come to me and put into action all those dangerously seductive promises your eyes are giving me, or do I have to come to you and make you make good those promises, because, I warn you, if I do have to then I shall be demanding payment with full interest penalties,' he added huskily.

For a moment Mariella couldn't do anything. Xavier was watching her as she had been watching him. Excitement exploded inside her. She took a step towards him and then another, measuring his reaction as best she could, but it wasn't easy given the extent of her own intense arousal.

She was only a breath away from him now, close enough to reach out her finger and draw the tip of it recklessly down his body, teasing the silky body hair.

'You don't know how much I've wanted to do this,' she breathed truthfully.

'No? Well, I certainly know how much I've wanted you to do it,' Xavier responded throatily, 'and how much I've wanted to...'

He gasped and shuddered as her fingertip stroked lower,

and suddenly in the space of one single heartbeat she was lying on the bed, with Xavier arching over her.

'Play with fire like that and you'll make us both burn,' he told her, his eyes darkening as he groaned. 'Do you know what seeing that look in your eyes does to me? Do you know how much I've wanted to see just what colour they turn when I touch you like this?'

Mariella hadn't realised just how ready she was for his intimate caress until she felt his hand stroke softly over her quivering belly, his fingers gently touching the swollen mound of her sex, his gaze pinioning hers as he parted the lips of her sex and began to caress her.

Mariella knew that she cried out, she knew too that her body arched to his touch actively seeking it, eagerly opening to it, but it was only a vague, distant knowledge, at the back of her awareness. Her self was concentrated on the mind-exploding battle to accept the intensity of her own feelings.

Frantically she reached for Xavier. Touching him, holding him, wrapping herself around him as she pressed passionate kisses against his skin, willing, aching for him to complete what he had begun.

And when he did enter her, moving into her, filling her moist sheathed muscles, filling her with such a soaring degree of pleasure that they and she clung to him, wanting to wring every infinitesimal sensation of pleasure from him, it was like nothing she had ever imagined feeling, a pleasure beyond any known pleasure, a sensation beyond any experienced sensation, a driven need that shocked her in its wanton compulsion as she urged him to drive deeper, harder, breaching every last barrier of her body until she knew instinctively that he could not and would not withdraw from her without giving her body the satisfaction it now craved.

They moved together, his thrusts carrying them both, delivering a pleasure so intense she could scarcely bear it, crying out against it at the same time as she abandoned herself to it.

She heard his guttural cry of warning and felt her body open up completely to him, the first tiny shudders of her orgasm sensitising her to the pulse of his, to the knowledge that she was receiving from him what she had so much wanted.

Was it that knowledge that made her orgasm so intense, so fierce that she felt almost as though she could not endure so much pleasure?

Long after it should have been over, the aftermath continued to send little shudders of sensation through her, shaking her whole body as she lay locked in Xavier's arms.

She had done it, instinctively she knew it. Her child, of the desert and of a man who was equally compelling, equally dangerous, had been given life.

RELUCTANTLY, MARIELLA OPENED her eyes. She could hear a shower running, and her whole body ached with an unfamiliar heaviness.

'So you are awake!'

She stiffened as she saw Xavier coming towards her, his hair damp from his shower, a towel wrapped carelessly round his hips.

Leaning towards her, he bent his head to kiss her. He smelled of soap and clean, fresh skin and her body quivered helplessly in reaction to him.

'Mmm...'

He kissed her again, more lingeringly, his hand stroking down over her bare arm.

The quivers became open shudders of erotic pleasure as he pulled the bedclothes back.

She had got what she wanted, and so surely she shouldn't be feeling like this now that there wasn't any need for her to want him!

The towel was sliding from his hips, quite plainly revealing the fact that he most definitely wanted her.

A sharp and unmistakable thrill of female excitement gripped her muscles.

It was just nature's way of making doubly sure, Mariella told herself hazily as his hand cupped her breast, his thumb and forefinger teasing the already eagerly taut crest of her nipple. That was all, and, since nature wanted to be doubly sure, then obviously she must give in to her urgings. Urgings that were demanding that she experience the pleasure Xavier had given her the night before, and right now…

His hands were on her hips, holding her, lifting her. Already Mariella was anticipating the feel of him inside her, longing for it and for him. Needing him.

'THERE WILL BE things we shall need to discuss once we return to the city.'

'Mmm…' Mariella agreed, too satiated to lift her head off the pillow as Xavier turned to brush a kiss across her mouth.

She looked so tempting lying there in his bed, her face soft with satisfaction and her eyes heavy with their lovemaking, he acknowledged, ruefully aware of the way in which his senses were still reacting to her.

It would be all too easy to let the desire between them flare into life again, but there were practicalities that had to be considered.

'Mariella.' The abrupt note in his voice caught her attention. 'Because of my position as leader of our tribe, I have always believed that I do not have the…freedoms of other men. I could never commit myself to a relationship with a woman who might not be able to understand or accept my duties and responsibilities to my people. Nor could I change my way of life, or...'

'Xavier, there's no need for you to say any more,' Mariella checked him swiftly. Her heart was pounding heavily, a sharp, bitter little pain, piercing her even though she was fighting against admitting to it, stubbornly refusing to listen to the message it was trying to give her.

'I would never ask you or any other man to do any such thing! And I can assure you that you need have no fear that I might misconstrue what's happened. I shan't. I am most definitely not looking for any kind of commitment from you.'

Only the commitment of conceiving his child, she admitted inwardly.

'In fact, commitment is the last thing I want.' Assuming a casualness that defied everything she had always inwardly believed in, she gave a small shrug and told him, 'We are both adults. We wanted to have sex. To satisfy a...a physical need... And...now that we have done so, I don't think there is any purpose in us holding a post-mortem, and even less in getting involved in needless discussions about the wherefores of why neither of us want a committed relationship. Truthfully, Xavier, I don't want to marry you any more than you want to marry me! In fact, I shall never marry.' Mariella delivered the words in a strong voice underpinned with determination.

'What?'

Why was Xavier looking at her like that? Where was the relief she had expected—the cool acceptance of her claim that they had come together merely to slake their sexual appetite for one another? Xavier was looking at her with a mingling of barely controlled fury and bitterness.

'What are you saying?' she heard him demanding savagely. 'You are not your sister, Mariella! You are not one of those shallow, surface-living women who think only of themselves; who give in to their need to experience what they want when they want, who go from man to man, bed to bed without…whose whole way of life—' He paused and shook his head.

'You are not like her! You don't even know what you are talking about! Mere physical sex is not something…'

Mariella could see and feel the intensity of his growing anger, and she could also feel her own increasingly disturbing reaction of panic and pain to it, but she refused to allow herself to be intimidated by them.

'I am not going to argue with you, Xavier. I know how I feel, and what I do and don't want from life.'

Well, that was the truth, wasn't it? She did know what she wanted, and she had every hope that last night had given her…

'Do you really expect me to believe that you drove all the way out here just because you wanted sex?'

'Why not?' Mariella shrugged. 'After all, I could hardly have come to your room at the villa, could I?' she pointed out, trying to make herself react as though she were the woman she was trying to be—a woman who thought nothing of indulging her sexual appetite as and when she wanted to do so!

'This was the perfect opportunity!'

Xavier was looking at her as though he would dearly love to make her take back her words, Mariella recognised uneasily. It had to be his male pride that was making him react in such an unexpected manner, she decided. Men were quite happy to use women for sexual pleasure without being emotionally committed to them, but apparently they didn't like it very much when they thought that they were the ones being used.

Her legs began to tremble shakily as she mentally digested his reaction and tried to imagine what he might say—and do if he knew that she hadn't even actually wanted him out of sexual lust, and that the desire that had really driven her had been her own female need to conceive his child!

Somehow instinctively she knew that the reaction she was seeing now would be nothing when compared with what he was likely to do were he ever to discover the truth!

The unexpected shrill sound of his mobile ringing broke into the thick silence stretching tensely between them.

Out of good manners Mariella turned away whilst he answered the call, but she could tell from the sound of his curt replies that it involved some kind of crisis.

Her instincts were confirmed when he ended the call and told her abruptly, 'There is a problem with the tribe—a quarrel between two of the younger men, which needs to be dealt with. I shall have to drive out to do so immediately.'

'That's okay. I can find my own way back to the city,' Mariella assured him.

'This matter isn't closed yet, Mariella,' he told her grimly. 'When I do return to the villa, we shall discuss it further!'

Mariella didn't risk making any response. There wasn't any need, not unless she wanted to provoke a further quarrel. The frieze was finished; there was nothing now to keep her in Zuran, no reason or need for her to stay, and she had already decided that she was going to make immediate plans to return home!

CHAPTER ELEVEN

'ELLA, you have to go! The prince will be mortally of-
fended if you don't and, besides, just think of the potential commissions you could be losing. I mean, I've done
some discreet checking on the guest list for this do, and
everyone who is everyone in the horse-racing world will
be there, plus some of the classiest A-list celebs on the
planet! This is going to be the most prestigious event on
the racing calendar this year, and here you are announcing that you don't want to go! I mean, why? You already
know just how impressed the prince is with your frieze,
and this is going to be its big unveiling. If you'd been hired
by the National Gallery itself you couldn't have got yourself more publicity for your work!'

Mariella could hear the exasperation in her agent's
voice, and ruefully acknowledged inwardly that she could
perfectly understand Kate's feelings.

However, Kate did not know that she had two very good
reasons for her reluctance to return to Zuran.

Xavier…and… Instinctively she glanced down her own
body. At three months, her pregnancy was not really showing as yet. She and the baby were both perfectly healthy,
her doctor had assured her, it was just that being so slight
she was not as yet showing very much baby bulge.

'Just wait another couple of months and you'll prob-

ably be complaining to me that you feel huge,' she had
teased Mariella.

Even now sometimes when she woke up in the morning she had to reassure herself that she was not fantasising, and that she actually was pregnant.

Pregnant... With a baby she already desperately wanted
and loved. Her baby! Her baby and Xavier's baby, she reminded herself warily.

But Xavier would never need to know! No one looking
at her could possibly know!

And if she was not careful she could potentially be in
danger of arousing more suspicions by not returning to
Zuran for the extravaganza that was to be the opening of
the new enclosure and the first public airing of her frieze
than by doing so.

Tanya for one would certainly have something to say
to her if she didn't go!

And of course it would be a perfect opportunity for her
to see Fleur, whom she still missed achingly. Her niece
would also always have a very, very special place in her
heart!

But against all this, and weighing very heavily on the
other side of the scales, was Xavier. Xavier whom disturb-
ingly she had spent far too much time thinking about since
her return home! Mystifyingly and totally contrary to her
expectations, not even the official knowledge that she had
conceived her much-wanted child had brought an end to
the little ache of longing and loneliness that now seemed
to haunt both her days and her nights. There was surely
no logical reason why she should actually physically ache
for Xavier now. And there was certainly no reason why increasingly she should feel such a deep and despairing emotional longing for him. Those kinds of feelings belonged to

someone who was in love! And she knew far better than to allow herself to do anything as foolish as fall in love!

She had actually begun to question, in her most emotional and anguished moments, whether what she was feeling could in some way be generated by the baby—a longing on his or her part for the father that he or she was never going to know. She had promised herself that her child would never suffer the anguish of being rejected by his or her father, because she had made sure there would be no father there to reject it. She would make sure right from the start that her baby would know that she would provide all the love it could possibly need! She would bring him or her up to feel so loved, so secure, so wanted, that Xavier's absence would have no impact on their lives whatsoever. Unlike her, her child would never suffer the pain of hearing his or her mother talk with such longing and need about the man who had abandoned them both, as she had had to do. Her child would never feel as she had done that somehow he or she was the cause of that father's absence; that, given the real choice, her mother would have preferred not to have had her and kept the love of the man who had quite simply not wanted the responsibility of a child!

'You must go,' Kate was insisting.

'You must come,' Tanya was pleading.

'Okay, okay, I give in,' she told Kate, grinning as her agent paused in mid-argument to look at her in silence, before breaking into a flurry of relieved plans.

'YOU'LL BE STAYING with us, of course,' Tanya was chattering excitedly as she bustled Mariella outside to the waiting limousine. 'I didn't bring Fleur because she's been cutting another new tooth. It's through now, but we had a bit of a bad night with her. I can't wait for the opening. It's going to be the highlight of our social calendar. Khalid has bought me the most fabulous dress. What are you going to wear? If you haven't got anything yet, we could go shopping—'

'No, it's okay, I've already got an outfit,' Mariella stopped her quickly, mentally grateful for the fact that Kate had insisted on taking her on a whirlwind shopping trip, following her decision to attend the opening, so that she could vet the outfit Mariella would be wearing, to make sure it made enough of the right kind of statement! Her small bulge might not show yet when she was dressed, but someone as close to her as her half-sister had always been would be bound to spot the differences in her body in the intimacy of a changing room with her wearing nothing more than her underwear!

Of course she was going to tell Tanya about her baby— ultimately—once she was safely back in England, and all the questions her sister was bound to ask about just who had fathered her coming baby could be answered over the telephone rather than in person! The last thing Mariella wanted to do was to risk betraying herself by a give-away expression.

She knew exactly what she was going to tell Tanya. She had already decided to claim that her child was the result of artificial insemination, the father an unknown sperm donor.

They were speeding along the highway towards the familiar outskirts of the city.

'How far is it to your new villa, Tanya?' Mariella asked her.

She had been receiving a constant stream of emails from her sister full of excitement about the new villa she and Khalid were having built, and which they had recently been due to move into.

'Oh, it's several miles up the coast from Xavier's. I'm really looking forward to moving into it now, but I must admit I'm a bit worried about how Fleur is going to adapt. She adores Hera, and to her Xavier's villa is her home and so—'

'What do you mean you're looking forward to moving in?' Mariella checked her anxiously. 'I thought you already had!'

'Well, yes, we were supposed to, but then all the furniture hasn't arrived yet, and so we're still living with Xavier. His great-aunt is visiting at the moment as well. You made a real hit with her, Ella—not like me. She's always singing your praises and in fact… I…'

Mariella could feel her heart, not just sinking, but literally plunging to the bottom of her ribcage with an almighty thump before it began to bang against her ribs in frantic panic. She wasn't prepared for this, she admitted. She wasn't armed for it, or protected against it.

The villa was ahead of them. It was too late for her to announce that she had changed her mind, or to demand that she be taken to the centre of the city where she could book into a hotel! The car was sweeping in through the gates.

Hazily Mariella noticed that the red geraniums she remembered tumbling from the urns in the outer courtyard had been changed to a rich vibrant pink to match the colour of the flowers of the ornamental vine softening the walls of the courtyard.

'Leave your luggage for Ali,' Tanya instructed her.

Where was the trepidation she should be feeling? Mariella wondered as, completely contrary to any kind of logic, the moment she stepped into the villa she immediately experienced a sense of well being, a sense of welcome familiarity, as though…as though she had come home?

'We'd better go straight in to see Tante Cecille!' Tanya pulled a face. 'I'll never hear the end of it if we don't.

She's even told them in the kitchen to bake some madeleines for you!'

Mariella had to bite down hard on her bottom lip to subdue the threatening weakness of her own emotional response. The last thing she wanted or needed right now was to be reminded in any way of the fact that she was so very much alone, so very bereft of family, unlike Xavier, who was not merely part of a large extended family group, but who also actively shared a large part of his life with them.

Treacherously Mariella found herself thinking about how a child might feel growing up in a household with so many caring adults, with aunts, uncles and cousins to play with…

'Ella, I'm so thrilled that you're here,' Tanya was telling her. 'I've really missed you! You're in the same room you had before. Xavier has given us our own suite of rooms whilst we're living here. Khalid says there's no way that he would agree to us living like they used to with separate men's and women's quarters, which is just as well because there's no way I would agree to it either!

'I couldn't do what Xavier does and go into the desert with the tribe.' Tanya gave a small shudder. 'The very thought appalls me. All that sand…and heat! And as for the camels! Ugh!' She pulled a distasteful face. 'Luckily Khalid feels exactly the same way! He can't understand why Xavier lets his life be dominated by a few promises his grandfather made, and neither can I. If Khalid was head of the family things would be very different…'

'Then perhaps it's as well that he isn't,' Mariella responded protectively, before she could stop herself.

She could see the way Tanya was looking at her, and she felt obliged to explain, 'Xavier is the guardian of some irreplaceable traditions, Tanya, and if he abandoned that responsibility a way of life that could never be resurrected could be totally lost…'

'A way of life? Spending weeks living in the desert, and having to do it every year! No, I can't think of anything worse. It might be traditional, but I still wouldn't do it! Well, there's no way it could ever be my way of life, anyway. I mean, can you imagine any woman wanting to live like that? Could you?'

Mariella didn't even have to pause to think about it.

'Not permanently, no, but in order to preserve something so important, and to support the man I loved, to be with him and share a very, very important part of his life, yes, I could and would.' Mariella hesitated, recognising that there was little point in trying to explain to her sister how much such a return to traditions, to the simplicity of such a lifestyle could do to rejuvenate a person in a very special and intensely personal, almost spiritual sense, to bring them back in touch with certain important realities of life. Tanya simply wouldn't understand.

'Yes?' Tanya stared at her. 'You're mad,' she told her, shaking her head. 'Just like Xavier. In fact…Tante Cecille is quite right. You and Xavier are two of a kind.'

Before Mariella could demand an explanation from Tanya of just how and when their similarities had been discussed, they were in the salon.

'Mariella, how lovely to see you again,' Madame Flavel exclaimed affectionately. Automatically as she embraced her Mariella held in her stomach, just as she had done when she and Tanya had hugged earlier. An automatic reflex, but one that wasn't going to conceal her growing bump for very much longer, Mariella acknowledged ruefully.

HALF AN HOUR later, holding Fleur whilst her niece beamed happily up at her, Mariella began to feel a little bit more relaxed. Xavier, after all, would be as keen to avoid spending time with her as she was with him—albeit for very different reasons! She might even not actually see him at all!

Totally involved in making delicious eye contact with Fleur, Mariella was oblivious to what was going on in the rest of the room until she heard Madame Flavel exclaiming happily, 'Ah, there you are, Xavier.'

Xavier! Automatically Mariella spun round, holding tightly onto Fleur more for her own protection than for the baby's, she recognised dizzily as she felt her whole body begin to tremble.

The sensation, the need slicing white-hot through her threw her into shocked panic. She couldn't be feeling like this. *Should* not be feeling like this. Should not be feeling this all-absorbing need to feed hungrily on the sight of every familiar feature, every slight nuance of expression, too greedy for them to savour them with luxurious slowness, aching for them; aching for him so intensely that the pain was sharply physical.

As the girl she had been before, she had fantasised naïvely about that wanting and about him, imagining, exploring in the privacy of her thoughts the potential of her secret yearnings for Xavier—she had never guessed where those feelings could lead.

But as she was now sharply aware she was not that girl any more. She was now a woman, a woman looking at the man who had been her lover, knowing just how his flesh lay against his bones, how it felt, how it tasted... how he touched and loved. And as that woman she was overwhelmed by the sheer force of her need to go to him, to be with him, to be part of him. Her knowledge of him, instead of slaking her desire, was actually increasing it, tormenting her with intensely intimate memories. She was no longer seeing him as a powerful distant figure, but as a man...*her* man!

But that wasn't possible. What did that mean about her feelings for Xavier?

'Xavier, I was just telling Ella how alike you and she are,' she heard Tanya commenting.

'Alike?'

Mariella could feel his gaze burning into her as he focused on her.

'In your attitudes to things,' Tanya explained. 'Ella, you really ought to have children of your own,' Tanya added ruefully. 'You are a natural mother.'

'I totally agree with you, Tanya.' Madame Flavel nodded.

Mariella could feel her face and then her whole body burning as they all turned to look at her, but it was Xavier's grim scrutiny that affected her the most as his glance skimmed her body, resting on the baby she was holding in her arms. The unbearable poignancy of knowing that in six months' time she would be holding his child as she was holding Fleur right now made her eyes burn with dangerous tears. What on earth was wrong with her? She was behaving as though...reacting as though...as though she were a woman in love. Totally, hopelessly, helplessly in love. But she wasn't! She wasn't going to let herself be!

BLEAKLY XAVIER WATCHED as Mariella cuddled Fleur. He had told himself that the discovery that she did not return his feelings would be enough to destroy them. And it should have been! But right now, if they had been alone...

The sickening feeling that had accompanied her unwanted thoughts was refusing to go away, and Mariella began to panic. She had suffered some morning sickness in the early weeks of her pregnancy, but these last few weeks she had felt much better. This nausea, though, wasn't anything to do with what was happening inside her body. No, this nausea was caused by her emotions! And what emotions! They surged powerfully inside her, inducing fear and panic, making her want to turn and run.

Automatically she had turned away from Xavier, unable to trust herself to continue facing him. Tanya had run to greet her husband who had just arrived.

'Ella,' Khalid greeted her warmly. 'We are so pleased that you are here, and I warn you that now that you are we shall not allow you to go easily. Tanya is already making plans to persuade you to move permanently to Zuran. Has she told you?'

Move permanently to Zuran! The shock of his disclosure made Mariella sway visibly, her face paling.

Xavier frowned as he saw her reaction. She looked as though she was about to pass out!

'Khalid, get some water,' Xavier demanded sharply, going immediately to Mariella's side and taking Fleur from her.

Just the feel of his hand touching her bare arm made her shudder with longing, and it seemed to Mariella as though the baby in her womb ached with the same longing that she did, for his touch and for his love.

She was vaguely conscious of being steered towards a chair and instructed to sit down, and then of a glass of water being handed to her.

'There's nothing wrong. I'm perfectly all right,' she protested frantically. The last thing she needed right now was to arouse any kind of suspicions about her health!

'Ella, you do look pale,' Tanya was saying worriedly.

'I'm just a bit tired, that's all,' Mariella insisted.

'You will probably feel better once you have had something to eat. We are going to have an informal family dinner this evening.'

'No,' Mariella refused agitatedly. The last thing she felt able to cope with right now was any more time spent in Xavier's company.

'Tanya, I'm sorry, but I just don't feel up to it. I'm rather tired…the flight…'

'Of course, *petite,* we understand,' Madame Flavel was assuring her soothingly, unintentionally coming to her rescue. 'Don't we, Xavier?' she appealed.

'Perfectly,' Mariella heard Xavier agreeing harshly.

ABRUPTLY MARIELLA OPENED her eyes. Her heart was thumping heavily. She had been dreaming about Xavier. She looked at her watch. It was only just gone ten o'clock. The others would probably just be sitting down for their evening meal. Her throat ached and felt raw, tight with the intensity of her emotions.

As she slid her feet out of the bed and padded to the window to look out into the shadowy garden she shivered in the coolness of the air-conditioning. It was there by the pool that Xavier had massaged her aching shoulders, and she had realised how much she'd wanted him. Because she had wanted his child, not because she loved him.

Her eyes burned dryly with pain. What she was feeling, what she was having to confront now, went way, way beyond the relief of easy tears.

So she was her mother's daughter, after all! She was to suffer the same pain as her mother—a pain she had inflicted on herself! How could she have been so stupid? How could she have been so reckless as to challenge fate? How could she have ignored everything that she knew about herself? Surely somewhere she must have realised that it was impossible for her to give herself to a man with the passionate intensity she had given herself to Xavier and not love him?

All she had wanted was to have a child, she insisted stubbornly. A child? No, what she had wanted was Xavier's child. And that alone should have told her, warned her...

With appalling clarity Mariella suddenly realised what she had done. Not so much to herself but to her child!

One day her child was going to demand to know about its father. When that happened, what answers was she going to be able to give?

Now she could cry. Slow, acid tears of guilt and regret, but it was too late to change things now.

'I'm so sorry,' she whispered, her hands on her stomach. 'Please, please try to forgive me...I love you so much...'

She had stolen the right to choose fatherhood from Xavier, and she had stolen from her child the right to be fathered...loved.

It was gone midnight when she finally stopped pacing the room and crawled into bed to fall into a shallow, exhausted sleep, riddled with guilt and anguished dreams.

'WELL, WHAT DO you think? How do I look?' Tanya demanded excitedly as she twirled round in front of Mariella in her new outfit.

'You look fabulous,' Mariella assured her truthfully.

'And so do you,' Tanya told her. Mariella forced a smile.

Her own dress with its simple flowing lines did suit her, but she was far more concerned about how well it concealed her shape than how well she looked in it. In less than half an hour they would be on their way to the gala opening of the prince's new hospitality suite at the racecourse, and Mariella would have given anything not to have to be there!

Tanya, on the other hand, couldn't wait, her excitement more than making up for Mariella's lack of it.

The last three days had been total torture for her. It would have been bad enough simply discovering that she loved Xavier without the additional emotional anguish of having to endure his constant presence. Every time she looked at him the pain grew worse and so did her guilt.

She had hardly been able to eat because of her misery and anxiety, and she couldn't wait to get on the plane that would take her home!

Under different circumstances, although she would have been nervous about the thought of the coming event, it would have been a very different kind of nervousness, caused purely by her anxiety about people's reaction to her work. Right now, she recognised ruefully, she hardly cared what they thought!

'Come on,' Tanya urged her. 'It's time to go.'

Reluctantly, Mariella got up.

She could feel Xavier's gaze burning into her as she walked into the courtyard where he and Khalid were already standing beside the waiting car.

The hot desert wind tugged at the thin silk layers of her full-length dress and immediately Mariella reached anxiously to hold them away from her body.

To her relief Xavier got into the front of the car, but she was still acutely conscious of him as Ali drove them towards the racecourse. Unlike Xavier, Khalid favoured a strong modern male cologne, but she could still smell beneath it the scent of Xavier's skin, and deep down inside her a part of her cried out in anguished pain and longing, aching despairingly for him.

'Poor Ella, you must be so nervous.' Tanya tried to comfort her, sensing her distress, but to Mariella's relief not realising the real cause of it. 'You've hardly eaten a thing since you arrived, and you look so pale.'

'TANYA IS RIGHT—YOU do look pale,' Xavier told Mariella grimly several minutes later when they had reached their destination and he had opened the car door for her, leaving her with no alternative but to get out. His hand was beneath her elbow, preventing her from moving away from him. Instinctively Mariella knew that he had been waiting for the opportunity to vent the anger he obviously felt towards her against her. She had seen it in his eyes every time he looked at her, felt it in the tension that crackled between them. 'What's wrong, Mariella? If it isn't food you want, then perhaps it's another appetite you want to have satisfied. Is that it? Are you hungry for sex?' he demanded harshly.

'No,' Mariella denied immediately, trying again to pull away from him. He was making sure that no one else could hear what he was saying to her, she recognised, and making sure too that she could not get away from him.

Had he deliberately waited until now? Chosen this particular time to launch his attack on her, when he knew she couldn't escape from him?

'No?' he taunted her. 'Then why are you trembling so much? Why do you look so hungrily at me when you think I am not aware of you doing so?'

'I am not...I do not,' Mariella replied. She could feel her face starting to burn and her heart beginning to pound.

'You're lying,' Xavier told her softly. 'And don't deny it. Unless you want to provoke me into proving to you that you are! Is that what you want, Mariella?'

'Stop it! Stop doing this to me,' Mariella demanded. She could hear her own voice shaking with emotion and was helplessly aware that it wouldn't be long before her body betrayed her by following suit.

'I spoke to your agent today. She told me that she was sure you'd be thrilled to learn that I want to commission you for a very special project. She certainly was especially when I told her how much I was prepared to pay to secure your exclusive…services.'

Mariella reeled from the shock of his taunting comment.

'Xavier, please,' she begged him fatally, her eyes widening as she saw the look of triumph leaping to life in his eyes.

'Please?' he repeated silkily.

'Xavier, Mariella, come on…' Tanya urged them.

'We're coming. I was just discussing a certain plan with Mariella,' Xavier said smoothly as he guided Mariella towards the throng of people making for the entrance to the suite.

'WELL, SISTER-IN-LAW, I think we can safely say that your frieze is an outstanding success,' Khalid commented, grinning at Mariella. 'Everyone is talking about it and it is very, very impressive!'

Mariella tried to respond enthusiastically, but she felt achingly tired from answering all the questions she had received about the frieze, and, besides, her whole nervous system was still on red alert just in case Xavier should suddenly reappear and continue his cynical verbal torment.

'Khalid and I are going to get something to eat, in a few minutes,' Tanya told her. 'Do you want to come with us?'

Nauseously Mariella shook her head. The last thing she wanted was food. She had been feeling sick all day and her stomach heaved at the very thought.

'Here comes the prince,' Tanya whispered as the royal party appeared.

'Mariella. My congratulations. Everyone is most impressed!'

As she acknowledged his praise Mariella suddenly realised that Xavier was with him. Her feeling of sickness increased, but grimly she refused to submit to it.

'Xavier has just been telling me that he has commissioned you to make a visual record of the everyday life of his people,' the prince was continuing. 'A truly excellent idea!' Smiling at her, he started to move on.

So that was what Xavier had meant! Already dropping her head in deference to the prince, Mariella suddenly raised it, intending to glare at Xavier, but instead she was overcome by a dizzying surge of weakness.

'Ella, what is it? What's wrong?' Tanya demanded anxiously. 'You look as though you're going to faint! Feeling sick…looking like you're going to faint—anyone would think you're pregnant!' Tanya laughed.

As her sister turned away Mariella realised that Xavier was looking straight at her, and she knew immediately from his expression that he had heard Tanya's teasing comment and that somehow he had guessed the truth!

The urge to turn and run was so strong that she suspected if the gallery had not been so crowded she would have done so. But once again Xavier seemed to be able to read her mind because suddenly he was standing beside her.

'Your sister isn't well,' she heard him telling Tanya curtly. 'I'm taking her back to the villa.'

'No,' Mariella protested, but it was too late. Khalid was urging Tanya to go with him to get something to eat, and Xavier was already propelling her towards the exit.

It was impossible for either of them to say anything in the car with Ali driving. 'This way,' Xavier told Mariella grimly once they were back at the villa, stopping her from seeking the sanctuary of her own room as his hand on the small of her back ushered her towards his own suite of rooms.

'You can't do this!' Mariella said shakily. 'I'm a single woman, remember, and—'

'A single woman who is carrying my child!' Xavier stopped her savagely as he opened the suite door and almost pushed her inside.

Mariella could feel herself starting to tremble. She didn't have the strength for this kind of fight. Not now and probably not ever!

'Xavier, I'm tired. It's been a long day.'

'Why the hell didn't you say something? Or were you hoping that by not eating and by exhausting yourself you could provoke a natural end to it?' he accused, ignoring her plea.

'No,' Mariella denied immediately, horrified. 'No! How dare you say that? I would never...' Tears filled her eyes. 'I wanted this baby,' she told him passionately. 'I...'

Abruptly she stopped, her expression betraying her as she saw the way he was looking at her.

'Would you mind repeating that?' he demanded with dangerous softness.

Nervously Mariella licked her lips.

'Repeat what?' she asked him.

'Don't play games with me, Mariella,' he warned her. 'You know perfectly well what I mean. You just said "I wanted this baby"..."wanted," rather than "want," which means...which means that it wasn't just sex you wanted from me, as you claimed, was it?

'What? Nothing to say?' he challenged her bitingly. 'Not even an "it was an accident"?'

Mariella bit down hard on her lower lip.

She wasn't going to demean herself by lying to him!

'You don't have to worry,' she tried to defend herself, her voice wobbling. 'I won't ever make any kind of claims on you, Xavier. I intend to take full responsibility for…for everything. I want to take full responsibility,' she stressed fiercely. 'There's no way I intend to let my baby suffer as I did through having a father who…'

'Your baby?' Xavier stopped her harshly. 'Your baby, Mariella, is my child! My child!'

'No!' Mariella denied immediately. 'This baby has nothing whatsoever to do with you, Xavier. He or she will be completely mine!'

'Nothing to do with me! I don't believe I'm hearing this,' Xavier breathed savagely. 'This baby…my baby has everything to do with me, Mariella. After all, without me he or she just could not exist! I'll make arrangements for us to be married as quickly and as quietly as possible, and then—'

'Married! No!' Mariella refused vehemently, her panic showing in her expression as she confronted him. 'I'm not going to get married, Xavier. Not ever. When my mother married my father, she believed that he loved her, that she could trust him, rely on him…but she couldn't. He left her… He left us both because he didn't want me.'

All the emotions she had been bottling up inside her whooshed out in a despairing stream of agonised denial, even whilst somewhere deep down inside her most guarded private self there was a deep burning pain at the thought of just how very, very much she wanted Xavier's total commitment for her baby and for herself. His total commitment and his enduring love! The pain of her own self-knowledge was virtually unbearable. She ached for him to simply take her in his arms and hold her safe, to keep her safe for ever, and yet at the same time her own self-conditioning was urging her to deny and deride those feelings to protect herself.

'I am not your father, Mariella, and where my child is concerned—' his mouth tightened '—in Zuran it is a father whose rights are paramount. I would be within my legal rights in ensuring that you are not permitted to leave the country with my child—either before or after his or her birth!'

Distraught, Mariella demanded passionately, 'Why are you doing this? Your own aunt told me that you had sworn never to marry or have children; that you didn't want a wife or children.'

'No,' Xavier stopped her curtly. 'It is true that I had decided not to marry, but not because I didn't want… The reason I had chosen not to marry was because I believed I could never find a woman who would love me as a man, with fire and passion and commitment, and that I wouldn't be able to find a woman also who would understand and accept my responsibilities to my people. I didn't think that such a woman could exist!'

'And because she doesn't…because I am carrying your child, you're prepared to marry me instead, is that it? I can't do it, Xavier. I won't, I won't be married, just because of the baby.' Her voice began to wobble betrayingly as her emotions overwhelmed her and to her own humiliation tears flooded her eyes and began to roll down her face. Helplessly Mariella lifted her hands to her face to shield herself, unable to bear Xavier's contemptuous response to her distress. It must be baby hormones that were making her cry like this, making her feel so weak and vulnerable!

'Mariella.'

Mariella froze with shock as she felt the warmth of Xavier's exhaled breath against her skin, as he crossed the space between them and took her in his arms.

'Don't!' His voice was rough with pain. 'I can't bear the thought of knowing that you and my child, the two people I love the most, will be lost to me, but I can't bear either knowing that I have forced you to stay with me against your will. When you came to me in the desert, gave yourself to me…it was as though you had read my mind. Shared my thoughts and my feelings, known how much I had wanted us to be together, and known too that I had been waiting for the right opportunity to approach you and tell you how I felt, but I was conscious of what had happened during your own childhood with your father. I wanted to win your belief in me, your trust of me… before I revealed to you how much I wanted to ask you to share my life! I knew how strong your sense of commitment was, your sense of responsibility, and I knew that the future of my people would rest safely in your hands. I thought that together you and I could…but I was wrong, as you made very clear to me… You didn't love me; you didn't even really want me. You merely wanted someone to father your child.

'I want and need both of you here with me more than I can find the words to tell you, but I cannot bear to see you so distressed. I shall make arrangements for you to return to England if that is what you want, but what I would ask you is that you allow me to play at least some part in my child's life, however small. I shall, of course, make financial provision for both of you…that is not just my duty, but my right! But at least once a year I should like your permission to see my child. To spend time with him or her. If necessary I shall come to your country to do so. And…'

Mariella fought to take in what he was saying. Xavier wanted her. Xavier loved her. In fact he loved her so much that he was prepared to put her needs and wishes above his own!

A new feeling began to whisper softly through her, a soft warmth that permeated every cell of her body, melting away all the tiny frozen particles of mistrust and pain that had been with her from the very first moment she had known about her father. A feeling so unfamiliar, so heady and euphoric that it made her literally tremble with happiness, and excitement unfurled and grew inside.

Instinctively her hand touched her belly. Could her baby feel what she was feeling? Was he or she right now uncurling and basking in the same glow of happiness that was engulfing her?

Xavier's hand covered hers and that small gesture brought immediate emotional tears to her eyes as she turned to look at him without any attempt to hide her emotions from him.

'I didn't know you loved me,' she whispered.

'You know now,' Xavier responded.

She could see the bleakness in his eyes and the pain. Her body could feel the warmth of his hand even through her own. Gently she pulled her own hand away and leaned into him so that he could feel the growing swell of their child, her gaze monitoring his immediate and intense reaction.

Xavier would never do what her father had done, instinctively she knew that, just as she knew too how much time she had wasted, how much that was so infinitely precious to her she had risked and nearly lost because of her frightened refusal to allow herself to believe that not all men were like her father.

Alongside her bubbling happiness she could feel another emotion she had to struggle to identify. It was freedom, she recognised; freedom from the burden she had been carrying around with her for so long, and it was Xavier who had given her that freedom by giving her his love, by being man enough, strong enough to reveal his vulnerability to her!

She took a deep breath and then held tightly to her courage and even more tightly to Xavier's arm.

'It isn't true what I said,' she told him simply. 'It wasn't just sex. I tried to pretend it was to myself because I was too afraid to admit how I really felt, but I think I knew even before, and then afterwards when I still wanted you...' Her skin turned a warm rose as she saw the way he was looking at her.

'Don't look at me like that,' she protested. 'Not yet, not until I've finished telling you... Otherwise...'

'Still wanted, in the past tense or...' Xavier pressed her huskily.

'Still wanted then,' Mariella informed him primly. 'And still want now,' she added, her own voice suddenly as husky and liquid with emotion as his had been. 'I still want you, Xavier!' she repeated. 'And I don't just want you, I need you as well. Need you and love you,' she finally managed to say, her voice so low that he had to bend his head to catch her shaky admission.

'You love me? But do you trust me, Mariella? Do you believe me when I tell you that I shall never, ever let you down or give you cause to doubt me? Do you believe me when I tell you that you and our child...our children, will always have my love and my commitment?'

Mariella closed her eyes and then opened them again.

'Yes,' she replied firmly, and her melting look of love told him that she meant it!

'Xavier,' she protested unconvincingly as he started to kiss her. 'The others will be coming back.'

'Shall I stop, then?' he asked her, brushing his lips tormentingly against her own.

'Mmm... No...' Mariella responded helplessly, sighing in soft pleasure as his hand covered her breast, his thumb probing the aroused sensitivity of her nipple. Her whole body turned liquid with desire, making her cling eagerly to him.

'Every night I've thought about you like this,' Xavier told her rawly. 'Wanted you…ached for you in my arms. Every night, and every day, and if I'd known that there was the smallest chance that you felt the same I would never have let you go. I warn you, Ella, that now that I do know I will never let you go.'

'I will never want you to,' Mariella responded emotionally. 'Take me to bed, Xavier,' she begged him urgently. 'Take me to bed and show me that this isn't all just a dream…'

She was in his arms and being carried from the salon into his bedroom almost before the words had left her mouth. And even if she had wanted to retract them it would have been impossible for her to do so with Xavier kissing her the way that he was, with all the passion and love, all the commitment she now recognised that she had secretly ached for all along.

EPILOGUE

'WELL, what do you think of your anniversary present?' Mariella asked Xavier lightly, whilst she watched him with a secret anxiety she was trying hard to hide.

She had been working on this special gift for him on and off ever since their marriage, only breaking off for their six-month-old son's birth and the early weeks of his life.

Xavier shook his head, as though he found it hard to comprehend what he was seeing. 'I knew you were working on something, but this...'

The stern note in his voice broke through her self-control, forcing her to reveal how much his approval meant to her. 'You don't like it—?'

'Like it! Mariella.' Reaching for her, Xavier wrapped her tightly in his arms.

'There is nothing, excluding your sweet self and our noisy and demanding young son, that I would value more,' he told her emotionally as he swung her round in his arms so that they could both look at the series of drawings she had spent the early hours of the morning displaying around their private salon to surprise him when he woke up on this, their anniversary morning.

As a wedding present from her new husband Mariella had asked to be allowed to travel in the desert with the tribe. Conscious of her pregnancy, Xavier had initially been reluctant to agree, but Mariella had been insistent. It had been on that journey that she had made the secret preliminary sketches for what was now a visual documentation of the tribe's way of life, a visual documentation that betrayed, not only her fine eye for detail, but also her love for the man whose people she had drawn.

'I do have a gift for you, although I haven't followed Tanya's advice and booked a luxury holiday,' Xavier told her ruefully.

Following the direction of his amused glance, Mariella laughed.

Fleur, who was now walking was sitting on the floor next to her six-month-old cousin, the pair of them deep in some personal exchange, which involved lots of shared giggles and some noisy hand-clapping from Ben.

'Don't you dare do any such thing. There's no way I want to be parted from these two!'

With Tanya and Khalid living around the corner, both the families saw a lot of each other, and the two young cousins could grow up together.

'I may have another present for you,' Mariella announced semi-hesitantly, the way her glance lingered on their son informing Xavier of just what she meant.

'What? We said we'd wait.'

'I know…but this time it's your fault and not mine. Remember your birthday, when you didn't want to wait until…'

'Mmm.' He did a rapid mental calculation. 'So in another seven months, then…'

'I think so… Do you mind?'

'Mind? Me? No way. Do you?'

'I've got my fingers crossed that I'm right,' Mariella admitted. 'Although I'm pretty sure that I am, and if I'm not…' she gave him a flirtatious look '…then I'm sure we can find a way of ensuring that I soon am! Anyway, what about *my* anniversary present? You still haven't told me what it is.'

'Come with me,' Xavier instructed her, bending to pick up their son and hand him to Mariella before lifting Fleur up into his own arms.

'Close your eyes and hold onto me,' Xavier said as he led her out into their own private courtyard, and through it to the new courtyard that had been developed behind it.

Mariella could smell the roses before he allowed her to open her eyes, and once he did so she drew in her breath in delight as she saw the new garden he had been having designed for her as a special surprise.

A softer and far more modern planting plan had been adopted for the new garden than the one favoured by Xavier's grandmother. The design was reminiscent of an English country garden with the flower beds filled with a variety of traditional plants, but it was the wonderful scent of the roses that most caught her attention.

'They're called "Eternity",' Xavier told her softly as she bent her head to touch the velvet-soft petals of the rose closest to her. 'And I promise that I shall love you for eternity, Mariella, and beyond it. My love for you is…eternal!'

Warm tears bathed Mariella's eyes as she smiled at him.

'And mine for you!' she whispered lovingly to him.

Silently, they walked through the garden together, his arm around her drawing her close, her head resting against his shoulder, the children in their arms.

* * * * *

THE SHEIKH'S
BLACKMAILED
MISTRESS

PROLOGUE

'OHHHH, NO!'

Her anxious warning protest had come too late, and now she was pressed hard against the very male body of the robed man who had been turning the corner at the same time from the opposite direction.

Her startled cry and the clear visual imprinting her eyes had relayed to her brain—of a tall, broad-shouldered and very arrogant-looking handsome male, with the most extraordinarily green eyes she had ever seen—was all there'd been time for before that image had been blanked out by her abrupt and far too intimate contact—visually and physically—with his body.

Now, with her face virtually buried against his shoulder, her senses were being assaulted by that intimacy in every sensory way that there was. She could feel the heat of his body, and smell its personal slightly musky male scent, mingled with the cool sharpness of the cologne he was wearing. She could feel, too, the heavy thud of his heart beating out a demand that called to her own heartbeat to follow it. Lean, strong fingers gripped her arm, bare flesh to bare flesh setting a panicky, firework-intense burst of lava-hot sensation spilling through her own body.

The manner in which they had collided had brought her up against him in such a way that she now realised she was leaning against one of his thighs, her own having somehow softened and parted to admit its muscular male presence. The lava flow changed from a rolling surge of heat into an explosion of female arousal that wrenched any kind of control over her body from her and claimed it for itself. Quivers of female recognition at his maleness were softening her flesh into his. Breathing was becoming a dangerously erotic hazard that leached her small soft moan of longing into the once sterile silence of the corridor.

She mustn't do this. She mustn't raise her head from the muscle-padded warmth of his shoulder to look up into his face. She mustn't let her desire-dazed gaze dwell yearningly on his mouth. She mustn't quiver and then sigh, and then place her hand on his chest, whilst lifting her gaze reluctantly from his mouth to his eyes, so that her own could whisper to him how much she ached to trace the sensuality of that full lower lip set beneath its sharply cut partner with her fingertip, or better still with her tonguetip, caressing it into a reciprocal hunger for the kiss she now wanted so badly.

No, she must not do any of those things—but she was doing them, and he was looking back at her as though he wanted exactly what she wanted, and for all the same reasons.

The air in the corridor hadn't changed, but she still shivered and trembled and then moaned as he lowered his head to hers, his free hand sliding into the untidy tangle of her honey-streaked curls.

She could feel the warmth of his breath against her skin—feel it and taste it, with its erotic mix of promised delights. Longingly she watched the slow descent of his mouth towards her own, savouring each millimetre of movement that brought him closer—until finally he stopped. Then she looked up at him, her face relaying a

message that was a mixture of female pride and passionate longing. His eyes blazed with emerald fire and the
pure intensity of male sexual arousal, burning the air between them.

Sam raised herself up on the tips of her toes, her lips
parting on a shaky breath of urgent need, clinging to his
robe as she did so to support herself. What she was inhal-
ing and tasting now was an aphrodisiac far stronger than
any wine.

He brushed her lips with his own, their touch warm and
hard and yet exquisitely sensual and caressing, and then
drew back to look at her. She moved closer, pressing herself
to him in a silent plea for more. Lifting her face towards
him, he kissed her briefly again, and then again, until finally he did what she knew she'd wanted him to do from
the first and drew her to him in a kiss that possessed her as
totally as the desert possessed those whose hearts it stole.

A commotion further down the corridor out of sight
from them had them springing apart. Her face on fire,
Sam fled, all too conscious of the fact that she was now
going to be even later for her appointment than she had
already been. Her heart was thumping with a mixture of
shock and disbelief.

She was here in the Arabian Gulf on business, not to
behave in the reckless and out-of-character way in which
she had just behaved.

Her impromptu trip out into the desert this morning
might have increased her longing to get this job she had
come so far to be interviewed for, but it had also meant
that she had not really left herself enough time in which to
get ready for the interview—which was why she had been
hurrying at speed down the hotel corridor in the first place.

Now she had less than half an hour in which to shower
and change and get to her appointment—and *that* was

why her heart was thudding so fast and so erratically, not because of what had just happened with the man she had bumped into.

What on earth had come over her?

After all, she knew perfectly well that if anything it was even more pertinent in this part of the world than it was in the west for a woman who wanted to be taken seriously professionally and respected to behave in a way that did not compromise her status—with no inappropriate sexual behaviour towards Arab men.

And as, according to the lectures she had attended to prepare herself for this interview, inappropriate behaviour here in the Arabian Gulf could mean something as simple as a woman reaching out to touch a man on the arm, or engaging him in eye contact, what she had just done definitely came under the heading of *very* inappropriate behaviour indeed.

Even now, despite that knowledge, and despite the fact that normally she wouldn't have dreamed of acting as she had—would indeed have been shocked if anyone had suggested she might—she was still so aware of the swollen ache deep inside her that even breathing as hard as she was doing right now was enough to make her grit her teeth. Uncharacteristic longings seemed to have taken control of her thought-processes. Longings which were making her wish…

Wish what? That he had taken her to a bedroom and made mad, passionate love to her? A bedroom? Mad, passionate love? Who was she kidding? The kind of behaviour she had just indulged in was not conducive to that kind of encounter—and it would be naïve of her not to understand that. She was weaving ridiculous fantasies inside her head of mutual overwhelming passion at first sight.

She needed bringing to her senses and some icy water thrown on the sexual heat that was now tormenting her.

What *was* this? She had heard that the desert could turn people crazy, but surely not after a mere couple of hours' viewing from the inside of a luxurious four-by-four air-conditioned vehicle? Oh, but he had been so handsome, and she had wanted him so much—still wanted him so much. She had never experienced anything remotely like the longing that had rolled over her when their bodies had made contact. It had been as though an electric surge of emotion had somehow bonded her to him, fusing them together, so that now she actually felt a physical pain, as though they had been forcibly wrenched apart.

One look into his eyes had been all it needed to complete her subjugation to what she had felt. If he had spoken to her then, and asked her to commit herself to him for the rest of her life, Sam suspected that she would quite willingly have agreed.

She tried to laugh herself out of her own emotional intensity, deriding herself for being silly and telling herself that she was probably simply suffering from too much sun. It wasn't much of an explanation for what she had felt, but it was way better than the alternative—which was to admit that with one single look she had fallen in love with a stranger to whom she would now be emotionally bound for ever.

CHAPTER ONE

VERE LOOKED through the window of his office in the palace of Dhurahn, thinking not of the beauty of the gardens that lay within his view, which had been designed by his late mother, but of the desert that lay beyond them. The familiar fierce need that was stamped into his bones was currently possessing him. He wanted to put aside the cares and complexities of rulership of a modern Arab state and enjoy instead that part of his heritage that belonged to the desert and the men who loved it.

Which in one sense he would soon be doing. In one sense, maybe, but not wholly and freely. On this occasion it was his responsibility to his country and his people that was taking him into what was known as the 'empty quarter' of the desert, to the boundary they shared there with the two of their Gulf neighbours.

As he crossed to the other side of his office to look down into the courtyard, where his household were preparing for his departure, the remote and aloof air that was so much a part of him, which those who did not know him thought of as regal arrogance, was very much in evidence. Vere felt the weight of his responsibility towards the birthright he shared with his twin brother very deeply. He was, after all, the elder of the two of them, and his nature had always

inclined him to take things more to heart and more seriously than Drax, his twin.

To Vere, ruling Dhurahn as their father and mother
would have wished was a duty that was almost sacred.

There had only been one previous occasion on which
his longing for the desert and the solace it offered him had
been as strong as it was now, and that had been the time
following the tragic death of his parents—his mother's
passing having hit him particularly hard. That thought
alone was enough to fill him with a savage determination
to tighten his control over his current feelings, which he
saw as a wholly unacceptable personal weakness.

It was unthinkable that his physical desire for the car-
nal pleasure afforded by one of those western women who
came to the Gulf ready to trade their bodies for the lifestyle they thought their flesh could buy—a woman ready to
give herself on the smallest pretext, shamelessly openly—
should have driven him to the point where he felt his only
escape from it could come from the same place where he
had sought solace for the loss of his mother. It was more
than unthinkable. It was a desecration, and a personal failure of the highest order.

It was more than half his own lifetime ago now since the
death of their parents, but for Vere as a teenager, struggling
to be a man and ultimately a ruler, with all the responsi-
bilites that meant, the loss of the gentle Irish mother who
had supplied the softening wisdom of her love against his
desire to emulate his father's strength, had been one that
had taken from him something very precious, leaving in
its place a need to protect himself from ever having to endure such pain again.

Some men might think that for a man in his position the
answer to the sexual hunger that was threatening to destroy
his self-control was to satisfy it via marriage or a mistress.

His brother Drax was, after all, already married, with his wife expecting their first child in the near future, and Drax had hinted to him that he would like to see Vere married himself.

Vere frowned as he watched the four-by-fours being loaded for the long overland drive to the empty quarter.

The initiative prompted originally by the Ruler of Zuran, to investigate and if necessary redefine the old borders that separated their countries from one another, and from the empty quarter, was one he fully supported. They all in their different ways held certain territorial rights over the empty quarter, but by long-held and unwritten tradition they tended to ignore them in favour of the last of the traditional nomad tribes, who had for centuries called the empty quarter home.

The Ruler of Zuran wanted to bring the small band of nomadic tribespeople within the protection of the opportunities for education and health welfare he provided for his own people, and to this end he had contacted his neighbours: the Emir of Khulua, and Vere and Drax.

His initiative was one that was very close to Vere's own heart, provided it could be accomplished without depriving the tribes of their right to their own way of life. The Emir, not wanting to be excluded even though he was a more old-fashioned and traditional ruler, had also indicated that he wanted to be involved in the project, and as a first step the Ruler of Zuran had funded the cost of a team of cartographers to thoroughly map out the whole of the area.

It had been the Emir who had suggested that whilst this was being done it might be a good idea to reassess and establish their own individual borders with one another, which met at the empty quarter.

It was a good idea that made sense—as long as the Emir, who was known for his skill at adapting situations to suit his own ends, did not make use of the re-mapping to claim territory that was not strictly his. During private talks with the Ruler of Zuran, both he and Drax had agreed to keep a very strict eye on any attempts the Emir might make to do that. As part of their agreed preventative measures against this it had been decided that each ruler should take it in turn to be involved 'on the ground' with the project, and now it was Vere's turn to drive out to the border region of the empty quarter.

A movement on the balcony above him caused Vere to look upwards, to where his twin brother Drax and his wife Sadie were standing. The sight of their happiness and their love for one another touched a place inside him he hadn't known existed until Drax had fallen in love.

As twins they had naturally always been close, but the car accident that had killed their parents when the brothers were in their teens had made the bond between them even stronger. In the eyes of the world he, as the elder twin, was the one to step into their father's shoes, but both he and Drax knew that it had always been their father's intention that they would share the rulership and the responsibility for Dhurahn. However, every country was expected to have a single figurehead—and that duty rested with him.

Up until recently the duty had never been one he considered irksome. Where Drax embraced modernity, especially in architecture and design, he preferred to cling to tradition. Where Drax was an extrovert, he was more of an introvert. Where Drax enjoyed the buzz of busy civilisation, he preferred the silent solitude of the desert. They were as all those who knew them best often said, two halves of one whole.

Like many cultured Arab men, Vere revered poetry and studied the verse of the great poets, but just recently—although he hated having to admit it—the beauty of those words had brought him more pain than pleasure.

Normally he would have welcomed the chance to spend time in the desert, embracing the opportunity it gave him to be at one with his heritage, but now the knowledge of how close the desert was brought him to those things within himself that he felt the most need to guard. It was making him feel irritable and on edge.

Because he knew that being in the desert would exacerbate that sense of emptiness and loss that lay within him, and with it his vulnerability?

Vere swung round angrily, as though to turn his back on his own unwanted thoughts. His pride hated having to acknowledge any kind of flaw, and to Vere what he was experiencing was a weakness. He wanted to wrench it out of himself and then seal it away somewhere, deprived of anything to feed on so it would wither and die.

But, no matter how hard he fought to deny it any kind of legitimacy, every time he thought he had succeeded in destroying it, it returned—like a multi-headed monster, infuriating him with the mirror it kept holding up to him, reflecting back his faults.

Generations of proudly arrogant male blood ran through Vere's veins. The moral code of that blood was burned into him by his own will. He came from a race that knew the value of self-control, of abstinence, of starving the body and the spirit in the eternal battle to survive in a harsh desert environment. Real men, the kind of man Vere had always considered himself to be, did not allow uncontrolled hungers of any kind to rule them. Not ever.

And certainly not in a hotel corridor, with an unknown woman, and in such a way that—

He wheeled round again, his body tight with anger, ignoring the harsh glare of the sun as it fell across his face, highlighting the jut of his cheekbones and the searing intensity of his gaze. Not for Vere the protection of designer sunglasses to shadow and colour reality.

Lust must surely be the most despicable of all human vices. It was certainly the cause of a great deal of human misery. Vere had always considered himself above that kind of selfish weakness. As the Ruler of Dhurahn he had to be. And yet he could not escape from the knowledge that for a handful of minutes he had been rendered so oblivious to his position by his own senses that nothing had mattered more to him than his desire for the woman he had held in his arms.

Another man might have shrugged his shoulders and accepted that he was a man, and thus vulnerable to the temptations of the flesh, but Vere's pride refused to accept that he could be so vulnerable, so prone to human frailty. He had fallen below the demands he made upon himself to meet certain standards. Others might not condemn him for doing so, but Vere condemned himself.

He wasn't entirely alone, though, in his belief that a man needed to prove he could withstand the most rigorous of tests before he could call himself a man and a leader of other men. There was an 'other' to share his belief, and that 'other' was the desert.

The desert had a way of drawing out a man and highlighting both his strengths and his weaknesses. Normally Vere looked forward to the time he could spend in the desert as a means of replenishing his sense of what he truly was—but right now he wasn't sure that he wanted to submit his current state to that test. He had found himself wanting, and he feared that so too would the desert—that he would no longer be at one with it, just as he could no longer feel at one with himself.

More than anything he wanted and needed to dismiss

the woman and the incident from his mind for ever—and then to deal with the damage she and it had done to his pride.

But the truth was he couldn't. The memory of her was branded into him and he couldn't seem to free himself from it—no matter how much he loathed and resented its presence. And her. He hadn't slept through a full night since it had happened. He didn't dare to let himself dream too deeply, fearing that if he did his dreams would be filled by her, and the ache of need he managed to control during the day would overpower him when he was asleep. It was bad enough having to acknowledge that every time he let his concentration slip the memory of her was there, waiting to taunt him. At its worst, that memory had him mentally lifting his hands to her body, determined to push her from him as he should have done all along, but knowing that in reality he would end up binding her to him.

How was it possible for one woman, a complete stranger, to invade the most private and strongly guarded recesses of his heart and mind and possess them, haunting and tormenting him almost beyond his own endurance?

It was mid-afternoon. He planned to leave for the desert camp of the surveyors as the sun began to set, so that he and his small entourage could make the most of the cooler night hours in which to travel. He had some work to do first, though, he reminded himself.

Whilst Drax and his wife occupied the new wing of the palace that Drax had designed for his own occupation before his marriage, Vere's personal apartments were in the older part of the palace, and had traditionally housed Dhurahn's rulers through several generations.

Thus it was that when he stood in the elegantly furnished and decorated private salon that lay behind the formal reception room where he held his public *divans*, to which his people were entitled to come and speak to him and be heard, he might be alone in the flesh, but in spirit the room was peopled with all those of his blood who had gone before him.

His formidable great-grandfather, who had ridden with Lawrence of Arabia and fought off all comers to maintain his right to his lands. His French grandmother, so elegant and cultured, who had bequeathed to him a love of art and design. And his own parents: his father, so very much everything that a true ruler should be—strong, wise, tender to those in his care—and his lovely laughing mother, who had filled his life with happiness and joy and the traditions of her homeland. Here in this room, at the heart of the palace and his life, he had always believed that he would never really be alone.

And yet now, thanks to one incident that was impossible to forget, that sense of comfort had been stolen from him and replaced with a stark awareness of his own inner solitude that he could not escape.

If he were reckless enough to close his eyes he knew that immediately he would be able to conjure up the feel of the thick silk of her wild curls beneath his hand, the scent of her woman's flesh—sweet and warm, iike honey and almonds—the stifled heat of her breath when her body discovered the maleness of his own. And most of all her eyes, so darkly blue that they'd caught exactly the colour of the desert sky overhead just before the sun finally burned into the horizon. A man could lose his reason if he looked too long at such a sky, or into such eyes…

Was that what he believed had happened to him? Vere grimaced, bringing himself abruptly back to reality. He was a modern man, born in an age of facts and science. The fact that he had turned a corner in a hotel corridor and bumped into a young woman with whom he had shared a kiss—no matter how intensely passionate and intimate, no matter how bitterly regretted—hardly constituted an act of fate that had the power to change his whole life. Unless he himself allowed that to happen, Vere warned himself.

He strode across the room and pulled at the double doors that opened into the wide corridor beyond it, its floor tiled in the mosaic style that was true Arab fashion.

His parents had instituted a tradition that these rooms were the preserve of themselves and their children and no one else. Normally Vere relished that privacy, but now for some reason it irked him.

Was that the reason for the deep-rooted and ever-present ache that pursued him even in his sleep? Tormenting him with images and memories—the smell of her, the feel of her in his arms, the feel of her body against his, the sound of her breathing, the scalding, almost unbearable heat of the moment their lips had met?

It was just a kiss—that was all… A mere kiss. A nothing—just like the woman with whom he had shared it. She hadn't even had the type of looks he found physically attractive. The type of women he liked to take to his bed were tall and soignée cool, worldly blondes—women who could satisfy him physically without involving him in the danger of them touching him emotionally.

Vere had never forgotten that loving a woman with the whole of his heart meant that ultimately he would be broken on the wheel of that love when she abandoned him. He had learned that with his mother's death, just as he had learned the pain that went with it. Better not to love at all ever again than to risk such agony a second time.

He still burned with shame to remember the nights he had woken from his sleep to find his face wet with tears and his mother's name on his lips. A man of fourteen did not cry like a child of four. Emotional weakness was some-

thing he had to burn out of himself, he had told himself.
And that was exactly what he had done. Until a chance
encounter in a hotel corridor had ripped off the mask he
had gone through so much trouble to fix to himself, and
revealed the unwanted need that was still inside him.

CHAPTER TWO

SAM STEPPED UNDER the surprisingly sophisticated shower in the 'bathroom' compartment of the traditional black tent that was her current personal accommodation, soaping her body and taking care not to waste any water when she rinsed herself off—even though she had been assured that, thanks to the efficiency of the Ruler of Zuran's desalination plants in Zuran, there was no need for them to economise on the water that was driven in to the camp almost daily in huge containers.

Sam had been over the moon with joy when she'd learned that against all the odds she had secured this so coveted job of working as part of the team of cartographers, anthropologists, statisticians, geologists and historians brought together to embark on what must surely be one of the most ambitious and altruistic ventures of its kind.

As a cartographer, Sam was part of the group that were re-mapping the borders and traditional camel caravan routes of this magical and ancient part of the world. Just the words 'the empty quarter' still brought a shiver of excitement down her spine. After all, hadn't her youthful desire to come to the Gulf initially sprung from reading about the likes of Gertrude Bell?

Normally Sam shared her comfortable and well-equipped accommodation with Talia Dean, one of the other three women who were also on the team, but the young American geologist had cut her foot two days ago, and was now hospitalised in Zuran.

Others before them had mapped the empty quarter and explored it, searching for hidden cities and routes, and the borders between the three Arabian states involved in the present exercise were already agreed and defined. However, modern technology combined with the excellent relations that existed between the three states meant that it was now possible, with satellite information combined with on-the-ground checks, to see what effect five decades of sandstorms that had passed since they were agreed might have had on the borders.

Now, with their evening meal over and the camp settling down for the night, Sam dried her newly showered body and then made her way into her blissfully air-conditioned tented bedroom.

Furnished with rich silk rugs and low beds piled high with velvet-covered cushions and throws, and scented with the most heavenly perfumes from swinging lanterns heated with charcoal, its combination of modern comfort-producing technology and traditional Bedouin tent produced an exotic if somewhat surreal luxury, which immediately struck the senses with its sharpness of contrast to the harshness of the desert itself.

But the desert also had its beauty. Some members of the team found the desert too harsh and unforgiving, but Sam loved it—even whilst she was awed by it. It possessed an arrogance that had already enslaved her, a ferocity that said *take me as I am, for I will not change.* There was something about it that was so eternal and powerful, so hauntingly beautiful, that just to look out on it brought a lump to her throat.

And yet the desert was also very cruel. She had seen falcons wheeling in the sky above the carcases of small animals, destroyed by the merciless heat of the sun. She had heard tales from the scarily expert Arab drivers supplied to the team, who were not allowed to drive themselves, of whole convoys being buried by sandstorms, never to be seen again, of oases there one day and gone the next, of tribes and the men who ruled them, so in tune with the savagery of the landscape in which they lived that they obeyed no law other than that of the desert itself.

One such leader was due to arrive in the camp tomorrow, according to the gossip she could not help but listen to. Prince Vereham al a' Karim bin Hakar, Ruler of Dhurahn, was by all accounts a man who was much admired and respected by other men. And desert men respected only those who had proved they were strong enough for the desert. Such men were a race apart, a chosen few, men who stood tall and proud.

She had been tired when she came to bed, but now— thanks to her own foolishness—she was wide awake, her body tormented by a familiar sweet, slow ache that was flowing through her as surely as the Dhurahni River flowed from the High Plateau Mountains beyond the empty quarter, travelling many, many hundreds of miles before emerging in its Plutonian darkness into the State of Dhurahn.

Why didn't she think about and focus on *that*, instead of on the memory of a kiss that by rights she should have forgotten weeks ago?

It had, after all, been three months—well, three months, one week and four and a half days, to be exact—since she had accidentally bumped into a robed stranger and ended up…

And ended up what? Obsessing about him three months later? How rational was that? It wasn't rational at all, was it? So they had shared an opportunistic kiss? No doubt both of them had been equally curious about and aroused by the cultural differences between them. At least that was what Sam was valiantly trying to tell herself. And perhaps she might have succeeded if she hadn't been idiotic enough immediately after the incident to fall into the hormone-baited trap of convincing herself that she had met and fallen in love with the one true love of her life, and that she was doomed to ache and yearn for him for the rest of her life.

What foolishness. A work of fiction worthy of any *Arabian Nights' Tale,* and even less realistic.

What had happened was an incident that at best should have simply been forgotten, and at worst should have caused her to feel a certain amount of shame.

Shame? For sharing a mere kiss with a stranger? That kind of thinking was totally archaic. Better and far more honest, surely, to admit the truth.

So what *was* the truth? That she had enjoyed the experience?

Enjoyed it?

If only it had been the kind of ephemeral, easy, lighter than light experience that could be dismissed as merely enjoyable.

But all it had been was a simple kiss, she told herself angrily.

A simple kiss was easily forgotten; it did not bury itself so deeply in the senses that just the act of breathing in an unguarded moment was enough to reawaken the feelings it had aroused. It did not wake a person from their sleep because she was drowning in the longing it had set free, like a subterranean river in full flood. It did not possess a person and her senses to the extent that she was possessed.

Here she went again, Sam recognised miserably. She was twenty-four years old—a qualified professional in a demanding profession, a woman who had so longed to train in her chosen field that she had deliberately refused to allow herself the distraction of emotional and physical relationships with the opposite sex, and had managed to do so without more than a few brief pangs of regret.

But now it was as though all she had denied herself had suddenly decided to fight back and demand recompense. As though the woman in her was demanding recompense for what she had been denied. Yes, that was it. That was the reason she was feeling the way she was, she decided with relief. What she was feeling had nothing really to do with the man himself, even though…

Even though what? Even though her body remembered every hard, lean line of his, every place it had touched his, every muscle, every breath, every pulse of the blood in his veins and the beat of his heart? And that was before she even began to think about his kiss, or the way she had felt as if fate had taken her by the hand and brought her face-to-face with her destiny and her soul mate. She was sure she would never have allowed herself to be subjected to such emotional intensity if she had stayed at home in England. Her loving but pragmatic parents, with their busy and practical lives, had certainly not brought her up to think in such terms.

If she was to re-experience that kiss now—that moment when she had looked into those green eyes and known that this was *it*, that neither she nor her life would ever be the same again, that somehow by some means beyond either her comprehension or her control, she was now *his*—it would probably not be anything like as erotic or all-powerful as she remembered. Imagination was a wonderful thing, she told herself. That she was still thinking about something she ought to have forgotten within hours of it happening only proved that she had far too much of that dangerous quality. After all, it wasn't as though she was ever likely to see him again—a stranger met by chance in a hotel corridor in a foreign country.

Instead of thinking about him, what she ought to be thinking about was tomorrow, when Sheikh Fasial bin Sadir, the cousin and representative of the Ruler of Zuran, who had been here at the camp since they had first arrived to oversee everything, would be handing over control of the project to Vereham al a' Karim bin Hakar, Sheikh of Dhurahn. In turn, in three months' time, he would be replaced by the nominated representative of the Emir of Khulua.

Sheikh Sadir was a career diplomat who had made it his business to ensure that both the camp and the work they were doing were run in a well-ordered and harmonious fashion. He had stressed to them—in perfect English—in an on-site briefing, that all three Rulers were determined to ensure that none of the small bands of nomads remaining in the empty quarter should in any way feel threatened by the work they were doing. That was why each working party would have with them an Arab guide, who would be able to speak with the nomads and reassure them about what was going on.

He had also gone on to tell them that whilst each state technically had rights over their own share of the empty quarter, where it came within their borders, it was accepted by all of them that the nomads had the right to roam freely across those borders.

Sam knew nothing about the Ruler of Dhurahn, but she certainly hoped he would prove to be as easy to work under as Sheikh Sadir. After all, she was already experiencing the problems that came with working alongside someone who was antagonistic towards her.

She gave a faint sigh. From the moment he had arrived four weeks ago, to take the place of one of the original members of the team who'd had to return home for personal reasons, James Reynolds had set out to wrong-foot her. He was two years her junior and newly qualified, and she had initially put his determination to question everything she said and did as a mere youthful desire to make his mark. So she hadn't checked him—more for the sake of his pride than anything else. She had assumed that he would soon realise that here they worked as a team, not as individuals trying to score points off one another, but instead of recognising that he was at fault James had started to become even more vocal in his criticism of her.

Sam really regretted ever having mentioned to James in conversation how interested she was in the origins of the river that flowed into and through Dhurahn. Since she had James had continually made references to it that implied she was spending the time she was paid for checking the status of the borders in trying, as James put it, 'to mess around with the source of a river that we all know is there', and in doing so avoiding doing any 'proper work'. Nothing could have been further from the truth.

'Take no notice of him,' Talia had tried to comfort her before she had injured herself. 'He obviously has issues with you, and that's his problem, not yours.'

'The trouble is that he's *making* it my problem,' Sam had told her. 'I really resent the way he's making such an issue of my interest in the source of the river—as though he thinks I've got some kind of ulterior motive.'

'I should just ignore him, if I were you,' Talia had told her. 'I mean, we've all heard the legend of how the river was first supposed to have been found—and who, in all honesty, wouldn't find it fascinating?'

Sam had nodded her head.

The story was that, centuries earlier, the forebears of Dhurahn's current Ruler, desert nomads, had been caught in a sandstorm and lost their way. After days of wandering in the desert, unable to find water, they had prayed to Allah to save them. When they had finished praying their leader had looked up and seen a bird perched on a rocky outcrop.

'Look,' he had commanded his people. 'Where there is life there must be water. Allah be praised!'

As he had spoken he had brought his fist down on a rock, and miraculously water had spouted from that rock to become a river that watered the whole of Dhurahn—the land he had claimed for his people.

'It's been proved now, of course, that the river runs underground for hundreds of miles before it reaches Dhurahn,' she'd reminded the other girl. 'The legend probably springs from the fact that a fissure of some kind must have allowed a spring to bubble up from underground. And luckily for Dhurahn it happened on their land.'

DAWN! HERE IN the desert it burst upon the senses fully formed, taking you hostage to its miracle, Vere acknowledged, as he brought his four-by-four to a halt so that he could watch it.

Naturally his was the first vehicle in the convoy, since it would be unthinkable for him to travel in anyone's dust. He had, in fact, left the others several miles behind him when he'd turned off the road that led to an oasis where the border-mapping team had set up camp, to drive across the desert itself instead.

As teenagers, both he and Drax had earned their spurs in the testosterone-fuelled young Arab male 'sport' of testing their skill against the treachery of the desert's sand dunes. Like others before them, they had both overturned a handful of times before they had truly mastered the art of dune driving—something which no one could do with the same panache as a desert-dwelling Arab.

These days, with modern GPS navigation systems, the old danger of losing one's bearings and dying from dehydration before one could be found wasn't the danger it had once been, but the desert itself could never be tamed.

The Oasis of the Doves, where the team was encamped, was just inside Dhurahn's own border, at the furthest end of a spear of Dhurahni land, which contained the source of the river that made so much of Dhurahn the lushly rich land that it was.

Their ancestors had fought hard and long to establish and hold on to their right to the source of the river, and many bitter wars had been fought between Dhurahn and its neighbours over such a valuable asset before the Rulers had sat down together and reached a legal and binding agreement on where their borders were to be.

Vere could remember his father telling him with a rueful smile that the family story was that their great-grandfather had in part legally secured the all-important strip of land containing the beginnings of the river that they had claimed by right of legend for so many generations because he had fallen passionately in love with the daughter of the English diplomat who had been sent to oversee the negotiations—and she with him. Lord Alfred Saunders had quite naturally used his diplomatic powers in favour of his own daughter once he had realised that she could not be dissuaded from staying with the wild young Arab with whom she had fallen in love.

It had been at Vere's insistence that the scientific and mapping teams had been housed in the traditional black tents of the Bedou, instead of something more westernised. It might be Drax who was the artist, but Vere's own eye was very demanding, and the thought of seeing anything other than the traditional Bedou tents clustered around an oasis affronted his aesthetic sense of what was due to the desert.

He restarted the four-by-four's engine and eased it easily and confidently down the steep ravine that lay ahead of him. His mother had always loved this oasis, and it was now protected by new laws that had been brought in to ensure that it remained as it was and would never, as some oases had, become an over-developed tourist attraction.

The oasis itself was a deep pool of calm water that reflected the colour of the sky. It was fringed with graceful plants, and the narrow path that skirted it was shaded by palm trees. Migrating birds stopped there to rest and drink, the Bedou nomads drove their herds here, and held their annual trading fairs here. Bedou marriage feasts took place here.

It was a place for the celebration of life, symbolised by the oasis itself—the preserver of life. But for once being here was not soothing Vere.

Instead he felt hauntingly aware of an emptiness inside himself, and the ache that emptiness was causing. How was it possible for him to feel like this when it wasn't what he wanted? He had grown so used to believing that he could control his own emotions that he couldn't accept that somehow his emotional defences had been breached. It shouldn't have been possible, and because of that Vere was determined to believe that it *wasn't* possible.

The pain he had felt on losing his parents had shocked and frightened him—something that he had never admitted to anyone, not even Drax, and something he had tried to bury deep within himself. He had reasoned at the time that it was because his father's death had made him Dhurahn's new ruler—a role that demanded for the sake of his people that he show them that he was their strength, that they could rely on him as they had relied on his father. How could he manifest that strength when alone in his room at night he wept for the loss of his mother? For the sake of Dhurahn and his people he'd forced himself to separate from his love for his mother and the pain of his loss. He had decided there must be a weakness within him that meant he must never, ever allow himself to become emotionally vulnerable through love, for the sake of his duty. He couldn't trust himself to put his duty above his own personal feelings should he fall in love and marry and then for any reason lose the woman he loved.

Those feelings and that decision still held as good for him now as they had done the day he had made them, sitting alone in his mother's private garden, sick with longing for her comfort. His father had worshipped and adored their mother, but Vere knew that, had he survived the accident, he would somehow have continued to be the Ruler of Dhurahn, not a grieving husband, because that was his absolute and predestined duty. The weakness within him, Vere had decided that day, was one he must guard against all his life. And as a young, passionately intense and serious-minded teenager it had seemed to him that the only way he could guarantee to do this would be to lock the gates of his heart against the risks that would come with falling in love. He could not trust himself to have the strength to put duty before love. That was his secret shame, and one he spoke of to no one.

Now, the discovery that, after so many years of believing he had conquered and driven out of himself the emotions and needs he feared, he was aching constantly for a woman he had met fleetingly and only once, was creating inside him an armed phalanx of warrior-like hostile emotions. Chief amongst these was the inner voice that told him that the woman had deliberately set out to arouse him, and that his lust for her was unacceptable and contemptible.

Sᴀᴍ ʜᴀᴅ ᴡᴏᴋᴇɴ up over an hour ago, with the first hint of dawn, and had been unable to get back to sleep. It would have been easy to blame her inability to sleep on the unease that James was causing her. Easy, but untrue, she admitted, as she pulled on the traditional black robe worn by Muslim women, which she had found so very useful as a form of protection against the sun and the sand.

She stepped barefoot out of the tent into the still coolness of the early morning.

Traditionally, all the members of a nomad tribe would have been up and busy at first light, to make the most of the cooler hours of the day before the sun rose too high in the sky for them to bear its heat, but in these days of air-conditioning units there was no need for anyone to rise early, and Sam knew from experience that she would have the early-morning peace of the oasis to herself.

A narrow pathway meandered along the water's edge, the ground flattened out in certain areas where animals came to drink. As Sam walked along the path a cloud of doves rose from the palm trees and then settled back down. A bird, so swift and graceful that all she saw was the flash of its wings, dipped down to the water and then rose up again with a small fish in its beak.

Sam turned a curve in the path and then came to such an abrupt halt that she almost fell over her own feet as she stared in disbelief at the man standing facing her. Her heart soared as easily as the doves on a surge of dizzying delight.

'You,' she breathed, helpless with longing.

CHAPTER THREE

WHAT A STRANGE THING the senses were in the way they could instantly recognise a person and then immediately cause one's body to react to that recognition, Sam thought giddily, as she stared across the space that divided them at the man who was looking back at her.

She had known he was tall, but she had not realised quite how tall. She had known how virile and broad-shouldered and how muscular his body was, but not how strong and corded those muscles would be with the morning sun delineating the power beneath the flesh.

She hesitated, engulfed by the intensity of her own emotional and sexual arousal, and torn between flight from it and submission to it. Nothing remotely like this had ever happened to her before—which, of course, was why she had tried to initially evade and then deny it. Now, though, she was face-to-face—quite literally—with a truth she could not escape, with a knowledge about herself and her emotions, and she had no idea how to cope with it.

How was it possible for her to feel the way she did? How was it possible for her to want him so completely and unreservedly that all she wanted to do was go to him and give herself into his keeping for ever?

It was crazy, reckless....dangerous. And if she had any sense she wouldn't be thinking such things. She looked at his mouth. Sense. What was that? Nothing that mattered. Not like the aching sweetness pouring through her.

'How did you find me?' She was filled with awe and delight, humbled and elated. Reality belonged to another universe, not this magical place she had suddenly stepped into, where a person's most secret dreams could come true.

Perhaps she *was* dreaming? Only in daylight now, instead of during the protective darkness of the night hours. If so, Sam knew that she did not want to wake up again— ever. Why had she wasted all those hours trying uselessly to convince herself that nothing life-transforming had really happened between them? Why had she not had more faith in what she felt? He obviously had, because here he was. He had found her. He had come for her. Joy flooded through her.

VERE FELT AS though he had been turned to stone. No, not stone—because stone could not have felt what he was feeling right now. Stone could not have been pierced by the sharp, immediate and intense male surge of overpowering need to take her, to let his body satisfy the elemental force that was filling his head with images of their bodies together: naked flesh to naked flesh, her head thrown back in ecstasy whilst he moulded her to him, shaping her with his hands, spreading open the softness of her eager thighs, possessing her as she was begging him to do, endlessly and erotically, as she cried out to him over and over again in her pleasure until it became his, until he knew even as fulfilment rushed through him that its satisfaction would never be enough, that like a drug once tasted he would need more, and then still more.

The young boy's fear translated into a grown man's savage anger against what gripped him. He had to get away from her.

SAM COULD HARDLY contain her emotions. They made her tremble like a gazelle scenting the hunter and knowing its fate. In another minute he would reach her and take her in his arms, and then… She started to walk towards him, her pace quickening with the intensity of her need to touch him and be touched by him. A wild thrill of excitement shot through her—only to turn to a sharp stab of shocked disbelief when, just as she had almost reached him, he abruptly turned his back on her and started to walk away.

Pain and confusion swirled through her, leaving her feeling unsteady and insecure, desperate to stop him from leaving her.

'No!'

The denial felt as though it had been torn from her heart, it hurt so much.

Another man had appeared from a side path and was coming between them, bowing low in front of him, to murmur respectfully, 'Highness.'

Highness?

Had she actually whispered her appalled dismay? Was that why he had turned to look at her, that brilliant emerald-green gaze homing in on her, transfixing her to the spot, unable to move, unable to do anything, until it had been removed from her and the two men were walking away from her back down the path.

SAM SEARCHED HER too pale expression in the mirror. If she didn't go and join the others soon, not only would she miss breakfast, she'd almost certainly have someone coming to ask why she wasn't there and if she was all right.

All right? She gave a small shiver. She wasn't sure she would ever be that again.

Had she actually seen him by the oasis, or had she only thought she had? Had he been merely a mirage, conjured

up by her own imagination? And if he had, what did that
tell her about the state she was in?

'SAM—AT LAST. I was just about to come and look for you
in case you'd overslept.'

The anxiety combined with just a hint of reproach in
the voice of Anne Smith, the female half of a pair of married statisticians who were part of the team, caused Sam
to give her an apologetic look.

'Sorry—' she began, but to her relief, before she was
obliged to come up with an explanation as to why she was
so late, Anne continued.

'You've never missed breakfast before, and with Sheikh
Sadir telling us that the Ruler of Dhurahn has arrived, and
that we are all to be formally presented to him, I was getting really worried that you wouldn't make it.'

At least now Sam knew the likely cause of his sudden
reappearance here at the oasis—as well as the reason he
had been in Zuran in the first place. He must be part of
the Ruler of Dhurahn's entourage.

She had been in a total state of shock after seeing him
so unexpectedly and then having him refuse to acknowledge her and walk away from her. It seemed ridiculous
now that she had actually thought that somehow or other
he had known she was there and come in search of her.
Patently it was quite impossible—as she had since told
herself. But at the time her sense of despairing anguish,
coming so quickly on the heels of her earlier euphoria, had
meant that it had been several minutes after he'd disappeared before she'd felt able to move. Even when she had,
her heart had been thudding so heavily and uncomfortably
that she had felt both sick and light-headed by the time she
had reached the privacy of her tent.

Now she wasn't even sure she could trust herself to have

actually seen him—not simply created the whole incident in the way that people lost in the desert and thirsting desperately for water saw mirages of what they so longed for.

The fact that she might be late for breakfast had been the last thing on her mind as she had semi-collapsed into a chair, her body going frantic with its wild message of longing, whilst her head and her heart burned with the pain of despair and humiliation.

Initially she had been glad that the shock of seeing him had left her so weak and shaky. If not for that, she suspected that her body, in its feverish heat of desire that seemed to have turned into a life force outside her own control, would have had her making a complete fool of herself and running after him—or, just as bad, running after a mirage. It was hard to say which would have offered her more humiliation.

Sam had stayed there in the chair for a long time, trying to understand what was happening to her—and, just as importantly, why. She wasn't the sort of person who became taken over either by an emotional or a sexual need so strong that it possessed her and threatened her self-control. How could one kiss be responsible for such a dramatic change in her personality? How could it have her indulging in ridiculous fantasies of love at first sight and soul mates?

Now she felt drained and on edge, exhausted physically and emotionally by what had happened, as weak as though she had been struck down by a powerful virus. Perhaps she had, she thought wildly. Perhaps someone somewhere had found the chemical formula that was responsible for sexual attraction and was trying it out on unsuspecting victims, causing them to suffer hallucinations.

Now she *was* being ridiculous, she warned herself as she followed Anne to the large tent that was used for meetings and general information announcements.

Anne, quite naturally, went to join her husband, who was seated with their colleagues, leaving Sam to find her own seat. Her heart sank when she saw that the only available space was next to James.

He gave her a superior look as she sat down next to him, and Sam realised too late that virtually everyone else in the tent was dressed formally—or at least as formally as the their desert situation would allow. The men were in long chinos and shirts, the women in sleeved tee shirts—some of them had even covered their heads.

They had been told at their original orientation meeting that although the Sheikh of Zuran did not expect them to abide by the Arab rules of dress whilst working in the desert, the other leaders might.

Had something been said to indicate that the Ruler of Dhurahn *did* expect them to dress more formally? Sam wondered in dismay, now acutely conscious of her own sleeveless tee shirt, and her very practical below the knee loose-fit multi-pocketed cargo pants. She had a fold-up wide brimmed canvas hat in one of the pockets, but no headscarf. It was too late now, though, to worry about her appearance. Two men were being ushered onto the slightly raised platform with its traditional Arab divans.

One of them was Sheikh Sadir, and the other...

Sam's heart literally missed a full beat, staggered through a half-beat and then missed another—rather as though she were a boxer who had been knocked off his feet.

It couldn't be, surely? But it *was*; the man accompanying Sheikh Sadir, and who he was treating with such obvious reverence, was none other than the man she had seen earlier—the man with whom she had exchanged that shockingly intimate kiss in the hotel corridor in Zuran. So he wasn't a mirage, then. She didn't know now whether to be glad or sorry about that.

Now, of course, she truly understood the importance of that reverent 'Highness' that had so shocked her earlier.

She felt James nudge her hard in her ribs, and realised that everyone was standing and lowering their heads. Somehow she managed to get to her own feet in time to hear Sheikh Sadir introducing the man as Prince Vereham al a' Karim bin Hakar, the Ruler of Dhurahn.

The Ruler of Dhurahn—Prince Vereham al a' Karim bin Hakar.

Not a mirage. Not a mere *man* at all, but a prince.

Sam recoiled in shock. This couldn't be happening. But of course it was.

Now she knew exactly why he had turned his back on her on the path this morning. Of course he didn't want to acknowledge her. He was the Ruler of an Arab state and she was a nobody—less than a nobody in his estimation, no doubt. What he had taken from her he had taken as carelessly as he might have plucked a fig from a tree, biting into it in his desire to enjoy its sweetness and then discarding it, his enjoyment of it over and forgotten.

The robed serving staff provided by the Ruler of Zuran were coming round in pairs, one carrying a tray of coffee cups, the other a tray of coffee and small sweet pastries.

Up above them on the dais, the Ruler of Dhurahn was also being served with coffee. Sam watched as the sleeve of the gold-embroidered black robe he was wearing over an immaculate crisp white full-length Arab shirt was swept back, to reveal a lean brown hand and a muscular forearm. Beads of sweat pierced her forehead and her upper lip. She felt sick and shaky. It was because she hadn't eaten any breakfast, she tried to reassure herself. But she knew deep down that wasn't the reason at all.

'We'll see a bit more action now that he's here,' James told her, helping himself to several of the small pastries with relish. 'Word has it that he's got his own reasons for being here, and that he's the kind to make sure he gets what he wants.'

Yes, he was very definitely that kind, Sam agreed mentally. And if he had wanted her... Stop that, she warned herself. Whatever foolish fantasies she might have entertained before—and they *had* been foolish—there could be no question of her continuing to entertain them now that she knew who he was.

He was standing up to speak, addressing them in un-accented crisply clear English as he reaffirmed what the cartographers amongst the team had already been told: namely, that the purpose of the exercise in which they were involved was not either to reassess or challenge the validity of already existing borders but to study the effect of the desert itself on those borders.

'Curious that he seems so keen to warn us that we aren't to question the existing borders, don't you think?' James asked Sam *sotto voce*, under cover of eating yet another pastry.

'Not really,' Sam denied. 'After all, we were told right from the start why we are here and all he's doing is reaffirming that.'

She didn't want to have to listen to James, and she certainly didn't want him obstructing her view of the Prince. And yet what was the point in her pathetic and painful desire to watch and listen to him, like an obsessed teenager fantasising about some out-of-reach pop idol?

Sheikh Sadir was now announcing that they were all to be presented to the Ruler of Dhurahn. Obediently everyone was shuffling out of their chairs to form a long line, going up to the dais, being introduced.

'Here—hold this for me a minute, will you?'

Before she could stop him James had thrust the sticky crumb-filled plate from which he had been eating his pastries towards her, before standing up and leaving her holding it.

Sam looked yearningly towards the rear exit to the tent. She was closer to it than she was to the dais. It would be easy enough for her to slip away and avoid the formal introduction. But of course it was impossible for her to do that. Apart from anything else it would be a grave breach of protocol, and indeed almost an insult to the Ruler.

She looked with distaste at the plate she was still clutching and then, feeling a bit guilty, bent down to slip it beneath the nearest chair before filing into the queue behind James.

IT WOULD BE her turn next. So far Sam had managed successfully to avoid looking directly at the new Ruler, but that hadn't stopped her heart thumping as heavily as though someone were wielding it like a sledgehammer, and now her palms were clammy with nervous perspiration. She was uncomfortably conscious of her bare shoulders and her casual attire. Would he think she had chosen to dress like this deliberately, as some kind of statement, or even worse in an attempt to lay claim to some kind of privileged status?

James was bowing his head. Sam heard him laugh, and then to her horror he turned to her and announced cheerfully, 'If you'll take my advice, Prince, you'll keep an eye on my fellow cartographer here. She's already been checking up on the source of your river. The next thing you know she'll probably be challenging your borders as well. Trust a woman to want to meddle, eh?'

Sam could feel herself shaking with a mixture of disbelief and furious outrage at James's wholly unprofessional and untruthful allegations. With a few supposedly casual words he had painted a picture of her for the man who was now in charge of their venture that could only mark her out as a troublemaker, determined to ignore the guidelines they had been given from the start—guidelines which the man now staring very hard and very coldly at her had only just repeated.

The words *That's not true* hovered on her tongue, only to be choked back. Any kind of protest or argument from her now would only make her position worse.

Ignoring James, she made a determinedly low obeisance to the Prince and said quietly, 'Highness, I am aware, of course, of the purpose of our being here, and I thank you and the other Rulers for granting us the opportunity to work here. It is a unique opportunity and a privilege to be permitted to learn something of the mystery of the desert.'

Without waiting to see what kind of reaction her words were receiving Sam backed away, waiting until her place in front of the Ruler of Dhurahn had been taken by someone else before straightening up ready to turn round. But before she did so she couldn't prevent her gaze from seeking his. She wanted to look at him as the woman she had been in the hotel corridor, and him to be the man who had looked back at her with such fierce, sensual hunger.

He was not that man now, though. Now he was an Arab prince. The Ruler of an Arab State—a man, his dismissive gaze was telling her, as far removed from her as it was possible for him to be. His cold refusal to engage visually with her, never mind acknowledge or recognise her, confirmed everything that Sam had already guessed. He didn't want to know. The look he had given her earlier on the path confirmed that he had recognised her as immediately as she had done him, but now he was letting

her know that he was the Ruler of Dhurahn and she was a
European woman he wanted to pretend he had never met.

It was an indication of just how foolish she was that
she actually felt achingly saddened to discover he was
the kind of prince who was ready to enjoy the sexual ad-
vantages of his power and position in private, but at the
same time determined to deny that he had availed himself
of them in public.

All these weeks while she had been dreaming her stupid dreams, suffering her tormented longings, no doubt he
had exorcised any desire she might have aroused in him
speedily and effectively with someone else. Or maybe with
several some one elses. No doubt to a man like him one
woman was much the same as another—a piece of flesh
to be used and then discarded.

IT WAS RELIEF that was burning that ice-cold fury into him,
Vere told himself. Relief because now he had good reason—had he needed it, which he didn't—to treat her with
disdain and suspicion, to make sure that he did not give
in to his unwanted physical desire for her. And it was only
physical, he assured himself.

EVERYONE HAD LEFT the tent now, and Sam looked round
for James. She might not have been able to say anything
in front of their visitor, but she certainly intended to tackle
James about the comments he had made—and sooner
rather than later.

Once she could see him she made her way determinedly
towards him, ignoring his cheerful, 'So, what do you think
of our new boss, then?'

'Why did you try to give the Prince the impression that
I've been questioning the legality of his country's rights

to the river, when we both know that I haven't done any such thing?' she demanded coolly.

'Oh, come on. It was just a bit of banter that's all.' He shrugged and shook his head. 'What is it with you women that makes you take everything so ruddy seriously and go all hormonal and emotional?'

His jibe about her being emotional found its mark, but she wasn't going to let let him see that.

'You've got equality now, you know,' he continued tauntingly. 'And that means—'

'I know exactly what equality means, James.' Sam stopped him, firmly taking charge of the conversation and fully intending to repeat her earlier demand that he explain his reasons for his comments to Prince Vereham. But before she could do so he had turned away from her to hail one of the other men.

A call for fellow male support? Sam wondered wryly, and her own inbuilt awareness of the bigger picture urged her to refrain from forcing a confrontation that could only lead to ill feeling. She had, after all, made her point and let him know that she was both aware of what he had done and annoyed about it. Involving herself in a battle of words that might descend into childish verbal gender taunts wouldn't do anything to enhance the professionalism on which she prided herself.

The triumphant smirk James was giving her still irked her, though. He plainly thought he had got away with something—and if she was honest so did she.

But she wasn't here to indulge in petty squabbles with a colleague who seemed to have unresolved issues with working alongside women on an equal footing—and she was certainly not here to moon around thinking about a man who had unequivocally proved that he neither wanted anything to do with her nor would have been worthy of her if he had been.

With her back ramrod-stiff with determination and pride, Sam made her way back to her tent.

Knowing that today was the day when control of the venture was handed from Zuran to Dhurahn, she had deliberately planned not to go out in the field but instead to work on her computer, so that she could compare the information she had gathered on the ground with that picked up by the GPS systems overlooking the area. Only then would she be in a position to start preparing a comparison between what the landscape showed now and what had been recorded over fifty years ago.

The three Rulers had thought of everything that might be needed in a practical sense to make the venture a success, providing everyone with power and internet access for their computers, so that within minutes of entering her tent Sam should have been accessing the GPS information she needed.

Instead, though, she was typing into an internet search engine the name of the Ruler of Dhurahn...

CHAPTER FOUR

THE FORMALITIES WERE OVER, and Sheikh Sadir and his entourage had taken their formal leave of him and begun their return journey to Zuran.

His own people were busy familiarising themselves with the site, and Vere had beside him the very latest print-outs of the reports on various initiatives being undertaken by those working on the joint venture.

By rights he should be studying those reports. One of them, after all, could have grave repercussions for him and for his country. Instead he had been studying a plan of the camp and a list of those living in it.

Vere frowned and stood up, walked over to the exit of his personal quarters and pulled back the opening, causing the guard standing outside to jump to attention.

His own tent was set apart from the others, shielded from view by palm trees and close to the oasis, as befitted his status, with the tents of his private entourage surrounding it.

Beyond them were the tents of the team working on the project, arranged in a neat pattern, with wide walkways between them and those tents that housed the communal areas set in the centre. By Vere's reckoning, from the plan he had been studying, the tent housing Ms Sam McLellan was several rows away from his own but, like his, backed onto the oasis.

The last thing he had been prepared for when he had arrived here had been that he would see her. He had recognised her instantly, of course, and he could still feel the shock of that recognition deep down within his own flesh. As always, when he was reminded against his will of his reaction to the kiss they had shared, Vere was filled with a furious need to deny that it had had any kind of long-lasting effect on him at all. It was unthinkable that he, who abhorred the modern relaxed attitude towards casual throwaway sex, should have been involved in such a situation in the first place, and it was his weakness in allowing that to happen on which he needed to focus—not the irrelevant fact that, try as he might, he could not force his body to give up its physical memory of her.

Even harder to admit was the emotional impact the event had had on him, unleashing all the inner insecurity that the loss of his mother had brought him. *No!* Vere could feel the angry denial exploding inside himself. He felt as though he had been plunged into a war within himself and against himself.

He had something far more important to think about than his unwanted desire for Sam McLellan.

Drax had telephoned to tell him that he had received information that suggested that the Emir of Khulua intended to try and win a bargaining tool for himself in future negotiations between their two countries, by paying a member of the team assessing the changes within the desert boundaries to suggest that Dhurahn had laid claim to lands to which in reality it had no legal rights.

Of course, as Drax had said and Vere knew, the Emir had no intention of going so far as to try to make a claim on such lands. He was a very astute man, after all, and he knew that it would be impossible for him to make such a claim stick. However, what he could do was use the laws of Arab protocol and interaction, to put pressure on Dhurahn to make favourable concessions in his favour, as public recompense for and acknowledgement of 'past dues owed', which would tie them up in protracted useless negotiations for years to come. It was the kind of subtle game of politics and power that men like the Emir loved.

Vere knew that the Ruler of Zuran would not think too kindly of either of them if he were to be drawn into such a quarrel—especially if it affected the ongoing development of Zuran as a tourist destination. The situation that might develop would be one that would demand a considerable amount of time and subtle negotiation. However, with Dhurahn's bid to host the Arab world's first independent financial sector and stock market now accepted, but still in its all-important first year and being monitored closely, Vere knew they could not afford either the time to become engaged in delicate convoluted negotiations with the Emir, nor the fall-out effect on their reputation if an outright argument were forced on them by him should they refuse to bargain.

It seemed perfectly obvious to Vere that the person in the Emir's pay had to be Samantha McLellan. She, after all, was a cartographer, and responsible for mapping any changes in the shared boundaries. She had also, according to her colleague, already been spreading rumours about the validity of those boundaries—even if she herself had denied it.

It was surely a logical step from knowing that to working out that the supposed accidental meeting between them in Zuran, when she had bumped into him, had been no accident at all and instead had been deliberately contrived.

No doubt she had hoped to tempt him into a sexual liaison with her that would have allowed her to cloud the issue of the borders even more with planned lies. Perhaps claiming that Vere had admitted to her that there were irregularities with them.

It wouldn't matter that it was untrue. The Emir would still be able to use it in his Machiavellian plan to cause discord and discredit. Honour and good faith were vitally important in the Middle East, and once lost they were impossible to recover.

Had she really thought that he would be so easily taken in? That he would be deceived on the strength of one passionately sensual kiss and the feel of her body against his, combined with a look that suggested she had found her world in him?

How many other men had she practised that look on? Pain shot through him, splintering into shards of unexpected agony which he forced himself to bear as punishment for having dropped his guard long enough to have registered her lying eyes.

He was, though, completely safe from any kind of vulnerability towards her, knowing what he did. It was totally impossible and completely beneath him for him to desire her now. Her duplicity was his salvation. His salvation? His pride reacted as though it had been spurred. He had no need to seek salvation from the likes of Sam McLellan, a woman whose morals and whose flesh were up for sale. Again anger burned fiercely inside him because she had dared to think he might be gullible enough to be taken in by her and her risible attempt to foster a sexual intimacy between them that she could use to manipulate him.

She must have been furious when her colleague had betrayed her with his comment about her views on the true legality of Dhurahn's borders. Vere had no doubt that she must have been acting on the Emir's orders, trying none too subtly to lay the foundations for some kind of spurious claim about their border based on some farcical trumpedup evidence.

However, much as he longed to confront her with what he knew, Vere realised he could not do so. The first thing she would do would be to tell the Emir, and he and Drax were both agreed that their best course of action at the moment was to gather together as much evidence of the Emir's plans as they could and then confront him privately, having first laid the whole thing before the Ruler of Zuran. That way they could avoid humiliating the Emir in public, whilst making it plain that they had seen through his machinations.

Vere had no doubt that in such circumstances the Emir would be forced to back down—if only so that he could save his own face.

Meanwhile Vere knew that his duty to his country meant that he must do all he could to find out exactly what Samantha McLellan was doing. Once he had, he would need to get her to admit that she was being paid by the Emir to corrupt the details of her research in order to throw doubt on Dhurahn's original borders.

And there was only one realistic way in which he could do that, Vere thought cynically.

A woman like her, who had been bribed by one man, could be bribed by another to betray him. So, much as the thought revolted him, he would have to let her think that he was not averse to being propositioned by her, Vere decidedly grimly. He would have to act as though he wanted her—as if he was completely taken in by her.

SAM PUSHED THE hair off her face and rubbed her eyes sleepily, before giving a shame-faced look at the screen in front of her. Had anyone told her four months ago that she would be doing something like this—scanning the internet and trying to pry into the private life of a man who had already made it clear that he wanted nothing whatsoever to do with her, a man who was a world away from the kind of man with whom she could realistically expect to share her life—she would have been appalled and defensive, instantly rejecting the very idea. She would have said, and genuinely believed, that she was far too well grounded, far too modern and way too practical to waste time doing something so pointless. Anyone who spent hours on the internet, pathetically prying into the life of a stranger, was surely to be pitied and told to get a life of their own.

What was it she was hoping to find out? She already knew exactly how he felt about her—or rather how he didn't. Trawling the internet wasn't going to alter that, given that he had made it so plain that he wanted nothing to do with her, was it?

Wasn't this the kind of thing that could lead to unhealthy and obsessive behaviour?

What did it matter what information about him the internet might hold? She had no intimate role to play in his life, nor he in hers.

Everything she was telling herself was quite true, Sam acknowledged, but she still couldn't quite bring herself not to give in to the temptation of looking. That was the trouble, wasn't it? she admitted to herself guiltily. Where he was concerned temptation seemed to be something she was incapable of resisting.

She had found any number of sites describing the history of the State of Dhurahn, but none of them contained any personal information about its current ruler.

She had also visited a site that gave a lavish description of Dhurahn's plans to create an independent Middle Eastern business and financial centre of excellence on land set aside for that purpose, complete with visuals of the office blocks and buildings. She had found, too, eloquent descriptions of the traditions of the country, preserved now and incorporated into national celebrations. There was even a piece about the current project, showing the original borders agreed when all three States had first been created.

But about Prince Vereham al a' Karim bin Hakar there was nothing—not even a photograph. Merely a clipped line in one of the free online encyclopaedias giving his date of birth, the names of his parents and grandparents, and the fact that the Rulers of Dhurahn had a tradition of choosing European women for their wives.

Sam's heart gave a small flurry of over-excited thuds as she re-read this information. *European* wives… Now she was being a fool.

Angry with herself for her silliness, she closed down the site and then opened up a new search for Khulua. Anne had mentioned that the state and its ancient ruins were well worth a visit. She had some leave days due in another month, and taking a short break away from the camp might do her good and bring her to her senses, Sam decided determinedly, as she checked out and then booked flights and a hotel for Khulua for a month ahead.

That done, Sam went to bring up the satellite map of the area which she used to work on.

As always when she studied this map, she was drawn to the area around the source of Dhurahn's river. She highlighted and magnified the river's source, fascinated all over again by her conviction that at some stage and for some reason the course of the river, not far from its source, had been changed. There might have been any number of reasons for this—none of them having any bearing on the state's border with Khulua—but Sam's natural curiosity burned to know exactly what that reason had been.

Logically there was no reason why the original course of the Dhurahni river should have been changed, which made her certainty that it had all the more mystifying.

The fact that Sam was engrossed in what she was doing, and had her back to the entrance to the tent, gave Vere the opportunity to stand and watch her unobserved before he started towards her.

As he began to walk in her direction, he knew he had certainly not made any sound that would have alerted her to his presence—and yet, as though he had commanded her to do so, within a heartbeat of him entering the tent she suddenly tensed and then swung round, saying, as she had done that morning when she had seen him by the oasis, '*You!* I mean… Your Highness,' Sam corrected herself quickly, half stumbling over the words as her brain struggled to come to grips with the fact that she had known he was there without hearing him or seeing him.

Her heart was thudding into her ribs so heavily that it almost hurt, and it was certainly making her feel weak and light-headed—or maybe that was caused by the fact that suddenly there didn't seem to be enough air in the tent for her to breathe properly, and what air there was had turned warmer, somehow, pressing against her and bringing with it unwanted memories of their first meeting.

Sam prayed that he wouldn't come any closer. She was already acutely aware of the sound of his breathing and the scent of his body. In trying to avoid looking into his eyes she had instead focused straight ahead. Now, though, she recognised that this was a mistake—because her eyes had impacted on his hands, strong and sinewy, with long fingers, hands that could easily support the weight of a hunting falcon, or secure the trembling body of a yearning woman. She was starting to tremble, sweat beading her forehead as unwanted images crashed through her de-

fences. She didn't think she could bear this. She really
didn't. But she must—or else risk giving him the opportunity to snub her again the way he had done earlier.

'I wanted to talk with you about this claim made by
your colleague that you are questioning the authenticity
of Dhurahn's borders,' Vere announced coldly, without
preamble.

His heart was thudding like blows on an anvil delivered
with a heavy hand. It was anger that was responsible for
the way he was feeling. Nothing else. There could not be
any other reason. Gifted as he was with the keen eyesight
that belonged to men of the desert, from where he had been
standing he had seen her booking a flight to Khulua, thus
confirming everything he had suspected.

Sam, though, was oblivious to what was going through
Vere's mind. All she could focus on was her own misery
and the situation she was in. She had feared, of course, that
as Dhurahn's Ruler he *would* challenge her about James's
comment, but she had assumed that it would be in a more
formal setting. She had thought that he would send for her,
perhaps, and demand that she explain herself—rather than
seek her out on his own, and in the privacy of her own
quarters, where she was far too aware of him as a man to
be able to concentrate on his status.

He was wearing that same fresh cologne he had been
wearing before and it was distracting her, painting images
into her thoughts that had no right to be there, and which
were certainly not appropriate for their current meeting.
She struggled to dismiss them and failed. She knew that if
she let her concentration slip even for a second she would
be remembering how it felt to be in his arms. And longing to be there again, despite what she knew? No, she denied immediately. But she knew she was lying to herself.

'I have never questioned Dhurahn's borders,' she told him truthfully.

'No? That was not the opinion of your colleague.'

She could see a glint of angry contempt in the gaze he was fixing on her. It drove her to defend herself.

'I have never questioned Dhurahn's borders, either publicly or privately.' she repeated, determinedly and fiercely.

His anger wasn't abating, and to her chagrin she heard herself continuing so weakly that she might just as well have been pleading with him for understanding.

'I don't think James realised how serious… That is to say, I think he was just making conversation…There is no valid reason why he should have said what he did.'

That wasn't the truth, was it? she challenged herself inwardly—and guiltily. Although it upset her to think it, she suspected that James had wanted to get her into trouble, and had said what he had deliberately, because of his own personal and unadmitted agenda.

She could see, though, that this man would never believe she was merely an innocent victim, and that he wasn't prepared to give her the benefit of the doubt. Not when she was pretty sure that he was already blaming her for another incident.

And did *she* think she was blameless there as well? Had she done everything she possibly could to avoid the intimacy they had shared? Had it all been down to him and him alone? Sam could feel her conscience prodding her. No, she didn't think that. Not after the way she had felt and behaved. But equally, if she wasn't blameless, then neither was all the blame hers either, was it? No matter how Prince Vereham al a' Karim bin Hakar was choosing to act now.

'James misunderstood what I was trying to say,' she added, for further emphasis of her point—even though she already knew that he wasn't really interested in giving her the opportunity to defend herself.

She could see that he was looking past her towards her computer, his frown deepening. For a moment, to her horror, she thought she might inadvertently have brought up one of the searches she had been doing on him, but when she glanced at the screen she was relieved to see that all it contained was her map of the source of the river.

He strode past her to focus on the screen.

'This is the source of the Dhurahni river.'

It was a statement more than a question.

'Yes,' Sam agreed.

'Why are you studying it? It flows quite plainly through Dhurahn, and only Dhurahn, and is therefore outside your remit for exploration and examination.' His voice was clipped, his manner hostile.

'Yes, I know,' Sam was forced to admit.

'So explain to me what this is all about.'

He wasn't just hostile, he was furious as well, Sam recognised miserably. But her tormentor hadn't finished.

'Why exactly do you feel it necessary to question the Dhurahni River's source?' he continued angrily. 'What are you hoping to prove, or gain. And why? What is the agenda behind this underhanded delving into something which has nothing whatsoever to do with you?'

Sam stared at him in horrified dismay.

'No—please, you don't understand,' she protested 'It isn't like that. It was just that…that I couldn't resist…' She could feel her face starting to burn as she realised the danger she was getting herself into. 'There's something about underground rivers that is so fascinating—especially those that travel so far—and I…'

Vere looked at her.

'It seems to me that you have a penchant for not resisting your own desires, Ms McLellan. Regardless of whether or not in doing so you are transgressing set boundaries.'

His words weren't just meant to refer to the river, Sam knew, and her face burned even more uncomfortably.

'There's no law that says that a person can't take an interest in natural phenomena,' she told him, somehow managing to find the gritty courage to reply in his own subtle double-speak. There—let him make what he wanted of that! 'Especially when I'm only doing it in my own time.'

Vere's mouth hardened, but he didn't say anything. It had been a mistake to let his emotions get the better of him. He had put her on her guard now, and it was unlikely that he was going to get her to admit that she was being paid to cause trouble for Dhurahn.

'I don't see why I shouldn't be interested in the river,' Sam continued determinedly. 'It's a vitally important resource for the area, after all, and I admit that I am curious about the fact that at some stage the course of the river appears to have been changed.'

'As you've just acknowledged, you are perfectly well aware that the river, and whatever may have happened to it, lies within Dhurahn's borders, and is therefore outside your mapping remit,' Vere told her coldly.

'Yes...' Sam was forced to admit.

'You are a professional cartographer. Don't think I would be the only person to question this excuse of "curiosity" you have given me.'

He was surely far more angry than the situation merited. He was so angry, in fact, that she could almost feel his fury raising the temperature inside the tent, and Sam had no illusions about the extent of the trouble she was in. He had spoken of her having an agenda, but Sam believed that any agenda belonged to *him* and related to what had happened between them. Was he looking for an excuse to have her dismissed? Removed from the camp and thus his vicinity?

'It is just curiosity. It is interesting, and—' she began to insist, only to have him cut her off with his savage voice.

'Interesting? To study and question something you have not been asked to involve yourself in—and I suspect using equipment and time that should have been used for something else? Interesting to whom, I wonder?'

He was losing it, Vere recognised. Going in a reckless headlong charge too far down a road that was strewn with potential hazards. But somehow he hadn't been able to stop himself. And he knew why. Despite the fact that he both wanted and needed to believe that this woman was someone he could not trust, against all the odds—against everything he had trained himself to think and be—something deep within him wanted to believe otherwise.

It was something he must root out and destroy.

Sam could feel the shock of his antagonism ricocheting through her. Despite the fact that he was wearing traditional Arab dress, any resemblance to some romantic image of a desert prince her imagination might once have conjured up collapsed like the fiction it was. Now that she was confronted with the reality, she could see a very twenty-first century, hard-edged and angry dominant male, ready to do battle for what he considered to be his. She suspected that if she didn't do something, and soon, she was going to find herself out of a job.

'I'm sorry if…if I've caused offence, or…or broken any rules.' She forced herself to apologise, inwardly hating having to be so submissive. But she didn't want to damage her career, and she wasn't going to let him penalise her just because he regretted what had happened in Zuran.

Did he think she didn't regret it even more? Did the sharp look he was giving her mean that he was aware that her apology might relate to more than her transgression over the possible diversion of the river?

'Where exactly is this supposed alteration of the course of the river? Show me,' Vere commanded, without making any response to her apology. He knew that he ought to be focusing on the plan he had made to win her over, instead of allowing his own revulsion at the thought that he might have revealed some vulnerability to her to drive his reactions.

He was standing far too close to her, Sam thought shakily, as she glanced at one of his hands on the back of her chair, and then at the palm of the other, flat on the small desk next to her computer.

She wasn't obliged to do as he was demanding. She could ask him to leave. He was, after all, in her private quarters, and she wasn't sure just how long her self-control could endure this sort of pressure.

As he himself had just pointed out, the information she had gathered was outside her working remit, and therefore she was under no obligation to share it with anyone. However, common sense told her that it would be extremely foolhardy of her to say as much. So, instead, she reached for her mouse and highlighted the area she had been examining, trying not to let her hand shake as she did so.

It was disconcerting having him stand half behind her and so close to her. More than disconcerting. She could feel the warmth of his breath against her skin as he leaned forward to take a closer look at the screen. It sent a frisson of unwanted sensual pleasure shivering over her skin, making her tense herself against its effect. She was aware, too, of the heat of his body and its maleness. And of the effect that maleness had already had on her. *Was* she aware of that, and the risk that came with it of humiliating herself a second time?

Sam was certainly conscious of the sharpness of the inner warning voice that was asking her that question, but at the same time another voice was whispering to her far more seductively that if she leaned back now her head would be resting against his shoulder, and then if he placed his hand on *her* shoulder he could turn her towards him...

Abruptly, something that was both a physical ache of longing and emotional anger against it jerked though her body and tightened. It was impossible for her to allow herself to feel and think like this. What had happened to her normal level headed common sense and dignity? It had been bad enough when she had been daydreaming about him, believing that he had shared her desire, but now she knew the truth her pride alone should be sufficient to stamp out any lingering feelings of physical longing she might have.

'It's here that I first noticed something,' she told him, somehow managing to sound far more in control and professional than she felt as she indicated the darker markings that showed where the channel was. But did her voice sound as thin with tension to him as it did to her? Had he noticed that her arm was stiff from the effort it took her to keep it out of contact with him whilst she moved the mouse?

Vere could have sworn that he was only looking at the screen, but somehow he could also see the soft fullness of her mouth, and the way her lips parted as she drew in that small shallow breath. Her breasts lifted. Soft, naturally curved breasts that made a man ache to cup his hands around them.

Furious with himself for the direction his thoughts were taking, Vere took refuge in attack.

'Do you seriously expect me to believe that a few scratches on a map are serious evidence of someone having tampered with the course of a river as fast-flowing as the Dhurahni?' he derided.

'These are GPS images,' Sam reminded him, stung by his criticism. 'Naturally they aren't easy to read, especially to the untrained eye.'

She was rewarded with a swift annihilating glance.

'I assure you that I am more than familiar enough with satellite images to be able to translate what these mean,' he said coldly.

'Then you will understand that the extent of the channel is much more defined when seen on the ground,' Sam retorted firmly, determined to show him that she was not going to be bullied out of her professional opinion.

'I am familiar with the source of the river, and I cannot say that I have ever noticed.' Now his tone was coldly dismissive.

It was plain that he did not like what she was saying, Sam recognised.

'Then perhaps you weren't looking in the right place.'

Or maybe he hadn't wanted to notice? Sam thought inwardly, wondering at the same time why this might be. After all, as he had said, both channels lay within the boundaries of Dhurahn, and it could not be disputed that the river ran exclusively through Dhurahn's land. But in some ways that made the fact that she was sure it had been altered all the more fascinating—at least to her.

She could feel the faint draught as he released the back of her chair before striding past her, turning round abruptly to face her, and then saying sharply, 'Maybe not.'

He was, Sam noticed, looking at his watch. She started to exhale unevenly in relief, assuming that he was about to leave, but instead to her dismay he informed her, 'After the evening meal tonight we shall drive out to the source of the river. It is a three-hour drive, and we shall camp there overnight. In the morning you can show me this supposed channel, and then we can return before the heat of the day.'

'No…' Sam croaked, panic gripping her. Her reaction was an immediate and instinctive grab for self-protection. *'What?'*

It was plain from both his expression and the disbelief in his voice that he wasn't used to having his orders questioned, Sam recognised, and now he was coming towards her.

Her panic increased, but shamefully now it was joined by another emotion—and this one was telling her that what she really wanted was for him to come even closer.

'No,' she repeated, denying her own emotions as much as his demand, as unwanted need threatened to swamp her protective panic. 'Don't come any closer…don't…. don't touch me.'

Wasn't what she really meant, *do* touch me—oh, please, please *do* touch me, and keep on touching me for ever…?

He had come to an abrupt halt several feet away from her and was looking at her as though she were an insect that had crawled out from beneath a stone, Sam thought. As though she were something unclean.

'Don't touch you?' he repeated, as though he could hardly believe she had spoken those words to him. 'Do you dare to believe that I would wish to?'

Torn between angry pride and stinging humiliation, Sam longed to have the kind of thick skin that would have enabled her to point out to him that there had been an occasion when he had done rather a lot more than merely touch her. But her own feelings of shamed guilt about the part she had played in that incident held her back, so instead she stayed silent. She wished she had not done so when he continued coldly, 'Well let me assure you that you need have no fear on that account. And before you humiliate yourself by referring to a certain incident that does neither of us any credit, let me tell you that it is certainly something I intend to forget. I would advise you to do the same.'

'There's no need to advise me to do anything. I had already forgotten it, Your Highness,' Sam lied through gritted teeth in fierce retaliation.

Her vehemence caught Vere off guard. He wasn't used to being challenged in any way or by anyone—except occasionally Drax. The fact that she had done so, and with such furious passion, was an unfamiliar enough experience for him without the additional unwanted knowledge that it underlined the fact that this woman seemed to have the knack of reacting in a way that he just wasn't prepared for. Even worse, she provoked him into behaving in a way that was totally out of character for him.

He had come in here with one purpose in mind, and that had been to get her off her guard enough for him to find a way to circumvent whatever it was the Emir was planning to do. Instead she had somehow or other forced him into a role that was a total surprise to him—and not a pleasant one either.

Vere did not like those kind of surprises. He liked to feel that he had the ability to read both situations and people well enough to be one step ahead of them, and thus prepared for what might happen. Sam's stubborn refusal to fit into the mould he had cast for her was infuriating.

She was lying about having forgotten their first meeting, of course. It was ridiculously obvious in everything she said and did, in every look she gave him, that she remembered it very well. He had a good mind to make her admit that to him—as well as admit why it had happened. Did she think he was a complete fool? Vere raged inwardly, his anger growing. Or did she think that by her pretence she could whet his appetite for more of the same?

Had she been lying in wait for him on that corridor? Had she believed that he would fall for that kind of ploy? Did she really think he was so emotionally vulnerable that he would be taken in by her and want her? Did she think that he was the kind of man who was so lacking in principles and pride that he would want what she had been so ready to offer?

Well, if so, she was certainly going to learn now how wrong she was and how totally immune he was to her, he decided furiously, and he strode past her and out of the tent. He ignored the inner voice trying to reason with him and remind him that he was supposed to be winning her confidence and getting under her guard.

CHAPTER FIVE

'SAM. THERE YOU ARE—could I have a word?'

Sam jumped guiltily. She had been so engrossed in her own thoughts—thoughts which revolved totally around having a certain person on his knees, begging her forgiveness for misjudging her—that she hadn't even heard Anne coming towards her until the other woman had spoken to her.

'Yes. Of course...'

'It's about James,' Anne confided, drawing her to one side as other members of the team walked past them on their way to the communal dining area for their evening meal.

'Ted thinks that he's been bringing alcohol into the camp and drinking it. He says he could smell it on James's breath the other morning, and he thinks he saw him drinking from a hip flask when they were out in the field, although of course he can't prove it.'

Sam could hear the dismay in Anne's voice.

'Oh, surely not,' she protested. 'We all know now that having alcohol here even for our own consumption is strictly forbidden. That was made plain to all of us when we were interviewed. James is very ambitious, and I can't see him doing anything that would damage his career.'

'Well, one would certainly like to think not—which is

why Ted is so concerned about him. Ted and I have spent a lot of time working in the Middle East, and I'm afraid that we have seen colleagues before develop a drink problem whilst they're out here, away from home. He's worried that James could be heading in that direction.'

'Just because Ted saw him drinking alcohol that doesn't mean he has a drink problem,' Sam felt bound to point out—although just why she should be defending James after the trouble he had got her into she had no idea.

'Of course not. But as I said Ted says there have been a couple of occasions on which he's been pretty sure he could smell drink on James's breath. He has tried to talk to him about it, but James brushed him off. In fact he was quite rude. I don't know if you've noticed, but sometimes his behaviour seems to be quite irrational. Neither of us likes telling tales out of school, but since you're working with him we agreed that we should have a word with you.'

'I'm glad you have,' Sam admitted. 'Not that there's anything I can do if he is drinking. I'm the last person he'd be likely to listen to.'

'Well, yes, but to be honest it was you we were thinking about rather than him. He does rather have a down on you. It was remarkably tactless of him to make the comment he did to the the Prince.'

'Yes,' Sam agreed ruefully. 'It was—especially as it wasn't even true.'

What she wasn't going to say to Anne was that she was beginning to wonder if James had been going through her work behind her back and had come across the satellite images of the river. From now on she intended to be far more careful about the access he had to her papers and her computer. Little as she liked to think he was looking for a means of getting her into trouble, she suspected that was exactly what he *was* doing—although she had no real idea why. If he did indeed have a drink problem then she genuinely felt very sorry for him. But she also knew that it was professional help he needed, not her sympathy.

'Come on—we'd better go and get some dinner. Have you heard yet when Talia is likely to be back?' Anne asked.

Sam shook her head. 'It's going to be several weeks, but more than that I don't know.'

The Smiths were a kind and thoughtful couple, and she appreciated the fact that, knowing she was now without a female companion, Anne had asked her to join them to eat. Not that she felt hungry. Not when she knew that after their evening meal she was going to have to give in to the demands of Prince Vereham al a' Karim bin Hakar and show him what she had discovered.

'I must say that I've never been on any field trip where we've been fed so well.' Anne laughed. 'I think I've actually put on weight.'

'The food *is* excellent,' Sam agreed.

Zuran was a world-renowned luxury holiday destination, and the Ruler of Zuran had provided them with the services of a gifted young chef. Fresh food was brought out for them every day, along with water, and Sam could well understand why Anne felt she'd gained a few pounds.

'I treated myself to a copy of the new Jane Austen DVD whilst we were in Zuran, but it's not Ted's cup of tea—so if you'd like to watch it with me after dinner…?' she offered.

'I'd love to,' Sam said truthfully. 'But I'm afraid I can't.' Trying not to sound as self-conscious as she felt, she told Anne, 'Prince Vereham al a' Karim bin Hakar has ordered me to accompany him on a field trip, and he wants to set off after dinner.'

If Anne was surprised, to Sam's relief she managed to keep it to herself, saying easily, 'Well never mind. Perhaps another time.'

There was no sign of James in the large air-conditioned tented 'dining room', nor any sign of the Ruler of Dhurahn either—but then it wasn't unusual for the high-ranking Arabs monitoring their work to eat separately from them. And of course Sam was relieved and delighted that he wasn't there. The last thing she wanted was to look up from her food to find that merciless cold green gaze focused on her.

'FINISHED ALREADY?' ANNE asked in surprise, when Sam touched her on the arm a little later, and explained that she was leaving.

'I've got to put a few things together. Somehow I don't think it would be a good idea to keep the Prince and his entourage waiting.'

'No,' Anne agreed. 'I don't think it would. I must say he is an outstandingly autocratically handsome man—very compelling, if somewhat austere, plus he has such presence. Jane Austen, I think, would have had a field-day with such a role model for a hero. You'd never think to look at him that Dhurahn is the most forward-thinking and democratically run Gulf State of them all, but Ted says that it is.'

Forward-thinking and democratic? No, she would certainly never have thought of describing the Ruler of Dhurahn as either of those things, Sam acknowledged grimly as she made her way back to her quarters to collect her laptop and everything else she felt she might need for her upcoming trip. Her *trip*? Didn't she mean her ordeal? Sam asked herself wryly.

VERE LOOKED AT his watch. His men should have loaded up the four-by-four with everything they would need by now. He had spoken to Drax and explained to his twin what he

had discovered, and Drax had promised to find out what
he could about Ms Samantha McLellan.

It was only after he had ended the call that Vere realised
he had said nothing to Drax about his own original meeting with 'Sam', as her colleagues appeared to call her. But
then why should he? What possible relevance to what was
happening now could that have? None whatsoever—other
than to underline for him the type of woman she was and
keep him on his guard against her.

A fresh surge of outrage and pride-fuelled fury burst
through him as he recalled how earlier in her tent she had
tried to pretend that she thought he had been going to
touch her. Did she really think she had the power to drive
him into such a state of arousal and need that he would
do such a thing. A man in his position? He could almost
hear his twin's soft laughter at his indignation. A small
rueful smile curled his mouth. Drax had always had the
knack of softening the burden imposed on him by his position. But the reality was that he was not just a man, he
was Dhurahn's ruler, and he had a duty to set his people
the right kind of example. He couldn't, for example, imagine his father, who had been so strong and so noble, indulging in the kind of behaviour *he* had descended to. But
then his father had had his mother, and the love they had
shared had been plain for everyone to see.

Love. He must never fall in love. Imagine, for instance,
if those hot, sharp pangs he had felt when he had held Ms
Samantha McLellan in his arms had not been lust but love?
How would he be feeling right now?

What? What was this? What on earth was he doing,
coupling Samantha McLellan and the word love together
in the same sentence?

'Everything is ready, Highness.'

Vere acknowledged the soft words of the man who had just salaamed his way into his tent with a brief nod of his head.

SAM HAD JUST finished packing a change of clothes into her backpack when the flap entrance to her tent was flung back to admit the Prince.

His curt, 'You are ready?' caused her to respond to him with an equally curt inclination of her head.

'Very well, then.'

He turned to leave, plainly expecting her to follow him, so Sam picked up her things and hurried after him. Irritatingly, the narrowness of the path and the bulk of what she was carrying made it impossible for her to do anything other than walk behind him, for all the world as though she was acknowledging his sexual superiority to her and following tamely. That was something she would certainly *never* do, she fumed, so engrossed in her own anger that she only just managed to stop herself from cannoning into him when he stopped alongside a large four-by-four. Bumping into him a second time was the last thing she needed to do right now——especially after his previous accusation.

Obviously he would be the one travelling in this enormous monster of a gas-guzzler, Sam decided, and searched round for the rest of the vehicles, looking confused when she couldn't see any.

'Something is wrong?' he was asking her impatiently.

Yes, just about everything, Sam thought ruefully, but shook her head and said instead, 'No.'

'Excellent. Give me your things, then, I'll put them in the back.'

Give *him* her things and *he* would put them in the back? Sam knew she was gaping at him as he took the laptop case from her unresisting grip. He was a prince, the Ruler of an Arab state. He was arrogant and demanding, and he was used to being waited on hand and foot, so no way could he have meant what he had said. But apparently he had, Sam realised, as he gestured to her to remove her backpack and then took it from her, carrying it as though it weighed nothing instead of the several heavy kilos her shoulders knew it did.

She could hear him opening the rear door of the four-by-four and then closing it again. He strode to the passenger door ignoring her. Sam looked wildly around herself wondering where on earth the vehicle that was to be her transport was, and if he would actually allow his own driver to drive off without her.

'If you're ready?'

It was more an impatient command than a request. Confused, Sam looked from his irritated stance beside the passenger door he was holding open to the empty seat, and then back to him again.

'You want me to get in?' she asked him

'It would seem a logical process, if we are to leave for our destination,' he agreed.

From the way he was looking at her, if she kept him waiting much longer he'd be bustling her into the passenger seat like a small child, Sam suspected, reluctantly stepping up to the door. Her, 'What about you?' was lost in the heavy thud of the door being closed by an impatient male hand.

She was reaching for her seat belt when the driver's door opened and he swung himself into the driver's seat, closing his own door as he did so.

He was driving them himself?

'What's wrong?'

'Where are the others?' she asked uncertainly.

'What others?'

'You mean that… But I thought…'

'You thought what? That after your earlier crass attempt to foster intimacy between us I wouldn't want to risk being alone with you? Somehow I think I'm capable of defending my own honour.'

Sam could feel her face burning with fury. She looked towards the door of the now moving vehicle, but of course it was too late for her to register a protest by trying to get out and walk off.

'What happened in that corridor was an accident…a mistake…'

'A mistake—yes, I agree. But an accident?'

'And as for you worrying about risking being alone with me—' She was so angry that the words she wanted to say had balled up as tightly in her throat as her fingers moved into tight fists against her palms. 'That is both offensive and ridiculous. After all, I'm not the one who arranged this trip, and I certainly wouldn't have chosen to make it alone with you.'

Vere knew perfectly well that she had a point, but the fact that she had made it still angered him. In fact, everything about her and her presence here, and the problems she was causing, infuriated him.

Her meddling in something that was nothing whatever to do with her, and her ridiculous claims about the source of the river, were obliging him to take time out of his already very busy life to check up on the situation, ready to head off any arguments the Emir might try to put forward.

He had no desire whatsoever to have her ideas brought into a more public arena, for others with their own agendas to get involved, and because of that he had been forced to make this trip alone with her—something he would never ordinarily have done.

When he came to the desert he liked to come alone—completely alone—so that he could replenish himself via his solitude with it.

He disliked sharing the desert—'his' desert—with anyone, but the thought of having to share it with this woman, who had already aggravated and irritated him to the point where he couldn't even close his eyes in sleep without her appearing in his dreams to infuriate him, inflamed his hostility towards her like a bur under a saddle. He came to the desert to cool his overheated thoughts and emotions, to live for a precious few days as a poet hermit, letting the desert reach out to him and unfold its mysteries to him.

None of that would be possible when he had to share its purity with a woman who bartered her flesh and her conscience for money—a woman who was the complete opposite of the kind of woman he admired.

But he *had* wanted her.

Briefly, foolishly, shamefully, and in a moment of lost self-control. It would not happen again.

SHE WOULD NEVER have agreed to this trip if she had known they were going to be alone, Sam fumed. He should have told her and given her the opportunity to refuse. But of course he was far too arrogant to do anything like that. So far as he was concerned his word was law. She frowned, remembering something, turning her head to look at him as she challenged him.

'I thought no one other than desert-qualified Arab drivers were allowed to drive members of the teams? Or don't the rules apply when one is the Ruler of one's own kingdom.'

She could see anger deepening the colour of his eyes. He obviously didn't like what she was saying one little bit. Did she really want to think of herself as the kind of

woman who was attracted to his kind of man? Of course
she didn't, she assured herself.

'I *am* a desert-qualified driver,' he told her coldly, looking away from her to switch on the car's satellite navigation and communication system, and using the earpiece
he had put on to say something in Arabic to the camp's
radio controller, effectively making it impossible for Sam
to rally and make a retort.

Good—she was glad that he was making it plain that
he didn't want to talk to her, because she certainly did not
want to talk to him! In fact she didn't want any kind of
contact with him at all!

THE FOUR-BY-FOUR MIGHT be the most comfortable vehicle
she had ever travelled in, with its air-conditioning and its
leather seats that could be electronically contoured to fit
one's own body for maximum support, but she certainly
wasn't going to be able to relax enough to enjoy that comfort, Sam admitted. And not just because of the number of
steep sand dune escarpments they were having to climb
and then descend as the Prince took what she could only
assume must be a shortcut to their destination.

There was also the fact that tonight they would be sharing a camp. Not, of course, that she had anything to fear
from him. She knew that. And she had made overnight
stays with other members of the team—it was part and
parcel of their work, after all, and taken as such by everyone concerned. Anne hadn't even blinked when Sam had
told her about this trip, for instance.

Other members of the team, Sam reminded herself.
Never just one person…just one man…*this* man…to whom,
no matter how hard she might try to deny it to herself, she
was dangerously vulnerable.

Not any more! That had been before, when she had

thought both of them were caught up in the same surge of mutual unstoppable passion that was beyond their control, when she had believed that they shared something very intimate and special, however out of character for her it had been. Then, of course, the thought of a night alone with him under the stars with only the desert and the night sky to witness their being together would have been her idea of heaven. Desert nights were cold—cold enough for two people who desired one another to positively need to share the heat of their bodies and their desire.

Sam couldn't think of anywhere more perfect than the desert, with all its powerful secrets, under the moon, with all its magical mystery, to consummate a love affair between two people who shared the same desire so intimately that they almost shared the same heartbeat. The male strength of the desert tamed by the female allure of the moon had surely been created to be together for an eternity that symbolised the best of human love.

Why was she letting herself think like this when she knew she could only hurt herself by doing so? It would have been hard enough for her had he merely ignored her, indicating that he wanted to pretend that embrace in the hotel corridor had never taken place. He had gone several steps further than that, though, with his criticism and accusations against her professionalism. He wasn't just indifferent to her, he actively disliked her. And she returned that dislike now, Sam told herself firmly.

Nothing could be more hellish, surely, than for two people to be alone together when their hostility towards one another was as strong as that between the Prince and herself. He had made his loathing of her very plain, and she was honour-bound to reciprocate it.

For some reason Sam suddenly felt very close to tears,

her heart as raw with pain as her throat would have been had she actually been crying.

It was pointless regretting now what couldn't be changed. All she could do was resolve to make sure in every single way she could that he had no further opportunity to throw in her face any accusation about her coming on to him sexually. That should be easy enough to do, surely? After all, she had been celibate virtually all her grown-up female life, so it wasn't as though she carried with her a fully awakened sexual lust that needed to be satisfied.

The irony of her situation was its own form of black humour. Here she was, a virgin still in the emotionally and sexually fulfilled sense. Her single experience of 'full sex' had been the fumbled and uncomfortable experience she had shared with a fellow undergraduate when she had traded her virginity for the right, as she had thought then, to call herself a woman. Being accused of attempting to seduce a man who any woman could see had at his disposal all the experience and sensuality that any woman could want in a lover was absurd.

Was that why she had succumbed to temptation so easily? Because in her heart of hearts she knew that she had deprived herself of a passionately loving journey into womanhood and secretly longed to experience its mystery? Had she looked at him and somehow believed that in his arms she could find what she had never had? It was less painful to think that than to think, as she had done initially and ridiculously, that they were fated to meet and be together.

Ridiculous, yes. But how very different things could have been if *he* had shared that shock of awareness and longing she had felt at their first touch. She would have given herself willingly—eagerly, in fact—into his hands, just for the joy of knowing the reality of true sensual pleasure and satisfaction, without asking anything from him other than his own reciprocal pleasure in their coming together. She could easily have lived off the sweetness of that remembered pleasure, storing it up inside her like the most precious of precious gifts, treasuring it and revering it for all her life as a time apart from reality, without expecting or needing anything else.

But he had not offered her that gift. Instead he had made accusations against her and humiliated her. Sam gave a small gasp of pain as her feelings pushed against the barriers she had tried to erect against them. This was definitely not the time to give in to her emotions, she warned herself.

VERE GLANCED TOWARDS the passenger seat. He prided himself on the excellence of his desert driving, and so far as he was aware he had done nothing to elicit the small sharp sound of pain from the woman seated next to him.

He looked at the satellite navigation system map and then checked the onboard compass. They were out of range of radio frequency now, but he had no fear of them not reaching their destination.

Vere had lied to Sam when he had told her that he knew nothing about the course of the river having been changed.

The source of the river had a deep-rooted significance for his family, and his parents had brought him and Drax here often. He and Drax had kept up the tradition, coming in the winter to camp beside the river their ancestor was supposed to have conjured up so magically from the rocks, and Vere was perfectly well aware of how and why the original course of the river had been changed. What he didn't know, though, was what interpretation Ms Sam McLellan intended to put on that change when, as the Emir's pawn, she started trying to make trouble for Dhurahn.

By the time they returned to the main camp tomorrow he would be in possession of that information, and he intended to have made sure that Sam McLellan knew that he would be merciless in destroying her credibility if he had to do so to protect his country and his people.

SAM GASPED AS the four-by-four suddenly seemed to surge up a slope so perpendicular that her heart was in her mouth. With every metre they climbed she held her breath, expecting at best to feel the wheels spin as they sank into the sand and at worst to find that they were sliding sideways back down the incline.

Vere seemed oblivious to her concern. In fact when she looked at him she could see that he was smiling grimly as though he was enjoying forcing the hostile terrain to accept his mastery. And then suddenly the pressure forcing her back in her seat was released as they crested the incline.

'There is our camp. We should be there in a few more minutes.'

The calm words gave no hint of the triumphant satisfaction she had sensed minutes earlier as he battled the steep hill.

Down below them Sam could see dozens of small pinpricks of light, whilst the moon revealed the outlines of two of the now familiar black Bedou tents.

Sam's eyes widened. She had assumed that they would have to make their own camp, but plainly she'd been wrong. People had obviously come out here ahead to establish the camp for them. The thought of others having to toil in the hot sun to set up this camp angered her, as well as underlining yet again the difference in their status.

'It all looks very welcoming,' she told him coolly. 'I hate to think of the waste of energy resources it must represent, though.'

Vere frowned. Dhurahn was arguably the most 'green' of all the states involved in the project. He and Drax were both committed to cutting Dhurahn's own greenhouse gases, and he didn't like Sam's coolly cynical comment.

'It's never a good idea to make assumptions—especially when one is doing so without the benefit of any real knowledge or expertise. For instance the lights you can see are solar fuelled, and water will be collected in the traditional way overnight from the change in temperature. Dhurahn is known as the greenstate of the gulf, and we take our responsibility to the environment very seriously.'

'But you drive a gas-guzzler,' Sam interrupted him, adding pointedly, 'but then of course as an Arab prince I dare say you feel it is your right.'

'Dhurahn does not have its own oil. This "gas-guzzler", as you call it, has been adapted to run in the most fuel efficient way possible. Along with our neighbours in Zuran, we are financing research into alternative eco-friendly fuels. I may be an Arab prince, Ms McLellan but I come from a people who know very well how to live alongside nature and respect it. As the Ruler of Dhurahn it is my privilege to honour the traditions of my people, rather than dishonour them by seeking to emulate the greedy consumerism that has caused so much human suffering.'

Sam opened her mouth to argue with him and then closed it again. What, after all, could she say? She had not expected him to be so fiercely determined about asserting his green credentials, and she felt slightly resentful of the way it seemed he had scored the moral high ground in having done so. How childish was that? Surely what was more important was his commitment to green issues, not her savouring a small moral victory. She had only wanted to be victorious because he kept on putting her down and making her feel small, making her feel that she had no value. But then to him she didn't, and she might as well accept that.

They had almost reached the small camp now, and Sam could see where the moon was reflected on a small pool of water beneath a rocky outcrop. She remembered seeing it when she had come out originally to look at the river. She had thought then that it was a beautiful spot, with vegetation around the pool framing it in a lush green halo, the rocks so old and worn smooth by time, that she had felt a sense of awe just looking at them. The privilege of seeing such beauty softened her mood, allowing her earlier irritation to slip from her. How could anyone not marvel at something like this? This was the reason she had wanted this posting—this miracle that was the desert when it bloomed.

'The spring for the pool must be underground,' she heard herself saying softly.

VERE LOOKED AT her. A look of shining reverence illuminated her face, and like the soft awe in her voice, it caught him off guard. As though a barrier within him had been removed, he could feel the swift flood of his own longing swirling powerfully through him. He wanted her! Angry denial gripped his insides, but the truth couldn't be ignored. Against everything he knew to be in his own best interests, and more importantly those of his people, he *did* want her.

He turned away from her. As a boy, he too had marvelled at the pool, thinking it magical, whereas Drax, as always more practically minded than him, had wanted to dive down and find out where the spring actually was.

'You will do no such thing,' their father had told them both sternly. 'It is far too dangerous. Besides, I can tell you that the spring is situated beneath the rocks. It ebbs and flows in a way known only to itself, but with a pull that is dangerously strong.'

Like the pull of this woman, whose presence he resented so much, on the desire within him that he could not subjugate to his will? How swiftly and treacherously that knowledge slid into his consciousness—the merest dart of awareness, yet as powerful as any narcotic and surely as compulsive, stealing away the mind's strength whilst feeding the heart's desire. It was, he knew, no matter how much he wished he did not have that knowledge, a pull that was capable of changing the course of his life for ever if he did not control it.

Vere's hands tightened on the steering wheel of the four-by-four, and then, with an abruptness that made Sam's body recoil against the sudden acceleration of the vehicle, he drove towards their camp.

CHAPTER SIX

COMFORTABLY SETTLED in the privacy of her own tent, Sam
reflected that whilst it had disconcerted her at first to discover that the two of them were to be the only occupants of
the well-organised camp, there were also certain benefits
to be found. Its quiet solitude after the busy hum of the
main camp was blissful, Sam thought, at least to someone
like her, who valued her privacy.

Here, she knew that she was unlikely to be disturbed
by a fellow worker wanting company. Deep down inside
Sam knew that she felt slightly cheated and disappointed
by the everyday activities of the main camp. But she knew
it was silly and almost childish of her to have imagined
that she would be experiencing true life in the desert, as
lived by its nomads, and she had to admit she welcomed
the camp's modern comforts.

The Prince had left her with the curt instruction that
he expected her to be ready at first light to drive out with
him to the place where she claimed the course of the river
had been altered, which meant that she ought now to be
in bed and asleep, ready for an early start, instead of sitting cross-legged on a cushion on the carpeted floor of her
tent, wearing the thin cotton robe she had put on after her
shower, her computer switched on in front of her.

Ostensibly she was checking her facts with regard to

the original course of the river and answering her e-mails, but she hadn't been able to resist the temptation to bring up the now familiar details of Dhurahn and its ruling family from her previous searches.

It wasn't really the foolish self-indulgence of a woman helplessly caught in the invisible web of one man's sexual aura that was driving her, she assured herself. Naturally she was curious about the background of a man who was behaving towards her with the kind of arrogance the Prince was.

Her breath caught in her throat as she suddenly found a new site, her whole attention focused on the screen as she learned from it what she had not realised before. Namely that he, the Ruler of Dhurahn, Prince Vereham al a' Karim bin Hakar, was the elder of a pair of twins. There were two of them? Surely it wasn't possible that the world could accommodate two such men, never mind one small country.

The site gave a few more details about them, including the information that their Bedouin ancestry was mixed with the French and Irish genes of their grandmother and their mother.

She frowned slightly as she read these facts. How did a man who obviously had such a strong commitment to his Arab heritage deal with such a potentially turbulent mixture of cultures within himself? Did it make him resent the cultural diversity within him or embrace it? Was he at war with that inheritance or at peace with it? And what kind of woman would most appeal to a man so complex?

He would father beautiful children.

A slow, hot ache slid through her body—a need that was surely elemental and universal, the need of a woman to bear the child of a man. Not any man, but *the* man.

Panic and denial shot through her. Now look what she had done! The computer, like a modern magical vessel of legend, had released genii in the shape of knowledge conjured up by her own thoughts, and it was too powerful for her to control.

Motherhood was something she had hoped to look forward to when eventually she met the man with whom she wanted to share her life, but it had certainly never dominated her thoughts or been a desire that drove her. Yet here she was thinking in terms of having *his* child, feeling her womb tighten with longing for that child and for him. What did that tell her?

Sam sat back from the computer, feeling slightly sick as the reality of exactly what it did mean was forced on her. There was only one reason she could ever want to conceive a specific man's child as powerfully as she did this man's.

She wanted his child because she had fallen head over heels in love with him. She started to panic. No. That wasn't possible. It *shouldn't* be possible. But somehow it certainly was.

This was crazy. It just wasn't logical to fall in love with someone on the strength of a single look followed by a single kiss—especially when that someone had made it clear that he had felt nothing for her other than dislike and contempt.

Crazy or not, it was what had happened to her, so she'd better get used to it and then work on some way of dealing with it.

Like what? Running away? Lying to herself and telling herself that she'd got it wrong, that she didn't really love him at all?

Why had this happened to her? She just wasn't the type. She was sensible, practical, she'd never believed in falling in love at first sight. She'd believed that love was something that should grow slowly and cautiously, as two people got to know one another. Love meant liking a person, respecting them and sharing goals with them. It meant......

It meant that she had known nothing about love at all, and now that she did she wished desperately that she hadn't found out.

IT WAS GONE midnight. Vere looked up from the maps he had been studying, forwarded to him in an e-mail attachment by Drax. The earlier dated map was the original one, drawn in the days when, after the end of the First World War the Ottoman Empire had originally been carved up. The map had been handed to his great-grandfather at the same time as he had been stealing the heart of another British diplomat's daughter. It showed the boundaries between all the Arab states, including their own. It also showed the original course of the Dhurahni River. Alongside it Vere had placed the second map, dated only a matter of months later, showing exactly the same boundaries but with the river diverted to a new course. In both maps the course of the river was well within their own border.

However, the Emir, being the wily manipulator that he was, would, Vere knew, use this alteration from the original to stir up trouble for them if he could, by hinting that if one supposedly innocent change had been made, and never revealed, what was to stop another, less innocent change being made and kept hidden.

How much had he paid Sam McLellan? However much it had been, the Emir would no doubt think he had got a real bargain. Vere had few doubts that initially all the Emir had hoped for at the very best would be to bribe the cartographer into dropping hints that the original borders had been tampered with. That would have been easy enough for her to do, given the changes that so many years of shifting desert sands had had on the landscape. But with the right kind of spin on it any change could quite easily be promoted as suspicious and underhand. Even if the allegation was retracted at a later date, the damage would have been done and Dhurahn's own reputation tarnished.

This matter of the change in course of the river put a whole new complexion on everything, and would add far more weight to any claim the Emir chose to make.

It would be easy enough for them to offer Sam more than the Emir had paid her, to 'forget' what she had discovered, but he and Drax had talked it over and they were both agreed that this was something they did not want to do. For one thing it ultimately weakened their truthful claim that the course of the river had had no effect whatsoever on their boundaries, and for another that was not the way they wanted to run their country.

Vere stood up and walked to the exit to his tent, stepping through it to breathe in the cool freshness of the night air. He stopped when he saw that there was a light on in Sam's tent.

What was she doing? Surely she ought to be asleep? He had already told her they had an early start in the morning. Could she have gone to bed and left her lamp on? Old habits died hard, and Vere and Drax's father had taught them when they were very young about the dangers of unattended oil lamps left in tents. Even though logically there was no need for him to be concerned, since a small generator was providing them with electricity, Vere was soon striding over to Sam's tent and flicking back the flap.

Once he had done so, the sight of Sam seated with her back to him, staring into a computer screen, had him walking towards her.

THIS TIME SAM was oblivious to his presence. She was staring at the screen without really seeing it as she battled against the reality being forced on her. She couldn't love him. It was—

The shadow falling across her computer screen made her react immediately and instinctively, turning round in alarm. The colour left her face and then returned in a surge of guilty heat as she tried to reach for her mouse to close the open window before showing what she had been viewing.

Vere was too quick for her, though, reaching out to stop her, his fingers curling round her wrist, the cool white crispness of his sleeve brushing against her. She saw that he had removed the plain white headdress he wore, secured by a black plaited rope, and that his hair beneath it was thick and dark, clean with health, and cut close into his neck at the back. She had an absurd longing to reach out and trace the line where it was cut so neatly against the strong muscles of his neck, and then to trace kisses along his collarbone whilst…

Frantically she wrenched her thoughts away from the sensual images forming inside her head and tried to focus instead on the grimness of the tight line around his mouth, rather than the shape of his mouth itself as he studied the information on her screen.

Sam's face burned as she realised that she had actually highlighted his own name.

'Why?' he demanded, after giving the screen a comprehensive look.

Sam understood perfectly well what he was asking her.

'I wanted to…to know now more about you…to understand why you are behaving towards me in the way that you are,' she answered him bravely. 'I didn't even know your full name.'

He looked back at the screen, indicating where she had highlighted his name and title.

'And you believe you have found it there?'

Sam was confused.

'What do you mean?'

'Those are my formal names. Vere is the name those closest to me know me by. It was my mother's choice—' Vere stopped sharply.

What was he doing? What had got into him? Why was he letting himself imagine how her lips might form the shortened version of his name, how her tongue-tip might taste, how it might sigh against his skin in a soft sound of pleasure.

'Vere,' Sam said, gasping a little when he released her wrist and then took the mouse from her to close down the site so fiercely that she started to overbalance.

As she struggled to stop herself from falling Vere moved faster, grasping her upper arms and hauling her to her feet. He was breathing rapidly, his fingers biting into her flesh. Sam thought that he might have cursed her under his breath, but she couldn't hear anything above the frantic pounding of her own heartbeat. She could smell the heat of his flesh and of their shared tension. It closed in around them, an invisible net of arousal and need meshing so tightly together that it was impossible to break free.

'No...' Sam heard the sound her lips had framed, but it was more a low moan of longing than any kind of denial, and the hands she had lifted to his chest weren't pushing him away.

'A thousand curses on you for doing this, and on me for wanting it,' Vere whispered harshly against her mouth, as she opened it for him with the inbuilt sensual knowledge of a woman who loved a man whose pride could only be humbled by his own need.

Feverishly their lips met and parted, only to meet again and again, until they were pressed body to body. Somehow Sam realised she had managed to open the buttons securing the front of his *kandora*, and her palms were now pressed flat against his chest. Her own robe had slipped from one shoulder, revealing the silky gleam of her pale skin and the curve of her breast, and the fabric was only kept from sliding down further because Vere's hand was on her, shaping the soft female texture of her flesh.

Her sensory receptors had gone into overload, her body a melting, swirling, frenzied mass of longing. A hundred thousand separate and acutely intense sensations filled her.

Now she could fulfil that earlier urge to touch her fingertips to his skin in awed delight and wonder. She pressed them against his collarbone. His flesh felt warm and sleek, the bone beneath it hard and solid, and her gaze fastened on the spasmodic pulse jerking against the flesh just beneath his jaw. Tenderly she kissed it, lost in her own loving pleasure before being flung tumultuously into sharp, agonised passion when he responded in kind, kissing her throat and then her shoulder. A swift shudder of pleasure flowed through her at the touch of his hand freeing her breast from its covering, followed by another that racked her more visibly when his palm took the weight of it and the pad of his thumb rubbed erotically over her eagerly swollen nipple.

By the time they kissed their way to her bed both of them were naked, and Sam's body was so erotically charged by the touch of Vere's hands that she was already engulfed by fierce shivers of pleasure.

The lamp was still on, casting its illumination over their bodies, causing Sam to suck in her breath when the movement Vere made to lift her away from himself and onto the bed revealed in clear detail every strongly muscled line of him to her. His flesh was warmly golden, and his chest was sleek with fine dark hair that made an erotic pathway down his body, drawing her eager gaze to the stiff thickness of his erection.

Was love always like this? she wondered dizzily. Did every woman who fell in love feel this mixture of tenderness and awe, this desire to see and touch and taste this male uniqueness? To feel this surge of need to know that no other woman would ever share his intimacy?

She was looking at him as every man wanted the woman he desired to look at him, Vere acknowledged, as he fought against the surging heat of his physical response to her. She was looking at him as though she had just seen the world's rarest and best treasure.

She was a very good actress, that was all, he warned. But his body wasn't listening to him and it was too late now to make it listen. Her skin was the colour of milk, spread against the soft coffee colour of the bedding. The honey blonde curls on her head were matched by those that nestled against her sex, providing a covering that served more to draw attention to the soft flesh beneath than conceal it. He lifted his hand and laid it over her sex, cupping it and feeling the heavy kick of heat that punched through him as she arched upwards. Her nipples were flushed a dark rose colour against her paleness, and when he softly pinched one of them she cried out in longing, and gripped his shoulders as she urged him down to her.

He could feel the bite of her nails against his skin like a goad, the slight pain they were inflicting underlining and enhancing the ferocity of his own passion. Like a dam newly breached it surged and boiled, flooding through him to sweep aside anything and everything that tried to stand in its way. It knew no master other than itself, and it dictated where he placed his lips, his hands, and the words of encouragement and enticement he whispered so passionately.

He tasted of musk and sweat, sharpened with salt where the cool night air touched the warm, nude male flesh that wasn't heated by her own body, and Sam knew that his scent would be with her for ever, just like every precious breath of time they were now sharing.

All the reasons she should not be doing this had been left behind, abandoned and unwanted. In the lamplight she could see the small indentations left on his skin by her nails. The sight filled her with an almost primitive surge of female triumph. He was hers now, his flesh bearing her mark of possession just as all the places of sensuality on her were receiving the brand of his touch.

He was bending his head, running his tongue over her nipples, first one and then the other. Both were now swollen and tight, gleaming damply from his caress.

He covered one with his mouth and tugged delicately on it, causing a burst of violent pleasure to galvanise her whole body as she felt the soft, deliriously erotic grate of his teeth against her sensitive flesh.

She must have cried out, because she could hear the echo of her longing shuddering round the tent. His every touch was a dizzying new pleasure previously unknown to her and unexplored. Nothing in that youthful fumble long ago had prepared her for this. It was all so new, like stumbling upon an unsuspected secret hoard of priceless treasure. She wanted to linger over every individual piece, taking her pleasure in it and from it, but at the same time she was being driven by an ever-increasing sense of urgency that would not rest.

Vere could feel the thundering jolt of his heart slamming into his chest. Why was he reacting like this? Like a boy with his first woman—all trembling hands and pounding heart, half afraid that his body was so out of control that he might end up disappointing her and shaming himself. The ability to be a considerate and accomplished lover was a skill he had set himself the task of learning as part of his journey along the road to manhood, along with many other things. His goal had been to gain that skill, not to take pleasure for himself, and now he was being overwhelmed by needs and sensations that were totally new to him.

He wanted her so badly. More than he had ever wanted anything or anyone. He wanted her, bone and soul deep, burned into him and branded on him in such a way that she would forever be a part of him. Like a fever, even when the desire left him it would be inside him, and he was powerless to stop that.

He reached out to cup her sex with his hand, his fingers trembling slightly as she yielded to his caress.

Sam moaned, her body trembling beneath the intensity of her need. She curled her fingers into her palms, silently willing him to touch her more intimately, and then realising when he did that even that was not enough to satisfy the hunger gnawing at her.

She was so soft, so wet, and his body wanted her so badly. *He* wanted her so badly, Vere admitted. And that need pushed aside all the barriers he had shored up against that admission and the full extent of his own subjugation to it swept over him. He had tried to avoid this, had even tried to stop it, but now, in a final moment of true knowledge of himself and his fate, Vere was face-to-face with the truth, heart to heart with the woman who had brought him to it, and there was no going back.

Vere positioned himself over her, unable to deny himself the pleasure of caressing her as he prepared to enter her. Her body welcomed him and embraced him so sweetly that it was like coming home to a place that was his and his alone. Each stroke, each thrust of their bodies as they came together, was a perfect meeting of two halves of one whole. This was his fate and he welcomed it.

This was it—this was what she had yearned and ached for, what she had been made for. Sam shivered with excitement as she felt each firm thrust of Vere's body within her own. How could anything be so perfect, so uplifting and emotionally intense that it filled her eyes with tears and made her throat ache with the sounds of her own joy? She could feel every movement of him within her, every particle of him, as though her own flesh was so extraordinarily sensitive to his that she was aware of even the smallest pressure of male muscle against the female flesh that contained him. It had been so long that this might as well have been her first time. But of course it was not. Then she had—

Sam tensed, horrified, as she suddenly remembered what neither of them had done and ought to have done.

'Stop!' she told Vere urgently.

He hadn't heard her, Sam recognised. He was so lost in his own desire and in her own... She struggled to do what her conscience was urging her to do, but it was far too late. She was as powerless as he was to resist the swift tide of ecstasy he was driving her to ride. If she had to stop now... But she couldn't. Instead she clung to him as she cried out when the pleasure became too intense and took her to the stars, then gasped and wept tears of joy whilst the final pulse of the satisfaction he had given her met the forceful surge of his completion.

THE HEAT OF their mutual desire had cooled now, and yet Vere was still here with her, still holding her—surely in a parody of the tenderness she secretly longed for and knew she could not expect. It was lust that had driven him to have sex with her, that was all. How could it possibly be anything else after the things he had said to her and the way he had behaved towards her?

He should go. Vere knew that—just as he knew he should never have come here in the first place. Had a part of him realised even before they had left the main camp that this would happen? Had he deliberately planned for this? He had certainly wanted it—and her. Everything about their coming together had been wrong, and yet everything about it and her had felt so very right—more right than he could ever possibly have imagined sexual intimacy to be for him. Lying here now, with her in his arms, for the first time since the death of his parents he felt at peace and complete.

What was this? He wasn't the kind of man who needed a woman to make him feel complete. He was the ruler of a small and vulnerable state: a man whose energies were needed to keep the delicate balance of power they shared with their neighbours.

Maybe so, but he was also a man, and right now all he wanted was to be that man and be with this woman. This woman who was causing him so much trouble—a woman who had been bought by another man. Vere knew that he should reject her and leave her, but somehow he couldn't. His emotional need to be with her surmounted what his head was telling him to do.

He lifted his hand to cup her face, feeling his heart turn over inside his chest when she turned her head to press a small fierce kiss into his palm. It was as though the sexual release of their lovemaking had opened a door into his emotions, allowing them to spill out from the place where he had locked them away. He had wanted her like this from that first heartbeat of recognition, that first look and touch. It was too late now to deny it. Something about her compelled and commanded him, overturning every barrier between them.

Sam looked at Vere with helpless adoration. He was being so tender, so very much the lover she had dreamed he would be from that first moment of seeing him. The awkward experience that had dealt with her physical virginity had done nothing to change the status of her emotional and sexual virginity—that was something she had only experienced now, in Vere's arms.

Sam knew without him having to say so that Vere wanted them to make love again—but she had no excuse this time. The practicalities had to be discussed and dealt with.

'No,' she told him gently, staying his hand as it moved down her body.

Immediately Vere withdrew slightly from her, the old wariness taking the place of his earlier mood. She was rejecting him, pushing him away, and he could feel the pain he had always dreaded tightening its grip on his heart.

'No?' he queried sharply.

'We shouldn't have done what we did the first time without taking proper precautions,' Sam told him.

'Precautions?'

Vere was looking at her as though she were speaking a foreign language, Sam thought.

'I'm not using any form of birth control,' she told him quietly. 'And then there's the matter of our mutual sexual health. I…. My last partner was my first, and that was a long time ago, so I know there is no question of me being a risk to you….' She was stumbling a little over her words now, self-conscious in the reality they were creating in a way she hadn't been during their physical intimacy.

Vere registered the surge of male pleasure it gave him to hear her hesitant admission about her lack of any real kind of sexual history, but it was pushed slightly to one side by his outrage that she should find it necessary to question his own sexual morality and healthiness.

Vere looked so affronted that had it not been for the seriousness of the situation Sam could almost have laughed.

'You cannot imagine that my sexual health could in any way put you at risk,' he challenged her.

'Why not?' Sam countered steadily. 'You're a sexually active man, after all.' Her voice might have sounded steady, but she was glad to be able to duck her head so that he couldn't look into her eyes and see there the pain it caused her to think of him with other women.

'How do you deduce that?' Vere demanded peremptorily. 'Since, by your own admission, I am only the second man you have given yourself to.'

'A man in your position is bound to…to have experienced more of life in every way than a woman in mine,' Sam answered him and then added huskily, 'besides, I cannot imagine that a man could…'

'Could what?' Vere demanded, when she suddenly went silent and refused to look at him.

'Could make love to a woman as beautifully as you made love to me without…without having a lot of previous experience,' Sam said reluctantly.

Somehow or other he had reached for her hand, was holding it tightly in his own.

'If the experience was beautiful then that was because of the uniqueness of what you brought to it yourself.'

Vere hesitated. He wanted to tell her how much her soft and honest words meant to him. He want to tell her too that he shared her feelings, but he had spent too long forcing himself to keep his emotions under control and hidden, sometimes even from himself.

'I assure you that there is no risk to your health from

the intimacy we have shared,' he told her briefly instead, then hesitated before adding, 'however, as to the risk of you conceiving my child...'

If she hadn't known how she felt about him before, she must know now. On hearing him say those words, at the thought of having his child, she felt her emotions close around her heart, the pressure of them like a giant fist, making the organ thud and kick. If only she might!

Sam knew she ought to be shocked by her own reckless thoughts, but the seed of an unexpected yearning had been placed inside her, and was already swelling and growing. An unplanned pregnancy was the last thing she needed in her life. But to have this man's child...his son...to have a part of him with her for ever...

Luckily for her that was unlikely to happen, Sam realised as she did a bit of quick mental arithmetic and then told Vere lightly, 'I doubt very much that I will have conceived, given the...the timing.'

'And if you have?' Vere challenged her.

'I haven't,' Sam insisted.

Abruptly Vere released her and turned away from her, getting up from the bed. The glow from the lamp lovingly illuminated every perfect male line of his body—but not as lovingly as she wanted to trace and kiss them with her fingers and her lips, Sam thought achingly. She didn't want him to leave her. She wanted him to stay with her and hold her, love her...

She wanted what she already knew she could not have, she warned herself as Vere reached for his clothes in silence.

Vere had no idea why Sam's assertion that she had not conceived his child should make him feel that dark bitterness and pain. All he did know was that it also made him feel angry and alone. Shamefully, it also made him feel that he wanted to take her back in his arms and make love to her until she was crying out to him to possess her. And this time when he did so he wanted to ensure that... That what? That he impregnated her with his seed? That her body, her womb, would ripen with it and with his child? The fierce clutch of savage joy at his heart was giving him a message that was totally at odds with the logical rejection inside his head.

He was Dhurahn's ruler. It was impossible for him to father a child, his first child, capriciously and outside marriage. How would he ever be able to assuage the guilt he would feel towards his people and towards that child—especially if it were a son—knowing he had deprived him of his birthright?

There must be no such child, and therefore no more unprotected sex. That meant no sex at all, since it was impossible for him to procure the protection they would need unless he made an incognito visit to Zuran.

Now he *was* being ridiculous, Vere told himself as he finished dressing and then strode towards the exit of the tent without turning round to say anything to Sam. He knew that if he did he would not be able to leave her.

He had gone and Sam was alone. Her eyes were burning with tears she was determined were not going to fall. It was all her own fault. She couldn't pretend to herself that she hadn't ached to know him as a lover because she had—from the very first moment she had bumped into him. And now she did know, she knew too that, no matter what happened in the rest of her life, no man would ever be able to take her to the heights Vere had shown her. Nor the depths of pain and despair she was now feeling because he had left her.

CHAPTER SEVEN

'AND AS YOU CAN SEE from the shape of the natural depression here, this must originally have been a deeper pool in the riverbed. My guess is that the river must at one time have cascaded down into it over this rocky outcrop to form a natural pool before flowing on.'

They were standing in the basin, in the shadow of the rock above them. Sam knew that her voice sounded stiff and over controlled as she underlined for him just why she was so sure that the course of the river had been changed. She focused straight ahead of herself, instead of turning to look at Vere. How could she behave naturally towards him now, after last night? She had barely slept, and had been unable to eat anything before he had driven her out here just as dawn was breaking. She felt so strung out by the intensity of her own emotions that just having to breathe separately from him, when all of her was screaming to be as physically and emotionally close to him as she could get, required her total concentration.

She could feel herself shaking with need. In an attempt to conceal it she bent down and picked up a handful of smooth pebbles.

'These must have been worn smooth by the river,' she told him. 'There is no other way that could have happened. The river must once have flowed into this pool and then out of it. You can even walk along what must have been the riverbed to the marshy area where it would have joined what is now the new course of the Dhurahni.'

It was obvious to Vere that she wasn't going to be persuaded that she was wrong—which meant he would need to find another way of neutralising the information she was selling to the Emir.

'We are over twenty miles from our border with Khulua, and you are talking about a change of direction in the river of a matter of a few hundred yards, if that. I fail to see what relevance it could possibly have,' he told her.

Vere's voice was clipped, and like Sam he avoided any eye contact. He had still noticed, though, how the breeze that sunrise always brought had stroked her hair, and he had been filled with a fierce, irrational need to tangle his own fingers in its silky length and bind her to him.

Her, this woman it made far more sense for him to despise rather than desire.

Last night she had given herself to him so sweetly and so completely, with such trust, that just holding her had touched and soothed sore places within himself, as though she possessed a magical ability to heal him.

No. Last night she had acted as only the most skilled of deceivers could act, and he was a fool for allowing himself to feel what he had felt.

Swiftly Vere clamped down on the argument raging inside him. He needed to think only as the Ruler of Dhurahn, and to remember the hard lesson the death of his mother had taught him. There was no place here for the man he had foolishly allowed himself to be the previous night— vulnerable, in need, responsive to a certain woman's hold on his senses to such an extent that everything else was forgotten.

Sam couldn't look at Vere. If she did... If she did, she

would end up begging him to hold her, and she must not do that. She had humiliated herself enough already. Last night had shown her yet again that she meant nothing to him. If he had used her to satisfy his lust then that was her own fault, for loving him so much that she had allowed him to do so.

She had to focus on being professional. Sam took a deep breath and then said firmly, 'It must have had some relevance to whoever changed it, and it's that that fascinates me. Why would anyone want to go to the trouble of altering it, especially in view of the work it must have involved? A new channel would have had to be cut through the rock, and that would have been expensive. To what purpose? No benefit could have been gained from it.'

'To your western mind, perhaps, but the Eastern mind thinks differently.'

Sam turned towards him, forgetting that she had promised herself she wouldn't look at him.

'So there *was* a reason?'

Her mouth looked soft and swollen still from his kisses, and the khaki shirt she was wearing couldn't conceal the aroused thrust of her nipples. Her face wore a tell-tale paleness that spoke of a night's sensual languor. The ache that was tormenting him immediately became a dervish-driven whirlwind of torture. He wanted her. He wanted to claim her now, here. He wanted— He stopped, knowing he wasn't free to feel like this, to need like this.

'Yes, there was a reason,' he agreed, forcing himself to deny the images that were tempting him. 'But it has nothing to do with protecting our right to the river, because that has never been necessary. The Dhurahni River belongs to Dhurahn. That is a legal reality that can never be changed or questioned.'

'Then why?'

Sam's persistence reactivated Vere's suspicions, and reminded him of why they were here.

It was plain to him that she was digging for information so that she could pass it on to the Emir. There was no need for him to answer her. But then neither was there any need to conceal the truth, since it was obvious that she was not going to allow herself to be persuaded that she was wrong.

Sam thought that he wasn't going to answer her. He was looking towards the rocks from where the water must once have flowed, down into the now dried-out pool in which they were standing, sheltered from the growing strength of the morning sun by the shadows cast by the rocks.

'There is a story that has been passed down through our family by word of mouth...'

The air had gone still, waiting for the sun's warmth—hungering for it, Sam guessed, in the same way that she hungered for Vere. Why had this happened to her? Why was fate subjecting her to this cruelty? Why couldn't she have loved another man? A different man? A man who might love her in return?

'When the borders between our states were originally drawn up,' Vere continued, 'my great-grandfather claimed as his wife the daughter of a British diplomat. It is said that after their marriage my ancestor and his bride spent their first night together as man and wife here, on their journey to Dhurahn city. A camp was set up, and my great-grandfather and his bride swam together alone here—for, as you have said, this was the course of the river then. It flowed over those rocks behind us and down into a pool here.

'The story goes that the pool was one of great beauty, fringed with all manner of plants and flowers, with an olive grove beyond it. The newly married couple consummated their vows to one another here in privacy, and it was here that their first child, a son, was conceived.

'Such was my ancestor's love for his wife that he commanded that the course of the river should be diverted, so that no other man could ever look upon the pool that held within it the memories of their love and her beauty, or imagine what anyone but him had the right to know. It was their special place, and he preferred to destroy it rather than let anyone else look upon it.'

'He must have loved her very much and…and very passionately' was all that Sam could manage to say.

'Yes,' Vere agreed.

Vere watched Sam from the protection of the shadows that cloaked his own expression. Last night, in giving herself to him, she had taken a part of him he could never reclaim. He had to admit that to himself because there was no way now he could evade that knowledge.

Without him knowing quite how, she had managed to touch his carefully protected emotions. But she was not someone with whom he could ever share his life, or to whom he could ever make a commitment. No matter how much he wanted her.

How could he do that when she was in the Emir's pay? Whatever his personal feelings, his duty was to his people and their best interests. The days were gone when a man like his great-grandfather had believed it was right to put his love for a woman above all else.

His *love* for a woman?

He did not love her. He could not—would not. It was impossible, unthinkable.

When he had guarded his heart against love he had thought he was protecting it from a woman who would know him as a man, a poet—someone to whom the desert was a sacred well from which he refilled his inner being— and that it would be her knowledge of this true essence of himself that would bind them together in mutual love.

She would love him *despite* the fact that he was a prince, not because of it, and she would share his belief that true honesty and trust were essential components of their love for one another. The woman would love him as his mother had loved his father—before and beyond anything or anyone else, even their children.

That woman was not this woman. He did not love this woman.

But his heart was thudding in sledgehammer-like blows, beating out a message that said he was lying to himself.

Having listened to Vere, Sam found that she was averting her gaze from the pool, not wanting to see the images Vere's story had brought to life. The young bride, her pale skin covered only by the water, and her husband, his skin darker, his body hardened by the desert and by tribal warfare, his passions aroused by his love for her. Their faces were concealed from her but their feelings were not.

To let her thoughts go further was too intrusive, and yet the images and the emotions they aroused in her couldn't be dismissed. Sam closed her eyes to shut them out, but when she opened them again the figures were still there, inside her imagination. Only now she could see their faces, and they belonged not to two unknown people but to herself and Vere. A shudder of naked longing racked her whole body.

The sun was fully risen now, its light sharpening the shadows glittering on the pebbles in the dried-out pool, now no more than an empty husk of what it had once been. It held no indication of the beauty it had known.

Vere looked at it and then looked away. His great-grandfather had loved passionately and intensely, and he had loved only one woman. To love like that was in his genes, a fate he could not avoid. But he must avoid it. He must not love this woman whom he could never trust.

Sam made a huge effort to redirect her thoughts to where they ought to be.

'If you knew the story behind the river, then why did you insist that I was wrong and that the course *hadn't* been changed?'

Her voice sounded low and strained in her own ears. She prayed that Vere wouldn't guess how difficult she was finding it to focus on what she was saying and the reason they were here.

'Why was it of so much interest to you that it had?' Vere countered, without answering her.

'Because I knew that I was *right* that it had been moved, and I knew that there had to be a reason.'

She was being very persistent. The Emir must have paid her very well indeed. So at least she had some kind of loyalty. Vere could feel the sharp acid bitterness of his own anger. It raked at his heart like wickedly sharp knives, driving him past caution.

'But of course you would have preferred that reason to be political rather than emotional?' he accused Sam bitingly.

Sam stared at him, not understanding his anger or his attack.

'Why do you say that?'

'Why do you think I say it?'

He was talking in riddles now, and Sam had no idea what they meant.

'I didn't have *any* preconceived idea about why the river had been re-routed. In fact that was part of what made it so intriguing. Logically there was no reason to move it. It isn't as though it forms part of a border, or is disputed in any way, but there had to be some motive. Everything must have a motive…'

What had been his for keeping his knowledge to himself and withholding it from her? she wondered. What had his motive been for sharing it with her now? Her instincts were warning her to be on her guard.

She was lying, of course. Vere knew it. She had to be. The only reason she had been interested in the changed course of the river was because the Emir was paying her to cause trouble for them. He knew that too.

How much had she told the Emir already? Had he, or those who had hired her on his behalf, suggested ways in which she might manipulate the facts to fit in with his personal agenda?

Had she hoped that by giving herself to him she could learn something that would aid the Emir's cause? The mere fact that he had slept with her so casually would be enough to discredit him and, via that, damage the reputation of their country. He had been a fool to let his desire for her overwhelm his judgement.

Vere thought quickly. He needed to protect Dhurahn against its current exposure to the Emir's schemes, and to negate the effect his relationship with the Emir's paid pawn might have. He needed to turn the tables on the Emir, and fast, and he thought he knew exactly how to do that.

If he were to establish Sam publicly as his official mistress, then who would place credence on any claims the Emir might try to make off the back of her investigations? No one.

Vere had no idea how such a plan had come to him. To take a person and use them without their knowledge for his ulterior purposes was ethically against everything he believed in. He wasn't doing this for himself, though, he reminded himself. He was doing it for Dhurahn.

Sam had shown herself willing to share his bed privately, so why should it make any difference to her if she shared it publicly? And their relationship would have to be shown publicly in order for it to benefit Dhurahn. The Heads of State would need to know that the 'expert witness' the Emir believed was secretly in his pocket was publicly in Vere's bed.

Publicly taking a mistress went against everything Vere held most dear, for he was a deeply private man, a man of pride and honour, but he knew that the only criticism of his actions would be his own. Drax would be more amused than shocked—all the more so if he believed that Vere genuinely felt desire for Sam—and Vere would keep from him the fact that his affair was a premeditated plan to outwit the Emir.

As for Sam herself... Vere frowned. He would make sure she was well reimbursed for her trouble, and that she knew she would be. All she needed to know was that he desired her and that he wanted her to be with him. If she was greedy and immoral enough to accept the Emir's bribe then she was hardly likely to turn down his offer, was she? A rich lover, ready to pay for the pleasure of having her in his bed, wasn't something she was going to turn her back on, was it? It was probably the kind of offer she had been hoping for from the start.

But, no matter how much he underpinned his decision with such thoughts, Vere knew that something deep inside him recoiled from it and felt tainted by it.

She had shown such trust and innocence last night, such sweetness in the way she had given herself to him so freely. Or had she? Had he simply allowed himself to think that because it was what he wanted to think? If things had been different, if *she* had been different, then his own future could have been so much happier than he had ever dreamed.

It was pointless thinking like that, Vere warned himself. He had a duty to do what must be done to protect Dhurahn.

'It's time we returned to the main camp,' he told Sam.

Sam nodded her head—but when she turned on her heel to start walking back to the four-by-four she slipped on the pebbles and lost her balance.

She could feel herself falling and cried out automatically—only to feel the breath leaking from her lungs as Vere reacted to her plight, catching hold of her and supporting her.

She looked up at him, intending only to thank him, she assured herself, but somehow her gaze slithered as helplessly to his mouth as her feet had done on the pebbles. And once there she couldn't remove it. Instead her imagination burned her senses with vivid images of a cool deep pool of water in which their naked bodies entwined as they swam together, before they stopped to stand body to body in its shallows, their hands and lips discovering one another.

'No...'

But it was too late. As though he had shared her intimate vision Vere was kissing her once, then twice, and then over and over again, as though his hunger for her was such that nothing could assuage it. Just like her hunger for him.

And when he did release her it was only to take her hand and lead her back to the four-by-four.

Neither of them spoke as he drove them back to the small camp. There was no need, Sam thought. She knew exactly what was in his mind, what he ached and yearned for, because the same thing was in her own.

In the cool shadows of her tent she watched as he undressed her, his lean long-fingered hands trembling visibly, but no more than her own fingers did when it was her turn to reach out and touch him.

Her body, knowing the delights ahead after last night, pulsed with eagerness and longing. Shrugging off the last of her clothes, she reached up to him, unable to wait any longer, urging him down towards her.

Outside the tent the sun scorched the earth in an embrace that was almost too much for it to bear. Inside, Sam lay in Vere's arms and felt that her desire for him was almost too much for her senses to bear. Several times tears scalded her eyes, and she cried out when Vere's touch carried her too close to her own pleasure.

'We mustn't,' she whispered to him. 'The risk…'

'Trust me, there will be no risk,' Vere soothed her, assuring himself that there would be no danger if he contented himself with simply pleasuring her and taking his own pleasure from that. He kissed her breasts and her belly, then moved lower, the tip of his tongue inscribing circles of indescribably intense pleasure against her thigh.

When he reached the swollen lips of her sex he stroked his fingertip along the length of its secrets. She was moist and ready, quickening to his touch, her flesh as sweet as fruit ripened to the moment of perfection. His hunger to taste her thundered through him, driving him beyond what he thought he knew of himself and what he was. It stripped away everything but his own need, forcing it and him into a single desire.

He tasted her with his tongue and then his lips. But even that wasn't enough to satisfy his need.

Unable to withstand her own pleasure, Sam cried out, her back arching and inviting. The feel of Vere sliding his body the length of hers made her sob with relief and cling to his shoulders. There was no need for her to urge him, though. He was already surging into her, filling her and completing her. He drove them both through their pleasure and beyond it to another level, and then another, each plateau more intense than the last, until finally all boundaries disappeared and they were at one with the universe, both of them oblivious to the risk they had taken.

SAM SURFACED SLOWLY through the layers of sleep that, when she had first closed her eyes, had cocooned her as securely as Vere's arms. Her body felt boneless and relaxed, and at the same time heavily sweet with the echoes of pleasure that clung to her like an invisible veil of sensation. She had never felt happier, nor more aware of how vulnerable she was. Of how finely balanced her emotions and senses were on the see saw edge of the intimacy she had shared with Vere. The heights and the depths were both there within her reach. With a single smile Vere could make her soar up to one and plunge down to the other.

Vere!

He was seated on the edge of the bed, fully dressed now, she realised, but with his head still bare. She could smell the freshly showered scent of his skin separating him from her, because her body was still perfumed with their intimacy.

'This can't be allowed to continue. For the Ruler of Dhurahn such clandestine behaviour is not fitting. Matters cannot continue as they are. Changes will have to be made.'

His harsh words plunged Sam down into the darkness of loss and despair. He was going to have her dismissed from her job, she recognised miserably.

She wanted to protest, but how could she? What could she say? No matter how much both of them might try to deny it, it was obvious that the sexual chemistry between them was too powerful for them to resist.

'I refuse to be forced to creep into your quarters under cover of darkness and then have to leave them again before the break of day, like some thief taking what he should not have. Instead I propose that you become my official mistress, and that I publicly acknowledge you as such. You will return with me to Dhurahn, where you will have your own suite of rooms in the royal palace. Your status will be recognised and respected. It is a great honour in the eyes of our people for a woman to be chosen to be their Ruler's mistress. You will share my life and my bed for as long as we continue to desire one another, and no one will dare to question our relationship.'

'You want me to be your mistress?' Sam could barely take in what he was saying, though she could feel the hollowness inside her filling with pain.

His *mistress*. How cold and unloving he made it sound—a union purely for sex, with no love or emotional bonding shared between them. There were no words from him to reassure her that, even if his position meant that he did not want to marry her, at least he cared enough to understand how important it was to her to know that he felt love for her.

'It seems a logical solution to a situation which we both know now is becoming untenable.'

She ought to turn him down and walk—no, run away from him just as far as she could, if only for the sake of her own pride. But how would she feel once she had done that? How would she feel back home in England, knowing she could have been with him? Would her pride sustain her then, when she was lying awake at night hungering for him?

It shocked her that she could feel like this, that there could even be any question of what she should do. What had happened to her inner belief that it was only within a secure and mutually committed, loving relationship that she would experience true sexual pleasure and satisfaction? What had happened to the conviction that for her a relationship without those things just wasn't worth having? That without being loved and loving in return, without being valued and valuing in return, there was no way she would want to be with a partner?

Vere offered her none of those things. Even his desire for her was a desire she felt he resented and in part blamed her for—a need which, when he wasn't being intimate with her, she suspected he felt extremely hostile towards.

Surely knowing all of these things her logic and common sense could only urge her in one direction. That direction being the opposite one from the one Vere was taking.

By rights she ought to be refusing him, telling him quite categorically that she had no wish to become his mistress. His *mistress*, she reminded herself. Not his lover. Even in choosing his wording Vere was offering her a position in his life which made them unequal.

But maybe it was understandable that he should withhold himself emotionally from her. A man in his position would have to be wary and careful. Women must throw themselves at him in their dozens. He had already accused her of doing exactly that, and said he wanted nothing more to do with her, but he had been the one who had instigated their lovemaking, and there Sam could find no fault with him at all. There, he had given her everything she had dreamed of in her wildest dreams and more.

She knew instinctively that it just wasn't possible for any other man to take her to such heights or show her such pleasures. No matter what she did from now on no one could ever match the sensuality of Vere's lovemaking. Her body would forever have desire for it and for him. Why not allow it to have what pleasure it could, even if she knew that ultimately that pleasure would be brought to an end?

She could live like that, couldn't she? She could endure the heights of sexual delight, knowing that what they had already shared had tipped her over the edge of fantasising about Vere into the painful reality of loving him, whilst Vere felt nothing emotionally for her. Was she sure she had the right degree of strength and self-discipline to separate her sexual fulfilment from the emotional barrenness of the relationship he was proposing without it destroying her?

But what if with time Vere should grow to love her? What if the sexual pleasure they shared led him to fall in love with her? Could she really bear to turn her back on the chance that that might happen?

The chance? It was a very small chance!

Yes, but it was there, wasn't it? And whilst it was there she could hope. Wasn't her love for him worth taking a risk for?

She gulped in a shallow breath of air and then exhaled, trying to steady her nerves.

'Some people might think it's an insult to a woman to offer her such a role,' she told Vere lightly.

'Might they? I doubt it. On the contrary. My opinion is that people will view the fact that I am publicly acknowledging you as a mark of my respect for you. Surely it is more insulting by far for me to be with you in secret, as though I feel that being with you shames me? As my mistress you will have status and position. Financially—'

'No!' Sam stopped him sharply. 'I don't want money to come into this. If I agree, then it is because...' She looked proudly at him. 'It is because I want you, not your money.'

'You say that, but if it is true then why do you hesitate? After all, I already know you want me.'

He had cut the ground from beneath her so neatly she had fallen straight into his trap, Sam acknowledged. She opened her mouth and then closed it again. Shaking her

head, she finally admitted, 'Since you put it like that, then
I don't suppose I can refuse, can I?'

'No,' Vere agreed softly. 'You can't. And nor would I
have allowed you to do so.'

CHAPTER EIGHT

SAM SUSPECTED that it wasn't just the motion of the helicopter Vere had summoned to transport them swiftly to Dhurahn that was making her feel slightly dizzy. From the second she had given her agreement to Vere's proposition things had moved so fast that Sam had barely had time to catch her breath at all.

When she had protested that she needed time to explain things to her colleagues, Vere had told her arrogantly that no explanation would be needed. The very fact that she was with him would be enough. And of course he had been right.

Anne, who had come to see her whilst she had been packing, had shaken her head and taken hold of Sam's hands in hers to say, almost maternally, 'Oh, my dear, are you sure?'

'That I'm doing the right thing? No,' Sam had admitted, choking back a small laugh. 'But I'm sure that if I don't go with him I shall regret it.'

'You're in love with him,' Anne had guessed. 'Well, I can't blame you. But these men are autocrats, my dear, and their way of life…'

'I know it won't last for ever,' Sam had told her bravely.

Anne had patted her hand without reassuring her, saying only, 'I do so hope that you won't end up being hurt.'

Would she end up being hurt? Sam wondered now, as they flew over the fertile area of land irrigated by the Dhurahni River. Or would the miracle she longed for occur and Vere fall in love with her?

Down below them she could see fields of crops, olive groves, and a wide, straight arterial road.

'Our farmers grow the crops that feed the tourists who flock to Zuran,' Vere told her, leaning across her slightly, his body hard against the softness of her own.

She had already noticed the respect with which she had been treated by the men who had accompanied Vere to the camp when he had escorted her from her tent to the helicopter. She shivered a little now, still not really able to take in the public change in her circumstances. All she wanted was Vere the man, as her lover and her love, but Vere was more than Vere the man; he was also the powerful Ruler. How would she fit in to his environment?

They were flying into what Sam assumed must be Dhurahn's airport.

Sam looked uncertainly at Vere, suddenly feeling very vulnerable and anxious.

'Are you sure this is a good idea?' she asked him. 'I mean, with you being Dhurahn's Ruler...and your brother...what will he—'

'Drax will thoroughly approve.'

Sam could see how Vere's expression softened and lightened when he mentioned his twin. She felt a small pang of jealousy. Vere loved his brother. She so desperately wanted him to love her. She knew so little about Vere's life, but she felt unable to ask too many questions. What did that tell her about the imbalance in their relationship?

The helicopter had come to rest. Vere touched her arm, indicating that she was to follow him.

By the time they were standing on the concrete runway a vehicle had pulled up in front of them, the driver getting out and salaaming to Vere before opening the car doors for them.

Sam didn't know quite what she had expected. Perhaps not exactly outriders and half an army, but certainly rather more formality.

She was even more bewildered when, instead of leaving the runway, they were driven over to a waiting plane. She looked at Vere questioningly.

'We're going to Zuran,' he told her, as they were ushered out of the car and towards a waiting plane, where he stopped to say something to the pilot as Sam was escorted on board by the flight attendants.

Sam had never flown in a privately owned jet before.

'The flight time to Zuran is one hour,' the male flight attendant was telling her as he offered her a glass of champagne, which she refused. She felt giddy enough already, without drinking alcohol.

She stared round the interior of the plane, her eyes widening at the luxury of its cream carpet and blue-grey walls. Instead of rows of seats there were plush-looking leather chairs and a desk.

'If you wish to rest, there is a bedroom here,' the steward continued, opening a door and ushering her towards it. Uncertainly Sam looked inside. The bedroom was luxuriously appointed, with its own *en suite* bathroom, and it was all Sam could do not to betray just how out of her depth she was beginning to feel in the midst of so much luxury. Would Vere expect to consummate their new relationship here? Her face began to burn and her heart pumped too fast.

'Perhaps you would like something else to drink?' the steward asked

'Just water…thank you,' Sam answered and then tensed,

knowing that Vere had entered the cabin even though she couldn't see him.

She turned round, her heart racing, whilst the steward made a deep obeisance. She waited for him to leave before she burst out shakily, 'I don't think I can do this. It was different in the desert, but I'm not—this...' She gestured helplessly around the cabin. 'This kind of thing...I don't think...I don't know anything about royal protocol, and even if I did that's not the way I want to live.'

'You'll get used to it,' Vere told her dismissively.

He couldn't afford for her to be having second thoughts now, and ruining his plans. Not when he was already aching for the hot sweet pleasure of holding her through the night, knowing she was his. Vere dismissed his unwelcome thoughts angrily. It was not for that reason that he was doing this.

'Dhurahn isn't Zuran,' he told Sam. 'We live relatively simply. Now, sit down and make yourself comfortable. We'll be taking off soon.'

Obediently Sam found that she was subsiding into one of the leather chairs and accepting the glass of water the steward had brought for her.

Their take-off was smooth and swift, and by the time they had eaten the meal the steward served them they had begun their descent into Zuran.

Here, though, when they left the aircraft they were met by several important-looking officials, then ushered to a waiting limousine with blacked-out windows and a motorcycle escort, the Zurani flag flying on its bonnet.

Sam hadn't thought to ask why they had come to Zuran, assuming it must be on some kind of state business, and she wasn't expecting it when they pulled up outside the entrance to what she knew to be Zuran's most exclusive and expensive shopping mall.

Uniformed flunkeys held open the doors for them, but when they stepped into the air-conditioned marble-floored mall it was completely empty of shoppers.

Bewildered, Sam turned to look at Vere.

'You're now my official mistress,' he told her. 'It will shame me if you are not appropriately clothed. The Ruler of Zuran has kindly offered to make the facilities of this mall available to us, so that you can be provided with all that is necessary.'

'You mean you've brought me here to buy me clothes?' Sam demanded angrily, too shocked to hide her feelings.

Vere frowned. She sounded more displeased than pleased. It was his understanding that women liked nothing better than a new designer wardrobe, and it irked him slightly that Sam was not reacting with more enthusiasm and appreciation.

'You can't have imagined that what you have will be suitable for your new role. Naturally my people will expect you to be dressed as befits that position.'

Sam wanted to tell him that she hated the thought of him paying for her clothes because it demeaned and hurt her, it turned her into an object—the appropriately dressed mistress—but a stunningly beautifully dressed young woman was coming towards them, making any further private conversation impossible.

'Highness,' she greeted Vere respectfully, before turning to Sam. 'I am to be your personal dresser, madam. If you would like to come this way, we have arranged a private room for you in which you can relax whilst clothes are brought for your inspection.'

AT LAST IT was over.

Sam refused to look at Vere as a team of sales assistants wrapped her new clothes in tissue paper. Her eyes felt dry, burning with the shamed tears she refused to let herself cry.

The clothes Vere had bought for her *were* beautiful—exquisite Chanel suits and tops, Jimmy Choo shoes, Vera Wang evening wear, and so much more, all of it designer label and all of it earning only a brief nod of the head from Vere after she had been dressed in them and then paraded in front of him.

With each successive humiliating nod of his head Sam had felt her outrage give way to misery, until her misery had been overtaken by what she felt now. The bleak certainty that she couldn't do this.

Vere frowned as he watched Sam's reaction to the growing pile of shiny bags and boxes. The more the quantity grew, the more she seemed to withdraw into herself—so much so that she was actually physically stepping back from the garments and from him. Her normal warmly vivacious expression had been replaced with blank withdrawal as she focused her gaze away from both her new clothes and him.

Vere might never have been responsible for providing a woman with a brand-new designer wardrobe before, but even without that experience he knew enough to recognise that this was not the reaction he might have expected.

Half a dozen men dressed in livery that wouldn't have disgraced a Hollywood extravaganza representing the court of an *Arabian Nights* Caliph had been summoned to carry Sam's new clothes. And it would take a fleet of limousines to ferry everything to the airport, Sam reflected bleakly, forcing herself to smile at the girls who had served her. After all, it wasn't their fault that she felt the way she did. It was her own.

She had been so naïve, never envisaging anything like this when she had let her heart rule her head and agreed to enter into this relationship with Vere. She was now beginning to recognise she would not be able to endure it. She didn't want to be his mistress, with all that that implied, she wanted to be his lover... No, that wasn't true, was it? What she really wanted, she acknowledged wretchedly, was to be his love, as he was hers. But she had already told herself that that was impossible. She had already said to herself that she accepted the limitations of what he was offering her and that she could live with them. Was she now saying that she had changed her mind and she couldn't?

Tears were burning her eyes behind the protection of her sunglasses. She felt so very alone. Her parents, living in their neat detached house in a London suburb, would never understand any of this.

She hesitated in mid-step and, as though he sensed her desire to flee, Vere reached out and took hold of her hand. He continued to hold it until they had reached the waiting limousine.

They got into it in mutual silence, and the first thing Vere did once they were inside it was close the partition that separated them from the driver, ensuring they could speak without being overheard.

'I can't do this,' Sam burst out as soon as Vere had closed the screen.

Vere's mouth compressed. 'You have already agreed.'

'That was when I thought...before...'

'Before what? Nothing has changed.'

'Of course it has. Have you any idea how humiliating it was to parade in front of you in those clothes, knowing that you would be paying for them, knowing that because I'm your mistress everyone will assume that you are paying me for sex.'

'That is often the assumption when a man takes a mistress.'

'That depends on how you define the word "mistress". I assumed that what you meant was that you wanted us to be lovers. Everything was so different when we were in the desert. There we were just two people who...who wanted one another. I love the desert. There's something so pure and pared-down about it. It makes you confront things about yourself—' Sam broke off and shook her head. 'Everything seemed so right there. Just the two of us and the desert. Nothing more. That's all I want from you, Vere. The right to be with you because it's what we both want. I don't want to be dressed up like...like an expensively wrapped trophy....'

Vere could hear the pain in her voice. It touched a place within him that he had thought protected from any touch. The desert stripped away the folly of consumerism and status and reduced a man to blood and bone and flesh. It demanded that a man meet it with only that. One either loved the desert or one feared it. Vere loved it.

He could feel the echo of Sam's emotional words striking a chord within him. It pierced the hard, protective wall he had built around his own emotions. Unwanted, dangerous thoughts and feelings pressed against that barrier, threatening it, fuelling Vere's anger against the woman who had caused them.

'It is too late to change your mind now,' he told her.

He knew that news of their shopping trip would reach the ears of the Emir, and that it would add substance to the fiction he wanted to create that Sam was indeed his mistress.

IGNORING THE GLOSSY magazines that had appeared in the jet's cabin whilst they had been in the shopping mall, Sam picked up the paperback she had bought for herself instead.

She had no idea where all the new clothes were, nor did she care. She felt weighed down with her own despair.

When Vere had asked her to be his official mistress she had envisaged long hours of sexual intimacy—not shopping trips followed by Vere involving himself in paperwork without so much as attempting to even kiss her. Admittedly the bedroom of his private jet couldn't provide the privacy she would have preferred, but if he really wanted her surely he would have managed to find some excuse to draw her in there to hold her and kiss her? He must know how alien and overwhelming she was finding all of this. After all, there couldn't be many young women in her position who wouldn't have been feeling the same.

Vere's mobile rang, showing the private number that belonged to his twin.

When he stood up and turned his back to her to take his call, Sam guessed that it must be personal and got up herself, heading for the bedroom cabin to give Vere privacy in which to take the call.

'Drax,' Vere welcomed his twin.

'I'm just about to leave for the Alliance of Arabic-Speaking Nations finance conference, but I thought I'd better let you know that the reports have come through from our agents on your Miss McLellan.'

Vere was on the point of denying that Sam was 'his', when he realised that it was hardly true any more. He needed to bring Drax up to speed with his decision.

However, before he could do so, Drax was continuing. 'We've drawn a blank, I'm afraid. Whoever it is who is in the Emir's pay it is definitely not Samantha McLellan. Our people have been over her life and her finances in microscopic detail, and there is nothing that can tie her into the Emir in any kind of way. Interestingly, though, they did discover that her computer has been hacked into whilst she's been working in the field, and their feeling is that someone has been very interested in her work.'

Sam was not in the Emir's pay.

Outrunning his shock was a wave of emotion that kicked away his defences. Now he had nothing to shield him from what she was doing to him. No way of protecting himself from the way she made him feel.

Vere struggled to wrest control from these sensations and focus on practical issues, regain some control.

'She raised the queries about the Dhurahni River being re-routed,' he managed to tell his twin. 'It could be that whoever is working for the Emir got to hear about them and thought there might be something there the Emir could use.'

'We'd better have her colleagues checked out, then,' Drax suggested.

'Yes,' Vere agreed. 'When do you expect to be back in Dhurahn?'

'I'm not sure. I've sent Sadie home ahead of me, so I don't intend to linger. She's got several weeks to go yet before the baby is due, of course, but much as I shall miss her she needs to rest—even though she insists she would rather be with me.'

'Drax?'

'Yes?'

'I'm on my way back to Dhurahn now, and I'm taking Samantha McLellan with me. It's a long story,' Vere added quickly, 'but—'

'Ah, you need say no more, brother.' Drax was laughing before Vere could tell him why he had planned to have Sam accompany him. 'I have been there myself, remember? I can tell from your voice what is happening... If you are having trouble persuading her to marry you, then...' Drax's voice faded, and then the connection was broken.

There was no point in trying to phone Drax back, Vere acknowledged. What, after all, could he say? Drax had obviously got hold of the wrong idea. Like everyone in love, Drax automatically assumed that everyone else wanted to share his exalted state. Besides, for once in his life Vere had something more important to think about than what his brother might think.

Sam was completely innocent of any wrong-doing.

The agents they employed were far too good at their job to make any mistakes, and Vere didn't even think of disputing what Drax had told him. So now he didn't need her as his mistress at all. There was no point in him establishing her in that role since she was not in the Emir's pay.

A mixture of emotions twisted through him. Fear, anger, hostility, all bound together by the ties linking him to his past and the loss of his mother. And joy, tenderness and guilt for misjudging her, woven like a gentle chain around his heart.

Out of habit, it was the older, darker emotions he allowed to claim him. They were the emotions he felt safe with. They did not require him to do anything other than go on believing as he had done for so long. They did not require a blind leap of faith. All they required and demanded was that he dismissed Sam from his life immediately.

It would be easy enough for him to tell her that he had changed his mind, and it would be a simple exercise for him to arrange for her to be taken back to the camp where she could resume her work. After all, there was no rational reason now to keep her with him, was there?

Immediately his emotions rejected the thought of letting her go. A sharp, unwanted stab of anguish pierced his heart at the thought of not having her in his life. His heart was hammering against his ribs and his whole body was tensed in rejection of the thought of losing her, whilst a battle raged within him between his need to protect himself and the desire Sam aroused within him.

He couldn't send her back, even if he wanted to, he reasoned to himself. The cartographer's position she had vacated had already been filled, and anyway, he could hardly expect her to simply carry on working at the camp as though nothing had happened. Those working with her were bound to ask questions. He surely had a duty to protect her from that.

But if he hadn't misjudged her in the first place... Though he'd had no option but to suspect her, given the circumstances, Vere defended himself.

And no option but to make love with her? His heart slammed into his ribs.

No, he had had no option there either—but for very different reasons.

He wasn't proud of what he had done, or of his own weakness, but it was for her sake and not his own that he intended to keep her with him in Dhurahn whilst he formulated some satisfactory way of compensating her for the damage his suspicions might have done to her career, as he now considered himself honour-bound to do.

And was that the only reason? Were his motives purely altruistic, and nothing whatsoever to do with his own feelings, his own desires?

She would be housed in her own quarters, and he would not intrude on those. He would find some way to ensure that her presence in Dhurahn was recognised as the professional visit of a qualified cartographer. The mouth of the Dhurahni where it reached the sea had never been properly mapped; silting had changed the course of river there. Mapping the coastline would be a very worthwhile project, and would surely go some way to redressing the harm he could have done her.

But he had already advertised the fact that she was his mistress.

She could be his lover *and* work professionally in Dhurahn. That way he could both make amends and keep her close to him. Close enough for them to...

To what?

That wasn't a question Vere could allow himself to answer.

She had told him, though, that she had changed her mind and no longer wanted to go with him. If he had any sense he would accept that and let her go.

But within a heartbeat he was reminding himself that she had only changed her mind about the outward image of her role, not about the inner, intimate living of it. She had said herself that she wanted him.

A hot surge of male need speared through him. They were already lovers. Would it really be so wrong for them to continue to be so? No one, least of all his twin, would deny him the right to set aside the responsibilities of rulership and simply be a man. And by needing her he was not really allowing himself to become vulnerable. Needing wasn't loving. He could need her without loving her. He did not love her. He would not love her. So there was really no reason why she should not stay, was there? Unless, of course, he secretly thought that he was in danger of loving her?

Of course he wasn't.

SAM HAD PUT as much distance as she could between herself and Vere, neither looking at him nor talking to him during the flight.

A group of officials were waiting to greet Vere as they left the jet. Sam deliberately kept herself in the shadows, which was surely the correct place for a mistress—espe-

cially one dressed like her, in the same serviceable clothes
she had taken with her to the desert. But even if she had
been able to bring herself to change into any of the new
clothes Vere had bought her she would still have hung
back, Sam knew.

She caught one of the officials, a young woman with
dark eyes that flashed liquid with longing whenever she
looked at Vere, staring at her. Unlike her, the woman was
standing tall with pride and self-respect, her sunglasses
perched on her head, all the better for Vere to admire those
magnificent tawny eyes of hers, Sam reflected miserably,
and the equally magnificent cleavage just teasingly hinted
at by the V in her crisp tailored shirt.

Why had she agreed to this? Sam asked herself wretchedly. It was obvious to her that she had been a fool to think
that Vere could ever come to love her. She had allowed
herself to be carried away by her own longing and the romance of the desert, where they had just been two people
unable to fight a mutual desire for one another. That, however, had merely been a desert mirage, that was all. The
reality was what was here in front of her now. And that
reality wasn't a man she had deceived herself into creating out of her own need, a man she could reach out to and
connect with, if only via his desire for her.

The reality was this stranger, dressed now not simply, as she had seen him in the desert, but wearing over
his plain white *dishdasha* a rich dark blue silk robe embroidered with gold thread, which he had put on before
they left the aircraft. There might not be a crown on his
head, but it might just as well be there. Both his manner
and that of those around him reflected what he was. Sam
could see in his expression hauteur, where before she had
seen merely a certain austere withdrawal which she had
translated as a sign of a complex and fascinating person-

ality. The hands Vere extended to those who had come to welcome him were covered in the same flesh that had touched her, but the heavy dark emerald ring glowing in the sunlight surely testified to the fact that those hands controlled the lives of others.

There was no place in this man's life for her. The days might have gone when an Eastern ruler installed his women in the seraglio, where no other male eyes could see them and where their days were wasted in an emptiness of waiting to be chosen to share his bed, but Sam suspected her role would be a traditional one nevertheless.

Dressed in her new clothes, she would be expected to live in the shadows, a symbol of her master's wealth and status, a toy for him to play with when the mood took him, to be returned to the shadows to wait for him to want her again.

VERE'S GAZE SEARCHED the small crowd, and came to rest on Sam's pale set face.

He could give instructions now that she was to be put on a plane home and, once he had compensated her financially for the disruption to her life, dismiss her from his thoughts. He could make amends for the loss of her job by ensuring that she was offered more lucrative work elsewhere. There were any number of ways in which he could ensure that he owed her nothing and had no moral obligations towards her. There was no logical reason for him to complicate his life by keeping her here.

No logical reason, no.

He gave a brief nod of his head. Two men stepped forward, bowing to Sam.

Miserably, Sam allowed herself to be guided towards yet another waiting limousine.

This time she was travelling in it alone, whilst Vere rode ahead of her in a different car, with two other men.

The road on which they were travelling was straight and wide. To one side of it lay the sea, a perfect shade of blue-green beneath the late-afternoon sunshine. To the other side lay what Sam presumed must be the City of Dhurahn, and then set aside from it was an area of tall modern glassfronted skyscrapers, located in what looked like landscaped gardens.

Their route was lined with palm trees set into immaculate flowerbeds with green verges. Through the dark tinted windows of the limousine she could see the people in the vehicles on the other side of the road turning to look at their cavalcade.

Up ahead of them Sam could see a huge wall, in which a pair of wrought-iron gates were opening to allow them through into a courtyard beyond them. The tails of the peacocks shaped in the wrought-iron gates shimmered in the sunlight just as richly as the real thing, the emerald-green of the stones set in them surely the exact shade of Vere's eyes. Vere. She must not think of him as Vere any more. She must think of him instead as the Ruler of Dhurahn. That way maybe she could distance herself properly from him.

A flight of polished cream marble steps led up to a portico, its heavy wooden doors already open and the steps themselves lined with liveried servants.

Vere was already out of his car and striding up the steps.

As she watched him disappear inside the doors, Sam could feel herself starting to panic. She felt lost, abandoned, vulnerable and alone. She also felt angry and resentful because of those feelings.

Someone was opening the car door. Reluctantly Sam got out.

One of the liveried men bowed respectfully. 'If you will come this way, please?'

Silently Sam followed him inside. The large hallway was cool and filled with shadows after the heat outside. Intricately carved shutters blocked the heat of the sunlight from coming through the windows. The marble floor was bare of rugs, and in the middle of it was a raised rectangular pool. The surface of the water was covered in creamy white rose petals. A traditional burning censer stood on one of the steps, giving off a warm spicy scent.

The only furniture in the room was several low divans with gilded legs and armrests, standing against the walls, their silk cushions a splash of colour against the plain white walls. Several sets of inner closed doors opened off the hallway, their dark wood carved with Arabic designs. Coloured glass lamps in fretted ironwork hung from the ceiling, along with several more censers.

'Welcome to Dhurahn, Madam,' said a small dark-haired girl with a soft voice, who seemed to have appeared out of nowhere to bow and gesture across the hallway. 'I am Masiri. If you will allow me, I shall show you to the women's quarters.'

The women's quarters! Sam shivered. But what else could she do but follow Masiri up the long flight of marble stairs and then along a gallery through which the hallway down below could only be seen through a protective fretted screen?

Another flight of stairs and another corridor, this one in the form of an upper veranda that overlooked an enclosed courtyard and garden. Sam caught her breath as she looked down into it, her misery momentarily forgotten as she admired its beauty. A fountain sent droplets of water upwards to sparkle in the sunlight before falling back to dimple the smooth surface of a pool. Large lazy goldfish half hidden

by water lily leaves basked in the warmth. The air was full
of the scent of the roses planted in the flowerbeds.

'His Highness Prince Vere lives in the old part of the
palace, whilst his brother His Highness Prince Drax lives
in the new part,' Masiri explained in careful English, adding, 'you are to have the rooms of the Lady Princess. It
was for her that her husband built the garden.'

Sam forced a smile and nodded her head, although she
had no real idea who Masiri meant.

The girl had stopped outside a pair of double doors, and
now opened them.

Reluctantly Sam stepped inside—and then stopped. The
room in which she was standing was a beautiful drawing
room, decorated as though it were in a classically styled
Georgian mansion. It was a woman's room, Sam saw at
once, its furniture delicate and feminine—a pretty ma-
hogany writing desk, a pair of matching sofa tables—and
there was even an embroidery screen and a sewing box.
A large gilt-framed mirror hung over an Adam-style fireplace; pale green watered silk covered the walls and hung
at the windows. A carpet woven in the same pattern and
colours as the plasterwork on the ceiling covered the floor.

The whole room was so elegant, its furnishings so obviously antique, that Sam could only gaze at her surroundings in bemusement and awe.

Smiling at her, Masiri led the way to another pair of
double doors telling Sam, 'Here is the bedroom for you,
madam.'

Dutifully Sam followed her.

The bedroom was decorated in the same style as the
drawing room, and in the same colours. The large bed had
pale green silk drapes lined in gold silk, and the bedspread
was green silk embroidered with gold.

'Here is a dressing room and a bathroom,' Masiri enun-

ciated carefully, indicating the doors on either side of the
bed. 'I go now and bring you coffee and some food.'

Sam nodded her head. Her head had started to ache.
She walked into the dressing room. Mirrored wardrobes
lined one wall, throwing back to her an image of herself
that depressed her. They had been travelling virtually all
day, and her serviceable long-sleeved khaki shirt and skirt
looked dull and dusty—and decidedly un-mistress-like.

She opened one of the wardrobe doors and then stiffened, quickly opening another. There, hanging up neatly,
were the clothes Vere had bought. They had obviously been
brought to the palace ahead of them and swiftly unpacked.

Another woman might welcome a life in which unseen hands performed every single necessary task and
all one had to do was allow oneself to be waited on, but
Sam didn't.

When Masiri returned with coffee and a plate of small
sweet pastries, Sam was waiting impatiently for her.

'I want to see His Highness,' she told her determinedly.
'There is something that I need to tell him.'

'You wish His Highness to come to you?' Masiri asked
uncertainly.

From the look on Masiri's face Sam suspected that she
viewed her request as a breach of protocol, but she didn't
care.

'Either he comes to me or you take me to him. It doesn't
matter which,' Sam told her firmly. 'But I must see him
as soon as possible.'

VERE LOOKED AT the note his PA had handed him and read
it quickly.

Sam wanted to see him. He looked down at his desk,
where his staff had neatly stacked that correspondence
they felt Vere would need to see most urgently.

He also should, as a matter of good manners, seek out his sister-in-law and enquire after her health. Drax would expect that of him at the very least. Sadie was a very modern young woman, who was determined to ensure that her husband and her brother-in-law did everything they could to promote sexual equality amongst their own people, and Vere supported her in that. And even if he had not done so, even if there had been issues on which they had clashed, he would have forgiven her them because of the love she had for his twin.

Initially Drax had brought her to Dhurahn as a bride for Vere, not himself, as part of his scheme to prevent them both from being forced into diplomatic marriages. Drax with the Emir's eldest daughter, and Vere with the Ruler of Zuran's youngest sister. Neither of them had welcomed their neighbours' marital plans, but they had agreed that they had to be dealt with tactfully and a plausible reason found for refusal. It had been Drax who had suggested that their best way out of the situation would be for them to provide *themselves* with wives, before either the Ruler or the Emir could broach the subject of formal negotiations.

When Drax had fallen in love with the prospective wife he had chosen for Vere, Vere had been happy for both of them—and happy for himself too. Drax's marriage meant that he could fob off both his neighbours' attempts to marry him into their families by pointing out that it was impossible for him to agree without risking offending one of them.

Ultimately he imagined that when he did marry it would be a diplomatic marriage, though one which he chose. The very thought of the vulnerability that falling in love brought made him stiffen his defences against it.

'You will not be able to escape your fate, brother,' Drax had teased him. 'You wait and see. You will follow the same path as our forebears and fall in love with a European woman. It is written into our genes, its course set into the stars. There is no escape.'

Drax was wrong, of course. Totally wrong.

He was, Vere realised, still holding his PA's note, telling him that Sam was asking to see him as a matter of urgency.

Just thinking about her waiting for him set off a reaction within him that underlined everything he was fighting against. She touched parts of him—his emotions, his self-control… Witness the way he had allowed her to urge his possession of her when he should have withdrawn. Vere could feel the colour crawling up under his skin even though he tried to suppress it. It was no use. He could not withstand the turbulent surge of desire that crashed through him, breaching every defence he tried to put up against it.

Images, scents, sounds filled his head, until his own breathing quickened in time to the remembered race of hers. He moved uncomfortably in his chair, all too aware of the heavy pulse of his erection. If he went to her now he wouldn't be able to trust himself not to touch her. But why *shouldn't* he touch her?

Without telling her the truth? Without giving her the opportunity to judge properly for herself whether or not she still wanted him? His parents would have abhorred such an attitude, and so too did he. If he went to her now… If he went to her now, feeling like this, he was afraid of what he might say and do. Better to wait until he was more in control of himself.

Vere crushed the note and then released it to drop onto his desk, ignoring it to focus on the other papers in front of him.

CHAPTER NINE

IT WAS SEVERAL HOURS since the sun had set. His desk was virtually clear, and Vere realised guiltily that he had not been to see Sadie.

It didn't take him long to walk through the old part of the palace and into the new modern wing that Drax had designed.

Sadie smiled when she saw him, offering to send for coffee for him, but Vere shook his head.

'You are well? Drax told me that you have been tired.'

'I am very well,' she assured him. 'And as for me being tired, yes, I was—but now that I am home I feel much better.'

Vere knew that she would have heard about Sam, but she was far too tactful to ask any questions. Unlike his twin.

'Drax is returning immediately after the conference ends,' he commented.

'I hope so.'

Vere remained with her for half an hour, but he could see that she was, as Drax had said, looking tired, so he didn't linger.

Now all he had to do was respond to Sam's earlier summons.

He had made up his mind that he must tell her the truth and admit how much he had misjudged and wronged her.

It had been easy to set aside his own strong moral scruples when he had believed that at least part of her reason for having sex with him was because she was in the Emir's pay, and therefore he had no responsibility towards her. But now he knew that was not the case, which meant that her desire for him must be genuine.

Whilst his flesh welcomed and indeed embraced that knowledge, his mind wanted to withdraw from it. And his emotions?

Vere cursed himself under his breath as he felt his body respond to the question with its now familiar ache for her.

SAM HAD WAITED for Vere for what had felt like hours, and then, when he hadn't appeared, she had showered the grime of the day from her tired body and wrapped herself in a towel, simply intending to sit in the drawing room for a few minutes.

Instead she had fallen asleep in the chair, and that was where Vere found her when he walked into the room.

She was lying with her head against the arm of the chair at an angle that could only result in her waking up with a stiff neck, and her hair looked damp, as though she had fallen asleep without drying it. Her lashes lay against her cheek in soft dark fans. Her lips parted naturally as she breathed, and in the dimly lit room the exposed flesh of her throat and shoulder gleamed with the luminescence of the purest mother-of-pearl.

Vere could feel his heart thudding as heavily as though it had become destabilised, crashing into his ribs with all the recklessness of a man about to haul himself over a precipice, oblivious to his own danger, driven only by a soul-deep need.

She looked so vulnerable and alone. There were

smudges beneath her eyes—had she been crying? He could feel the weight of his own guilt.

Somehow he managed to wrench his thoughts back to where they should be. She was just a sleeping woman, that was all.

A sleeping woman whom he had held in his arms in the tranquillity that had followed the intensity of their shared orgasm. He could remember how it had felt to have her burrowing against him, wanting and needing him, finding her security in being with him. Trusting him.

Shame vied inside him with a feeling of almost melancholic sweetness that poured softly through his veins like warmed honey. Now was not the time to disturb her, and possibly distress her with what he had to say. His admissions and her questions could wait until morning. Though he couldn't leave her there to sleep so uncomfortably.

He leaned down, lifting her from the chair, his intention merely to carry her over to the bed and then leave her.

However, he had barely taken more than a couple of steps when she woke up, stiffening, and then relaxing as she said his name with recognition and relief.

She reached out to hold on to him, turning her own body into his. 'I'm so glad you're here.' Her voice was soft with sleep and contentment. Automatically Vere tightened his hold on her.

Sleepily Sam clung to Vere's strength as he carried her into the bedroom and towards the bed. She had been so angry, so determined to tell him that she wanted to leave, but somehow now that he was here, and she was in his arms, that anger had evaporated like the pools of water created overnight by the cold desert air, disappearing in the morning heat of the sun as though they had never been.

She loved him so much. Surely with that love she would

be able to show him how much she needed the respect that came from knowing he valued her and cared about her.

He was placing her on the bed. Lovingly she reached up to him, twining her arms round his neck as the towel slipped away from her body, and she breathed out his name against his skin in a soft sound of pleasure.

He must not stay here, Vere warned himself. But as he reached to unclasp her hands from behind his neck Sam pressed her mouth against his in a kiss of sweet command, the tip of her tongue tormenting the closed line of his lips with eager little impatient caresses.

Vere could feel his resolve crumbling to dust—less than dust. It was nothing, gone, forgotten as he let her tease him into submitting to her pleasure. Her tongue slipped between his parted lips, causing Vere to shudder in violent need as it found his and flirted with it, coaxing and cajoling. In the moonlight Vere could see the stiff tightness of her nipples, erect with arousal, and the curve of her breast demanding the cup of his hand around its soft weight. He probed the urgent thrust of her nipple with the pad of his thumb, stroking it, rubbing it erotically, feeling her going wild with sexual excitement. Her tongue meshed with his, submitting to its control of their pleasure. Her hands were trying to push away the fabric that was coming between her and his flesh. She moaned beneath his kiss, her whole body trembling.

He reached out with his free hand to caress the curve of her hip, his own body gripped by unbearable need when she arched upwards, opening her thighs to offer him the gift of her desire for him.

Her sex pulsed with the frantic demand that was throbbing through his own aroused flesh. She was moist and hot, crying out to him when he touched her.

It was more than he could endure.

He undressed quickly and Sam wound her arms around him, pressing her body close to him and kissing every bit of him she could reach…his throat, his shoulder, his chest, and then, to his shock, his belly, making his already hard erection swell and stiffen even more. Abandoning the last of his clothes, Vere picked her up and placed her down on the bed, his mouth against her breast, tightening around her nipple and drawing rhythmically on it whilst Sam gasped and cried out that it was too much pleasure for her to bear.

Her body was already convulsing into the beginning of her orgasm when he entered her, and he felt her flesh tighten on him and possess him, until his cry of release mingled with her own.

'Oh, Vere. I knew right from the start that it would be like this for us.' Sam clung to him emotionally, her voice reflecting the intensity of her experience whilst her heartbeat slowed back down to its normal rate.

How could she not love him and want him to love her after what they had just shared? She felt so bonded with him, so very aware of how much he completed her in ways that no one else ever could. During their lovemaking she had given herself to him, completely and totally. This was how she would want their child to be conceived, in an act of total commitment and giving, so that it would be born carrying that gift of love within its genes.

'Stay with me,' she whispered.

How had it come to this? Vere wondered helplessly as his arms closed round her, holding her to him. This wasn't what he had intended when he had come to her.

Wasn't it? Did he really believe that? Or had he known all along what the outcome would be once he touched her?

Soon Sam had fallen asleep. Vere rested his chin on top of her head. It felt so right, being here with her like this—*she* felt so right. A sensation as though a rock was being lifted away from a guarded, painful place inside him eased gently though him.

'Stay with me,' she had asked him, those words like a tender healing touch on a sore place, overlaying his own painful teenage cry to his parents of, 'Don't leave me'.

SAM WOKE UP abruptly, her hand on the empty space in the bed where Vere should have been. He had gone, left her. The pain inside her was raw and cruel.

She could smell coffee, and the shutters to the French doors had been opened to let in the bright morning light. She pulled on her robe, its long filmy sleeves covering her arms, and stepped through the open doors into the enclosed private courtyard garden.

The sun warmed her skin, and bees hummed busily as they worked. Sam paused to breathe in the scent of a newly opened rose. A shadow fell across the path, and her heart turned over inside her chest in a leap of joy.

'Vere!'

He was showered, his hair still damp, and the smell of soap was on his skin as he came and stood beside her.

'I want to talk to you,' he told her quietly.

Vere had been awake before dawn, lying with Sam's body a sweet weight in his arms, whilst a much heavier and less pleasant weight lay on his conscience.

It had been his own manservant who had discreetly brought fresh coffee and fruit.

'If it's about the clothes—' Sam began, but Vere shook his head

'No, it isn't about the clothes. When we first met in Zuran you had no idea who I was, did you?'

'No, I didn't,' Sam agreed truthfully.

Vere exhaled.

'I know you thought...that is, you suggested...I don't

normally…I couldn't help myself,' Sam admitted. 'I looked at you and I knew that my life had changed for ever.'

How could he ever have thought of her as duplicitous? Her honesty shone from her, shaming him.

'I…I felt…something too.'

It astonished Vere that he should make such an admission, but he had been compelled to do so, unable to deny the words that had surely come from his conscience.

'Not that I wanted to.'

'No. I could tell that,' Sam agreed. But something had changed. She could sense it, although she wasn't sure yet what it was. She knew what she was hoping it was. Perhaps miracles could happen? Perhaps Vere could love her? Not just physically desire her.

'Before I left here for your camp we'd been alerted to the fact that someone within the camp was in the pay of the Emir of Khulua. The Emir is our neighbour, and on the surface there is cordiality between us, but he is of the old school and likes nothing better than to create situations, which he can work to his advantage. We'd been warned that he was likely to raise questions about the legitimacy of our shared borders. Not because he genuinely believes they are not legitimate. They are. No, what he was looking to do was to put us in a defensive position.'

Sam listened, wondering if his natural concern about such a matter had been responsible for the way he had behaved towards her initially when he had arrived at the camp. Perhaps what she had thought was hostility had merely been anxiety and preoccupation. She could understand that this was a serious matter for him as the Ruler of Dhurahn.

Vere's expression was very grave, and he was speaking slowly, as though he was having to choose his words with great care.

'When I discovered that you had been questioning the course of the Dhurahni River—'

'You were very angry with me?' Sam supplied for him. She shook her head and then reached out to him, placing her hand on his arm. 'I was hurt at the time, because I didn't understand why you were angry. I understand now that you've explained about the Emir, though. Do you know who it is the Emir has been paying?'

Here was the opportunity, the opening he needed. A gut-wrenching pain tore at him. She was being so tender and understanding. She had no idea how little he deserved her concern, or how badly he had maligned her in his own thoughts. But soon she would.

'I believed that I did.' Vere turned away from her. He couldn't bear to look at her when he told her. He didn't want to see the warmth die from her eyes to be replaced by the condemnation he knew he deserved.

Sam could feel the first prickle of an uneasy sense of anxiety, and dread chilled through her body.

Something was wrong. In fact something was very wrong indeed.

'When I saw you on the path by the oasis I didn't want to recognise you. What had happened between us in Zuran wasn't something I wanted to remember—nor was it fitting behaviour for the son my parents would have expected me to be.'

Vere could see the pain in her eyes, and it shocked him to realise how much he wanted to take that pain away from her. He put his hands on her upper arms, struggling not to allow himself to be distracted by the soft smoothness of her skin beneath the sleeves of her robe,

Sam bit into her bottom lip. She was being over-emotional, she knew, but it hurt knowing that he had had such a low opinion of her.

'The truth was that I hadn't forgotten you—because I couldn't. Your memory was embedded in my senses. But I couldn't let it stay there. I needed a reason to make myself resist you. It was no longer enough for me to tell myself that my desire was something I had to control. Out of that need I convinced myself that *you* were the Emir's tool and in his pay.'

Sam's face had lost its colour. She looked every bit as shocked and upset as he had imagined she would. She pulled back from him and he let her go.

'You thought that of me? But you made love to me… you asked me to be your mistress.' Sam was stumbling over the words, trembling as she spoke them, desperately wanting to hear him say that she had misheard him.

'I believed it was my duty to…to get close enough to you to find out what you were doing.'

Sam could feel horror dripping through her, numbing her at first, and then seizing her with a gigantic pain that held her like a vice, allowing her no escape.

'No…' she protested.

She wanted to turn and run, to hide herself from him. But there was no escape. He was speaking again, paralysing her where she stood.

'I decided that the best way to undermine the Emir would be for me to publicly take you, his tool, as my mistress.'

Vere heard her small whimper, like that of a small creature caught in the cruel talons of a hawk.

'I had to put Dhurahn first.'

Sam listened in silence. Was that an explanation or an excuse? she wondered. Did she even care any more? He had hurt her more than she deserved, and certainly more than she could endure. He had used her, knowing she'd believed he wanted her.

From somewhere she summoned the last shreds of her pride to demand, 'Why are you telling me this now?'

'Because whilst we were on our way here my brother rang to say that the investigations I had ordered showed that it wasn't possible for you to be in the Emir's pay. I have wronged you, and for that I can only apologise and beg your forgiveness. Naturally I shall make whatever recompense is needed to ensure that your career does not suffer because of this. As a cartographer—'

'My *career*?' Sam stopped him as she battled against her pain. 'How do you propose to recompense me for my loss of pride and self-respect? For the fact that you let me think you wanted me, and that you—'

She couldn't go on. Tears flooded her eyes, emotion suspending her voice.

Vere went to her.

'No!' She denied him as he made to take her in his arms, beating her fists impotently against his chest in an agony of distraught despair, forcing Vere to let her go.

She had turned away from him, heading back inside the palace, when it happened: a darting movement, liquid and quicksilver, then Sam's shocked cry, the telltale puncture wound in her leg. Then his own reaction as he reached her and told her not to move, knowing what even the slightest action would send the snake's venom speeding fatally towards her heart.

'Keep still and trust me,' he told her, pausing only to call for help before he dropped down on his haunches to take hold of her leg and place his mouth against the puncture marks, desperately trying to suck the poison from them.

Vere's voice had become oddly distorted and echoy, his expression contorted. She tried to move, but his fierce command of, 'No—keep still,' ricocheted through her.

Servants alerted by Vere's cry came hurrying towards

them, but even whilst he told them to summon his doctor Vere didn't take his gaze off Sam, fixing it on her as though by doing so he could fill her with his own strength and somehow keep her alive until she could be given the necessary antidote to the snake's poison.

The gardens were kept rigorously free of snakes, but somehow this one—one of the most poisonous of all—had got in. Vere could feel his heart thudding and pumping with the life force that Sam so badly needed. If he could have opened his veins and given her life he knew he would have done so. She was everything to him. Without her he was nothing, his life an empty wasteland.

Like a desert sandstorm whipped up by the winds of fate the truth stormed through him, refusing to allow him to deny its existence any longer.

He loved her.

Vere's eyes burned with emotion. He couldn't lose her. Not now—not when he loved and needed her so much.

He could feel the beat of Sam's heart slowing down. Her pulse was so weak it was barely there. He would not lose her. He would *not*.

The doctor arrived, his expression grave and taut with concern. In the space of the time it took him to reach into his case for the antidote Sam's lips turned blue.

The doctor put down the hypodermic needle.

'No!' Vere denied fiercely. *'No!'*

'Highness, it is too late.'

The doctor's voice held a finality that Vere could not accept. Images, memories flooded through his heart: the messenger who had brought them the news of their parents' death, the long flight he and Drax had had to make to accompany their bodies back to Dhurahn for their state funeral, the grief and anger that had possessed him ever since. He could not lose Sam as well. He could not. His hand tightened on her wrist, and miraculously he felt a pulse; her chest lifted slightly.

'Look,' he commanded.

Nodding his head, the doctor reached for the syringe.

CHAPTER TEN

SAM PUT DOWN THE BOOK she had been trying to read. She was sitting in the elegant drawing room that Vere had told her had been decorated for his great-grandmother. She had eaten her solitary dinner, and now she looked at her watch.

Vere had been so loving and tender towards her whilst she had been recovering, coming to talk to her often and letting her know that it was her colleague James who had been the Emir's pay. But now that she had been pronounced fully well and allowed to get up out of bed he had retreated into a coldness that left her feeling desperately hurt and confused. She hadn't seen him at all today, apart from one brief visit during which he had made no attempt to hold her or even talk properly to her. His voice had been sharp and somehow almost hostile.

She was beginning to feel that she must have imagined that moment when she had opened her eyes to find him sitting at her bedside, had thought she had heard him whispering to her that he loved her and feared to lose her. She must have done, because he certainly wasn't behaving as though he loved her now. She suspected that he regretted having spoken such words to her. But why? He must know that she loved *him*. After all, she hadn't made any attempt to hide her feelings from him.

Was it really only a little over twenty-four hours since

he had sat with her in the darkness of her room, holding her hand and cupping her face in his hands, whispering emotionally how much she meant to him?

'I can't wait for Dr Sayid to pronounce you fully fit. My bed has been as empty without you as my heart and my life would be if I lost you. I yearn to be with you, flesh to flesh, heart to heart and mind to mind. With nothing between us, no barriers to separate us.'

Sam's heart turned over now, just replaying those words inside her head. Vere was such a passionate lover. Going into his arms was like opening a door into their own secret special world.

And yet now that Dr Sayid had pronounced her properly well, instead of taking her to his bed, as she so longed for him to do, Vere was ignoring her.

Why?

She ought to try and find out, Sam knew, but she just didn't think she had the courage—even though a part of her said that she should find it. By staying here without knowing the truth of what Vere's feelings were she was cheating them both, not just herself. Vere needed to be free to share his life with a woman he loved, and she was not that woman.

Her close brush with death had changed her, Sam recognised, making her all too aware of her physical vulnerability and the uncertainty of life, but at the same time giving her new emotional strength and an unshakable belief in the importance and value of love.

Like life itself, true love should not be treated lightly nor taken for granted. It demanded respect and the most tender of care.

She had had plenty of time to think about his life and the role she could reasonably expect to play in it whilst she had been recovering from the snake bite, and now that she was over the initial shock of his revelations about his misjudgement of her she was desperately trying to see past them and focus instead on the care he had shown her whilst she was ill. A care, she comforted herself, which must indicate that she meant *something* to him.

VERE STOOD IN front of the formal state portrait of his parents. It dominated the palace's formal audience room. It was here that subjects traditionally came to speak to their Ruler, and to have their voices heard.

The portrait was extraordinarily lifelike. During the early months after their death Vere had often come here to look at it, almost as though by focusing on the couple it would somehow bring them back to life. But of course he had known that this was not possible, and he had always left the room feeling as though he couldn't bear the weight of his own pain.

It was in this room, beneath this portrait, that he had made a solemn mental vow that he must separate himself from his own vulnerability for the sake of his people, and that he must never allow himself to fall in love.

How could he rule wisely and properly if he was constantly in fear of life taking from him the person he loved? He could not.

But he had broken that vow in loving Sam, hadn't he?

Vere knew he would never forget how he had felt when he had thought she was dying. He had had a vision then of his own future, his life stretching out ahead of him as a barren wasteland of nothingness.

But he could not afford that kind of vulnerability. Like someone once burned, he was mortally afraid of the remembered pain and of suffering it again. Better to live without the warmth of fire than to risk the agony it could inflict.

He couldn't keep Sam here now. He knew that. It was too dangerous.

A protective veil had been ripped away from inside his heart, allowing him to see what was hidden inside it. He couldn't pretend to himself any longer that it was only physical desire he felt for her, and that it was therefore safe to keep her with him in his life and in his bed.

He couldn't send her away yet, though. Not until he was one hundred percent sure that she was fully recovered. It was all very well for Dr Sayid to say that she was, but Vere suspected that she still wasn't restored to full physical strength. And besides, where would she go? How would she support herself?

A surge of protective urgency so strong that it caught him off guard thundered through him. He looked up at his parents' portrait. His father's arm rested protectively around his mother. The gesture reflected just how he wanted to keep Sam within the protection of his own love. But who could protect him from the pain he would suffer if he should lose her for any reason?

The only person who could do that was himself, by not loving her in the first place.

CHAPTER ELEVEN

IT WAS TWO DAYS NOW since Sam had been told she was fully recovered, but she hadn't seen Vere even once during that time... Tears pricked at Sam's eyes. She felt abandoned and rejected, not knowing what she had done to cause Vere to treat her in such a way.

She put down the book she had been pretending to read and got up to wander aimlessly round the room, relieved to have someone else to talk to when Masiri appeared with a tray of coffee.

'I am sorry I am late,' she apologised. 'Only the Princess called me and I had to go...'

'The Princess?' Sam queried uncertainly.

Vere had made no mention of any princess living in the palace.

'Yes.' Masiri nodded her head vigorously. 'The Princess. She is the wife of His Highness. She has been away, visiting her own country, but now she has returned.'

Sam's whole body had gone icy cold with shock.

Vere was *married*?

'The Princess is the Prince's wife?' Sam could hear herself stammering, as the answer to her question as to why Vere was ignoring her became all too apparent.

'Yes,' Masiri confirmed.

Why hadn't Vere told her he was married?

Did she really need to ask herself that?

He hadn't told her because she was just his lover, his mistress, and men—especially men like Vere—did not discuss their wives with the women they chose to sleep with outside their marriage.

But Vere had told her he loved her.

That was what men told their lovers. And now that his wife was back he was regretting having said those words to her and wanted to back off from her. She hadn't even really been his mistress, had she, never mind had his love? After all, the real reason he had brought her here had nothing to do with him wanting her.

It was as though two separate people were arguing inside her head. One the shamed, betrayed woman deeply in love, the other her cynical bitterly angry counterpart, savage with fury at the part she had unwittingly been forced to play in another woman's marriage.

'The Princess…?'

Masiri was looking at her, waiting for her to continue, but Sam knew that she had no right to ask the questions burning her heart.

'It doesn't matter,' she told Masiri tonelessly.

Vere was married. Another woman had the right to call herself his wife, to share his life and his bed. Another woman. Never in the wildest reaches of her imagination had Sam ever envisaged herself playing the role of 'the other woman'. If she had known right from the start that Vere was married…if he had told her…then she would never have…

She would never have *what*? Fallen in love with him? Gone to bed with him? Accepted his protection as her lover? At which one did she draw the line?

Sam felt sick with horror and shame.

She couldn't stay here now. She would have to leave. It

nauseated her to think what she had done. And what about
Vere? How could he have done such a thing? Or did he expect his wife to understand that he had taken Sam to bed
for the sake of Dhurahn, and that because of that it didn't
mean anything? Would *she* be able to accept that if she
had been his wife? Or would it haunt her for the rest of
her days that her husband might be lying to her and might
have wanted that other woman?

The man she had thought Vere was could never have
behaved as Vere had.

His behaviour was unforgivable, and he had dragged
her down into its nastiness with him.

Sam knew that she would have left there and then but
for the fact that Vere had taken charge of her passport for
sakekeeping. She would have to wait until she could see
him.

The smell of the coffee Masiri had poured for her before leaving the room was making her feel suffocated and
sick. She badly needed some fresh air. She half ran and
half stumbled into the pretty courtyard garden, now thankfully free of snakes.

She skirted the fish pond, hurrying down the path that
led past it, unable to bear looking at it. Then she noticed
for the first time that, almost obscured by the roses that
smothered it, there was a high wrought-iron gate in the
far wall of the garden.

What lay beyond it? Sam wondered absently, automatically going to look, pleased with any distraction from her
thoughts on the horror of the reality of her situation.

At first all she could see was another garden, more modern in concept than the one she was in, ornamented with
sleek pieces of artwork in stone and metal set in beds of
gravel planted with grasses and spiky plants. Water jet-
ted upwards in a thin straight plume from some unseen

source. As she turned away she saw Vere, coming from the far corner of the garden. She drew in her breath. He was dressed in European clothes—a business suit that emphasised the breadth of his shoulders—and the greenery surrounding him threw shadows across his face. Sam waited for her heart to give its normal eager kick of recognition and joy, but strangely it didn't.

He was turning his head away from her, without having seen her, holding out his hand to someone.

A woman came slowly towards him, wearing a white dress, a hat covering her head. She was very obviously pregnant, leaning into him and then smiling up at him. He was putting his arm around her to support her, bending his head to kiss her on the forehead, his hand resting protectively on her swollen body.

The desire to be violently sick cramped Sam's insides. Unable to watch any longer, she turned and ran.

SAM HAD NO idea how long she had been sitting there in the garden. She knew that every now and again her body shuddered violently of its own accord, and that in between those shudders her forehead broke out into a sweat. She knew too that she felt slightly light-headed. Light-headed, but oh, so very heavy-hearted.

Was Vere still with his wife? Was he cradling her and their child, his hand resting on the womanly flesh that held the new life they had created together, as it had done when she had seen them in the garden? Her teeth started to chatter together, but it was far from cold.

She could hear light footsteps on the path. Masiri, no doubt, coming to see where she was and if she wanted more coffee.

She stood up clumsily, the colour leaving her face as

PENNY JORDAN   333

she stepped forward and saw that it wasn't Masiri but Vere's wife.

'Oh, I'm sorry—I've startled you and I didn't mean to.'

She had a light musical voice, and her smile was warm and genuine. 'I've seen you walking in the garden, and I've been dying to come and talk to you. You're English as well, aren't you?'

Sam nodded her head, completely unable to speak.

'I shouldn't really be doing this, of course.' She laughed, a soft, indulgent sound. 'Vere won't approve at all, and will be cross with me, I know, but I was so curious about you I couldn't resist.'

Sam fought to match her calm, easy manner, feeling as though she had strayed into some surreal and alien world

'Yes. Yes, you must have been curious.'

'I can't stay very long.' She patted her stomach and pulled a face. 'Vere's been worrying that I might go into labour before my due date. I'm Sadie, by the way. I do hope that we're going to be friends.'

Friends!

'Yes,' Sam agreed, wondering inwardly what on earth she was saying. She could never, ever be a friend to Vere's wife. This was tearing her apart, destroying her. How could his wife be so nice to her? Unless...maybe she didn't know that Vere had made love to her? Yes, that must be it, Sam decided feverishly. She didn't know. Vere must have lied to her. How could it hurt so much, loving a man she knew wasn't worthy of that love?

'I'd better go,' Sadie was saying. 'I don't want Vere to come and catch me here with you.'

Sam could feel herself trembling violently as she watched Sadie walk back the way she had come.

She had to get away from here. If only she could access her passport, Sam thought. She would do anything to es-

cape her searing pain and equally searing guilt about having slept with Sadie's husband. She didn't have anything
much to pack, as she certainly didn't intend to take with
her the clothes Vere had bought for her, even if she had
given in and worn them these last few days.

Where was Vere now? With his wife? Reassuring her
that she and their child were all that mattered to him? Was
he whispering to Sadie the words of love and passion he
had whispered to her? She would have to go and see him
to demand that he return her passport, but she didn't have
any fears now that he would try to prevent her from leaving. He would probably be all too relieved to see her go.

Sam went back to her room and asked Masiri to have a
message sent to Vere, telling him that she had to see him
urgently.

VERE HAD BEEN on the point of getting together with his
twin so that Drax could update him on his recent trip when
he was informed of Sam's wish to see him 'urgently'.

Sam's use of the word 'urgently' produced within him a
dangerous mix of volatile emotions, dominated by a recklessly urgent need of his own that had very little to do with
dry dialogue and everything to do with a very male pos-
sessive instinct.

He had to confront his vulnerability, Vere decided.
Avoiding any kind of contact with Sam was a coward's
way of dealing with the situation. A coward who was too
weak to send her away, not strong enough to trust his own
self-control. He inclined his head and gave instructions for
Sam to be brought to his office.

THE FACT THAT Vere was seeing her in his office told her
everything she needed to know, thought Sam as she was
bowed into it, to find Vere seated at his desk, apparently

engrossed in reading some documents he had in front of him.

He couldn't have made it more obvious that it was over between them, and of course Sam knew exactly why. Beneath her pain the volcano of her pride sent up a lava-hot surge of protective anger.

'It's all right Vere,' she told him. 'I haven't come to beg you to take me to bed, or to remind you about what you said to me when I was ill.'

Sam had the satisfaction of seeing the way the muscle in his jaw tensed beneath the lash of her latter comment.

'All I want is my passport.'

He was looking at her now, a flicker of something unreadable briefly darkening his eyes before he averted his gaze.

'So silly of me to feel concerned that I might be burdening you with my unwanted love, and *that* is why you haven't been anywhere near me for the last couple of days, when the real reason is that your wife has returned to the palace. And so very naïve of me not to have guessed that you were married.'

She loved him. But then of course he knew that, because he now knew her. He knew that without loving a man she could not and would not give herself in the way she had given herself to him.

A pain, slow and sharp and unending, was piercing him. He must endure it, because it was the price he had to pay for his future without her, and for the emotional security that future without Sam would bring him.

'Your wife—*Sadie*—came to see me.' Sam gave a laugh that was too high-pitched and haunted with despair. 'She seemed to like me. She said she wanted us to be friends.'

All Vere had to do to stop her pain was tell her that she'd got it wrong and that Sadie was Drax's wife. All he had to do to stop his own pain was take her in his arms and tell her that *she* was the one he loved, the one he would always love.

All he had to do to cross the chasm that separated his past from a future filled with love was to push his way past that mental imagine of his mother's body, her face frozen into an unnatural calm by the undertaker's skill. It had been his duty to see her—a horror from which he had protected Drax by taking it upon his shoulders alone.

Only he knew how often during those hours it had been touch and go for Sam. He had seen that memory reform inside his head, with Sam's face replacing his mother's. A fierce shudder ripped through him.

No wonder he shivered at the thought of his wife befriending her, thought Sam bitterly.

'I'm packed and ready to leave, so if you will give me my passport I'm sure you'll be only too happy to see that I get the first empty seat on a plane leaving for Zuran.' Her head lifted proudly as she spoke. Not for the world was she going to let him see the heartache she was feeling inside.

It was the perfect solution to a situation that had become untenable and, if he was honest, unbearable. Far better to let Sam think the worst of him, for her to walk away from him despising and hating him—for her sake. Perhaps, in fact, that was the best gift he could give her. He had no idea just how she had come to think that Sadie was his wife, but it made sense to let her go on thinking so.

He opened one of the drawers in his desk and removed her passport, placing it down on the desk between them and then withdrawing from it.

Sam could almost taste her own bitterness. He obviously didn't even want to risk touching her fingers.

How could she still care, knowing as she did what kind of cheat he was?

Where was her self-respect? Crushed, like her dreams, beneath the weight of her heavy heart.

Vere pressed the buzzer that would summon one of his aides, telling him when he arrived to organise a car to take Sam to the airport.

'By the time you reach the airport a flight will have been arranged for you.' Even if that meant sending her out of Dhurahn in the royal jet, Vere decided, as he started to stand up. 'My brother is waiting to see me, so if you will excuse me I will leave my PA to escort you to your car.'

It was over, thought Sam shakily. Over? How could it ever be over when she still loved him? her heart protested. But she could not listen to it, because if she did she would surely shame herself utterly and completely by going to him, clinging to him, begging him... It *was* over. It had to be.

Somehow Sam managed to follow the aide, who was already leaving the room.

She was leaving—just as he had wanted her to do. Now there would be no risk, no struggle between the two opposing forces within him. In severing the link between them he had severed himself—freed himself from a lifetime of fear that she might ultimately abandon him.

He was glad she had gone. From his office window he could see her, getting into the waiting car. She was hesitating, looking over her shoulder and then up towards where he was. Immediately Vere stepped back from the glass.

He must go and see Drax. They had important matters to discuss—matters that involved Dhurahn and its future, matters which he as its Ruler needed to give his full attention to.

The car would have left the palace now, and would be travelling down the Royal Highway. It wasn't very far to the airport, and the plane that would take Sam to Zuran had been delayed to wait for her. And then she would be gone—for ever.

'No!'

The tortured sound of his own denial was thrown back to him by the walls of his office. Vere reached for the telephone.

CHAPTER TWELVE

THEY HAD ALMOST reached the airport. Soon she would be gone from Dhurahn, never to return.

The driver brought the car to an abrupt halt and then did a U-turn, and before Sam could so much as knock on the privacy screen separating them they were speeding back the way they had just come.

Back in the palace courtyard, a servant sprang to open the car door for her. Two aides were waiting to escort her swiftly inside—aides or jailers? Sam wondered apprehensively as they walked either side of her, down now familiar corridors, taking her, she realised, to Vere's private quarters.

Outside the double doors they stopped and knocked, and then opened them for her.

She didn't want to go through them, but somehow she discovered that she had.

Behind her the doors were closed, and she was left confronting Vere.

'Why have you done this?' she demanded.

Her heart was thudding and thundering out of beat, and the loud, out-of-control thump was surely totally betraying her.

'Because I had to,' said Vere.

She had never seen him looking like this before, his

emotions clearly revealed in his expression—so clearly that Sam felt as though he was willing her to look at him and see what was there.

She shouldn't be here with him. It was far too dangerous. She took a step backwards, but it was too late; she had hesitated for too long. And now she was in Vere's arms, and he was kissing her with a raw passion more intimate than anything he had shown her before.

Sam knew she should resist and object, but shockingly she was winding her arms round his neck, pressing her body into his and giving herself up to his kiss.

'I couldn't let you go.'

The words, thick, unsteady and wholly honest, tore at her heart.

Such simple words to elicit so many complex feelings. Simple words that were very dangerous. Words that were forbidden between them.

Tears filled Sam's eyes.

'You shouldn't have done this. It's wrong.'

'I love you,' Vere told her fiercely, ignoring her protest.

'You can't. You mustn't.'

It was his own words given back to him. How easy it was now to dismiss them as foolish shadows with no base in reality. Just like his own adolescent fears.

'You have a wife and…soon you will have a child…' A child. What about her own secret? The one that had begun so recently as a joyous hope and had now become a guilty fear—because her baby, if there was to be one, would never know its father or receive his love.

'No. Sadie is not my wife, Sam. She is married to my brother Drax.'

Sam's head swam with the enormity of the message those simple words carried.

'That can't be true.'

'It is true,' Vere insisted. 'And if you won't believe me then I shall ask Drax and Sadie to tell you themselves.'

He meant what he was saying. Sam could see that.

'If you aren't married, then why did you let me think that you were?'

Sam couldn't keep the pain out of her voice and, hearing it, Vere ache with guilt, and with his own desire to hold her and assure her that he would never hurt her again. How best could he explain to her the complexity of the turmoil he had experienced since meeting her?

Whilst he hesitated Sam broke the silence, her voice hesitant and heavy with sadness. 'I love you, Vere,' she told him quietly. 'You know that, I know. But I can't... I'm not emotionally equipped to be in a relationship with someone who blows hot one moment and cold the next.'

And more importantly, she could not and would not take that risk for their child—although of course she wasn't going to tell him that. Just as she wasn't going to tell him of her growing suspicions that she might be pregnant.

Shakily she continued, 'I accept that originally you believed you had good reason to be suspicious of me, and that because of that there were times when you backed off from me. But afterwards, once you knew the truth...'

Would she understand if he told her his truth? Would she love him enough to accept his vulnerability and understand it? He had to take the risk and tell her, Vere knew. He had to make that pledge, give that trust—to her and to their future. Vere wanted so badly to touch her and hold her, but he dared not, because he knew that if he did he would never be able to let her go.

Instead he exhaled and began, 'Your presence was a reminder of...something I didn't want to admit.'

'What something?' Sam asked him. Her mouth had

gone dry and her heart was pounding unsteadily and uncomfortably.

'My...my vulnerability.'

Vere's voice was terse.

He had never been able to talk about how it had felt to lose his parents, but his conscience was forcing him to acknowledge that he owed Sam at least some kind of honesty. And besides...to his own surprise he discovered that a part of him actually wanted to tell her.

'Drax and I were in our early teens when our parents were killed in an accident. We were a very close family. My parents were very much in love with one another. To lose them so unexpectedly and in such a way was a terrible shock, but we were their sons—our father's heirs. We had a duty to our people and our country that had to come before our grief.'

His pain was tearing at Sam's heart.

He made a helpless gesture with his hand.

'It is so hard to say or explain. We had our duty, but we had our own feelings as well. For me there was...there was fear and anger as well as loss. We had loved them so dearly. Our mother especially... She was...very loving... very warm. We were of that age when we were just beginning to think ourselves too old to be her "boys" any more, and yet at the same time inside we still needed her comfort. When it was taken from us... The pain of such a loss goes very deep. I... For me it was easier to shut myself off from the risk of it happening again. This isn't easy for me to say, Sam, and I know it won't be easy for you to hear, but there are things I have to tell you that need to be said, so please bear with me?'

Her throat tight with anxiety, Sam nodded her head.

'I didn't want to love you,' Vere admitted. 'In fact I fought every way I knew not to. At first I thought it would be enough for me to simply deny my feelings and to re-name them lust.'

Sam winced.

'But then after your snake bite, when you were so close to death, that fabrication was ripped from me. All that mattered to me was that you lived, and that you didn't leave me. But even that was not enough to keep me from my path to self-destruction. Even though I knew that I loved you, and I couldn't deny those feelings any longer, I still fought against giving in—as I saw it—to that love.'

'Why?' Sam challenged him.

When he didn't reply, she made her own assumption and said bleakly, 'I suppose it was because you felt I wasn't the right person for…for a Ruler?'

'No,' Vere assured her swiftly, and truthfully. 'You must never think that. I knew you were the right person for me, and for Dhurahn. I knew you were the perfect person for me, Sam, in fact the only person for me. That was why I fought so hard against loving you. The truth is that the reason I believed I didn't dare allow myself to love you lies in my past and in the death of my parents. I was a young adolescent, just at that stage of being torn between a desire for manhood and a fear of how swiftly I was moving towards it—especially in view of the fact that my father was preparing me for the responsibilities of rulership.

'My mother understood this. She was the only person I felt able to admit my feelings to. As the eldest son and the elder brother I felt I had a duty to be strong. I knew my father loved me, but as with most boys of that age I felt a need to match him emotionally, man to man, and that meant not allowing him to see that I sometimes felt vulnerable and fearful of the future. Of course I realise now that he would have known this, having no doubt come through the same experience himself—and that that, in fact, was why he was trying to prepare me.

'There can never be a good time to lose one's parents, and to say that I simply wasn't prepared to lose mine when I did, that I didn't have the resources in place within me to cope, would be an understatement. The loss of my mother in particular left me feeling abandoned and vulnerable. My feelings overwhelmed and frightened me. But I was Dhurahn's Ruler. I had to be tough.'

Sam made a small sound of loving compassion and told him, 'You were a boy...'

'I was Dhurahn's new Ruler,' Vere corrected her gently.

Sam's tender heart ached with sadness for him.

'The only way I could cope was to tell myself that what I was going through was the worst it could ever be—the worst it would ever be. Because I would never allow myself to be so vulnerable again. I told myself that I must never love someone so much that losing them could affect me so deeply and painfully.

'What happened between us in that hotel corridor in Zuran breached defences I had believed were indestructible. I told myself to ignore what I had felt and simply pretend that it and you did not exist. But the memory of you kept me awake at night, tormenting and mocking me. I told myself what I felt was merely physical attraction, and I despised myself for wanting you. It was a relief and an escape route to be able to tell myself that you had an ulterior motive, and that I must therefore despise you and be suspicious of you. But love has a mind and an instinct of its own. Something no doubt my mother would have told me, if she had lived long enough to guide me through the treacherous currents of adolescence. My love wasn't so easily dismissed or forced into accepting convenient lies.

'I was perched on top of a landslide that would sweep

away all my false beliefs, and that is exactly what did happen when you were bitten. The thought of losing you demolished all my defences. I was forced to admit that I loved you.'

'But as soon as I was well again you backed off from me.'

'Shedding the protective skin one has worn for so many years isn't easy or painfree. Doubts flooded into the space left by my destroyed defences. Yes, I loved you—but that did not mean that you would never leave me. My old fear was still there, and if I'm honest perhaps a part of it will always remain. But what I do know now is that I would rather live with that fear than without you. That is if you can bring yourself to love and marry a man who is so very unworthy of you.'

'You want to marry me?'

'I want to commit to you in every way there is,' Vere said softly.

'When you came to me and told me you wanted to leave I told myself that your going was the best thing that could happen to me. But the minute I visualised you getting on board that plane and leaving me for good I knew that in truth it was the worst, that my life would be meaningless without you. You are my joy, Sam, not my fear. You are my future and not my past.'

'I couldn't stay, thinking you were married,' she whispered to him. 'Not when I loved you so much myself, and not when I wanted your child so desperately.'

Sam looked up at him. He had moved closer, so that their bodies were only a breath apart.

Dared she tell him what she had feared she must keep to herself?

Sam swallowed painfully.

If they were to have a future together then it had to be built on trust and honesty.

'And, most of all, not when I thought that maybe you had already given me that child,' she told him simply.

Vere's reaction was everything she could have hoped for and more. He reached for her, holding her protectively, his eyes brilliant with emotion.

'You are carrying our child?'

'I think so, and I hope so—although it is too early to be sure.'

'My love!' His voice was hoarse with emotion.

'Oh, Vere.'

She loved him so much. But right now Sam knew that her greatest need was to comfort the boy he had been, to take the hand of the man he had become and help him walk free of the shadows of the past into the healing light of the sun.

She went to him and gripped his arms, raising herself up on her toes to kiss him gently, in commitment and in love.

'You are mine. And I warn you that I shall never let you go,' Vere whispered against her lips, before taking the initiative from her and kissing her so intimately that her own passionate response to him left her clinging weakly to him. 'We belong together, you and I, Sam.'

'That's what I felt the first time we met,' Sam told him emotionally. 'And now we are together, and we always will be.'

'Always,' Vere agreed firmly, knowing that it was the truth, and that he could trust in it and in her.

The journey to self-acceptance that he had begun so long ago was now finally completed.

* * * * *